ANGELOLOGY

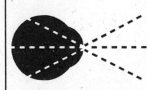

ANGELOLOGY

DANIELLE TRUSSONI

THORNDIKE PRESS

A part of Gale, Cengage Learning

GALE
CENGAGE Learning™

Detroit • New York • San Francisco • New Haven, Conn • Waterville, Maine • London

Copyright © Danielle Trussoni, 2010.

Thorndike Press, a part of Gale, Cengage Learning.

ALL RIGHTS RESERVED

This is a work of fiction. Names, characters, places, and incidents either are the product of the author's imagination or are used fictitiously, and any resemblance to actual persons, living or dead, business establishments, events, or locales is entirely coincidental.

Thorndike Press® Large Print Thriller.

The text of this Large Print edition is unabridged.

Other aspects of the book may vary from the original edition.

Set in 16 pt. Plantin.

Printed on permanent paper.

LIBRARY OF CONGRESS CATALOGING-IN-PUBLICATION DATA

Trussoni, Danielle.
  Angelology / by Danielle Trussoni.
    p. cm. — (Thorndike Press large print thriller)
  ISBN-13: 978-1-4104-2541-6 (alk. paper)
  ISBN-10: 1-4104-2541-X (alk. paper)
  1. Nuns — Fiction. 2. Angels — Fiction. 3. Armageddon —
Fiction. 4. Large type books. I. Title.
  PS3620.R93A83 2010b
  813'.6—dc22

                                                    2009051097

Published in 2010 by arrangement with Viking, a member of Penguin Group (USA) Inc.

Printed in the United States of America
1 2 3 4 5 6 7 14 13 12 11 10

For Angela

One of the original branches of theology, angelology is achieved in the person of the angelologist, whose expertise includes both the theoretical study of angelic systems and their prophetic execution through human history.

The angelologists examined the body. It was intact, without decay, the skin as smooth and as white as parchment. The lifeless aquamarine eyes gazed heavenward. Pale curls fell against a high forehead and sculptural shoulders, forming a halo of golden hair. Even the robes — the cloth woven of a white shimmering metallic material that none of them could identify exactly — remained pristine, as if the creature had died in a hospital room in Paris and not a cavern deep below the earth.

It should not have surprised them to find the angel in that preserved condition. The fingernails, nacreous as the inside of an oyster shell; the long smooth navel-less stomach; the eerie translucency of the skin — everything about the creature was as they knew it would be, even the positioning of the wings was correct. And yet it was too lovely, too vital for something they had studied only in airless libraries, prints of quattrocento paintings spread before them like road maps. All their professional lives they had waited to see it. Although not one of them would have admitted so, they secretly suspected to find a monstrous corpse, all bones and fiber shreds, like something unearthed from an archaeological dig. Instead there was this: a delicate tapering hand, an aquiline nose, pink lips pressed in a frozen kiss. The angelologists hovered above the body, gazing down in anticipation, as if they expected the creature to blink its eyes and wake.

THE FIRST SPHERE

To you this tale refers,
Who seek to lead your mind
Into the upper day,
For he who overcomes should
Turn back his gaze
Toward the Tartarean cave,
Whatever excellence he takes with him
He loses when he looks below.

— Boethius,
The Consolation of Philosophy

December 23, 1999, 4:45 A.M.

Evangeline woke before the sun came up, when the fourth floor was silent and dark. Quiet, so as not to wake the sisters who had prayed through the night, she gathered her shoes, stockings, and skirt in her arms and walked barefoot to the communal lavatory. She dressed quickly, half asleep, without looking in the mirror. From a sliver of bathroom window, she surveyed the convent grounds, covered in a predawn haze. A vast snowy courtyard stretched to the water's edge, where a scrim of barren trees limned the Hudson. St. Rose Convent perched precariously close to the river, so close that in daylight there seemed to be two convents — one on land and one wavering lightly upon the water, the first folding out into the next, an illusion broken in summer by barges and in winter by teeth of ice. Evangeline watched the river flow by, a wide strip of black against the pure white snow. Soon morning would gild the water with sunlight.

Bending before the porcelain sink, Evangeline splashed cold water over her face, dispelling the remnants of a dream. She could not recall the dream, only the impression it made upon her — a wash of foreboding that left a pall over her thoughts, a sensation of loneliness and confusion she could not explain. Half asleep, she peeled away her heavy flannel night shift and, feeling the chill of the bathroom, shivered. Standing in her white cotton briefs and cotton undershirt (standard garments ordered in bulk and distributed biyearly to all the sisters at St. Rose), she looked at herself with an appraising, analytic eye — the thin arms and legs, the flat stomach, the tousled brown hair, the golden pendant resting upon her breastbone. The reflection floating on the glass before her was that of a sleepy young woman.

Evangeline shivered again from the cool air and turned to her clothing. She owned five identical knee-length black skirts, seven black turtlenecks for the winter months, seven black short-sleeved cotton button-up shirts for the summer, one black wool sweater, fifteen pairs of white cotton underwear, and innumerable black nylon stockings: nothing more and nothing less than what was necessary. She pulled on a turtleneck and fitted a bandeau over her hair, pressing it firmly against her forehead before clipping on a black veil. She stepped into a pair of nylons and a wool skirt, buttoning, zipping, and straightening the wrinkles in one quick, unconscious gesture. In a matter of seconds, her private self disappeared and she became Sister Evangeline, Franciscan Sister of Perpetual Adoration. With her rosary in hand, the metamorphosis was complete. She placed her nightgown in the bin at the far end of the lavatory and prepared to face the day.

Sister Evangeline had observed the 5:00 A.M. prayer hour each morning for the past half decade, since completing her formation and taking vows at eighteen years of age. She had lived at St. Rose Convent since her twelfth year, however, and knew the convent as intimately as one knows the temperament of a beloved friend. She had her morning route through the compound down to a science. As she rounded each floor, her fingers traced the wooden balustrades, her shoes skimming the landings. The convent was always empty at that hour, blue-shadowed and sepulchral, but after sunrise St. Rose would swarm with life, a beehive of work and devotion, each room glistening with sacred activity and prayer. The silence would soon abate — the staircases, the community rooms, the library, the communal cafeteria, and the dozens of closet-size bed-chambers would soon be alive with sisters.

Down three flights of stairs she ran. She could get to the chapel with her eyes closed.

Reaching the first floor, Sister Evangeline walked into the imposing central hallway, the spine of St. Rose Convent. Along the walls hung framed portraits of long-dead abbesses, distinguished sisters, and the various incarnations of the convent building itself. Hundreds of women stared from the frames, reminding every sister who passed by on her way to prayer that she was part of an ancient and noble matriarchy where all women — both the living and the dead — were woven together in a single common mission.

Although she knew she risked being late, Sister Evangeline paused at the center of the hallway. Here, the image of Rose of Viterbo, the saint after whom the convent had been named, hung in a gilt frame, her tiny hands folded in prayer, an evanescent nimbus of light glowing about her head. St. Rose's life had been short. Just after her third birthday, angels began to whisper to her, urging her to speak their message to all who would listen. Rose complied, earning her sainthood as a young woman, when, after preaching the goodness of God and His angels to a heathen village, she was condemned to die a witch. The townspeople bound her to a stake and lit a fire. To the great consternation of the crowd, Rose did not burn but stood in skeins of flame for three hours, conversing with angels as the fire licked her body. Some believed that angels wrapped themselves about the girl, covering her in a clear, protective armor. Eventually she died in the flames, but the miraculous intervention left her body inviolable. St. Rose's incorrupt corpse was paraded through the streets of Viterbo hundreds of years after her death, not the slightest mark of her ordeal evident upon the adolescent body.

Remembering the hour, Sister Evangeline turned from the portrait. She walked to the end of the hallway, where a great wooden portal carved with scenes of the Annunciation separated the convent from the church. On one side of the boundary, Sister Evangeline stood in the simplicity of the convent; on the other rose the majestic church. She heard the sound of her footsteps sharpen as she left carpeting for a pale roseate marble veined with green. The movement across the threshold took just one step, but the difference was immense. The air grew heavy with incense; the light saturated blue from the stained glass. White plaster walls gave way to great sheets of stone. The ceiling soared. The eye adjusted to the golden abundance of Neo-Rococo. As she left the convent, Evangeline's earthly commitments of community and charity fell away and she entered the sphere of the divine: God, Mary, and the angels.

In the beginning years of her time at St. Rose, the number of angelic images in Maria Angelorum Church struck Evangeline as excessive. As a girl she'd found them overwhelming, too ever-present and overwrought. The creatures filled every crook and crevice of the church, leaving little room for much else. Seraphim ringed the central dome; marble archangels held the corners of the altar. The columns were inlaid with golden halos, trumpets, harps, and tiny wings; carved visages of putti stared from the pew ends, hypnotizing and compact as fruit bats. Although she understood that the opulence was meant as an offering to the Lord, a symbol of their devotion, Evangeline secretly preferred the plain functionality of the convent. During her formation she felt critical of the founding sisters, wondering why they had not used such wealth for better purposes. But, like so much else, her objections and preferences had shifted after she took the habit, as if the clothing ceremony itself caused her to melt ever so slightly and take a new, more uniform shape. After five years as a professed sister, the girl she had been had nearly faded away.

Pausing to dip her index finger into a fount of holy water, Sister Evangeline blessed herself (forehead, heart, left shoulder, right shoulder) and stepped through the narrow Romanesque basilica, past the fourteen Stations of the Cross, the straight-backed red oak pews, and the marble columns. As the light was dim at that hour, Evangeline followed the wide central aisle through the nave to the sacristy, where chalices and bells and vestments were locked in cupboards, awaiting Mass. At the far end of the sacristy, she came to a door.

Taking a deep breath, Evangeline closed her eyes, as if preparing them for a greater brightness. She placed her hand on the cold brass knob and, heart pounding, pushed.

The Adoration Chapel opened around her, bursting upon her vision. Its walls glittered golden, as if she had stepped into the center of an enameled Fabergé egg. The private chapel of the Franciscan Sisters of Perpetual Adoration had a high central dome and huge stained-glass panels that filled each wall. The central masterpiece of the Adoration Chapel was a set of Bavarian windows hung high above the altar depicting the three angelic spheres: the First Sphere of Seraphim, Cherubim, and Thrones; the Second Sphere of Dominions, Virtues, and Powers; and the Third Sphere of Principalities, Archangels, and Angels. Together the spheres formed the heavenly choir, the collective voice of heaven. Each morning Sister Evangeline would stare at the angels floating in an expanse of glittering glass and try to imagine their native brilliance, the pure radiant light that rose from them like heat.

Sister Evangeline spied Sisters Bernice and Boniface — scheduled for adoration each morning from four to five — kneeling before the altar. Together the sisters ran their fingers over the carved wooden beads of their seven-decade rosaries, as if intent to whisper the very last syllable of prayer with as much mindfulness as they had whispered the first. One could find two sisters in full habit kneeling side by side in the chapel at all times of the day and night, their lips moving in synchronized patterns of prayer, conjoined in purpose before the white marble altar. The object of the sisters' adoration was encased in a golden starburst monstrance placed high upon the altar, a white host suspended in an explosion of gold.

The Franciscan Sisters of Perpetual Adoration had prayed every minute of every hour of every day since Mother Francesca, their founding abbess, had initiated adoration in the early nineteenth century. Nearly two hundred years later, the prayer persisted, forming the longest, most persistent chain of perpetual prayer in the world. For the sisters, time passed with the bending of knees and the soft clicking of rosary beads and the daily journey from the convent to the Adoration Chapel. Hour after hour they arrived at the chapel, crossed themselves, and knelt in humility before the Lord. They prayed by morning light; they prayed by candlelight. They prayed for peace and grace and the end of human suffering. They prayed for Africa and Asia and Europe and the Americas. They prayed for the dead and for the living. They prayed for their fallen, fallen world.

Blessing themselves in tandem, Sisters Bernice and Boniface left the chapel. The black skirts of their habits — long, heavy garments of more traditional cut than Sister Evangeline's post–Vatican II attire — dragged along the polished marble floor as they made way for the next set of sisters to take their place.

Sister Evangeline sank into the foam cushion of a kneeler, the cover of which was still warm from Sister Bernice. Ten seconds later Sister Philomena, her daily prayer partner, joined her. Together they continued a prayer that had begun generations before, a prayer that ran through each sister of their order like a chain of perpetual hope. A golden pendulum clock, small and intricate, its cogs and wheels clicking with soft regularity under a protective glass dome, chimed five times. Relief flooded Evangeline's mind: Everything in heaven and earth was perfectly on schedule. She bowed her head and began to pray. It was exactly five o'clock.

In recent years Evangeline had been assigned to work in the St. Rose library as assistant to her prayer partner, Sister Philomena. It was an unglamorous position to be sure, not at all as high-profile as working in the Mission Office or assisting in Recruitment, and it had none of the rewards of charity work. As if to emphasize the lowly nature of the position, Evangeline's office was located in the most decrepit part of the convent, a drafty section of the first floor down the hall from the library itself, with leaky pipes and Civil War–era windows, a combination that led to dampness, mold, and an abundance of head colds each winter. In fact, Evangeline had been afflicted with a number of respiratory infections in the past months, causing her a shortness of breath that she blamed entirely on drafts.

The saving grace of Evangeline's office was the view. Her worktable abutted a window on the northeast side of the grounds, overlooking the Hudson River. In the summer her window would perspire, giving the impression that the exterior world was steamy as a rain forest; in the winter the window would frost, and she would half expect a rookery of penguins to waddle into sight. She would chip the thin ice with a letter opener and gaze out as freight trains rolled alongside the river and barges floated upon it. From her desk she could see the thick stone wall that wrapped about the grounds, an impregnable border between the sisters and the outside world. While the wall was a remnant from the nineteenth century, when the nuns kept themselves physically apart from the secular community, it remained a substantial edifice in the FSPA imagination. Five feet high and two feet wide, it formed a stalwart impediment between worlds pure and profane.

Each morning after her five o'clock prayer hour, breakfast, and morning Mass, Evangeline stationed herself at the rickety table under the window of her office. She called the table her desk, although there were no drawers to its credit and nothing approximating the mahogany sheen of the secretary in Sister Philomena's office. Still, it was wide and tidy, with all the usual supplies. Each day she straightened her calendar blotter, arranged her pencils, tucked her hair neatly behind her veil, and got to work.

Perhaps because the majority of the St. Rose mail came in regard to their collection of angelic images — the main index of which was located in the library — all convent correspondence ended up in Evangeline's care. Evangeline collected the mail each morning from the Mission Office on the first floor, filling a black cotton bag with letters and returning to her desk to sort them. It became her duty to file the letters in an orderly system (first by date, then alphabetically by surname) and respond to inquiries on their official St. Rose stationery, a chore she completed at the electric typewriter in Sister Philomena's office, a much warmer space that opened directly upon the library.

The job proved quiet, categorical, and regular, qualities that suited Evangeline. At twenty-three, she was content to believe that her appearance and character were fixed — she had large green eyes, dark hair, pale skin, and a contemplative demeanor. After professing her final vows, she had chosen to dress in plain dark clothing, a uniform she would keep the rest of her life. She wore no adornments at all except for a gold pendant, a tiny lyre that had belonged to her mother. Although the pendant was beautiful, the antique lyre finely wrought gold, for Evangeline its value remained purely emotional. She had inherited it upon her mother's death. Her grandmother, Gabriella Lévi-Franche Valko, had brought the necklace to Evangeline at the funeral. Taking Evangeline to a bénitier, Gabriella had cleaned the pendant with holy water, fastened the necklace around Evangeline's throat. Evangeline saw that an identical lyre glimmered at Gabriella's neck. "Promise me you will wear it at all times, day and night, just as Angela wore it," Gabriella had said. Her grandmother pronounced Evangeline's mother's name with a lilting accent, swallowing the first syllable and emphasizing the second: An-*gel*-a. She preferred her grandmother's pronunciation to all others and, as a girl, had learned to imitate it perfectly. Like Evangeline's parents, Gabriella had become little more than a powerful memory. The pendant, however, felt substantial against her skin, a solid connection to her mother and grandmother.

Evangeline sighed and arranged the day's mail before her. The time had arrived to get down to work. Choosing a letter, she sliced the envelope with the silver blade of her letter

24

opener, tapped the folded paper onto the table, and read it. She knew instantly that this was not the sort of letter she usually opened. It did not begin, as most of the regular convent correspondences did, by complimenting the sisters on their two hundred years of perpetual adoration, or their numerous works of charity, or their dedication to the spirit of world peace. Nor did the letter include a charitable donation or the promise of remembrance in a will. The letter began abruptly with a request:

Dear St. Rose Convent Representative,

In the process of conducting research for a private client, it has come to my attention that Mrs. Abigail Aldrich Rockefeller, matriarch of the Rockefeller family and patron of the arts, may have briefly corresponded with the abbess of St. Rose Convent, Mother Innocenta, in the years 1943–1944, four years before Mrs. Rockefeller's death. I have recently come upon a series of letters from Mother Innocenta that suggests a relationship between the two women. As I can find no references to the acquaintance in any scholarly work about the Rockefeller family, I am writing to inquire if Mother Innocenta's papers were archived. If so, I would like to request that I might be allowed to visit St. Rose Convent to view them. I can assure you that I will be considerate of your time and that my client is willing to cover all expenses. Thank you in advance for your assistance in this matter.

Yours,
V. A. Verlaine

Evangeline read the letter twice and, instead of filing it away in the usual manner, walked directly to Sister Philomena's office, took a leaf of stationery from a stack upon her desk, rolled it onto the barrel of the typewriter, and, with more than the usual vigor, typed:

Dear Mr. Verlaine,

While St. Rose Convent has great respect for historical research endeavors, it is our present policy to refuse access to our archives or our collection of angelic images for private research or publication purposes. Please accept our most sincere apologies.

Many Blessings,
Evangeline Angelina Cacciatore, FSPA

Evangeline signed her name across the bottom of the missive, stamped the letter with the official FSPA seal, and folded it into an envelope. After typing out the New York City address on an envelope, she affixed a stamp and placed the letter on a stack of outgoing mail balanced at the edge of a polished table, waiting for Evangeline to take it to the post office in New Paltz.

The response might be perceived by some as severe, but Sister Philomena had specifically instructed Evangeline to deny all access to the archives to amateur researchers, the number of which seemed to be growing in recent years with the New Age craze for guardian angels and the like. In fact, Evangeline had denied access to a tour bus of women and men from such a group only six months before. She didn't like to discriminate against visitors, but there was a certain pride the sisters took in their angels, and they did not appreciate the light cast upon their serious mission by amateurs with crystals and tarot decks.

Evangeline looked at the stack of letters with satisfaction. She would post them that very afternoon.

Suddenly something struck her as odd about Mr. Verlaine's request. She pulled the letter from the pocket of her skirt and reread the line stating that Mrs. Rockefeller may have briefly corresponded with the abbess of St. Rose Convent, Mother Innocenta, in the years 1943–1944.

The dates startled Evangeline. Something momentous had occurred at St. Rose in 1944, something so important to FSPA lore that it would have proved impossible to overlook its significance. Evangeline walked through the library, past polished oak tables adorned with small reading lamps to a black metal fireproof door at the far end of the room. Taking a set of keys from her pocket, she unlocked the archives. Was it possible, she wondered as she pushed the door open, that the events of 1944 were in some way related to Mr. Verlaine's request?

Considering the amount of information the archives contained, they were given a miserly allotment of space in the library. Metal shelves lined the narrow room, storage boxes arranged neatly upon them. The system was simple and organized: Newspaper clippings were filed in the boxes on the left side of the room; convent correspondence and personal items such as letters, journals, and artwork of the dead sisters to the right. Each box had been labeled with a year and placed chronologically on a shelf. The founding year of St. Rose Convent, 1809, began the procession, and the present year of 1999 ended it.

Evangeline knew the composition of the newspaper articles well, as Sister Philomena had assigned her the laborious task of encapsulating the delicate newsprint in clear acetate. After so many hours of trimming and taping and filing the clippings in acid-free cardboard boxes, she felt considerable chagrin at her inability to locate them immediately.

Evangeline recalled with precise and vivid detail the event that had occurred at the beginning of 1944: In the winter months, a fire had destroyed much of the upper floors of the convent. Evangeline had encapsulated a yellowed photograph of the convent, its roof eaten away by flames, the snowy courtyard filled with old-fashioned Seagrave fire engines as hundreds of nuns in serge habits — attire not altogether different from that still worn by Sisters Bernice and Boniface — stood watching their home burn.

Evangeline had heard stories of the fire from the Elder Sisters. On that cold February day, hundreds of shivering nuns stood on the snow-covered grounds watching the convent melt away. A group of foolhardy sisters went back inside the convent, climbing the east-wing staircase — the only passageway still free of fire — and threw iron bed frames and desks and as many linens as possible from the fourth-floor windows, trying, no doubt, to salvage their more precious possessions. The sisters' collection of fountain pens, secured in a metal box, was thrown to the courtyard. It cracked upon hitting the frozen ground, sending inkwells flying like grenades. They had shattered upon impact, exploding in great bursts of colored splotches on the grounds, red, black, and blue bruises bleeding into the snow. Soon the courtyard was piled high with debris of twisted bed springs, water-soaked mattresses, broken desks, and smoke-damaged books.

Within minutes of detection, the fire spread through the main wing of the convent, swept through the sewing room, devouring bolts of black muslin and white cotton, then moved on to the embroidery room, where it incinerated the folds of needlework and English lace the sisters had been saving to sell at the Easter Bazaar, and then finally arrived at the art closets filled with rainbows of tissue paper twisted into jonquils, daffodils, and hundreds of multicolored roses. The laundry room, an immense sweatshop inhabited by industrial-size wringers and coal-heated hot irons, was completely engulfed. Jars of bleach exploded, fueling the fire and sending toxic smoke throughout the lower floors. Fifty fresh-laundered serge habits disappeared in an instant of heat. By the time the blaze had burned down to a slow, steamy stream of smoke by late afternoon, St. Rose was a mass of charred wood and sizzling roof tin.

At last Evangeline came upon three boxes marked 1944. Realizing that news of the fire would have spilled over into the middle months of 1944, Evangeline pulled down all three, stacked them together, and carried them out of the archives, bumping the door closed with her hip. She strode back to her cold, dreary office to examine the contents of the boxes.

According to a detailed article clipped from a Poughkeepsie newspaper, the fire had started from an undetermined quadrant of the convent's fourth floor and spread through the entire building. A grainy black-and-white photograph showed the carcass of the convent, beams burned to charcoal. A caption read, *"Milton Convent Ravaged by Morning Blaze."* Reading through the article, Evangeline found that six women, including Mother Innocenta, the abbess who may or may not have been in correspondence with Mrs. Abigail Rockefeller, had died of asphyxiation.

Evangeline took a deep breath, chilled by the image of her beloved home engulfed in flames. She opened another box and paged through a sheaf of encapsulated newspaper clippings. By February 15 the sisters had moved into the basement of the convent, sleeping on cots, bathing and cooking in the kitchen so that they could assist in repairing the living quarters. They continued their regular routine of prayer in the Adoration Chapel, which had been left untouched by the fire, performing their hourly adoration as if nothing had happened. Scanning the article, Evangeline stopped abruptly at a line toward the bottom of the page. To her amazement she read:

Despite the near-total destruction of the convent proper, it is reported that a generous donation from the Rockefeller family will allow the Franciscan Sisters of Perpetual Adoration to repair St. Rose Convent and their Mary of the Angels Church to their original condition.

Evangeline put the articles into their boxes, stacked them one on top of the other, and returned them to their home in the archive. Edging to the back of the room, she found a box marked EPHEMERA 1940–1945. If Mother Innocenta had had contact with anyone as illustrious as Abigail Rockefeller, the letters would have been filed among such papers. Evangeline set the box on the cool linoleum floor and squatted before it. She found all variety of records from the convent — receipts for cloth and soap and candles, a program of the 1941 St. Rose Christmas celebrations, and a number of letters between Mother Innocenta and the head of the diocese regarding the arrival of novices. To her frustration, there was nothing more to be found.

It was possible, Evangeline reasoned as she returned the documents to their correct box, that Innocenta's personal papers had been filed elsewhere. There were any number of boxes in which she might find them — Mission Correspondence or Foreign Charities seemed especially promising. She was about to move on to another box when she spied a pale envelope tucked below a pack of receipts for church supplies. Pulling it out, she saw that it was addressed to Mother Innocenta.

The return address had been written in elegant calligraphy: *"Mrs. A. Rockefeller, 10 W. 54th Street, New York, New York."* Evangeline felt the blood rush to her head. Here was proof that Mr. Verlaine had been correct: A connection between Mother Innocenta and Abigail Rockefeller did, in fact, exist.

Evangeline looked carefully at the envelope and then tapped it. A thin paper fell into her hands.

December 14, 1943

Dearest Mother Innocenta,

I send good news of our interests in the Rhodope Mountains, where our efforts are by all accounts a success. Your guidance has helped the progress of the expedition enormously, and I daresay my own contributions have been useful as well. Celestine Clochette will be arriving in New York early February. More news will reach you soon. Until then, I am sincerely yours,

A. A. Rockefeller

Evangeline stared at the paper in her hands. It was beyond her understanding. Why would someone like Abigail Rockefeller write to Mother Innocenta? What did "our interests in the Rhodope Mountains" mean? And why had the Rockefeller family paid for the restoration of St. Rose after the fire? It made no sense at all. The Rockefellers, as far as Evangeline knew, were not Catholic and had no connection to the diocese. Unlike other wealthy Gilded Age families — the Vanderbilts came immediately to mind — they did not own a significant amount of property in the vicinity. Yet there had to be some explanation for such a generous gift.

Evangeline folded Mrs. Rockefeller's letter and put it into her pocket. Walking from the archives into the library, she felt the difference in temperature in an instant — the fire had overheated the room. She removed the letter she had written to Mr. Verlaine from the stack of mail waiting to be posted and carried it to the fireplace. As the flame caught the edge of the envelope, painting a fine black track into the pink cotton bond, an image of the martyred Rose of Viterbo appeared in Evangeline's mind — a flitting figment of a willowy girl withstanding a raging fire — and disappeared as if carried away in a swirl of smoke.

The A train, Eighth Avenue Express, Columbus Circle station, New York City

The automatic doors slid open, ushering a gust of freezing air through the train. Verlaine zipped his overcoat and stepped onto the platform, where he was met by a blast of Christmas music, a reggae version of "Jingle Bells" performed by two men with dreadlocks. The groove mixed with the heat and motion of hundreds of bodies along the narrow platform. Following the crowd up a set of wide, dirty steps, Verlaine climbed to the snow-blanketed world aboveground, his gold-wire-rimmed eyeglasses fogging opaque in the cold. Into the arms of an ice-laden winter afternoon he rose, a half-blind man feeling his way through the churning chill of the city.

Once his glasses cleared, Verlaine saw the holiday shopping season in full swing — mistletoe hung at the subway entrance, and a less-than-jolly Salvation Army Santa Claus shook a brass bell, a red-enameled donation bucket at his side. Christmas lights scored the streetlamps red and green. As masses of

New Yorkers hurried past, scarves and heavy overcoats warming them against the icy wind, Verlaine checked the date on his watch. He saw, to his great surprise, that there were only two days until Christmas.

Each year hordes of tourists descended upon the city at Christmas, and each year Verlaine vowed to stay away from midtown for the entire month of December, hiding out in the cushioned quiet of his Greenwich Village studio. Somehow he had coasted through years of Manhattan Christmases without actually participating in them. His parents, who lived in the Midwest, sent a package of gifts each year, which he usually opened as he spoke with his mother on the phone, but that was as far as his Christmas cheer went. On Christmas Day he would go out for drinks with friends and then, sufficiently tipsy on martinis, catch an action movie. It had become a tradition, one he looked forward to, especially this year. He'd worked so much in the past months that he welcomed the thought of a break.

Verlaine jostled through the crowd, slush clinging to his scuffed vintage wing tips as he progressed along the salt-strewn walkway. Why his client had insisted upon meeting in Central Park and not in a warm, quiet restaurant remained beyond his imagination. If it weren't such an important project — indeed, if it were not his only source of income at the moment — he would have insisted upon mailing in his work and being done with it. But the dossier of research had taken months to prepare, and it was imperative that he explain his findings in just the right manner. Besides, Percival Grigori had dictated that Verlaine follow orders to the letter. If Grigori wanted to meet on the moon, Verlaine would have found a way to get there.

He waited for traffic to clear. The statue at the center of Columbus Circle rose before him, an imposing figure of Christopher Columbus poised atop a pillar of marble, framed by the sinuous, barren trees of Central Park. Verlaine thought it an ugly, overmannered piece of sculpture, gaudy and out of place. As he walked past, he noticed a stone angel carved into the base of the plinth, a marble globe of the world in its fingers. The angel was so lifelike that it appeared as if it would come unmoored from the monument entirely, lift over the bustle of taxis, and rise into the smoky heavens above Central Park.

Ahead, the park was a tangle of leafless trees and snow-covered walkways. Verlaine went past a hot-dog vendor warming his hands over a gust of steam, past nannies pushing baby carriages, past a magazine kiosk. The benches at the edge of the park were empty. Nobody in his right mind would take a walk on such a cold afternoon.

Verlaine glanced at his watch again. He was late, something he wouldn't worry about under normal circumstances — he was often five or ten minutes behind schedule for appointments, attributing his tardiness to his artistic temperament. Today, however, timing mattered. His client would be counting the minutes, if not the seconds. Verlaine straightened his tie, a bright blue 1960s Hermès with a repeating pattern of yellow fleurs-de-lis that he had won on an eBay auction. When he was uncertain about a situation or felt that he might appear ill at ease, he tended to choose the quirkiest clothes in his closet. It was an unconscious response, a bit of self-sabotage that he noticed only after it was too late. First dates and job interviews were particularly bad. He would show up looking as if he'd stepped out of a circus tent, with every article of clothing mismatched and too colorful for the situation at hand. Clearly this meeting had made him jittery: In addition to the vintage tie, he wore a red pin-striped button-up shirt, a white corduroy sport jacket, jeans, and his favorite pair of Snoopy socks, a gift from an ex-girlfriend. He had really outdone himself.

Pulling his overcoat closer, glad that he could hide behind its soft, neutral gray wool, Verlaine took a deep breath of cold air. He clutched the dossier tight, as if the wind might tear it from his fingers, and walked deeper through the whorls of snowflakes into Central Park.

Beyond the rush of Christmas shoppers, obscured in a pocket of icy tranquillity, a ghostly figure waited upon a park bench. Tall, pale, brittle as bone china, Percival Grigori appeared to be little more than an extension of the swirling snow. He lifted a white silk square from the pocket of his overcoat and, in a violent spasm, coughed into it. His vision trembled and blurred with each seizure and then, in an instant of respite, resumed focus. The silk square had been stained with drops of luminous blue blood, vivid as chipped sapphires in snow. There was no more denying it. His situation had grown increasingly serious in the past months. As he tossed the bloodied silk onto the sidewalk, the skin of his back chafed. His discomfort was such that each small movement felt like an instance of torture.

Percival looked at his watch, a solid-gold Patek Philippe. He'd spoken to Verlaine only the previous afternoon to verify the meet-

39

ing and had been very clear about the time — twelve o'clock sharp. It was now 12:05. Irritated, Percival leaned into the cold park bench, tapping his cane on the frozen sidewalk. He disliked waiting for anyone, let alone a man he was paying so well. Their telephone conversation the day before had been perfunctory, functional, without pleasantries. Percival disliked discussing business matters over the telephone — he could never quite trust such discussions — yet it took some restraint to resist inquiring after the details of Verlaine's findings. Percival and his family had amassed extensive information about dozens of convents and abbeys across the continent over the years, and yet Verlaine claimed he had come across something of interest just up the Hudson.

Upon their first meeting, Percival had assumed Verlaine to be fresh from business school, a climber who dabbled in the art market. Verlaine had rather wild curly black hair, a self-deprecating manner, and a mismatched suit. He struck Percival as artistic in the way that men were at that time of life — everything from his attire to his manners was too youthful, too trendy, as if he had not yet found his place in the world. He certainly was not the sort Percival usually found working for his family. He later learned that, in addition to his specialization in art history, Verlaine was a painter who taught part-time at a university, moonlighted at auction houses, and took consulting work to get by. He clearly thought himself to be something of a bohemian, with a bohemian lack of punctuality. Nevertheless, the young man had shown himself to be skilled at his work.

Finally Percival spotted him hurrying into the park. As he reached the bench, Verlaine extended his hand. "Mr. Grigori," he said, out of breath. "Sorry to be late."

Percival took Verlaine's hand and shook it, coolly. "According to my exceedingly reliable watch, you are seven minutes late. If you expect to continue to work for us, you will be on time in the future." He met Verlaine's eye, but the young man didn't appear chastened in the least. Percival gestured in the direction of the park. "Shall we walk?"

"Why not?" Glancing at Percival's cane, Verlaine added, "Or we could sit here, if you'd like. It might be more comfortable."

Percival stood and followed the snow-dusted sidewalk deeper into Central Park, the metal tip of the cane clicking lightly upon the ice. Not so very long ago, he had been as handsome and strong as Verlaine and wouldn't have noticed the wind and frost and cold of the day. He remembered once, on a winter walk through London during the 1814 freeze, with the Thames solid and the winds arctic, that he had strolled for miles, feeling as warm as if he were indoors. He was a different being then — he had been at the height of his strength and beauty. Now the chill in the air made his body ache. The pain in his joints drove him to push himself forward, despite the cramping in his legs.

"You have something for me," Percival said at last, without looking up.

"As promised," Verlaine replied, pulling an envelope from under his arm and presenting it with a flourish, his black curls falling over his eyes. "The sacred parchments."

Percival paused, uncertain of how to react to Verlaine's humor, and weighed the envelope in the palm of his hand — it was as large and heavy as a dinner plate. "I very much hope you have something that will impress me."

"I think you'll be quite pleased. The report begins with the history of the order I described on the telephone. It includes personal profiles of the residents, the philosophy of the Franciscan order, notes on the FSPA's priceless collection of books and images in their library, and a summary of the mission work they do abroad. I've cataloged my sources and made photocopies of original documents."

Percival opened the envelope and sifted through the pages, glancing absently at them. "This is all rather common information," he said, dismissive. "I fail to see what could have drawn your attention to this place to begin with."

Then something caught his attention. He

pulled a bundle of papers from the envelope and paged through them, the wind ruffling the edges as he unfolded a series of drawings of the convent — the rectangular floor plans, the circular turrets, the narrow hallway connecting the convent to the church, the wide entrance corridor.

"Architectural drawings," Verlaine said.

"What variety of architectural drawings?" Percival asked, biting his lip as he flipped through the pages. The first had been stamped with a date: December 28, 1809.

Verlaine said, "From what I can tell, these are the original sketches of St. Rose, stamped and approved by the founding abbess of the convent."

"They cover the convent grounds?" Percival asked, examining the drawings more closely.

"And the interiors as well," Verlaine said.

"You found these where?"

"In a county-courthouse archive upstate. Nobody seemed to know how they ended up there, and they'll probably never notice that they're gone. After a little searching, I found that the plans were transferred to the county building in 1944, after a fire at the convent."

Percival looked down at Verlaine, the faintest hint of challenge in his manner. "And you find these drawings significant?"

"These are not really your run-of-the-mill drawings. Take a look at this." Verlaine directed Percival to a faint sketch of an octagonal structure, the words ADORATION CHA-PEL written at the top. "This is particularly fascinating. It was drawn by someone with a great eye for scale and depth. The structure is so precisely rendered, so detailed, that it doesn't fit at all with the other drawings. At first I thought it didn't belong with the set — it's too different in style — but it has been stamped and dated, like the others."

Percival stared at the drawing. The Adoration Chapel had been rendered with enormous care — the altar and entrance had been given particular attention. A series of rings had been drawn within the Adoration Chapel plan, concentric circles that radiated one from the next. At the center of the spheres, like an egg in a nest of protective tissue, was a golden seal. Flipping through the pages of drawings, Percival found that a seal had been placed upon each sheet.

"Tell me," he said, placing his finger upon the seal. "What, do you suppose, is the meaning of this seal?"

"That interested me, too," Verlaine said, reaching into his overcoat and removing an envelope. "So I did a little more research. It is a reproduction of a coin, Thracian in origin, from the fifth century B.C. The original was uncovered by a Japanese-funded archaeological dig in what is now eastern Bulgaria but was once the center of Thrace — something of a cultural haven in fifth-century Europe.

The original coin is in Japan, so I have nothing but this reproduction to go by."

Verlaine opened the envelope and presented Percival with an enlarged photocopied image of the coin.

"The seal was put on the architectural drawings over one hundred years *before* the coin was discovered, which makes this seal — and the drawings themselves — rather incredible. From the research I've done, it seems that this image is unique among Thracian coins. While most from that period depict the heads of mythological figures like Hermes, Dionysus, and Poseidon, this coin depicts an instrument: the lyre of Orpheus. There are a number of Thracian coins in the Met. I went to see them myself. They're in the Greek and Roman Galleries, if you're interested. Unfortunately, there is nothing quite like this coin on display. It's one of a kind."

Percival Grigori leaned on the sweat-slicked ivory knob of the cane, attempting to contain his irritation. Snow fell through the sky, fat, wet flakes that drifted through the tree branches and settled upon the sidewalk. Clearly Verlaine did not realize how irrelevant the drawings, or the seal, were to his plans.

"Very well, Mr. Verlaine," Percival said, straightening himself the best he could and fixing Verlaine with a severe gaze. "But surely you have more for me."

"More?" Verlaine asked, perplexed.

"These drawings you've brought are interesting artifacts," Percival said, returning them to Verlaine with a dismissive flourish, "but they are secondary to the job at hand. If you have obtained information connecting Abigail Rockefeller to this particular convent, I expect you have sought access? What progress there?"

"I sent a request to the convent just yesterday," Verlaine said. "I'm waiting for the response."

"Waiting?" Percival said, his voice rising in irritation.

"I need permission to enter the archives," Verlaine said.

The young man displayed only a slight hesitation, a hint of color in his cheeks, the faintest bafflement in his manner, but Percival seized upon this insecurity with furious suspicion. "There will be no waiting. Either you will find the information that is of interest to my family — information that you have been given ample time and resources to discover — or you will not."

"There's nothing more I can do without access to the convent."

"How long will it take to gain access?"

"It isn't going to be easy. I'll need formal permission to get in the front door. If they give me the go-ahead, it could take weeks before I find anything worthwhile. I'm planning to take a trip upstate after the New Year. It's a long process."

Grigori folded the maps and returned them to Verlaine, his hands shaking. Suppressing his annoyance, he removed a cash-filled envelope from the inside pocket of his overcoat.

"What's this?" Verlaine asked, looking at the contents, his astonishment apparent at finding a pack of crisp hundred-dollar bills.

Percival put his hand upon Verlaine's shoulder, feeling a human warmth that he found foreign and alluring. "It is a bit of a drive up," he said, leading Verlaine along the walkway toward Columbus Circle, "but I believe you have time to make it before nightfall. This bonus will compensate for the inconvenience. Once you've had a chance to complete your work and have brought me verification of Abigail Rockefeller's association with this convent, we will continue our discussion."

St. Rose Convent, Milton, New York

Evangeline walked to the far end of the fourth floor, beyond the television room to a rickety iron door that opened upon a set of mildewed steps. Mindful of the softness of the wood, she followed the steps up, moving with the curvature of the damp stone wall until she stood in a narrow, circular turret high above the convent's grounds. The tower was the only piece of the original structure remaining in the upper floors. It grew from the Adoration Chapel itself, rose in a twist of spiraled stairs past the second and third floors and opened up on the fourth floor, giving the sisters access from their bedroom chambers straight to the chapel. Although the turret had been designed to offer the sisters a direct path to their midnight devotionals, it had long been abandoned for the main staircase, which had the benefit of heat and electricity. Although the fire of 1944 had not reached the turret, Evangeline sensed smoke lingering in the rafters, as if the room had inhaled the sticky tar of the fumes and stopped breathing. Electrical wiring had never been installed, and the only light came from a series of lancet windows with heavy, handmade leaded glass that spanned the east curve of the tower. Even now, at midday, the room was consumed by an icy darkness as the relentless north wind rattled against the glass.

Evangeline pressed her hands upon the chilled windowpane. In the distance, anemic winter sunshine fell over a rise of rolling hills. Even the sunniest of December days cast a pall over the landscape, as if light passed through an unfocused lens. In the summer months, an abundance of brightness collected upon the trees each afternoon, giving the leaves an iridescent hue that winter light, no matter how bright, could not match. A month before, perhaps five weeks, the leaves had been brilliant umber, red, orange, yellow, a quiltwork of color reflected in the brown glass of river water. Evangeline imagined day-trippers from New York City taking the passenger train along the east side of the Hudson, gazing at the lovely foliage on their way to pick apples or pumpkins. Now the trees were bare, the hills covered with snow.

Evangeline took refuge in the tower only rarely, at best once or twice a year, when her thoughts drew her away from the community at large and sent her in search of a quiet place to think. It was not the usual order of things for one of the sisters to steal away from the group for contemplation, and Evangeline would often feel remorse for her actions for days after. And yet she could not stay away from the turret completely. Upon each visit she noticed how her mind attenuated, how her thoughts became clear and sharp as she ascended the steps, and even clearer as she peered over the landscape of the convent.

Standing at the window, she recalled the dream that had woken her that morning. Her mother had appeared to her, speaking softly in a language Evangeline could not comprehend. The ache she'd felt when she tried to hear her mother's voice again had remained with her all morning, and yet she did not remonstrate with herself for thinking of her mother. It was only natural. Today, the twenty-third of December, was Angela's birthday.

Evangeline remembered only fragments of her mother — Angela's long blond hair; the sound of her rapid, mellifluous French as she spoke on the telephone; her habit of leaving a cigarette in a glass ashtray, the air filling with nets of smoke that dissolved before Evangeline's eyes. She recalled the incredible height of her mother's shadow, a diaphanous darkness moving upon the wall of their fourteenth arrondissement apartment.

On the day her mother died, Evangeline's father picked her up from school in their red Citroën DS. He was alone, and this was unusual in itself. Her parents had the same line of work, a calling Evangeline knew now to be extremely dangerous, and they rarely went anywhere without each other. Evangeline saw at once that her father had been crying — his eyes were swollen and his skin ashen. After she climbed into the backseat of the car, arranging her coat and dropping her bookbag on her lap, her father told her that her mother was no longer with them. "She has left?" Evangeline asked, feeling a desperate confusion fill her as she tried to understand what he meant. "Where has she gone?"

Her father shook his head, as if the answer were incomprehensible. He said, "She has been taken from us."

Later, when Evangeline understood fully that Angela had been abducted and killed, she could not quite understand why her father had chosen the words he had. Her mother had not simply been taken: Her mother had been murdered, extinguished from the world as thoroughly as light leaves the sky when the sun sinks behind the horizon.

As a girl, Evangeline had not had the ability to understand how young her mother had been when she'd died. With time, however, she began to measure her own age in relation to Angela's life, holding each year as a precious reenactment. At eighteen, her mother had met Evangeline's father. At eighteen, Evangeline had taken vows as a Franciscan Sister

51

of Perpetual Adoration. At twenty-three, the age Evangeline had reached at present, her mother had married her father. At thirty-nine, her mother had been killed. In comparing the timelines of their lives, Evangeline wove her existence around her mother as if she were wisteria clinging to a trellis. No matter how she tried to convince herself that she had been fine without her mother and that her father had managed the best he could, she knew that in every minute of every day Angela's absence lived in her heart.

Evangeline was born in Paris. They lived together — her father and mother and Evangeline — in an apartment in Montparnasse. The rooms of the apartment were burned upon her memory so vividly that she felt as if she'd lived there yesterday. The apartment rambled, each room connecting to the next, with high, coffered ceilings and immense windows that filled the space with a granular gray light. The bathroom was abnormally large — as big as the communal lavatory at St. Rose, at least. Evangeline remembered her mother's clothes hooked upon the bathroom wall — a lightweight spring dress and a brilliant red silk scarf knotted about the hanger's neck and a pair of patent-leather sandals placed below them, arranged as if worn by an invisible woman. A porcelain bathtub crouched at the center of the bathroom, compact and heavy as a living thing, its lip glistening with water, its clawed feet curled.

Another memory Evangeline held close, playing and replaying it in her mind as if it were a film, was of a walk she had taken with her mother the year of her death. Hand in hand they went along the sidewalks and cobblestone streets, moving so fast that Evangeline had to jog to keep up with Angela's stride. It was spring, or so she guessed from the colorful abundance of flowers in the window boxes hanging from the apartment blocks.

Angela had been anxious that afternoon. Holding Evangeline's hand tightly, she led her through the courtyard of a university — at least Evangeline had believed it to be a university, with its great stone portico and the abundance of people lounging in the courtyard. The building appeared exceptionally old, but everything in Paris seemed ancient compared to America, especially in Montparnasse and the Latin Quarter. Of one thing, however, she was certain: Angela was searching for someone in the masses of people. She dragged Evangeline through the crowd, squeezing her hand until it tingled, signaling that she should hurry to keep up. Finally a middle-aged woman greeted them, stepping close and kissing her mother on both cheeks. The woman had black hair and her mother's lovely, chiseled features, softened only slightly by age. Evangeline recognized her grandmother, Gabriella, but knew that she was not allowed to speak to her. Angela and Gabriella had quarreled, as they often did, and Evangeline knew not to put herself between them. Many years later, when both she and her grandmother lived in the United States, Evangeline began to learn more about Gabriella. It was only then that she came to understand her grandmother with some clarity.

Although so many years had passed, it still upset Evangeline that the one thing she recalled from the walk with her mother with extreme precision struck her as bizarrely mundane — the gleaming leather of her mother's brown knee-high boots worn over a pair of faded blue jeans. For some reason Evangeline could recall everything about the boots — the stacked heels, the zippers that tracked from ankle to calf, the sound the soles made upon brick and stone — but she could not for the life of her recall the shape of her mother's hand, the curve of her shoulders. Through the haze of time, she had lost the essence of her mother.

What tortured Evangeline perhaps most of all was that she had lost the ability to recall her mother's face. From photographs she knew that Angela had been tall and thin and fair, her hair often tucked up in a cap in a way that Evangeline associated with gamine French actresses of the 1960s. But in each picture, Angela's face appeared so different that Evangeline had difficulty creating a composite image. In profile her nose seemed sharp and her lips thin. At three-quarters her cheeks were full and high, almost Asian. When looking directly at the camera, her big blue eyes overwhelmed all else. It seemed to Evangeline that the structure of her mother's face shifted with the light and position of the camera, leaving nothing solid behind.

Evangeline's father had not wished to discuss Angela after her death. If Evangeline inquired about her, he would often simply turn away, as if he had not heard her speak. Other times, if he had opened a bottle of wine with their dinner, he might relate a tantalizing piece of information about her — the way Angela would spend all night at her laboratory and return to the apartment at sunrise. How she would become so engrossed in her work that she would leave books and papers wherever they fell; how she wished to live near the ocean, away from Paris; the happiness Evangeline had brought her. In all the years they lived together, he had discouraged any substantial discussion of her. And yet when Evangeline asked about her mother, something in his demeanor opened, as if welcoming a spirit that brought pain and comfort in equal measure. Hating and loving the past, her father seemed both to welcome Angela's ghost and to persuade himself that it did not exist at all. Evangeline was certain that he had never stopped loving her. He had never remarried and had few friends in the United States. For many years he made a weekly call to Paris, talking for hours in a language that Evangeline found so gorgeous and musical that she would sit in the kitchen and simply listen to his voice.

Her father had brought her to St. Rose when she was twelve, entrusting her to the women who would become her mentors, encouraging her to believe in their world when, if she were honest with herself, faith seemed like a precious but unattainable substance, one possessed by many but denied to her. Over time Evangeline came to understand that her father valued obedience above faith, training above creativity, and restraint above emotion. Over time she had fallen into routine and duty. Over time she had lost sight of her mother, her grandmother, herself.

Her father visited her often at St. Rose. He sat with her in the community room, frozen upon the couch, watching her with great interest, as if she were an experiment whose outcome he wished to observe. Her father would stare intently into her face as if it were a telescope through which, if he strained his vision, he might view the features of his beloved wife. But, in truth, Evangeline looked nothing at all like her mother. Instead her features had captured the likeness of her grandmother, Gabriella. It was a likeness her father chose to ignore. He had died three years before, but while he had lived, he held steadfastly to the conviction that his only child resembled a ghost.

Evangeline squeezed the necklace in her hand until the sharp point of the lyre drove deep into the skin of her palm. She knew she must hurry — she was needed in the library, and the sisters might wonder where she had gone — and so she let thoughts of her parents recede and focused upon the task at hand.

Bending to the floor, she slid her fingers over the rough brickwork of the turret wall until she felt the slightest movement in the third row from the floor. Inserting the flat of a fingernail into a groove, she levered the loose brick and pulled it from the wall. From the space Evangeline removed a narrow steel box. The very act of touching the cold metal relieved her mind, as if its solidity contradicted the insubstantial quality of memory.

Evangeline set the box before her and lifted the top. Inside was a small diary bound with a leather strap and fastened with a golden clasp molded in the shape of an angel, its body long and thin. A blue sapphire marked the angel's eye, and the wings, when pressed, released the latch so that the pages fell open upon her lap. The leather was worn and scuffed and the binding flexible. On the first page, the word ANGELOLOGY had been stamped in gold. As she flipped through the pages, Evangeline's eye skimmed over hand-drawn maps, notes scribbled in colored inks, sketches of angels and musical instruments drawn in the margins. A musical score filled a page at the center of the notebook. Historical analysis and biblical lore filled many pages, and in the last quarter of the notebook there grew a mass of numbers and calculations that Evangeline did not understand. The diary had belonged to her grandmother. Now it belonged to Evangeline. She ran her hand over the leather cover, wishing she could understand the secrets inside.

Evangeline withdrew a photograph tucked in the back of the diary, a snapshot of her mother and grandmother, arms wrapped around each other. The picture had been taken the year of Evangeline's birth — she had compared the date stamped upon the border of the photograph with her own birthday and had come to the conclusion that her mother had been three months pregnant at the time, although her condition wasn't at all apparent. Evangeline gazed upon it, her heart aching. Angela and Gabriella were happy in the photo. She would give anything, trade everything she had, to be with them again.

Evangeline took care to return to the library with a cheerful expression, hiding her thoughts as best she could. The fire had gone out, and a draft of cold air swept from the stone fireplace at the center of the room and tickled the edges of her skirt. She retrieved a black cardigan from her worktable and wrapped it about her shoulders before going to the center of the rectangular library to investigate. The fireplace was well used in the long, cold winter months, and one of the sisters must have left the flue open. Rather than close the flue, Evangeline opened it fully. She took a piece of the knotty pine stacked in the log rack, placed it in the middle of an iron grating, and lit kindling paper around it. Clasping the brass handles of the bellows, she blew a few subtle gusts of air until the fire, encouraged, caught.

Evangeline had spent very little time studying the angelic texts that had brought St. Rose Convent such renown in theological circles. Some of these texts, such as histories of angelic representation in art and works of serious angelology, including modern copies of medieval angelological schema and studies of Thomas Aquinas's and St. Augustine's views on the role of the angels in the universe, had been in the collection from the 1809 founding. A number of studies on angelmorphism could also be found among the stacks, although these were quite academic and did not catch the interest of many of the sisters, especially the younger generation, who (truth be told) did not spend much time on angels at all. The softer side of angelology was also represented, despite the cold eye the community cast upon the New Agers: There were books on the various cults of angel veneration in the ancient and modern world as well as the phenomenon of guardian angels. There were also a number of art books filled with plates, including an exceptional volume of Edward Burne-Jones's angels that Evangeline loved in particular.

On the opposite wall from the fireplace there stood a rostrum for the library ledger. Here the sisters wrote the titles of books they removed from the stacks, taking as many as they wished to their cells and returning them at will. It was a haphazard system that somehow worked perfectly well, with the same intuitive matriarchal organization that marked the convent. It was not always thus. In the nineteenth century — before the ledger — books had come and gone without systemization, piling up on whatever shelf space was available. The mundane task of finding a work of nonfiction was as much a matter of luck as an impromptu miracle. The library was given over to such chaos until Sister Lucrezia (1851–1923) imposed alphabetization at the turn of the twentieth century. When a later librarian, Sister Drusilla (1890–1985), suggested the Dewey decimal system, there was a general outcry. Rather than succumb to gross systemization, the sisters agreed to the ledger, writing each book's title in blue ink on the thick paper.

Evangeline's interests were more practical, and she would rather pore over the lists of local charities run by the sisters — the food bank in Poughkeepsie, the Spirit of World Peace Study Group in Milton, and the St. Rose–Salvation Army Annual Clothes Drive that had drop-off locations from Woodstock to Red Hook. But like all the other nuns who took vows at St. Rose, Evangeline had learned the basic facts about angels. She knew that angels were created before the earth formed, their voices ringing through the void as God molded heaven and earth (Genesis 1:1–5). Evangeline knew that angels were immaterial, ethereal, filled with luminosity, and yet they spoke in human language — Hebrew according to Jewish scholars, Latin or Greek according to Christian. Although the Bible had only a handful of instances of angelophony — Jacob wrestling an angel (Genesis 32:24–30); Ezekiel's vision (1:1–14); the Annunciation (Luke 1:26–38) — these moments were wondrous and divine, instances when the gossamer curtain between heaven and earth ripped and all of humanity witnessed the marvel of ethereal beings. Evangeline often wondered at this meeting of man and angel, the material and immaterial brushing against each other like wind against the skin. In the end she concluded that trying to capture an angel in the mind was a bit like scooping water with a sieve. And yet the sisters of St. Rose had not given up the effort. Hundreds and hundreds of books about angels lined the shelves of their library.

To Evangeline's surprise, Sister Philomena joined her at the fire. Philomena's body was as round and dappled as a pear, her height reduced by osteoporosis. Recently Evangeline had become concerned about Sister Philomena's health when she began to forget meetings and misplace her keys. The nuns of Philomena's generation — known by the younger generation as the Elder Sisters — were not able to retire from their duties until much later in life, so dramatically had the order's numbers decreased in the years after the Vatican II reforms. Sister Philomena in particular always appeared overworked and agitated. In some ways Vatican II had robbed the older generation of retirement.

Evangeline herself believed the reforms beneficial for the most part — she had been free to choose a comfortable uniform over the old-fashioned Franciscan habit and had participated in modern educational opportunities, taking a degree in history from nearby Bard College. The opinions of the Elder Sisters, by contrast, seemed frozen in time. Yet, strange as it seemed, Evangeline held views that were often similar to those of the Elder Sisters, whose opinions had been formed during the Roosevelt era and the Depression and World War II. Evangeline found she admired the opinions of Sister Ludovica, their oldest sister at 104, who would command Evangeline to sit at her side and listen to stories of the old days. "There was none of this laissez-faire, do-what-you-want-to-with-your-time nonsense," Sister Ludovica would say, leaning over in her wheelchair, her thin hands shaking slightly on her lap. "We were sent to orphanages and parochial schools to teach before we knew the subject! We worked all day and prayed all night! There was no heat in our cells! We bathed in cold water and ate cooked oats and potatoes for supper! When there were no books, I memorized all of John Milton's *Paradise Lost* so that I could recite his lovely, lovely words to my class: 'Th' infernal Serpent; he it was whose guile, / Stirred up with envy and revenge, deceived / The mother of mankind, / What time his pride / Had cast him out from Heaven, with all his host / Of rebel Angels, by whose aid, aspiring / To set himself in glory above his peers, / He trusted to have equalled the Most High, / If he opposed, and with ambitious aim / Against the throne and monarchy of God, / Raised impious war in Heaven and battle proud, / With vain attempt.' Did the children memorize Milton, too? Yes! Now, I am sad to say, education is all fun and games."

Still, despite their vast differences in opinion about the changes, the sisters lived as a harmonious family. They were protected from the vicissitudes of the outside world in ways that seculars were not. The St. Rose land and buildings had been bought outright in the late nineteenth century, and despite the temptation to modernize their quarters, they did not borrow on the property. They produced fruits and vegetables on the grounds, their henhouse gave four dozen eggs a day, and their pantries were filled with preserves. The convent was so secure, so abundantly stocked with food and medicine, so well equipped for their intellectual and spiritual needs, that the sisters sometimes joked that if a second Flood were to encompass the Hudson River Valley, it would be possible for the women of St. Rose Convent simply to bolt the heavy iron doors at the front and back entrances, seal the windows tight, and pray on as usual for many years to come in their own self-sustaining ark.

Sister Philomena took Evangeline by the arm and led her to her office, where, stooping over her work area, the dolman sleeves of her habit brushing the keys of the typewriter, she searched through the papers for something. Such hunting about her office was not unusual. Philomena was nearly blind, with thick glasses that occupied a disproportionate portion of her face, and Evangeline often helped her to locate objects that were hidden in plain sight. "Perhaps you can help me," Sister Philomena said at last.

"I am happy to assist," Evangeline said, "if you tell me what to look for."

"I believe we received a letter regarding our angelic collection. Mother Perpetua had a telephone call from a young man in New York City — a researcher or consultant or something of that nature. He claims to have written a letter. Has such a letter come across your desk? I know I would not have missed it had I found such an inquiry. Mother Perpetua wants to be sure we are consistent with St. Rose policy. She would very much like a response sent at once."

"The letter came today," Evangeline said.

Sister Philomena peered through the lenses of her glasses, her eyes large and watery as she strained to see Evangeline. "You have read it, then?"

"Of course," Evangeline said. "I open all mail the instant it arrives."

"It was a request for information?"

Evangeline was not used to being questioned so directly about her work. "Actually," she said, "it was a request to visit our archives in search of specific information about Mother Innocenta."

A dark look passed over Philomena's face. "You've replied to the letter?"

"With our standard response," Evangeline said, leaving out the fact that she had destroyed the letter before mailing it, an act of duplicity that felt deeply foreign. It was unsettling —

her ability to lie to Philomena with such ease. Nevertheless, Evangeline continued, "I am aware that we do not allow amateur research in the archives," she said. "I wrote that it is our standard policy to refuse such requests. Of course, I was polite."

"Fine," Philomena said, examining Evangeline with particular interest. "We must be very careful when we open our home to outsiders. Mother Perpetua gave specific orders to block all inquiries."

Evangeline was not at all surprised that Mother Perpetua took such a personal interest in their collection. She was a gruff and distant figure at the convent, one whom Evangeline did not see often, a woman with strong opinions and a heady management style whom the Elder Sisters admired for frugality and faulted for modern vision. Indeed, Mother Perpetua had pushed for the Elder Sisters to implement the more benign Vatican II changes, urging them to discard their cumbersome woolen habits for those of lighter fabrics, a suggestion they did not take.

As Evangeline turned to leave the office, Sister Philomena cleared her throat, a sign that she had not finished quite yet and that Evangeline should stay just a moment longer. Philomena said, "I have worked in the archives for many years, my child, and have weighed each request with great care. I have turned away many pesky researchers and writers and pseudo religious. It is a great responsibility to be the guardian at the gate. I would like you to report all unusual correspondence to me."

"Of course," Evangeline said, confused by the zeal in Philomena's voice. Her curiosity getting the better of her, Evangeline added, "There is one thing I was wondering, Sister."

"Yes?" Philomena responded.

"Was there anything unusual about Mother Innocenta?"

"Unusual?"

"Something that would inspire interest in a private research consultant whose specialty is art history?"

"I haven't the slightest notion what might interest such people, my dear," Sister Philomena said, clucking her tongue as she walked to the door. "I would hope that the history of art is filled with enough paintings and sculptures to occupy an art historian indefinitely. Yet, apparently, our collection of angelic images is irresistible. One can never be too careful, child. You will inform me if there are any new requests?"

"Of course," Evangeline said, feeling her heart beat unnaturally fast.

Sister Philomena must have taken note of her young assistant's distress and, stepping closer, so that Evangeline could smell something vaguely mineral about her — talcum powder, perhaps, or arthritis cream — she took Evangeline's hands, warming them between her chubby palms. "Now, there is no reason for worry. We won't let them in. Try as they might, we will hold the door closed."

"I'm sure you're right, Sister," Evangeline said, smiling despite her bewilderment. "Thank you for your concern."

"You're welcome, child," Philomena said, yawning. "If something more should come up, I'll be on the fourth floor the remainder of the afternoon. It is nearly time for my nap."

The instant Sister Philomena had left, Evangeline was thrown into a morass of guilt and speculation over what had just occurred between them. She regretted that she had misled her superior in such a manner, but she also wondered at Philomena's strange reaction to the letter and the intensity of her desire to keep visitors away from St. Rose's holdings. Of course Evangeline understood the necessity of protecting the environment of contemplative calm they all worked hard to create. Sister Philomena's reaction to the letter had seemed excessive, but what had inspired Evangeline to lie in such a bold and unjustifiable fashion? Yet, there it was, a fact: She had lied to an Elder Sister. Even this breach had not assuaged her curiosity. What was the nature of the relationship between Mother Innocenta and Mrs. Rockefeller? What had Sister Philomena meant when she said that they would not "open our home to outsiders"? What harm could possibly come from sharing their beautiful collection of books and images? What did they have to hide? In the years Evangeline had spent at St. Rose — nearly half her life — there had been nothing at all out of the ordinary. The Franciscan Sisters of Perpetual Adoration led exemplary lives.

Evangeline slid her hand into her pocket and pulled out the thin, weathered onionskin letter. The writing was florid and slick — her eyes slid across the arches and dips of the cursive with ease. *"Your guidance has helped the progress of the expedition enormously, and I daresay my own contributions have been useful as well. Celestine Clochette will be arriving in New York early February. More news will reach you soon. Until then, I am sincerely yours, A. A. Rockefeller."*

Evangeline reread the letter, trying to understand its meaning. She folded the thin paper carefully, securing it in her pocket, knowing that she could not continue her work until she understood the significance of Abigail Rockefeller's letter.

Fifth Avenue, Upper East Side, New York City

Percival Grigori tapped the tip of his cane as he waited for the elevator, a rhythm of sharp metallic clicks pounding out the seconds. The oak-paneled lobby of his building — an exclusive prewar with views of Central Park — was so familiar that he hardly noticed it any longer. The Grigori family had occupied the penthouse for over half a century. Once he might have registered the deference of the doorman, the opulent arrangement of orchids in the foyer, the polished ebony and mother-of-pearl elevator casement, the fire sending a spray of light and warmth across the marble floor. But Percival Grigori noticed nothing at all except the pain crackling through his joints, the popping of his knees with each step. As the doors of the elevator slid open and he hobbled inside, he regarded his stooped image in the polished brass of the elevator car and looked quickly away.

At the thirteenth floor, he stepped into a marble vestibule and unlocked the door to the

70

Grigori apartment. Instantly the soothing elements of his private life — part antique, part modern, part gleaming wood, part sparkling glass — filled his senses, relaxing the tension in his shoulders. He threw his keys onto a silk pillow at the bottom of a Chinese porcelain bowl, shrugged his heavy cashmere overcoat into the lap of an upholstered banister-back chair, and walked through the travertine gallery. Vast rooms opened before him — a sitting room, a library, a dining hall with a four-tiered Venetian chandelier suspended overhead. An expanse of picture windows staged the chaotic ballet of a snowstorm.

At the far end of the apartment, the curve of a grand staircase led to his mother's suite of rooms. Peering up, Percival discerned a party of her friends gathered in the formal sitting room. Guests came to the apartment for lunch or dinner nearly every day, impromptu gatherings that allowed his mother to hold court for her favorite friends from the neighborhood. It was a ritual she had grown more and more accustomed to, primarily because of the power it gave her: She selected those people she wished to see, enclosed them in the dark-paneled lair of her private quarters, and let the rest of the world go on with its tedium and misery. For years she had left her suite only on rare occasions, when accompanied by Percival or his sister, and only at night. His mother had grown so comfortable with the arrangement, and her circle had become so regular, that she rarely complained of her confinement.

Quietly, so as not to draw attention to himself, Percival ducked into a bathroom at the end of the hallway, shut the door softly behind him, and locked it. In a succession of quick movements, he discarded a tailored wool jacket and a silk tie, dropping each piece of clothing onto the ceramic tiles. Fingers trembling, he unbuttoned six pearlescent buttons, working upward to his throat. He peeled away his shirt and stood to full height before a large mirror hung upon the wall.

Running his fingers over his chest, he felt a mélange of leather strips weaving one over the other. The device wrapped about him like an elaborate harness, creating a system of stays that, when fully fastened, had the overall appearance of a black corset. The straps were so taut they cut into his skin. Somehow, no matter how he fastened it, the leather cinched too tightly. Struggling for air, Percival loosened one strap, then the next, working the leather through small silver buckles with deliberation until, with a final tug, the device fell to the floor, the leather slapping the tiles.

His bare chest was smooth, without navel or nipples, the skin so white as to appear cut from wax. Swiveling his shoulder blades, he could see the reflection of his body in the mirror — his shoulders, his long thin arms, and the sculpted curve of his torso. Mounted at the center of his spine, matted by sweat, deformed by the severe pressure of the harness, were two tender nubs of bone. With a mixture of wonder and pain, he noted that his wings — once full and strong and bowed like golden scimitars — had all but disintegrated. The remnants of his wings were black with disease, the feathers withered, the bones atrophied. In the middle of his back, two open wounds, blue and raw from chafing, fixed the blackened bones in a gelatinous pool of congealed blood. Bandages, repeated cleanings — no amount of care helped to heal the wounds or relieve his pain. Yet he understood that the true agony would come when there was nothing left of his wings. All that had distinguished him, all that the others had envied, would be gone.

The first symptoms of the disorder had appeared ten years before, when fine tracks of mildew materialized along the inner shafts and vanes of the feathers, a phosphorescent green fungus that grew like patina on copper. He had thought it a mere infection. He'd had his wings cleaned and groomed, specifying that each feather be brushed with oils, and yet the pestilence remained. Within months his wingspan had decreased by half. The dusty golden shimmer of healthy wings faded. Once, he had been able to compress his wings with ease, folding his majestic plumage smoothly against his back. The airy mass of golden feathers had tucked into the arched grooves along his spine, a maneuver that rendered the wings completely undetectable. Although physical in substance, the structure of healthy wings gave them the visual properties of a hologram. Like the bodies of the angels themselves, his wings had been substantial objects utterly unimpaired by the laws of matter. Percival had been able to lift his wings through thick layers of clothing as easily as if he had moved them through air.

Now he found that he could no longer retract them at all, and so they were a perpetual presence, a reminder of his diminishment. Pain overwhelmed him; he lost all capability for flight. Alarmed, his family had brought in specialists, who confirmed what the Grigori family most feared: Percival had contracted a degenerative disorder that had been spreading through their community. Doctors predicted that his wings would die, then his muscles. He would be confined to a wheelchair, and then, when his wings had withered completely and their roots had melted away, Percival would die. Years of treatments had slowed the progression of the disease but had not stopped it.

Percival turned on the faucet and splashed cool water over his face, trying to dissipate the fever that had overtaken him. The harness helped him to keep his spine erect, an increasingly difficult task as his muscles grew weak. In the months since it had become necessary to wear the harness, the pain had only grown more acute. He never quite got used to the bite of leather on his skin, the buckles as sharp as pins against his body, the burning sensation of ripped flesh. Many of their kind chose to live away from the world when they became ill. This was a fate Percival could not begin to accept.

Percival took Verlaine's envelope in his hands. Feeling its heft with pleasure, he disemboweled the dossier with the delicacy of a cat feasting upon a trapped bird, tearing open the paper with slow deliberation and placing the pages upon the marble surface of the bathroom sink. He read the report, hoping to find something that might be of use to him. Verlaine's summary was a detailed and thorough document — forty pages of single-spaced lines forming a black, muscular column of type from beginning to end — but from what he could see there was nothing new.

Putting Verlaine's documents back in the envelope, Percival took a deep breath and slipped the harness over his body. The tight leather caused much less trouble now that his color had returned and his fingers had grown steady. Once dressed, he saw that he'd ruined all hope of being presentable. His clothes were wrinkled and sweat-stained, his hair fell into his face in a messy blond sweep, his eyes were bloodshot. His mother would be mortified to see him so careworn.

Smoothing his hair, Percival left the bathroom and set out to find her. The sounds of crystal glasses clinking, the hum of a string quartet, and the shrill laughter of her friends became louder as he ascended the grand staircase. Percival paused at the edge of the room to catch his breath — the slightest effort drained his strength.

His mother's rooms were always filled with flowers and servants and gossip, as if she were a countess holding a nightly salon, but Percival found the gathering under way to be even more elaborate than he had expected, with fifty or more guests. A cantilevered ceiling rose above the party, the skylights' usual brightness dimmed by a cap of snow. The walls of the upper floor were lined with paintings his family had acquired over the course of five hundred years, most of which the Grigoris had chosen from museums and collectors for their private enjoyment. The majority of the paintings were masterworks, and all were original — they had provided expert copies of the paintings to be circulated through the world at large, taking the originals for themselves. Their art required meticulous care, everything from climate control to a team of professional cleaners, but the collection was well worth the trouble. There were a number of Dutch masters, a few from the Renaissance, and a smattering of nineteenth-century engravings. An entire wall at the center of the sitting room held the famous Hieronymus Bosch triptych *The Garden of Earthly Delights,* a wonderfully gruesome depiction of paradise and hell. Percival had grown up studying its grotesqueries, the large central panel depicting life on earth providing him with early instruction on the ways of humanity. He found it particularly fascinating that Bosch's depiction of hell contained gruesome musical instruments, lutes and drums in various stages of dissection. A perfect copy of the painting hung at the Museo del Prado in Madrid, a reproduction Percival's father had personally commissioned.

Gripping the ivory head of his cane, Percival made his way through the crowd. He usually put up with such debauchery but felt now — in his current condition — that it would be difficult to make it across the room. He nodded to the father of a former schoolmate — a member of his family's circle for many centuries — standing at a remove from the crowd, his immaculate white wings on display. Percival smiled slightly at a model he had once taken to dinner, a lovely creature with pellucid blue eyes who came from an established Swiss family. She was far too young for her wings to have emerged, and so there was no way to glean the full extent of her breeding, but Percival knew her family to be old and influential. Before his illness had struck, his mother had tried to convince him to marry the girl. One day she would be a powerful member of their community.

Percival could tolerate their friends from old families — it was to his benefit to do so — but he found their new acquaintances, a collection of nouveau riche money managers, media moguls, and other hangers-on who had insinuated themselves into his mother's good graces, to be loathsome. They were not like the Grigoris, of course, but most were close enough to be sympathetic to the delicate balance of deference and discretion the Grigori family required. They tended to gather at his mother's side, inundating her with compliments and flattering her sense of noblesse oblige, ensuring that they would be invited to the Grigori apartment the next afternoon.

If it were up to Percival, their lives would be kept private, but his mother could not endure being alone. He suspected that she surrounded herself with amusement to stave off the terrible truth that their kind had lost their place in the order of things. Their family had formed alliances generations before and depended upon a network of friendships and relations to maintain their position and prosperity. In the Old World, they were deeply, inextricably connected to their family's history. In New York, they had to re-create it everywhere they went.

Otterley, his younger sister, stood by the window, a dim light falling over her. Otterley was of average height — six feet three inches — thin, and zipped into a low-cut dress, a bit much but in keeping with her taste. She'd pulled her blond hair back into a severe chignon and had painted her lips a bright pink that seemed a little too young for her. Otterley had been stunning once — even more lovely than the Swiss model standing nearby — but had burned through her youth in a hundred-year spree of parties and ill-suited relationships that had left her — and their fortune — significantly diminished. Now she was middle-aged, well into her two-hundredth year, and despite her efforts to conceal it, her skin had the appearance of a plastic mannequin's. Try as she might, she couldn't recapture the way she had looked in the nineteenth century.

Seeing Percival, Otterley sauntered to his side, slid a long bare arm through his arm, and led him into the crowd as if he were an invalid. Every man and woman in the room watched Otterley. If they had not done business with his sister, they knew her from her work on various family boards or by the incessant social calendar she maintained. Their friends and acquaintances were wary of his sister. No one could afford to displease Otterley Grigori.

"And where have you been hiding?" Otterley asked Percival, narrowing her eyes in a reptilian stare. She had been raised in London, where their father still resided, and her crisp British accent had a particularly sharp sting when she became irritated.

"I doubt very much that you're feeling lonely," Percival said, glancing at the crowd.

"One is never alone with Mother," Otterley replied, tart. "She makes these things more elaborate each week."

"She's here somewhere, I assume?"

Otterley's expression hardened in irritation. "Last I checked, she was receiving admirers at her throne."

They walked to the far end of the room, past a wall of French windows that seemed to invite one to step through their thick, transparent depths and float out above the foggy, snow-laden city. Anakim, the class of servants the Grigoris and all well-bred families kept, stepped in their path and cut away. *More champagne, sir? Madam?* Dressed entirely in black, the Anakim were shorter and smaller-boned than the class of beings they served. In addition to their black uniforms, his mother insisted that they wear their wings exposed, to distinguish them from her guests. The difference in shape and span was marked. Whereas the pure class of guests had muscular, feathered wings, the servants' wings were light as film, webs of gossamer tissue that appeared washed in sheets of gray opalescence. Because of the wings' structure — they resembled nothing so much as the wings of an insect — the servants flew with precise, quick movements that allowed great accuracy. They had huge yellow eyes, high cheekbones, and pale skin. Percival had witnessed a flight of Anakim during the Second World War, when a swarm of servants had descended upon a caravan of humans fleeing the bombing of London. The servants ripped the wretched people apart with ease. After this episode Percival understood why the Anakim were believed to be capricious and unpredictable beings fit only to serve their superiors.

Every few steps Percival recognized family friends and acquaintances, their crystal champagne flutes catching the light. Conversations melted into the air, leaving the impression of one continual velvety drone of gossip. He overheard talk of holidays and yachts and business ventures, conversation that characterized his mother's friends as much as the flash of diamonds and the sparkling cruelty of their laughter. The guests looked upon him from every corner, taking in his shoes, his watch, pausing to examine the cane and finally — seeing Otterley — realizing that the sick, disheveled gentleman was Percival Grigori III, heir to the Grigori name and fortune.

Finally they reached their mother, Sneja Grigori, stretched out upon her favorite divan, a beautiful and imposing piece of Gothic furniture with serpents carved into the wood frame. Sneja had gained weight in the decades since her move to New York and wore only loose, flowing tunics that draped against her body in silken sheets. She'd splayed her lush, brilliant-colored wings behind her, folded and arranged to great effect, as if displaying the family's jewels. As Percival approached, he was nearly blinded by their luminosity, each delicate feather shimmering like a sheet of tinted foil. Sneja's wings were the pride of the family, the height of their beauty proof of the purity of their heritage. It was a mark of distinction that Percival's maternal grandmother had been endowed with multicolored wings that stretched over thirty-six feet, a span that had not been seen in a thousand years. It was rumored that such wings had served as models for the angels of Fra Angelico, Lorenzo Monaco, and Botticini. Wings, Sneja had once told Percival, were a symbol of their blood, their breeding, the predominance of their position in the community. Displaying them properly brought power and prestige, and it was no small disappointment that neither Otterley nor Percival had given Sneja an heir to carry on the family endowment.

Which was precisely the reason it annoyed Percival that Otterley hid her wings. Instead of displaying them, as one would expect, she insisted upon keeping them folded tight against her body, as if she were some common hybrid and not a member of one of the most prestigious angelic families in the United States. Percival understood that the ability to retract one's wings was a great tool, especially when in mixed society. Indeed, it gave one the ability to move in human society without being detected. But in private company it was an offense to keep one's wings hidden.

Sneja Grigori greeted Otterley and Percival, lifting a hand so that it might be kissed by her children. "My cherubs," she said, her voice deep, her accent vaguely Germanic, a remnant of her Austrian childhood in the House of Hapsburg. Pausing, she narrowed her eyes and examined Otterley's necklace — a globular pink diamond solitaire sunk in an antique setting. "What a superior piece of jewelry," she said, as if surprised to find such a treasure about her daughter's neck.

"Don't you recognize it?" Otterley said, lightly. "It is one of Grandmother's pieces."

"Is it?" Sneja lifted the diamond between her thumb and forefinger so that light played off the faceted surface. "I would think I should recognize it, but it seems quite foreign to me. It is from my room?"

"No," Otterley replied, her manner guarded.

"Isn't it from the vault, Otterley?" Percival asked.

Otterley pursed her lips, giving him a look that told him at once that he had given his sister away.

"Ah, well, that would explain its mystery," Sneja said. "I haven't been to the vault in so long I've completely forgotten its contents. Are all of my mother's pieces as brilliant as this?"

"They are lovely, Mother," Otterley said, her composure shaken. Otterley had been taking pieces from the vault for years without their mother noticing.

"I simply adore this piece in particular," Sneja said. "Perhaps I will have to make a midnight trip to the vault? It may be time to do an inventory."

Without hesitation Otterley unfastened the necklace and placed it in her mother's hand. "It will look stunning on you, Mother," she said. Then, without waiting for her mother's reaction, or perhaps to mask the anguish of giving up such a jewel, Otterley turned on her stiletto heels and slinked back into the crowd, her dress clinging to her as if wet.

Sneja held the necklace to the light — it burst into a ball of liquid fire — before dropping it into her beaded evening clutch. Then she turned to Percival, as if suddenly recalling that her only son had witnessed her victory. "It is rather funny," Sneja said. "Otterley thinks I am unaware that she's been stealing my jewelry these twenty-five years."

Percival laughed. "You haven't let on that you've known. If you had, Otterley would have stopped ages ago."

His mother waved the observation away as if it were a fly. "I know everything that goes on in this family," she said, adjusting herself on the divan so that the arch of a wing caught the light. "Including the fact that you have not been taking proper care of yourself. You must rest more, eat more, sleep more. Things cannot simply go on as usual. It is time to make preparations for the future."

"That is precisely what I have been doing," Percival said, annoyed that his mother insisted upon directing him about as if he were in his first century of life.

"I see," Sneja said, evaluating her son's irritation. "You have had your meeting."

"As planned," Percival said.

"And that is why you have come upstairs with such a sour look — you wish to tell me about the progress you've made. The meeting did not go as planned?"

"Do they ever?" Percival said, though his disappointment was plain. "I admit: I had higher hopes for this one."

"Yes," Sneja said, looking past Percival. "We all did."

"Come." Percival took his mother's hand and helped her from the divan. "Let me speak to you alone for a moment."

"You cannot talk to me here?"

"Please," Percival said, glancing at the party with repulsion. "It is completely impossible."

With her audience of admirers captivated,

Sneja made a great show of leaving the divan. Unfurling her wings, she stretched them away from her shoulders so that they draped about her like a cloak. Percival watched her, a tremor of jealousy stopping him cold. His mother's wings were gorgeous, shimmering, healthy, full-plumed. A gradation of soft color radiated from the tips, where the feathers were tiny and roseate, and moved to the center of her back, where the feathers grew large and glittering. Percival's wings, when he'd had them, had been even larger than his mother's, sharp and dramatic, the feathers precisely shaped daggers of brilliant, powdery gold. He could not look at his mother without longing to be healthy again.

Sneja Grigori paused, allowing her guests to admire the beauty of her celestial attribute, and then, with a grace Percival found marvelous, his mother drew the wings to her body, folding them to her back with the ease of a geisha snapping closed a rice-paper fan.

Percival led his mother down the grand staircase by the arm. The dining-room table had been stacked with flowers and china, awaiting his mother's guests. A small roasted pig, a pear in its mouth, lay amid the bouquets, its side carved into moist shelves of pink. Through the windows Percival could see people hurrying below, small and black as rodents pushing through the freezing wind. Inside, it was warm and comfortable. A fire burned in the fireplace, and the faint sound of muted conversation and soft music descended upon them from upstairs.

Sneja arranged herself in a chair. "Now, tell me: What is it you want?" she asked, looking more than a little annoyed at being escorted away from the party. She took a cigarette from a platinum cigarette case and lit it. "If it is money again, Percival, you know you'll have to speak with your father. I haven't the slightest idea how you go through so much so quickly." His mother smiled, suddenly indulgent. "Well, actually, my dearest, I do have some idea. But your father is the one you must speak to about it."

Percival took a cigarette from his mother's case and allowed her to light it for him. He knew the moment he inhaled that he had made a mistake: His lungs burned. He coughed, trying to breathe. Sneja pushed a jade ashtray to Percival so that he could extinguish the cigarette.

After recovering his breath, he said, "My source has proved useless."

"As expected," Sneja said, inhaling the smoke from her cigarette.

"The discovery he claims to have made is of no value to us," Percival said.

"Discovery?" Sneja said, her eyes widening. "Exactly what kind of new discovery?"

As Percival elaborated upon the meeting,

outlining Verlaine's ridiculous obsession with architectural drawings of a convent in Milton, New York, and an equally infuriating preoccupation with the vagaries of ancient coins, his mother ran her long, chalk-white fingers over the polished lacquer table, then stopped abruptly, astonished.

"It is amazing," she said at last. "Do you really believe he found nothing of use?"

"What do you mean?"

"Somehow, in your zeal to trace Abigail Rockefeller's contacts, you've missed the larger point entirely." Sneja crushed out her cigarette and lit another. "These architectural drawings may be exactly what we're looking for. Give them to me. I would like to see them myself."

"I told Verlaine to keep them," Percival said, realizing even as he spoke them that those words would enrage her. "Besides, we ruled St. Rose Convent out after the 1944 attack. There was nothing left after the fire. Surely you don't imagine we missed something."

"I would like to be able to see for myself," Sneja said, without bothering to mask her frustration. "I suggest we go to this convent at once."

Percival jumped at an opportunity to redeem himself. "I have taken care of it," he said. "My source is en route to St. Rose this very instant to verify what he's found."

"Your source — he is one of us?"

Percival stared at his mother a moment, unsure how to proceed. Sneja would be furious to learn he had placed so much faith in Verlaine, who was outside their network of spies. "I know how you feel about using outsiders, but there is no cause to worry. I've had him thoroughly checked."

"Of course you have," Sneja said, exhaling cigarette smoke. "Just as you've had the others checked in the past."

"This is a new era," Percival said. He measured his words carefully, determined to remain calm in the face of his mother's criticism. "We are not so easily betrayed."

"Yes, you are correct, we live in a new era," Sneja retorted. "We live in an era of freedom and comfort, an era free of detection, an era of unprecedented wealth. We are free to do as we wish, to travel where we wish, to live as we wish. But this is also an era in which the best of our kind have become complacent and weak. It is an era of sickness and degeneration. Not you, nor I, nor any one of the ridiculous creatures hanging about in my sitting room are above detection."

"You think I have been complacent?" Percival said, his voice rising despite his efforts. He took his cane in hand and prepared to leave.

"I don't believe you can possibly be anything else in your condition," Sneja said. "It is essential that Otterley will assist you."

"It is only natural," Percival said. "Otterley has been working on this as long as I have."

"And your father and I have been working on it long before that," Sneja said. "And my parents were working on it before I was born, and their parents before them. You are just one of many."

Percival tapped the tip of his cane on the wooden floor. "I should think my condition brings a new urgency."

Sneja glanced at the cane. "It is true — your illness brings new meaning to the hunt. But your obsession to cure yourself has blinded you. Otterley would never have given up those drawings, Percival. Indeed, Otterley would be at this convent now, verifying them. Look at all the time you have wasted! What if your foolishness has cost us the treasure?"

"Then I will die," he said.

Sneja Grigori placed her smooth white hand upon Percival's cheek. The frivolous woman he had escorted from the divan hardened into a statuesque creature filled with ambition and pride — the very things he both admired and envied in her. "It will not come to that. I will not allow it to come to that. Now go and rest. I will take care of Mr. Verlaine."

Percival stood and, leaning heavily upon his cane, hobbled from the room.

St. Rose Convent, Milton, New York

Verlaine parked his car — a 1984 Renault he'd bought secondhand during college — before St. Rose. A wrought-iron gate cut across the passageway to the convent, leaving him no choice but to climb over a thick limestone wall that surrounded the grounds. Up close, St. Rose proved to be much as he had imagined it: isolated and serene, like a castle enchanted in a spell of sleep. Neo-Gothic arches and turrets lifted into the gray sky; birch and evergreen trees rose on all sides in tight protective clusters. Moss and ivy clung upon the brickwork, as if nature had embarked upon a slow, insatiable campaign to claim the structure as its own. At the far end of the grounds, the Hudson edged alongside a riverbank crusted with snow and ice.

As he walked up a snow-dusted cobblestone path, Verlaine shivered. He felt unnaturally cold. The sensation had come over him the moment he left Central Park, and it had remained heavy and stifling throughout the drive to Milton. He had blasted the heat in his car in an attempt to shake off the chill, and still his hands and feet remained numb. He could not account for the effect the meeting had had upon him or why it unsettled him to discover how truly ill Percival Grigori really was. There was something eerie and disturbing about Grigori, something that Verlaine couldn't put his finger upon. Verlaine had a strong sense of intuition about people — he could discern much about a person within minutes of an introduction, and he rarely wavered from his initial impressions. From their first meeting, Grigori had provoked a strong physical reaction in Verlaine, so strong that he felt instantly weakened in Grigori's presence, empty and lifeless, without a trace of warmth.

The meeting earlier that afternoon had been their second, and it might, Verlaine surmised with relief, be their last. If he himself didn't terminate their arrangement — which would happen very soon if this research trip went as planned — there was a real chance that Grigori wouldn't be around much longer anyway. Grigori's skin had appeared so colorless that Verlaine could see networks of blue veins through the thin, pale surface. Grigori's eyes had burned with fever, and he could only just hold himself up on his cane. It was absurd that the man would leave his bed, let alone conduct business meetings outside in a blizzard.

More absurd, however, was his sending Verlaine to the convent without the prerequisite preparations in place. It was impetuous and unprofessional, just the sort of thing Verlaine should have expected from a delusional art collector like Grigori. Standard research protocol required that he get permission to visit private libraries, and this library would be even more conservative than most. He imagined that the St. Rose library would be small, quaint, filled with ferns and hideous oil paintings of lambs and children — all the cheesy décor that religious women found charming. He guessed the librarian to be about seventy years old, somber and gnarled, a severe and pasty creature who would hold no appreciation whatsoever for the collection of images she guarded. Beauty and pleasure, the very elements that made life bearable, were surely not to be found at St. Rose Convent. Not that he'd been to a convent before. He came from a family of agnostics and academics, people who kept their beliefs closed up within themselves, as if speaking of faith would cause it to disappear altogether.

Verlaine climbed the wide stone steps of the convent's entrance and rapped upon a set of wooden doors. He knocked twice, three times, and then searched for a doorbell or speaker system, something to draw the attention of the sisters, but found nothing. As someone who left the door of his apartment unlocked half the time, he found it odd that a group of contemplative nuns would employ such iron-clad security. Annoyed, he walked to the side of the building, removed a photocopy of the architectural plan from his interior pocket, and began to look over the drawings, hoping to locate an alternate entrance.

Using the river as a touchstone, he found that the main entrance should have been located on the southern side of the building. In reality the entrance was on the western façade, facing the main gate. According to the map (as he now thought of the drawings), the church and chapel structures should dominate the back of the grounds, the convent forming a narrow wing in the front. But unless he had read the sketches incorrectly, the buildings were situated in a different configuration entirely. It became more and more apparent that the architectural plans were at odds with the structure before him. Curious, Verlaine walked the perimeter of the convent, comparing the solid brick contours with those in pen and ink. Indeed, the two buildings were not at all as they should be. Instead of two distinct structures, he found one massive compound molded together in a patchwork of old and new brick and mortar, as if the two buildings had been sliced and jointed in a surreal collage of masonry.

What Grigori would make of it, Verlaine

couldn't say. Their first meeting had been at an art auction, where Verlaine assisted in the sale of paintings, furniture, books, and jewelry belonging to famous Gilded Age families. There had been a fine set of silver belonging to Andrew Carnegie, a set of gold-trimmed croquet mallets engraved with Henry Flagler's initials, and a marble statuette of Neptune from the Breakers, Cornelius Vanderbilt II's Newport mansion. The auction was a small affair, with bids coming in lower than expected. Percival Grigori caught Verlaine's attention when he bid high on a number of items that had once belonged to John D. Rockefeller's wife, Laura "Cettie" Celestia Spelman.

Verlaine knew enough about the Rockefeller family to realize that the lot of items Percival Grigori had bid upon was not special. And yet Grigori had wanted it very badly, driving the price well above its reserve. Later, after the last lots had been sold, Verlaine had approached Grigori to congratulate him on his purchase. They fell into discussing the Rockefellers, then continued their dissection of the Gilded Age over a bottle of wine in a bar across the street. Grigori admired Verlaine's knowledge about the Rockefeller family, expressed curiosity about his research into the MoMA, and asked if he would be interested in doing private work on the subject. Grigori took his telephone number. Verlaine became Grigori's employee soon after.

Verlaine had a special affection for the Rockefeller family — he had written his Ph.D. dissertation on the early years of the Museum of Modern Art, an institution that would not have existed without the vision and patronage of Abigail Aldrich Rockefeller. Originally Verlaine's study of art history had arisen from an interest in design. He took a few classes in the art history department at Columbia, then a few more, until he found that his attention turned from modern design to the ideas behind modernism — primitivism, the mandate to break from tradition, the value of the present over the past — and eventually to the woman who had helped build one of the greatest museums of modern art in the world: Abigail Rockefeller. Verlaine knew perfectly well, and his adviser had often reminded him, that he was not an academic at heart. He was incapable of systematizing beauty, reducing it to theories and footnotes. He preferred the vibrant, heart-stopping color of a Matisse over the intellectual rigidity of the Russian formalists. Over the course of his graduate work, he had not become more intellectual in the way he viewed art. Instead, he had learned to appreciate the motivation behind creating it.

In working on his dissertation, he had come to admire Abigail Rockefeller's taste and, after years of research on the subject, felt himself to be a minor expert on the Rockefeller family's dealings in the art world. A portion of his dissertation had been published in a prestigious academic art journal the year before, which led to a teaching contract at Columbia.

Assuming that everything went as planned, Verlaine would clean up the dissertation, find a way to give it a more general appeal, and, if the stars aligned, publish it one day. In its present form, however, it was a mess. His files had grown into a tangle of information, with facts and miscellaneous bits of portraiture knotted up together. There were hundreds of copied documents saved in folders, and somehow Grigori had persuaded him to copy, for Grigori's personal purposes, nearly every piece of data, every document, every report he'd found in compiling his research. Verlaine had believed his files to be exhaustive, and so it came as a surprise when he discovered that, during the very years he specialized in, the years when Abigail Rockefeller was heavily involved in her work with the Museum of Modern Art, there had been a correspondence between Mrs. Rockefeller and St. Rose Convent.

Verlaine discovered the connection on a research trip he'd taken to the Rockefeller Archive Center earlier in the year. He'd driven twenty-five miles north of Manhattan to Sleepy Hollow, a picturesque town of bungalows and Cape Cods on the Hudson River. The center, perched upon a hill overlooking twenty-four acres of land, was housed in a vast stone mansion that had belonged to John D. Rockefeller Jr.'s second wife, Martha Baird Rockefeller. Verlaine parked the Renault, threw his backpack over one shoulder, and climbed the steps. It was a wonder how much money the family had accumulated and how they had been able to surround themselves with seemingly endless beauty.

An archivist checked Verlaine's research credentials — a Columbia University instructor's ID with his adjunct status clearly marked — and led him to the second-floor reading room. Grigori paid well — one day of research would cover Verlaine's rent for a month — and so he took his time, enjoying the peacefulness of the library, the smell of the books, the archive's orderly system of distributing files and folios. The archivist brought boxes of documents from the temperature-controlled vault, a large concrete annex off the mansion, and placed them before Verlaine. Abby Rockefeller's papers had been divided into seven series: Abby Aldrich Rockefeller Correspondence, Personal Papers, Art Collections, Philanthropy, Aldrich/Greene Family Papers, Death of Abby Aldrich Rockefeller, and Chase Biography. Each part contained hundreds of documents. The sheer volume of papers would take weeks to sort through. Verlaine dug in, taking notes and making photocopies.

Before embarking on the trip, he had reread everything he could find about her, intent to discover something original that might help him, some piece of information that had not been claimed by other historians of modern art. He had read various biographies and knew a considerable amount about her childhood in Providence, Rhode Island, her marriage to John D. Rockefeller Jr., and her subsequent life in New York society. He'd read descriptions of her dinner parties and of her five sons and one rebellious daughter, all of which seemed dull compared to her artistic interests and passions. Although the particulars of their lives could not be more different — Verlaine lived in a studio apartment and ran a haphazard and precarious financial existence as a part-time college instructor while Abby Rockefeller had married one of the richest men of the twentieth century — he had come to feel a certain closeness with her. Verlaine felt he understood her tastes and the mysterious passions that drove her to love modern painting. There would not be much in her personal life that hadn't been examined a thousand times over. He knew full well that there was little hope of his finding anything new for Grigori. If he were to strike gold — or at least discover a fragment of material that might be useful to his boss — it would be a major piece of luck.

And so Verlaine bypassed the batches of papers and letters that had been pillaged by scholars, crossing the Chase Biography files off his list and turning to the box pertaining to art acquisition and the planning of the MoMA — the Art Collections, Series III: Inventories of artworks bought, donated, lent, or sold; Information pertaining to Chinese and Japanese prints and American folk art; Notes from dealers on the Rockefeller art collection. After hours of reading, however, he found nothing exceptional in the material.

Finally Verlaine sent back the boxes of Series III and asked the archivist to bring Series IV: Philanthropy. He had no concrete reason for doing so, except that Rockefeller's charitable donations were perhaps the only element that he had not overexamined, as they tended to be dry sheets of accounting. When the boxes arrived and Verlaine began to work through them, he found that despite the dull subject matter, Abby Rockefeller's voice intrigued him nearly as much as did her taste in paintings. He read for an hour before discovering a strange set of letters — four missives folded among a mess of papers. The letters were tucked among reports of charitable donations, neatly folded in their original envelopes without commentary or addenda. In fact, Verlaine realized, turning to the catalog for that series, the letters were entirely undocumented. He couldn't account for them, and yet there they were, yellowed with age, delicate to the touch, giving off a dusty powder on his fingers as if he'd touched the wings of a moth.

He unfolded them and pressed them flat under the glow of the lamp to see them more clearly. Instantly he understood the reason behind the oversight: The letters had no direct relation to Abigail Rockefeller's family, society life, or artistic work. There was no definite category at all for such letters. They were not even written by Abigail Rockefeller, but by a woman named Innocenta, an abbess at a convent in Milton, New York, a town he had never heard of before. He learned, upon checking an atlas, that Milton was only a few hours north of New York City on the Hudson River.

As Verlaine read the letters, his wonder grew. Innocenta's handwriting was spidery and old-fashioned, featuring narrow European numerals and pinched, looping letters, obviously scratched out with nib and ink. From what Verlaine could gather, Mother Innocenta and Mrs. Rockefeller had shared an interest in religious work, charity, and fundraising activities, much as any two women in their respective positions might. Innocenta's tone started out as one of deference and polite humility but grew warmer with each letter, suggesting that a regular communication had transpired between the women. He could find nothing overt in the letters to substantiate this, but it was his hunch that some piece of religious art was at the bottom of it all. Verlaine became more and more certain that these letters would lead him somewhere, if only he could understand them. They were exactly the sort of discovery that could assist his career.

Quickly, before the archivist had a chance to observe him, Verlaine slid the letters into the interior pocket of his backpack. Ten minutes later he was speeding home toward Manhattan, the stolen papers lying exposed upon his lap. Why he had taken the letters was a mystery even then — he had no motivation other than that he'd desperately wanted to understand them. He knew that he should have shared his discovery with Grigori — the man had paid him to make the trip, after all — but there seemed little concrete information to relay, and so Verlaine decided to tell Grigori of the existence of the letters later, once he had verified their importance.

Now, standing before the convent, he was flummoxed once again as he compared the architectural drawings with the physical structure before him. Sheets of winter light fell across the pages of sketches, the spiky shadows of birch trees stretching upon the surface of the snow. The temperature was falling quickly. Verlaine turned up the collar of his overcoat and set out on his second trip around the compound, his wing tips soaked from slush. Grigori was right about one thing: They could learn nothing more without gaining access to St. Rose Convent.

Halfway around the building, Verlaine discovered a set of ice-glazed steps. Down he walked, grasping a metal railing so as not to slip. A door stood in the hollow of a vaulted stone entranceway. Giving the knob a twist, Verlaine found the door unlocked, and a moment later he was in a dark, damp space that smelled of wet stone, rotting wood, and dust. When his eyes had adjusted to the dim light he closed the door, securing it firmly behind him before walking through an abandoned corridor and into St. Rose Convent.

Whenever visitors arrived, the sisters relied upon Evangeline to act as the liaison between the realms of sacred and profane. She had a talent for putting the uninitiated at ease, an air of youth and modernity the other sisters lacked, and she often found herself translating the internal workings of the community to outsiders. Guests expected to be greeted by a nun wrapped in full habit, black-veiled, with dour leather lace-up shoes, a Bible in one hand and a rosary in the other — an old woman who carried all the sadness of the world upon her face. Instead they were met by Evangeline. Young, pretty, and sharp-minded, she quickly disabused them of their stereotype. She would make a joke or comment upon some item in the newspaper, breaking the image of severity the convent presented. On the occasions when Evangeline led guests through the winding corridors, she would explain that theirs was a modern community, open to new ideas. She would explain that despite their traditional habits, the middle-aged sisters wore Nikes for their morning walks by the river in autumn or Birkenstocks as they weeded the flower gardens in the summer. Exterior appearances, Evangeline would explain, meant little. The routines established two hundred years ago, rituals revered and maintained with ironclad persistence, were what mattered most. When seculars became startled by the quiet of their halls, the regularity of their prayers, and the uniformity of the nuns, Evangeline had the ability to make it all appear quite normal.

That afternoon, however, her manner took on another aspect altogether — never before had she been more surprised to find someone standing in the doorway of the library. A rustle of movement at the far end of the room had brought the person's intrusion to her attention. Turning, she discovered a young man leaning against the door, gazing at her with unusual interest. A feeling of alarm sharp as electricity shot through her. Tension grew in her temples, a sensation that manifested itself as a blurring in her vision and a slight ringing in her ears. She straightened her posture, unconsciously assuming the role of guardian of the library, and faced the intruder.

Although she could not say how, Evangeline understood that the man standing at the library door was the very same man whose letter she had read that morning. It was odd that she should recognize Verlaine. She had pictured the author of the letter as a wizened professor, gray-haired and paunchy, whereas the man before her was much younger than she would have guessed him to be. His wire-rimmed glasses, his unruly black hair, and the hesitant way he waited at the door struck her as boyish. How he had gained entrance into the convent and, even more curious, how he'd found his way to the library without being intercepted by one of the sisters struck Evangeline as wholly mysterious. She did not know if she should greet him or call for assistance in escorting him from the building.

She straightened her skirt with care and determined that she would perform her duties to the letter. Walking to the door, she fixed him with a cool stare. "May I assist you in some way, Mr. Verlaine?" Her voice sounded odd, as if she were hearing it through a wind tunnel.

"You know who I am?" Verlaine said.

"It is not so difficult to deduce," Evangeline replied, her manner more severe than she intended it to be.

"Then you know," Verlaine said, his cheeks flushing, a sign of self-consciousness that made Evangeline soften toward him despite herself, "that I spoke with someone on the telephone — Perpetua, I think her name was — about visiting your library for research purposes. I also wrote a letter about arranging a visit."

"My name is Evangeline. It was I who received your letter, and I am therefore quite aware of your request. I am also aware that you spoke with Mother Perpetua of your intentions to conduct research on the premises, but as far as I know, you have not been given permission to access the library. In fact, I am not entirely certain of how you got in here at all, especially at this time of day. I can understand how one might wander into restricted areas after Sunday Mass — the public is invited to worship with us, and it has happened before, some curious person sightseeing in our private quarters — but in the middle of the afternoon? I am surprised you did not encounter any of the sisters on your way to the library. In any case, you must register in the Mission Office — that is the protocol for all visitors. I think we had better go there immediately, or at least speak with Mother Perpetua, just in case there is some —"

"I'm sorry," Verlaine interrupted. "I know that this is out of line and that I shouldn't have come at all without permission, but I'm hoping that you'll help me. Your expertise might get me out of a rather difficult situation. I certainly didn't come here to cause you trouble."

Evangeline looked at Verlaine a moment, as if trying to gauge his sincerity. Then, gesturing to the wooden table near the fireplace, she said, "There is no trouble that I cannot handle, Mr. Verlaine. Sit, please, and tell me what I can do to help you."

"Thank you." Verlaine slid into a chair while Evangeline took the one opposite. "You probably know from my letter that I'm trying to find proof that a correspondence took place between Abigail Rockefeller and the abbess of St. Rose Convent in the winter of 1943."

Evangeline nodded, recalling the text of the letter.

"Yes, well, I didn't mention it in my letter, but I'm in the process of writing a book — actually, it was my doctoral dissertation, but I'm hoping to turn it into a book — about Abigail Rockefeller and the Museum of Modern Art. I've read nearly everything published about the subject, and many unpublished documents, and a relationship between the Rockefellers and St. Rose Convent is not referenced anywhere. As you can imagine, such a correspondence could be a significant discovery, at least in my corner of academia. It's the kind of thing that could change my career prospects entirely."

"That is very interesting," Evangeline said. "But I fail to see how I can help you."

"Let me show you something." Verlaine dug in the inside pocket of his overcoat and placed a sheaf of papers on the table. The papers were filled with drawings that upon first glance appeared to be little more than a series of rectangular and circular shapes but became, once she looked more closely, the representation of a building. Smoothing the papers with his fingers, Verlaine said, "These are the architectural plans for St. Rose."

Evangeline leaned over the table to see the paper clearly. "These are the originals?"

"Yes indeed." Verlaine turned the pages to show Evangeline the various sketches of the convent. "Dated 1809. Signed by the founding abbess."

"Mother Francesca," Evangeline said, drawn to the age and intricacy of the plans. "Francesca erected the convent and founded our order. She designed much of the church herself. The Adoration Chapel was entirely her creation."

"Her signature is on every page," Verlaine said.

"It is only natural," Evangeline replied. "She was something of a Renaissance woman — she would have insisted upon approving the plans herself."

"Look at this," Verlaine said, spreading the papers over the surface of the table. "A fingerprint."

Evangeline leaned closer. Sure enough, a small, smudged oval of ink, its center as tight and knotted as the core of an aged tree, stained the yellowed page. Evangeline entertained the thought that Francesca herself might have left the print.

"You have studied these drawings carefully," Evangeline observed.

"There is one thing I don't understand, though," Verlaine said, leaning back in his chair. "The arrangements of the buildings are significantly different from their placement in the architectural plans. I walked around outside a little, comparing the two, and they diverge in fundamental ways. The convent used to be in a different location on the grounds, for example."

"Yes," Evangeline said. She had become so engrossed in the drawings that she forgot how wary Verlaine made her feel. "The buildings were repaired and rebuilt. Everything changed after a fire burned the convent to the ground."

"The fire of 1944," Verlaine said.

Evangeline raised an eyebrow. "You know about the fire?"

"It's the reason these drawings were taken out of the convent. I found them buried in a repository of old building plans. St. Rose Convent was approved for a building permit in February 1944."

"You were allowed to take these plans from a public-records repository?"

"Borrow them," Verlaine said, sheepish. Pressing the seal with the edge of his fingernail so that a slim crescent formed on the foil seal, he asked, "Do you know what this seal marks?"

Evangeline looked closely at the golden seal.

It was positioned at the center of the Adoration Chapel. "It is roughly where the altar is," she said. "But it doesn't seem exactly precise."

She assessed Verlaine, scrutinizing him with renewed interest. Whereas she had initially thought him little more than an opportunist come to pillage their library, she realized now that he had the innocence and candor of a teenage boy on a treasure hunt. She could not fathom why this should make her warm to him but it did.

She certainly did not intend to signal any such warmth to Verlaine. But he seemed less hesitant, as if he'd detected a shift in her feelings. He was staring at her from behind the smudged lenses of his glasses as if seeing her for the first time. "What is that?" he asked, without taking his eyes from her.

"What is what?"

"Your necklace," he said, moving closer.

Evangeline pulled away, afraid that Verlaine might touch her, nearly knocking over a chair in the process.

"I'm sorry," Verlaine said. "It's just that —"

"There is nothing more I can tell you, Mr. Verlaine," she said, her voice cracking as she spoke.

"Hold on a second." Verlaine riffled through the architectural drawings. Pulling a leaf from the stack, he presented it to Evangeline. "I think your necklace has said it all."

Evangeline took the paper and straightened

it on the table before her. She found a brilliant likeness of the Adoration Chapel, its altar, its statues, its octagonal shape rendered precisely as the original she had seen each day for so many years. Affixed to the drawing, at the very center of the altar, there was a golden seal.

"The lyre," Verlaine said. "Do you see? It's the same."

Her fingers trembling, Evangeline unfastened the pendant from about her neck and placed it carefully on the paper, the golden chain trailing behind it like the glimmering tail of a meteor. Her mother's necklace was the twin of the golden seal.

From her pocket Evangeline removed the letter she had found in the archives, the 1943 missive from Abigail Rockefeller to Mother Innocenta, and placed it on the table. She did not understand the connection between the seal and the necklace, and the chance that Verlaine might know suddenly made her anxious to share her discovery with him.

"What's this?" Verlaine asked, picking it up.

"Perhaps you can tell me."

But as Verlaine opened the crinkled paper and scanned the lines of the letter, Evangeline suddenly doubted herself. Recalling Sister Philomena's warning, she wondered if perhaps she truly was betraying her order by sharing such a document with an outsider.

She had the sinking feeling that she was making a grave mistake. Yet, she merely watched him with growing anticipation as he read the paper.

"This letter confirms the relationship between Innocenta and Abigail Rockefeller," Verlaine said at last. "Where did you find it?"

"I spent some time in the archive this morning after I read your request. There was no doubt in my mind that you were wrong about Mother Innocenta. I was certain that no such connection existed. I doubted that there would be anything at all relating to a secular woman like Mrs. Rockefeller in our archives, let alone a document that confirmed the correspondence — it is simply extraordinary that physical evidence would remain. In fact, I went into the archive to prove that you were wrong."

Verlaine's gaze remained fixed upon the letter, and Evangeline wondered if he'd heard a word she'd said. Finally he took a scrap of paper from his pocket and wrote his telephone number on it. "You said you found only one letter from Abigail Rockefeller?"

"Yes," Evangeline said. "The letter you just read."

"And yet all of the letters from Innocenta to Abigail Rockefeller were responses. That means there are three, perhaps four, Rockefeller letters somewhere in your archive."

"You honestly believe we could have over-looked such letters?"

Verlaine gave her his telephone number. "If you find anything, would you call me?"

Evangeline took the paper and looked at it. She did not know what to tell him. It would be impossible for her to call him, even if she were to find what he was looking for. "I'll try," she said at last.

"Thanks," Verlaine said, gazing at her with gratitude. "In the meantime, do you mind if I make a photocopy of this one?"

Evangeline picked up her necklace, refastened it about her neck, and led Verlaine to the library door. "Come with me."

Escorting Verlaine into Philomena's office, Evangeline removed a leaf of St. Rose stationery from a stack and gave it to Verlaine. "You may transcribe it onto this," she said.

Verlaine took a pen and got to work. After he'd copied the original and returned it to Evangeline, she could detect that he wished to ask her something. She had known him all of ten minutes, and yet she could understand the turn his mind had taken. At last he asked, "Where did this stationery come from?"

Evangeline lifted another sheet of the thick pink paper from the stack next to Philomena's desk and held it between her fingers. The top section of the stationery was filled with Baroque roses and angels, images she'd seen a thousand times before. "It's just our standard stationery," she said. "Why?"

"It is the same stationery that Innocenta used for her letters to Abigail Rockefeller," Verlaine said, taking a clean sheet and examining it more closely. "How old is the design?"

"I've never thought about it," Evangeline said. "But it must be nearly two hundred years old. The St. Rose crest was created by our founding abbess."

"May I?" Verlaine said, taking a few pages of the stationery and folding them into his pocket.

"Certainly," Evangeline said, perplexed by Verlaine's interest in something she found to be quite banal. "Take as many as you'd like."

"Thanks," Verlaine said, smiling at Evangeline for the first time in their exchange. "You're probably not supposed to help me out like this."

"Actually, I should have called the police the moment I saw you," she said.

"I hope there's some way I can thank you."

"There is," Evangeline said as she ushered Verlaine to the door. "You can leave before you are discovered. And if you are by chance found by one of the sisters, you did not meet me or set foot in this library."

St. Rose Convent, Milton, New York

Still more snow had accumulated while Verlaine was inside the convent. It drifted from the sky in sheets, collecting upon the svelte arms of the birch trees and hiding the cobblestone walkway from view. Squinting, he tried to locate his blue Renault in the darkness beyond the locked wrought-iron gate, but there was little light and his vision could not compete with the thickening snow. Behind him the convent had disappeared in a haze; ahead he saw nothing but a deepening void. Negotiating the new ice under his shoes as best he could, Verlaine edged his way out of the convent grounds.

The crisp air in his lungs — so delicious after the stifling warmth of the library — only served to add to the exuberance he felt about his success. Somehow, to his astonishment and delight, he had pulled it off. Evangeline — he couldn't bring himself to think of her as Sister Evangeline; there was something too alluring, too intellectually engaging, too

116

feminine about her for her to be a nun — had not only given him access to the library but she had shown him the very item he'd most hoped to find. He'd read Abigail Rockefeller's letter with his own eyes and could now say with certainty that this woman had indeed been working on a scheme of some sort with the sisters of St. Rose Convent. Although he hadn't been able to get a photocopy of the letter, he recognized the handwriting as authentic. The result would surely satisfy Grigori and — more important — bolster his own personal research. The only thing that could have topped this would have been if Evangeline had given him the original letter outright. Or, better yet, if she had produced as many letters from Abigail Rockefeller as he possessed from Innocenta — and given him those originals outright.

Ahead, past the bars of the gate, a sweep of headlights broke through the blur of snow-flakes. A matte black Mercedes SUV pulled into sight, parking next to the Renault. Verlaine ducked sidelong into a thicket of pine trees, an act of instinct that sheltered him from the harsh headlights. From a needling crevice between the trees, he watched as a man wearing a stocking cap followed by a bigger, blond man carrying a crowbar emerged from the vehicle. The physical revulsion Verlaine had felt earlier in the day — from which he had only just fully recovered — returned at the sight of them. In the headlights' glare, the men appeared more menacing, larger than was possible, their silhouettes blazing a brilliant white. The contrast of illumination and shadow hollowed their eyes and cheeks, giving their faces the stark aspect of carnival masks. Grigori had sent them — Verlaine knew this the moment he saw them — but why on earth he had done so was beyond him.

Using the edge of the crowbar, the taller man brushed at a line of snow clinging to one of the Renault's windows, running the metal tip over the glass. Then, with a show of violence that startled Verlaine, he brought the crowbar down upon the window, shattering the glass with one swift crack. After clearing away the shards, the other man reached inside and unlocked the door, each move quick and efficient. Together the two of them went through the glove compartment, the backseat, and, after popping it open from inside, the trunk. As they tore through his belongings — disemboweling his gym bag and loading his books, many on loan from the Columbia University library, into the SUV — Verlaine realized that Grigori must have sent his men to steal Verlaine's papers.

He wouldn't be driving back to New York City in his Renault, that was for certain. Endeavoring to get as far away from these thugs as possible, Verlaine dropped to his hands and knees and crawled along the ground, the soft snow crunching under his weight. As he crept through the thick evergreens, the sharp scent of pine sap filled his senses. If he could remain under the cover of the forest, following the shadowy path back toward the convent, he might escape unnoticed. At the edge of the trees, he stood up, his breathing heavy and his clothes mottled with packed snow: A stretch of exposed space between the forest and the river gave him no choice but to risk exposure. Verlaine's only hope was that the men were too preoccupied with destroying his car to notice him. He ran toward the Hudson, looking over his shoulder only after he'd reached the edge of the bank. In the distance the thugs were getting into the SUV. They hadn't driven off. They were waiting for Verlaine.

The riverbed was frozen. Looking at his wing tips — the leather now completely drenched — he felt a rush of anger and frustration. How was he supposed to get home? He was stuck in the middle of nowhere. Grigori's monkeys had taken all his notebooks, all his files, everything he'd been working on for the past years, and they'd trashed his car in the process. Did Grigori have any idea how hard it was to find replacement parts for a 1984 Renault R5? How was he supposed to walk through this wilderness of snow and ice in a pair of slippery vintage shoes?

He navigated the terrain, striding south alongside the riverbank, taking care not to fall. Soon he found himself standing before a barricade of barbed wire. He supposed that the fence marked the boundaries of the convent's property, a spindly and sharp extension of the massive stone wall that surrounded the St. Rose grounds, but for him it was yet another obstacle to his escape. Pressing the barbed wire with his foot, Verlaine climbed over, snagging his coat.

It wasn't until he had walked for some time and had left the convent grounds for a dark, snow-covered country road that he realized he'd sliced his hand climbing over the fence. It was so dark that he couldn't make out the cut, but he guessed it to be bad, perhaps in need of stitches. He removed his favorite Hermès tie, rolled up his bloodied shirtsleeve, and wrapped the tie around the wound, forming a tight bandage.

Verlaine had a terrible sense of direction. With the snowstorm obscuring the night sky, and his utter ignorance of the small towns along the Hudson, he had no idea of where he was. Traffic was sparse. When headlights appeared in the distance, he stepped from the gravel shoulder into the trees at the edge of the forest, hiding himself. There were hundreds of small roads and highways, any one of which he might have stumbled upon. Yet he couldn't help but worry that Grigori's men, who by now would be looking for him in earnest, could drive by at any moment.

His skin had already grown raw and chapped from the wind; his feet had gone numb as his hand began to throb, and so he stopped to examine it. As he tightened his tie around the wound, he noticed with stunned detachment the elegance with which the silk absorbed and retained the blood.

After what felt like hours, he came across a larger, more heavily trafficked county highway, two lanes of cracked concrete with a sign that posted the speed limit — fifty-five miles per hour. Turning toward Manhattan, or what he assumed was the direction of Manhattan, he walked along the ice and gravel shoulder, wind biting into his skin. Traffic grew heavier as he walked. Semitrucks with advertisements painted across their trailers, flatbed trucks piled high with industrial cargo, minivans, and compacts sped past. Exhaust mixed with the frigid air, a thick, toxic soup that made it painful for him to breathe. The seemingly endless stretch of highway ahead, the bitter wind, the mind-numbing ugliness of the scene — it was as if he had fallen into a piece of nightmarish postindustrial art. Walking faster, he scanned the passing traffic, hoping to flag a police car, a bus, anything that would get him out of the cold. But the traffic moved by in a relentless, aloof caravan. Finally Verlaine stuck out his thumb.

With a whoosh of hot, gaseous air, a semi slowed and stopped a hundred yards or so ahead, the brakes creaking as the tires ground to a halt. The passenger door was flung open, and Verlaine broke into a run toward the brightly lit cab. The driver was a fat man with a great tangled beard and a baseball cap who eyed Verlaine sympathetically. "Where you headed?"

"New York City," Verlaine said, already basking in the warmth of the cab's heater.

"I'm not going that far, but I can drop you in the next town, if you'd like."

Verlaine tucked his hand deep into his coat, obscuring it from view. "Where's that?" he asked.

"About fifteen miles south in Milton," the driver said, looking him over. "Looks like you've had a hell of a day. Hop in."

They drove for fifteen minutes before the truck driver pulled over, letting him off on a quaint, snowy main street with a stretch of small shops. The street was utterly deserted, as if the entire town had shut down due to the snowstorm. The shop windows were dark and the parking lot before the post office empty. A small tavern on a corner, a beer sign illuminated in the window, gave the only sign of life.

Verlaine checked his pockets, feeling for his wallet and keys. He'd buttoned the envelope of cash into an interior pocket of his sport jacket. Removing the envelope, he checked to be sure he hadn't lost the money. To his relief, it was all there. His anger grew, however, at the thought of Grigori. What had he been doing, working for a guy who would track him down, bust up his car, and scare the hell out of him? Verlaine was beginning to wonder if he'd been crazy for getting involved with Percival Grigori at all.

The Grigori penthouse, Upper East Side, New York City

The Grigori family had acquired the penthouse in the late 1940s from the debt-ridden daughter of an American tycoon. It was large and magnificent, much too big for a bachelor with an aversion to large parties, and so it had come as something of a relief when Percival's mother and Otterley began to occupy the upper floors. When he had lived there alone, he had spent hours alone playing billiards, the doors closed to the movement of servants brushing through the corridors. He would draw the heavy green velvet drapes, turn the lamps low, and drink scotch as he aligned shot after shot, aiming the cue and slamming the polished balls into netted pockets.

As time passed, he remodeled various rooms of the apartment but left the billiard room exactly as it had been in the 1940s — slightly tattered leather furniture, the transmitter-tube radio with Bakelite buttons, an eighteenth-century Persian rug, an abundance of musty old books filling the cherrywood shelves, hardly any of which he had attempted to read. The volumes were purely decorative, admired for their age and value. There were calf-bound volumes pertaining to the origins and exploits of his many relations — histories, memoirs, epic novels of battle, romances. Some of these books had been shipped from Europe after the war; others were acquired from a venerable book dealer in the neighborhood, an old friend of the family transplanted from London. The man had a sharp sense for what the Grigori family most desired — tales of European conquest, colonial glory, and the civilizing power of Western culture.

Even the distinctive smell of the billiard room remained the same — soap and leather polish, a faint hint of cigar. Percival still relished whiling away the hours there, calling every so often for the maid to bring him a fresh drink. She was a young Anakim female who was wonderfully silent. She would place a glass of scotch next to him and sweep the empty glass away, making him comfortable with practiced efficiency. With a flick of his wrist, he would dismiss the servant, and she would disappear in an instant. It pleased him that she always left quietly, closing the wide wooden doors behind her with a soft click.

Percival maneuvered himself onto a stuffed armchair, swirling the scotch in its cut-crystal glass. He straightened his legs — slowly, gently — onto an ottoman. He thought of his mother and her complete disregard for his efforts in getting them this far. That he had obtained definite information about St. Rose Convent should have given her faith in him. Instead Sneja had instructed Otterley to oversee the creatures she'd sent upstate.

Taking a sip of scotch, Percival tried to telephone his sister. When Otterley did not pick up, he checked his watch, annoyed. She should have called by now.

For all her faults, Otterley was like their father — punctual, methodical, and utterly reliable under pressure. If Percival knew her, she had consulted with their father in London and had drawn up a plan to contain and eliminate Verlaine. In fact, it wouldn't surprise him if his father had outlined the plan from his office, giving Otterley whatever she needed to execute his wishes. Otterley was his father's favorite. In his eyes she could do nothing wrong.

Looking at his watch again, Percival saw that only two minutes had passed. Perhaps something had happened to warrant Otterley's silence. Perhaps their efforts had been thwarted. It wouldn't be the first time they had been lured into a seemingly innocuous situation only to be cornered.

He felt his legs pulsing and shaking, as if the muscles rebelled against repose. He took another sip of scotch, willing it to calm him, but

nothing worked when he was in such a
Leaving his cane behind, Percival drew h
self up from the chair and hobbled to a boo
shelf, where he removed a calf-bound volume
and placed it gently upon the billiard table.
The spine creaked when he pressed the cover
open, as if the binding might pop apart. Percival had not opened *The Book of Generations*
in many, many years, not since the marriage
of one of his cousins had sent him searching
for family connections on the bride's side —
it was always awkward to arrive at a wedding
and be at a loss for who mattered and who did
not, especially when the bride was a member
of the Danish royal family.

The Book of Generations was an amalgama-
tion of history, legend, genealogy, and pre-
diction pertaining to his kind. All Nephilistic children received an identical calf-bound
volume at the end of their schooling, a kind
of parting gift. The stories told of battle, of
the founding of countries and kingdoms, of
the binding together in pacts of loyalty, of the
Crusades, of the knighthoods and quests and
bloody conquests — these were the great stories of Nephilistic lore. Percival often wished
that he had been born in those times, when
their actions were not so visible, when they
were able to go about their business quietly,
without the danger of being monitored. Their
power had been able to grow with the aid of
silence, each victory building upon the one

before. The legacy of his ancestors ere, recorded in *The Book of Genera-*

state.
m-

l read the first page, filled with bold here was a list of names document- ... sprawling history of the Nephilistic bloodline, a catalog of families that began at the time of Noah and branched into ruling dynasties. Noah's son Japheth had migrated to Europe, his children populating Greece, Parthia, Russia, and northern Europe and securing their family's dominance. Percival's family was descended directly from Javan, Japheth's fourth son, the first to colonize the "Isles of the Gentiles," which some took to mean Greece and others believed to be the British Isles. Javan had six brothers, whose names were recorded in the Bible, and a number of sisters, whose names were not recorded, all of whom created the basis of their influence and power throughout Europe. In many ways *The Book of Generations* was a recapitulation of the history of the world. Or, as modern Nephilim preferred to think, the survival of the fittest.

Looking over the list of families, Percival saw that their influence had once been absolute. In the past three hundred years, however, Nephilistic families had fallen into decline. Once there had been a balance between human and Nephilim. After the Flood they'd been born in almost equal numbers. But Nephilim were deeply attracted to humans and had married into human families, causing the genetic dilution of their most potent qualities. Now Nephilim possessing predominantly human characteristics were common, while those who had pure angelic traits were rare.

With thousands of humans born for every one Nephilim, there was some debate among good families about the relevance of their human-born relations. Some wished to exclude them, push them further into the human realm, while others believed in their value, or at least their use to the larger cause. Cultivating relations with the human members of Nephilim families was a tactical move, one that might yield great results. A child born to Nephilim parents, without the slightest trace of angelic traits, might in turn produce a Nephilistic offspring. It was an uncommon occurrence, to be sure, but not unheard of. To address this possibility, the Nephilim observed a tiered system, a caste relating not to wealth or social status — although these criteria mattered as well — but to physical traits, to breeding, to a resemblance to their ancestors, a group of angels called the Watchers. While humans carried the genetic potential to create a Nephilistic child, the Nephilim themselves embodied the angelic ideal. Only a Nephilistic being could develop wings. And Percival's had been the most magnificent anyone had seen in half a millennium.

He turned the pages of *The Book of Generations,* stopping randomly at a middle section of the book. There was an etching of a noble merchant dressed in velvets and silks, a sword cocked in one hand and a bag of gold in the other. An endless procession of women and slaves knelt around him, awaiting his command, and a concubine stretched out upon a divan at his side, her arms draped over her body. Caressing the picture, Percival read a one-line biography of the merchant describing him "as an elusive nobleman who organized fleets to all corners of the uncivilized world, colonizing wilderness and organizing the natives." So much had changed in the past three hundred years, so many parts of the globe subdued. The merchant would not recognize the world they lived in today.

Turning to another page, Percival happened upon one of his favorite tales in the book, the story of a famous uncle on his father's side — Sir Arthur Grigori, a Nephilim of great wealth and renown whom Percival recalled as a marvelous storyteller. Born in the early seventeenth century, Sir Arthur had made wise investments in many of the nascent shipping companies of the British Empire. His faith in the East India Company alone had brought him enormous profit — as his manor house and his cottage and his farmlands and his city apartments could well attest. While he was never directly involved in overseeing his business ventures abroad, Percival knew that his uncle had undertaken journeys around the globe and had amassed a great collection of treasures. Travel had always given him great pleasure, especially when he explored the more exotic corners of the planet, but his primary motive for distant excursion had been business. Sir Arthur had been known for his Svengali-like ability to convince humans to do all he asked of them. Percival arranged the book in his lap and read:

Sir Arthur's ship arrived just weeks after the infamous uprising of May 1857. From the seas to the Gangetic Plain, in Meerut and Delhi and Kanpur and Lucknow and Jhansi and Gwalior, the Revolt spread, wreaking discord among the hierarchies that governed the land. Peasants overtook their masters, killing and maiming the British with sticks and sabers and whatever weapons they could make or steal to suit their treachery. In Kanpur it was reported that two hundred European women and children were massacred in a single morning, while in Delhi peasants spread gunpowder upon the streets until they appeared covered in pepper. One imbecilic fellow lit a match for his bidi, blowing all and sundry to pieces.

Sir Arthur, seeing that the East India Company had fallen into chaos and fearing that his profits would be affected, called the Governor-General to his apartments one afternoon to discuss what might be done between them to rectify the terrible events. The Governor-General, a portly, pink man with a penchant for chutney, arrived in the hottest hour of the day, a flock of children about him — one holding the umbrella, another holding a fan, and yet another balancing a glass of iced tea upon a tray. Sir Arthur received him with the shades drawn, to keep away the glare of both the sun and curious passersby.

"I must say, Governor-General," Sir Arthur began, "a revolt is no great greeting."

"No, sir," the Governor-General replied, adjusting a polished gold monocle over a bulbous blue eye. "And it is no great farewell, either."

Seeing that they understood one another very well, the men discussed the matter. For hours they dissected the causes and effects of the revolt. In the end Sir Arthur had a suggestion. "There must be an example made," he said, drawing a long cigar from a balsam box and lighting it with a lighter, an imprint of the Grigori family crest etched upon its side. "It is essential to drive fear into their hearts. One must create a spectacle that will terrify them into compliance. Together we will choose a village. When we are through with them, there will be no more revolts."

While the lesson Sir Arthur taught the British soldiers was well known in Nephilistic circles — indeed, they had been practicing such fear-generating tactics privately for many hundreds of years — it was rarely used on such a large group. Under Sir Arthur's deft command, the soldiers rounded up the people of the chosen village — men, women, and children — and brought them to the market. He chose a child, a girl with almond eyes, silken black hair, and skin the color of chestnuts. The girl gazed curiously at the man, so tall and fair and gaunt, as if to say, Even among the peculiar-looking British, this man is odd. Yet she followed after him, obedient.

Oblivious to the stares of the natives, Sir Arthur led the child before the prisoners of war — as the villagers were now called — lifted her into his arms, and deposited her into the barrel of a loaded cannon. The barrel was long and wide, and it swallowed the child entirely — only her hands were visible as they clung tight to the iron rim, holding it as if it were the top of a well into which she might sink.

"Light the fuse," Sir Grigori commanded. As the young soldier, his fingers trembling, struck a match, the girl's mother cried out from the crowd.

The explosion was the first of many that morning. Two hundred village children — the exact number of British killed in the Kanpur massacre — were led one by one to the cannon. The iron grew so hot that it charred the fingers of the soldiers dropping the heavy bundles of wiggling flesh, all hair and fingernails, into the shaft. Restrained at gunpoint, the villagers watched. Once the bloody business was through, the soldiers turned their muskets upon the villagers, ordering them to clean the market courtyard. Pieces of their children hung upon the tents and bushes and carts. Blood stained the earth orange.

News of the horror soon spread to the nearby villages and from those villages to the Gangetic Plain, to Meerut and Delhi and Kanpur and Lucknow and Jhansi and Gwalior. The Revolt, as Sir Arthur Grigori had foretold, quieted.

Percival's reading was interrupted by the sound of Sneja's voice as she leaned over his shoulder. "Ah, Sir Arthur," she said, the shadow of her wings falling over the pages of the book. "He was one of the finest Grigoris, my favorite of your father's brothers. Such valor! He secured our interests across the globe. If only his end had been as glorious as the rest of his life."

Percival knew that his mother was referring to Uncle Arthur's sad and pathetic demise. Sir Arthur had been one of the first in their family to contract the illness that now afflicted Percival. His once-glorious wings had withered to putrid, blackened nubs, and after a decade of terrible suffering his lungs had collapsed. He had died in humiliation and pain, succumbing to the disease in the fifth century of life, a time when he should have been enjoying his retirement. Many had believed the illness to be the result of his exposure to various lower breeds of human life — the wretched natives in the various colonial ports — but the truth of the matter was that the Grigoris did not know the origin of the illness. They knew only that there may be a way to cure it.

In the 1980s Sneja had come into possession of a human scientist's body of work devoted to the therapeutic properties of certain varieties of music. The scientist had been named Angela Valko and was the daughter of Gabriella Lévi-Franche Valko, one of the most renowned angelologists working in Europe. According to Angela Valko's theories, there was a way to restore Percival, and all their kind, to angelic perfection.

As was her wont, Sneja appeared to be reading her son's mind.

"Despite your best efforts to sabotage your

own cure, I believe that your art historian has pointed us in the right direction."

"You've found Verlaine?" Percival asked, closing *The Book of Generations* and turning to his mother. He felt like a child again, wishing to win Sneja's approval. "Did he have the drawings?"

"As soon as we hear from Otterley, we will know for certain," Sneja said, taking *The Book of Generations* from Percival and paging through it. "Clearly we overlooked something during our raids. But make no mistake, we will find the object of our search. And you, my angel, will be the first to benefit from its properties. After you are cured, we will be the saviors of our kind."

"Magnificent," Percival said, imagining his wings and how lush they would be once they had returned. "I will go to the convent myself. If it is there, I want to be the one to find it."

"You are too feeble." Sneja glanced at the glass of scotch. "And drunk. Let Otterley and your father handle this. You and I will stay here."

Sneja tucked *The Book of Generations* under her arm and, kissing Percival on the cheek, left the billiard room.

The thought of being trapped in New York City during one of the most important moments of his life enraged him. Taking his cane, he walked to the telephone and dialed

Otterley's number once more. As he waited for her to answer, he assured himself that his strength would soon return. He would be beautiful and powerful once more. With the restoration of his wings, all the suffering and humiliation he had endured would be transformed to glory.

St. Rose Convent, Milton, New York

Making her way past the crowd — sisters on their way to work and sisters on their way to prayer — Evangeline tried to maintain equilibrium under the scrutinizing eyes of her superiors. There was little tolerance for public displays of emotion at St. Rose — not pleasure, fear, pain, or remorse. Yet hiding anything at all in the convent proved virtually impossible. Day after day the sisters ate, prayed, cleaned, and rested together, so that even the smallest change in the happiness or anxiety of one sister transmitted itself throughout the group, as if conducted by an invisible wire. Evangeline knew, for example, when Sister Carla was annoyed — three tension lines appeared about her mouth. She knew when Sister Wilhelmina had slept through her morning walk along the river — a restrained glassiness weighed upon her gaze during Mass. Privacy did not exist. One could only wear a mask and hope that the others were too busy to notice.

The enormous oak door that connected

the convent to the church stood open night and day, big as a mouth waiting to be fed. Sisters traveled between the two buildings at will, transposing themselves from the gloomy convent to the glorious luminescence of the chapel. To Evangeline, returning to Maria Angelorum throughout the day always felt like going home, as if the spirit were released just slightly from the constraints of the body.

Trying to ease her panic at what had occurred in the library, Evangeline paused at the bulletin board that hung beside the church door. One of her responsibilities in addition to her library duties was the preparation of the Adoration Prayer Schedule, or APS for short. Each week she wrote down the sisters' regular time slots, careful to mark variations or substitutions, and posted the APS on the large corkboard listing the roster of alternate Prayer Partners in case of illness. Sister Philomena always said, "Never underestimate our reliance upon the APS!" — a statement Evangeline found to be quite correct. Often the sisters scheduled for adoration at night would walk the hallway between the convent and the church in pajamas and slippers, white hair tied up in plain cotton scarves. They would check the APS, glance at their wristwatches, and hurry on to prayer, assured in the soundness of the schedule that had kept perpetual prayer alive for two hundred years.

Taking solace in the exactitude of her work,

Evangeline left the APS, dipped a finger in holy water, and genuflected. Walking through the church, she felt calmed by the regularity of her actions, and by the time she approached the chapel, she felt a sense of renewed serenity. Inside, Sisters Divinia and Davida knelt at the altar, prayer partners from three to four. Sitting at the back, careful not to disturb Divinia and Davida, Evangeline took her rosary from her pocket and began to count the beads. Soon her prayer took rhythm.

For Evangeline — who had always endeavored to assess her thoughts with a clinical, incisive eye — prayer was an opportunity for self-examination. In her childhood years at St. Rose, long before she had taken vows and with them the responsibility of her five o'clock prayer shift, she would visit the Adoration Chapel many times a day for the sole purpose of trying to understand the anatomy of her memories — stark, frightening recollections she often wished to leave behind. For many years the ritual had helped her to forget.

But this afternoon's encounter with Verlaine had shaken her profoundly. His inquiries had brought Evangeline's thoughts, for the second time that day, back to an event she wished to forget.

After her mother's death, Evangeline and her father had moved to the United States from France, renting a narrow railroad apartment in Brooklyn. Some weekends they would take the train to Manhattan for the day, arriving early in the morning. Pushing through turnstiles, they followed the crowded tunnel walkways and emerged into the bright street aboveground. Once in the city, they never took taxis or the subway. Instead they walked. For blocks and blocks across the avenues they went, Evangeline's eyes falling upon chewing gum wedged in the cracks of the sidewalk, briefcases and shopping bags and the endlessly shifting movement of people rushing to lunch dates, meetings, and appointments — the frantic existence so different from the quiet life she and her father shared.

They had come to America when Evangeline was seven years old. Unlike her father, who struggled to express himself in English, she learned their new language quickly, drinking in the sounds of English, acquiring an American accent with little difficulty. Her first-grade teacher had helped her with the dreaded *th,* a sound that congealed upon Evangeline's tongue like a drop of oil, impeding her ability to communicate her thoughts. She repeated the words "this," "the," "that," and "them" over and over until she said them properly. Once this difficulty had disappeared, her pronunciation rang as clear and perfect as that of children born in America. When they were alone, she and her father spoke in Italian, her father's native language, or French, her mother's, as if they were still living in

Europe. Soon, however, Evangeline began to crave English as one craves food or love. In public she returned her father's melodic Italian words with new, flawlessly articulated English.

As a child, Evangeline had not realized that their trips to Manhattan, taken many times a month, were more than pleasurable excursions. Her father said nothing of their purpose, only promising to take her to the carousel in Central Park, or to their favorite diner, or to the Museum of Natural History, where she would marvel at the enormous whale suspended from the ceiling, catching her breath as she examined the exposed underbelly. Although these day trips were adventures to Evangeline, she realized as she got older that the real purpose for their journeys to the city revolved around meetings between her father and his contacts — an exchange of documents in Central Park, or a whispered conversation in a bar near Wall Street, or lunch with a table of foreign diplomats, all of them speaking in rapid, unintelligible languages as they poured wine and traded information. As a child, she had not understood her father's work or his growing dependence upon it after her mother died. Evangeline simply believed that he brought her to Manhattan as a gift.

This illusion fractured one afternoon the year she was nine years old. The day was brilliantly sunny, with the first sharpness of winter woven into the wind. Instead of walking to an agreed-upon destination, as they normally did, they had walked over the Brooklyn Bridge, her father leading her silently past the thick metal cables. In the distance, sunlight slid over the skyscrapers of Manhattan. They walked for miles, finally stopping at Washington Square Park, where her father insisted they rest for a moment on a bench. Her father's behavior struck Evangeline as extremely odd that afternoon. He was visibly edgy, and his hands shook as he lit a cigarette. She knew him well enough to understand that the slightest nervous reflex — the twitch of a finger or his trembling lips — revealed a well of hidden anxiety. Evangeline knew that something was wrong, and yet she said nothing.

Her father had been handsome as a young man. In pictures from Europe, his dark curly hair fell over one eye, and he wore impeccable, finely tailored clothing. But that afternoon, sitting there shaking on a bench in the park, he seemed to have become, all at once, old and tired. Taking a square of cloth from his trouser pocket, he dabbed sweat off his forehead. Still she remained silent. If she had spoken, it would have broken an implicit agreement between them, a silent communication that they had developed after her mother had died. That was their way — a tacit respect of their mutual loneliness. He would never tell her the truth about what worried him. He did not confide in her. Perhaps it was her father's strange condition that made her pay particular attention to the details of that afternoon, or perhaps the magnitude of what happened that day had caused her to relive it time and time again, searing the events into her memory, because Evangeline could recall each moment, each and every word and gesture, even the smallest shift in her feelings, as if she were still there.

"Come," her father said, tucking the pocket square into his jacket and standing suddenly, as if they were late for an appointment.

Leaves crunched under Evangeline's patent-leather Mary Janes — her father insisted that she dress in the fashion he felt appropriate for a young girl, which left her with a wardrobe of starched cotton pinafores, pressed skirts, tailored blazers, and expensive shoes shipped to them from Italy, clothes that separated her from her classmates, who wore jeans and T-shirts and the latest brand of tennis shoes. They walked into a dingy neighborhood with bright-colored signs advertising CAPPUCCINO, GELATO, VINO. Evangeline recognized the neighborhood at once — they had come to Little Italy often in the past. She knew the area well.

They stopped before a café with metal tables strewn upon the sidewalk. Taking her hand, her father led her into a crowded room where a warm gust of sweet-smelling steam fell upon them. The walls were filled with black-and-white pictures of Italy, the frames gilded and ornate. At the bar, men drank espresso, newspapers spread before them, hats pulled low over their eyes. A glass case filled with desserts drew Evangeline's attention — she stood before it, hungry, wishing her father would allow her to choose from the frosted cakes arrayed like bouquets under soft lights. Before she had a chance to speak, a man stepped from behind the bar, wiped his hands upon a red apron, and shook her father's hands as if they were old friends.

"Luca," he said, smiling warmly.

"Vladimir," her father said, returning the man's smile, and Evangeline knew that they must indeed have been old friends — her father rarely displayed affection in public.

"Come, have something to eat," Vladimir said in heavily accented English. He pulled out a chair for her father.

"Nothing for me." Her father gestured to Evangeline as she sat. "But I believe my daughter has her eye on *i dolci.*"

To Evangeline's delight, Vladimir opened the glass case and allowed her to choose whatever she wished. She took a petite pink frosted cake with delicate blue marzipan flowers scattered over its surface. Holding the plate as if it might break in her hands, she walked to a high metal table and sat, her Mary Janes folded against the legs of a metal parlor chair, the thick planks of the wooden floor shining below. Vladimir brought her a glass of water and set it near her cake, asking her to be a good girl and wait there while he spoke to her father. Vladimir struck her as ancient — his hair was pure white and his skin heavily lined — but there was something playful in his manner, as if they shared a joke. He winked at Evangeline, and she understood that the two men had business to attend to.

Happy to comply, Evangeline worked a spoon into the heart of the cake and found it filled with a thick, buttery cream that tasted ever so slightly of chestnuts. Her father was fastidious about their diet — they did not spend money on such extravagant confections — and so Evangeline grew up without a taste for rich food. The cake was a rare treat, and she endeavored to eat very slowly, to make it last as long as possible. As she ate, her attention distilled to a single act of pure enjoyment. The warm café, the noise of the patrons, the sunlight burnishing the floor bronze — all of this receded from her perception. Surely she would not have noticed her father's conversation either, if it had not been for the intensity with which he spoke to Vladimir. They sat a few tables away, near the window, close enough that she could hear.

"I have no choice but to see them," her father said, lighting a cigarette as he spoke. "It has been nearly three years since we lost Angela." Hearing him speak her mother's name was such a rarity that it stopped Evangeline cold.

"They have no right to keep the truth from you," Vladimir said.

At this her father inhaled deeply from the cigarette and said, "It is my right to understand what happened, especially after the assistance I gave during Angela's research, the midnight interruptions when she was in her lab. The stress it caused during her pregnancy. I was there in the beginning. I supported her decisions. I also made sacrifices. As has Evangeline."

"Of course," Vladimir said. He called over a waiter and ordered coffee. "You have the right to know everything. All I ask you to consider is whether this information is worth the risk you take to obtain it. Think of what might happen. You are safe here. You have a new life. They have forgotten about you."

Evangeline studied her cake, hoping her father would not notice the intense interest his conversation had aroused. They simply did not speak of her mother's life and death. But when Evangeline leaned forward, eager to hear more, she set the table off balance. The glass of water fell to the floor, chunks of ice skittering upon the parquet. Startled, the men stared at Evangeline. She tried to mask her shame by wiping the water from the table with a napkin and going back to her cake, as if nothing at all had happened. With a look of reproach, her father shifted in his chair and resumed the conversation, oblivious that his attempts at secrecy only made Evangeline more intent to hear him.

Vladimir sighed heavily and said, "If you must know, they are holding them in the warehouse." He spoke so quietly that Evangeline could just barely hear his voice. "I got a call last night. They have three of them, one female and two males."

"From Europe?"

"They were captured in the Pyrenees," Vladimir said. "They arrived here late last night. I was going to go myself, but, to be honest, I cannot bring myself to do it any longer. We are growing old, Luca."

A waiter stopped at their table and placed two cups of espresso before them.

Her father sipped his espresso. "They are still alive, yes?"

"Very much so," Vladimir said, shaking his head. "I hear they are horrifying creatures — very pure. I don't understand how they managed to transport them to New York. In the old days, it would have taken a ship and full crew to get them here so quickly. If they are of the pure stock that they claim, it would be nearly impossible to contain them. I didn't think it possible."

"Angela would have known more about the

details of their physical capabilities than I," her father said, folding his hands before him and staring out the plate-glass window as if Evangeline's mother might appear into the sun-filled pane before him. "It was the focus of her studies. But I believe there is a growing consensus that the Famous Ones have been growing weaker, even the purest of them. Perhaps they are so weak they can be captured with more ease."

Vladimir bent closer to her father, his eyes wide. "Do you mean to say that they are dying out?"

"Not exactly dying out," her father said. "But there has been speculation that their vitality is in serious decline. Their strength is diminishing."

"But how is that possible?" Vladimir asked, astonished.

"Angela used to say that one day their blood would be mixed too thoroughly with human blood. She believed that they would become too like us, too human to maintain their unique physical properties. I believe that it is something along the lines of negative evolution — they have reproduced with inferior specimens, human beings, far too often."

Her father put out his cigarette in a plastic ashtray and took another sip of his espresso.

"They can retain the traits of angels only so long, and only if they do not interbreed. The time will come when their humanity will overtake them and all of their children will be born with characteristics that can only be described as inferior — shorter life spans, susceptibility to disease, a tendency toward morality. Their last hope will be to infuse themselves with pure angelic traits, and this, as we know, is beyond their abilities. They have been plagued by human traits. Angela used to speculate that the Nephilim are beginning to feel emotion as humans do. Compassion, love, kindness — everything that we define ourselves by may be emerging in them. In fact," her father concluded, "they consider this a great weakness."

Vladimir leaned back in his chair and folded his hands upon his chest, as if thinking this over. "Their demise is not impossible," he said at last. "And yet how can we say what is and is not possible? Their very existence defies the intellect. But we have seen them, you and I. We have lost much to them, my friend." Vladimir met her father's eye.

Her father said, "Angela believed that the Nephilistic immune system reacted negatively to human-made chemicals and pollutants. She believed that these unnatural elements worked to break down the cellular structures inherited from the Watchers, creating a form of deadly cancer. Another theory she had was that the change in their diet over the past two hundred years has altered their body chemistry, thus affecting reproduction. Angela had studied a number of the creatures with degenerative diseases that severely shortened their life span, but she did not come to any definitive conclusion. Nobody knows for certain what is causing it, but whatever the cause, the creatures are surely desperate to stop it."

"You know very well what will stop it," Vladimir said, his voice soft.

"Exactly," her father said. "To that end, Angela even began testing many of your theories, Vladimir, to determine whether your musicological speculations had a biological significance as well. I've suspected that she was on the brink of something monumental and that this is why she was killed."

Vladimir fingered his demitasse. "Celestial musicology is no weapon. Its uses as such are wishful thinking at best, not to mention inordinately dangerous to pursue. Angela of all people should have known this."

"They may be inordinately dangerous," her father said, "but think of what would happen if they found a cure for the degeneration. If we are able to prevent it, they will lose their angelic properties and become closer to human beings. They will suffer sickness, and they will die."

"I just don't believe it is happening on that level," Vladimir said, shaking his head. "It's wishful thinking."

"Perhaps," her father said.

"And even if it were happening," Vladimir

said. "What would it mean for us? Or for your daughter? Why would you jeopardize the happiness you have for the sake of uncertainties?"

"Equality," her father said. "We would be free of their treacherous hold on our civilization. We would have control of our destiny for the first time in modern history."

"A wonderful dream," Vladimir said, wistful. "But a fantasy. We cannot control our destiny."

"Perhaps it's God's plan to weaken them slowly," her father said, ignoring his friend. "Perhaps he chose to exterminate them over time rather than wipe them out suddenly, in one clean sweep."

"I tired of God's plans years ago," Vladimir said, weary. "And so, Luca, did you."

"You will not come back to us, then?"

Vladimir looked at her father for a moment, as if measuring his words. "Tell me the truth — are my musicological theories what Angela was working with when they took her?"

Evangeline started, unsure if she'd heard Vladimir correctly. Angela had been gone for years, and still Evangeline did not know the precise details of her mother's death. She shifted in her chair to get a better look at her father's face. To her surprise, his eyes had filled with tears.

"She was working on a genetic theory of Nephilistic diminishment. Angela's mother, whom I blame for all of this as much as I blame anyone, sponsored the bulk of the work, found funding, and encouraged Angela to take over the project. I suppose Gabriella thought it the safest niche in the organization — why else would she hide her away in classrooms and libraries if she didn't think it prudent? Angela assisted in developing models in laboratories — under her mother's observation, of course."

"You blame Gabriella for the abduction?" Vladimir said.

"Who can say who is to blame? She was at risk everywhere. Her mother certainly did not protect her from them. But each day I live with the uncertainty. Is Gabriella to blame? Am I? Could I have protected her? Was it a mistake to allow her to pursue her work? That, my old friend, is why I must see the creatures now. If anyone can understand this sickness, this horrid addiction to learning the truth, it is you."

Suddenly a waiter came to Evangeline's table, blocking her view of her father. She had been so involved in listening to him that she'd completely forgotten her cake. It lay half eaten, the cream seeping from the center. The waiter cleared the table, wiping up the remainder of the spilled water and, with a cruel efficiency, taking away the cake. By the time Evangeline turned her gaze back to her father's table, Vladimir had lit a cigarette. Her father's seat was empty.

Noticing her distress, Vladimir waved her to come to his side. Evangeline jumped from her chair, searching for her father.

"Luca has asked me to watch you while he is gone," Vladimir said, smiling kindly. "You may not remember, but I met you once when you were a very little girl, when your mother brought you to our quarters in Montparnasse. I used to know your mother quite well in Paris. We worked together, briefly, and were dear friends. Before I spent my days making cakes, I was a scholar, if you can believe it. Wait a moment, and I will show you a picture I have of Angela."

As Vladimir disappeared into the back room of the café, Evangeline hurried to the door and ran outside. Two blocks away, through crowds of people, she caught sight of her father's jacket. Without a thought of Vladimir, or of what her father would say if she caught him, she rushed into the crowd, running past shops, convenience stores, parked cars, vegetable stands. At the corner she stepped into the street, nearly tripping over a curb. Her father was ahead; she could see him plainly in the crowd.

He turned a corner and walked south. For many blocks Evangeline followed, passing through Chinatown and into ever more industrial buildings, pushing onward, her toes pinching in her tight leather shoes.

Her father stopped at the end of a dingy,

trash-strewn street. Evangeline watched him pound upon the doorway of a great corrugated-steel warehouse. Preoccupied with whatever business was at hand, he didn't notice her walking toward him. She was almost close enough to call out to him when a door swung open. He stepped inside the warehouse. It happened so quickly, with such finality, that for an instant Evangeline stopped in her tracks.

Pushing the heavy door open, she stepped into a dusty corridor. She climbed a set of aluminum stairs, balancing her weight carefully, lightly, so that the soles of her shoes would not alert her father — or whoever else was in the depths of the warehouse — to her presence. At the top of the stairs, she crouched down, resting her chin upon her knees, hoping that no one would discover her. In the past years, all his efforts had been to keep Evangeline at a distance from his work. Her father would be furious if he knew she had followed him there.

It took a moment for her eyes to adjust to the sunless, airless space, but when they did, she saw that the warehouse was vast and empty, except for a group of men standing below three suspended cages, each one as big as a car. The cages were hung with steel chains from steel girders. Inside, trapped like birds in cubes of iron mesh, were three creatures, each in a cage. One of them appeared to be nearly insane with rage — it clutched the bars and screamed obscenities at its captors standing below. The other two were listless, lying limp and sullen, as if drugged or beaten into submission.

Studying them more closely, Evangeline saw that the creatures were completely naked, although the texture of their skin, a luminescent membrane of clarified gold, made them seem encased in pure light. One of the creatures was female — she had long hair, small breasts, and a tapering waist. The other two were male. Gaunt and hairless, with flat chests, they were taller than the female and at least two feet taller than the size of a grown man. The bars of the cage were smeared in a glittering, honeylike fluid that dripped slowly down the metal and onto the floor.

Evangeline's father stood with the men, his arms crossed. The group appeared to be doing some kind of scientific experiment. One man held a clipboard, another had a camera. There was a large lit board with three sets of chest X-rays clipped to it — the lungs and rib cage stood out in ghostly white against a faded gray background. A nearby table held medical equipment — syringes and bandages and numerous tools Evangeline could not name.

The female creature began to pace in her cage, still screaming at her captors, tearing at her flowing blond hair. Her gestures were executed with such strength that the bearing chain creaked and groaned above the cage, as if it might break. Then, with a violent movement, the female creature turned her body. Evangeline blinked, unable to believe her eyes. At the center of her long, lithe back grew a pair of sweeping, articulated wings. Evangeline covered her mouth with her hands, afraid that she might call out in surprise. The creature flexed her muscles, and the wings opened, spreading the entire length of the cage. White and sweeping, the wings shone with mellowed luminosity. As the cage swayed under the angel's weight, tracing a slow parabola through the stagnant air, Evangeline felt her sense sharpen. Her heartbeat pounded in her ears; her breath quickened. The creatures were lovely and horrifying at once. They were beautiful, iridescent monsters.

Evangeline watched the female pace the length of her cage with wings unfurled, as if the men below her were little more than mice she might swoop down upon and devour.

"Release me," the creature growled, her voice grinding, guttural, anguished. The tips of her wings slid through the interstices of the cage, sharp and pointed.

Evangeline's father turned to the man with the clipboard. "What will you do with them?" he asked, as if referring to a net filled with rare butterflies.

"We won't know where to send the remains until we've had the final test results."

"Most likely we'll send them back to our labs in Arizona for dissection, documentation, and preservation. They certainly are beauties."

"Have you made any determinations about their strength? Do you see any signs of diminishment?" Evangeline's father asked. Evangeline could detect a strain of hope in his questions, and although she could not be certain, she felt that this had something to do with her mother. "Something in their fluid tests?"

"If you're asking whether they have the strength of their ancestors," the man said, "the answer is no. They're the strongest of their kind that I've seen in years, and yet their vulnerability to our stimuli is pronounced."

"Wonderful news," Evangeline's father said, stepping closer to the cages. Addressing the creatures, his voice became commanding, as if speaking to animals. "Devils," he said.

This drove one of the male creatures from his lethargy. He wrapped his white fingers around the bars of the cage and pulled himself to full height. "Angel and devil," he said. "One is but a shade of the other."

"There will come a day," Evangeline's father said, "when you will disappear from the earth. One day we will be rid of your presence."

Before Evangeline could hide, her father turned and walked quickly toward the stairs. Although she had been careful to obscure herself at the top of the stairwell, she had not planned her exit. She had no choice but to scamper down the stairs, through the door, and out into the brilliantly sunny afternoon. Blinded by the light, she ran and ran.

Milton Bar and Grill, Milton, New York

As Verlaine pushed his way through a crowded barroom, the pounding in his head dissolved in a wash of country music. He was frozen stiff, the cut on his hand seared, and he hadn't eaten a thing since breakfast. If he were in New York, he would be getting takeout from his favorite Thai restaurant or meeting friends for a drink in the Village. He would have nothing to worry about other than what he should watch on television. Instead he was stuck in a dive bar in the middle of nowhere, trying to figure out how he was going to get himself out of there. Still, the bar was warm and gave him a place to think. Verlaine rubbed his hands together, trying to bring life back to his fingers. If he could unthaw, perhaps he would be able to sort out what in the hell he was going to do next.

Taking a table at a window overlooking the street — it was the only isolated spot in the place — he ordered a hamburger and a bottle of Corona. He drank the beer quickly, to warm himself, and ordered another. The second beer he drank slowly, allowing the alcohol to bring him back to reality little by little. His fingers tingled; his feet thawed. The pain of his wound lessened. But by the time his food arrived, Verlaine felt warm and alert, better equipped to sort out the problems before him.

He took the piece of paper from his pocket, placed it upon the laminate table, and reread the sentences he had copied. Pale, smoky light flickered over his weather-beaten hands, the half-full bottle of Corona, the pale pink paper. The communication was short, only four direct, unadorned sentences, but it opened a world of possibilities for Verlaine. Of course, the relationship between Mother Innocenta and Abigail Rockefeller remained mysterious — clearly they had collaborated upon some project or another and had found success in their work in the Rhodope Mountains — but he could foresee a large paper, perhaps even an entire book, about the object the women had brought back from the mountains. What intrigued Verlaine nearly as much as the artifact, however, was the presence of a third person in the adventure, someone named Celestine Clochette. Verlaine tried to recall if he had come across a person by that name in any of his other research. Could Celestine have been one of Abigail Rockefeller's partners? Was she a European art dealer? The prospect of understanding the triangle was the very reason he loved the history of art: In every piece there lay the mystery of creation, the adventure of its distribution, and the particularities of its preservation.

Grigori's interest in St. Rose Convent made the information all the more perplexing. A man like Grigori could not possibly find beauty and meaning in art. People like that lived their entire lives without understanding that there was more to a van Gogh than record-breaking sales at an auction. Indeed, there must be a monetary value to the object in question, or Grigori wouldn't spend a moment of his time trying to hunt it down. How Verlaine had gotten mixed up with such a person was truly beyond his understanding.

Gazing outside, he searched the darkness beyond the pane. The temperature must have fallen again; the heat from the interior of the room reacted with the cold window, creating a layer of condensation on the glass. Outside, the occasional car drove by, its taillights leaving a trail of orange in the frost. Verlaine watched and waited, wondering how he would get back home.

For a moment he considered calling the convent. Perhaps the beautiful young nun he'd met in the library would have a suggestion. Then the thought struck him that she, too, might be in some kind of danger. There was always the chance that the thugs he'd seen at the convent might go inside looking for him. Yet there was no way they could possibly know where he had gone in the convent, and surely they wouldn't know he'd spoken to Evangeline. She had not been happy to see him and would probably never speak to him again. In any event, it was important to be practical. He needed to get to a train station or find a bus that would get him back to the city, and he doubted that he would find either of those in Milton.

St. Rose Convent, Milton, New York

Evangeline did not know Sister Celestine well. At seventy-five, she was wheelchair-bound and did not spend much time among the younger nuns. Although she made an appearance each day at morning Mass, when one of the sisters would push her wheelchair to the front of the church, Celestine resided in a position of isolation and protection as sacrosanct as a queen's. Celestine always had her meals delivered to her room, and from time to time Evangeline had been dispatched to Celestine's cell from the library, a stack of poetry books and historical fiction in her arms. There were even the occasional works in French that Sister Philomena had secured by interlibrary loan. These, Evangeline had noted, made Celestine particularly happy.

As Evangeline walked through the first floor, she saw that it had filled with sisters at work, a great mass of black-and-white habits shuffling along under the weak light of bulbs encased in metal sconces as they performed their daily chores. Sisters swarmed the hallways, opening broom closets, brandishing mops and rags and bottles of cleaning agents as they set about the evening chores. The sisters tied aprons at their waists and rolled up their dolman sleeves and snapped on latex gloves. They shook the dust from drapery and opened windows to dissuade the perennial mildew and moss of their damp, cool climate from taking hold. The women prided themselves on their ability to carry out a great deal of the convent's labor themselves. The cheerfulness of their evening chore groups somehow disguised the fact that they were scrubbing and waxing and dusting, and instead it created the illusion that they were contributing to some marvelous project, one of much larger significance than their small individual tasks. Indeed, it was true: Each floor washed, each banister finial polished became an offering and a tribute to the greater good.

Evangeline followed the narrow steps from the Adoration Chapel up to the fourth floor. Celestine's chamber was one of the largest cells in the convent. It was a corner bedroom with a private bathroom containing a large shower equipped with a folding plastic platform chair. Evangeline often wondered whether Celestine's confinement freed her from the burden of daily participation in community activities, offering her a pleasant reprieve from duties, or if isolation made Celestine's life in the convent a prison. Such immobility struck Evangeline as horribly restrictive.

She knocked on the door, giving three hesitant raps.

"Yes?" Celestine said, her voice weak. Celestine was born in France — despite half a century in the United States, her accent was pronounced.

Evangeline stepped into Celestine's room, closing the door behind herself.

"Who is there?"

"It's me." She spoke quietly, afraid to disturb Celestine. "Evangeline. From the library."

Celestine was nestled into her wheelchair near the window, a crocheted blanket in her lap. She no longer wore a veil, and her hair had been cut short, framing her face with a shock of white. On the far side of the room, a humidifier spewed steam into the air. In another corner the hot coils of a space heater warmed the room like a sauna. Celestine appeared to be cold, despite the blanket. The bed was made up with a similar crocheted throw, typical of the blankets made for the Elder Sisters by the younger ones. Celestine narrowed her eyes, trying to account for Evangeline's presence. "You have more books for me, do you?"

"No," Evangeline said, taking a seat next to Celestine's wheelchair, where a stack of books sat on a mahogany end table, a magnifying glass atop the pile. "It looks like you've got plenty to read."

"Yes, yes," Celestine said, looking out the window, "there is always more to read."

"I'm sorry to disturb you, Sister, but I was hoping to ask you a question." Evangeline pulled the letter from Mrs. Rockefeller to Mother Innocenta out of her pocket and flattened it upon her knee.

Celestine folded her long white fingers together upon her lap, a gold FSPA signet ring glinting on her ring finger, and stared blankly at Evangeline with a cool, assessing gaze. It was possible that Sister Celestine could not remember what she had eaten for lunch, let alone events that had occurred many decades before.

Evangeline cleared her throat. "I was working in the archives this morning and found a letter that mentions your name. I don't really know where to file it — I was wondering if you would help me to understand what it is about, so that I can put it in its proper place."

"Proper place?" Celestine asked, doubtful. "I don't know if I can be much help at putting anything in its proper place these days. What does the letter say?"

Evangeline gave the page to Sister Celestine, who turned the thin paper over in her hands.

"The glass," she said, fluttering her fingers toward the table.

Evangeline placed the magnifying glass in her hands, watching Celestine's face intently as the lens moved over the lines, transforming the solid paper into a sheet of watery light. It was clear by her expression that she was struggling with her thoughts, although Evangeline could not say if the words on the page had caused the confusion. After a moment Celestine laid the magnifying glass in her lap, and Evangeline understood at once: Celestine recognized the letter.

"It is very old," Celestine said at last, creasing the paper and resting her blue-veined hand over it. "Written by a woman named Abigail Rockefeller."

"Yes," Evangeline said. "I read the signature."

"I am surprised you found this in the archives," she said. "I thought they had taken everything away."

"I was hoping," Evangeline ventured, "that you might shed some light on its meaning."

Celestine sighed deeply and turned her eyes, framed by folds of wrinkled skin, away. "This was written before I came to live at St. Rose. I didn't arrive until early 1944, just a week or so before the great fire. I was weak from the journey, and I didn't speak a word of English."

"Do you happen to know why Mrs. Rockefeller would send such a letter to Mother Innocenta?" Evangeline persisted.

Celestine pulled herself up in the wheelchair, straightening the crocheted blanket about her legs. "It was Mrs. Rockefeller who brought me here," she said, her manner guarded, as if she might give too much away. "It was a Bentley we arrived in, I believe, although I have never known much about cars made outside of France. It was certainly a vehicle befitting Abigail Rockefeller. She was a plump, aged woman in a fur coat, and I could not have been more her opposite. I was young and unspeakably thin. In fact, dressed as I was in my old-fashioned Franciscan habit — the variety they still wore in Portugal, where I had taken my vows before embarking upon my journey — I looked much more like the sisters gathered at the horseshoe driveway in their black overcoats and black scarves. It was Ash Wednesday. I remember because crosses of black ash marked the sisters' foreheads, blessings from the Mass conducted that morning.

"I will never forget the greeting I received from my fellow sisters. The crowd of nuns whispered to me as I passed by, their voices soft and encompassing as a song. *Welcome,* the sisters of St. Rose Convent whispered. *Welcome, welcome, welcome home.*"

"The sisters greeted me in a similar way upon my arrival," Evangeline said, recalling how she had wished for nothing more than that her father would take her back to Brooklyn.

"Yes, I recall," Celestine said. "You were so very young when you came to us." She paused, as if comparing Evangeline's arrival with her own. "Mother Innocenta welcomed me, but then I realized that the two women were acquainted already. And when Mrs. Rockefeller replied, 'It is lovely to meet you at last,' I wondered suddenly if the sisters had been welcoming me at all, or if it was Mrs. Rockefeller who had won their attention. I was aware of the sight I presented. I had dark black circles under my eyes, and I was many kilograms underweight. I could not say what had caused more harm — the deprivations in Europe or the journey across the Atlantic."

Evangeline strained to imagine the spectacle of Celestine's arrival. It was a struggle to picture her as a young woman. When Celestine had come to St. Rose Convent, she had been younger than Evangeline was at present. "Abigail Rockefeller must have been anxious for your well-being," Evangeline offered.

"Nonsense," Celestine replied. "Mrs. Rockefeller pushed me forward for Innocenta's inspection as if she were a matron presenting her debutante daughter at her first ball. But Innocenta merely propped open the heavy wooden door at a great angle, anchoring it with her weight so that the mass of sisters could return to their work. As they passed, I smelled chores on their habits — wood polish, ammonia, taper wax — but Mrs. Rockefeller didn't seem to heed this. What did capture her fancy, I recall, was the marble statue of

170

the Archangel Michael, his foot crushing the head of a serpent. She placed a gloved hand upon the statue's foot and ran a finger delicately across the exact point of pressure that would crack the demon's skull. I noticed the double strand of creamy pearls nestled in her grizzled neck, buttery orbs glinting in the dim light, objects of beauty that, despite my usual immunity to the material world, caught my attention for a moment and held it. I could not help but note how unfair it was that so many children of God could languish ill and broken in Europe, while those in America adorned themselves with furs and pearls."

Evangeline stared at Celestine, hoping that she would continue. Not only had this woman known of the relationship between Innocenta and Abigail Rockefeller, she appeared to be at the very center of it. Evangeline wanted to ask her to go on but was afraid that any direct questioning might put Celestine on guard. Finally she said, "You must know quite a lot about what Mrs. Rockefeller wrote to Innocenta."

"It was my work that brought us to the Rhodopes," Celestine said, meeting Evangeline's eyes with a sharpness that unsettled her. "It was my efforts that led us to what we found in the gorge. We were careful to be sure that everything went as planned in the mountains. They didn't overtake us, which was a great relief to Dr. Seraphina, our leader. It was our greatest worry — to be captured before we made it to the gorge."

"The gorge?" Evangeline asked, growing confused.

"Our planning was meticulous," Celestine continued. "We had the most modern equipment and cameras that allowed us to document our discoveries. We took care to protect the cameras and the film. The findings were all in order. Wrapped in cloth and cotton. Very secure, indeed." Celestine stared out the window as if measuring the rise of the river.

"I'm not sure I understand," Evangeline said, hoping to prod Celestine to explain. "What cavern? What findings?"

Sister Celestine met Evangeline's eyes once more. "We drove through the Rhodopes, entering through Greece. It was the only way during the war. The Americans and British had begun their bombing campaigns to the west, in Sofia. The damage was growing each week, and we knew it was possible that the gorge could be hit, although not likely, of course — it was one cave in thousands. Still, we pushed everything into motion. It all happened very quickly once the funding from Abigail Rockefeller was secure. All of the angelologists were summoned to continue their efforts."

"Angelologists," Evangeline said, turning the phrase over. Although it was a familiar word, she did not dare admit this to Celestine.

If Celestine detected a change in Evangeline, she did not let on. "Our enemies did not attack us at the Devil's Throat, but they tracked our return to Paris." Celestine's voice grew animated, and she turned to Evangeline, her eyes wide. "They began to hunt us immediately. They put their networks of spies to work and captured my beloved teacher. I could not stay in France. It was too dangerous to remain in Europe. I had to come to America, although I had no desire at all to do so. I was given the responsibility of bringing the object to safety — our discovery was left to my care, you see, and there was nothing I could do but flee. I still feel that I betrayed our resistance by leaving, but I had no choice. It was my assignment. While others were dying, I took a boat to New York City. Everything had been prepared."

Evangeline struggled to mask her reaction to these bizarre details of Celestine's history, but the more she heard, the more difficult it was to remain silent. "Mrs. Rockefeller assisted you in this?" she asked.

"She arranged for my passage out of the inferno that Europe had become." This was the first direct answer she had given to Evangeline. "I was smuggled to Portugal. The others were not so lucky — I knew even as I departed that the ones left behind were doomed. Once they found us, the horrid devils killed us. That was their way — vicious, evil, inhuman creatures! They would not rest until we were exterminated. To this day we are hunted."

Evangeline stared at Celestine, aghast. She did not know much about the Second World War or how it pertained to Celestine's fears, but she worried that such agitation might bring her harm. "Please, Sister, everything is fine. I assure you that you're safe now."

"Safe?" Celestine's eyes were frozen in fear. "One is never safe. *Jamais.*"

"Tell me," Evangeline said, her voice steady to mask her growing distress. "What danger do you speak of?"

Celestine's voice was little more than a whisper as she said, *"'A cette époque-là, il y avait des géants sur la terre, et aussi après que les fils de Dieu se furent unis aux filles des hommes et qu'elles leur eurent donné des enfants. Ce sont ces héros si fameux d'autrefois.'"*

Evangeline understood French: indeed, it was her mother's native tongue, and her mother had spoken to her exclusively in French. But she had not heard the language spoken in more than fifteen years.

Celestine's voice was sharp, rapid, vehement as she repeated the words in English. "'There were giants in the earth in those days, and also after that, when the sons of God came in unto the daughters of men, and they bare children to them, the same became mighty men which were of old, men of renown.'"

In English the passage was familiar to Evangeline, its placement in the Bible clear in her mind. "It is from Genesis," she said, relieved that she understood at least a fraction of what Sister Celestine was saying. "I know the passage. It occurs just before the Flood."

"Pardon?" Celestine looked at Evangeline as if she had never seen her before.

"The passage you quoted from Genesis," Evangeline said. "I know it well."

"No," Celestine said, her gaze suddenly full of animosity. "You do not understand."

Evangeline placed her hand on Celestine's, to calm her, but it was too late — Celestine had worked herself into a fury. She whispered, "In the beginning, human and divine relations were in symmetry. There was order in the cosmos. The legions of angels were filed in strict regiments; man and woman — God's most adored, made in his own image — lived in bliss, free from pain. Suffering did not exist; death did not exist; time did not exist. There was no reason for such elements. The universe was perfectly static, and pure in its refusal to move forward. But the angels could not rest in such a state. They grew jealous of man. The dark angels tempted humanity out of pride, but also to cause God pain. And so the angels fell as man fell."

Realizing that it would only do more harm to allow Celestine to continue such madness, Evangeline pulled at the letter resting under Celestine's trembling fingers, removing it with deliberation. Folding it into her pocket, she stood. "Forgive me, Sister," she said. "I did not mean to disturb you in this fashion."

"Go!" Celestine said, shaking violently. "Go at once and leave me in peace!"

Confused and more than a little afraid, Evangeline closed Celestine's door and half walked, half ran down the narrow hallway to the stairwell.

Most afternoons Sister Philomena's naps lasted until she was called to dinner, and so it was little surprise, then, that the library was empty when Evangeline arrived, the fireplace cold and the trolley stacked with volumes waiting to be returned to their shelves. Ignoring the mess of books, Evangeline endeavored to build a fire to warm the frigid room. She stacked two pieces of wood in the grating, packing the underbelly with crumpled newspaper, and struck a match. Once the flames began to catch, she stood and straightened her skirt with her small, cold hands, as if smoothing the fabric might help her gain focus. One thing was certain: She would need all the concentration she could muster to bring herself to sort through Celestine's story. She removed a piece of folded paper from the pocket of her skirt, unfolded it, and read the letter from Mr. Verlaine:

In the process of conducting research for a private client, it has come to my attention that

Mrs. Abigail Aldrich Rockefeller, matriarch o͏ Rockefeller family and patron of the arts, m. have briefly corresponded with the abbess of St. Rose Convent, Mother Innocenta, in the years 1943–1944.

It was nothing more than a harmless note asking to visit St. Rose Convent, the kind of letter institutions with collections of rare books and images received on a regular basis, the kind of letter that Evangeline should have responded to with a swift and efficient refusal and, once posted, should have forgotten forever. Yet this simple request had turned everything upside down. She was both wary and consumed by the intense curiosity she felt about Sister Celestine, Mrs. Abigail Rockefeller, Mother Innocenta, and the practice of angelology. She wished to understand the work her parents had performed, and yet she longed for the luxury of ignorance. Celestine's words had echoed deeply within her, as if she had come to St. Rose for the very purpose of hearing them. Even so, the possible connection between Celestine's history and her own caused Evangeline the most profound agitation.

Her one consolation was that the library was utterly still. She sat at a table near the fireplace, placed her pointy elbows upon the wooden surface, and rested her head in her hands, trying to clear her mind. Although the fire had risen, a trickle of freezing air seeped

fireplace, creating a current of in-
... it and biting cold that resulted in a
...ixture of sensations upon her skin.
... to reconstruct Celestine's jumbled
...y as best she could. Taking a piece of
paper and a red marker from a drawer in the
table, she jotted the words in a list:

Devil's Throat Cavern
Rhodope Mountains
Genesis 6
Angelologists

When in need of guidance, Evangeline was
more like a tortoise than a young woman —
she retreated into a cool, dark space inside
herself, became completely still, and waited
for the confusion to pass. For half an hour,
she stared at the words she had written —
*"Devil's Throat, Rhodope Mountains, Genesis
6, Angelologists."* If anyone had told her the
previous day that these words would be written by her, confronting her when she least
expected them, she would have laughed. Yet
these very words were the pillars of Sister Celestine's story. With Mrs. Abigail Rockefeller's
role in the mystery — as the letter she'd found
implied — Evangeline had no choice but to
decipher their relation.

While her impulse was to analyze the
list until the connections magically revealed
themselves, Evangeline knew better than to

wait. She crossed the now-warm library and removed an oversize world atlas from a shelf. Opening it upon a table, she found a listing for the Rhodope Mountains in the index and turned to the appropriate page at the center of the atlas. The Rhodopes turned out to be a minor chain of mountains in southeastern Europe spanning the area from northern Greece into southern Bulgaria. Evangeline examined the map, hoping to find some reference to the Devil's Throat, but the entire region was a mottle of shaded bumps and triangles on the map, signifying elevated terrain.

She recalled that Celestine had mentioned entering the Rhodopes through Greece, and so, running her finger south, to the sealocked Grecian mainland, Evangeline found the point where the Rhodopes rose from the plains. Green and gray covered the areas near the mountains, pointing to a depressed level of population. The only major roads seemed to emerge from Kavala, a port city on the Thracian Sea where a network of highways extended to the smaller towns and villages in the north. Moving her eye to the south of the mountain chain and down into the peninsula, she saw the more familiar names of Athens and Sparta, places she'd read of in her study of classical literature. Here were the ancient cities she had always associated with Greece. She'd never heard of the remote sliver of mountain that fell over its northernmost border with Bulgaria.

Realizing that she could learn only so much about the region from a map, Evangeline turned to a set of careworn 1960s encyclopedias and located an entry on the Rhodope Mountains. At the center of the page, she found a black-and-white photograph of a gaping cave. Below the photo she read:

The Devil's Throat is a cavern cut deep into the core of the Rhodope mountain chain. A narrow gap sliced into the immense rock of the mountainside, the cavern descends deep below the earth, forming a breathtaking shaft of air in the solid granite. The passageway is marked by a massive internal waterfall that cascades over the rock, leveling to form a subterranean river. A series of natural enclosures at the bottom of the gorge have long been the source of legend. Early explorers reported strange lights and feelings of euphoria upon entering these discrete caves, a phenomenon that may be explained by pockets of natural gases.

Evangeline went on to find that the Devil's Throat had been declared a UNESCO landmark in the 1950s and was considered an international treasure for its vertiginous beauty and its historical and mythological ⸱tance to the Thracians, who lived in the area in the fourth and fifth centuries B.C. While the physical descriptions of the cave were interesting enough, Evangeline was curious to know more about its historical and mythological importance. She opened a book of Greek and Thracian mythology, and after a number of chapters describing recent archaeological digs into Thracian ruins, Evangeline read:

The ancient Greeks believed that the Devil's Throat was the opening to the mythological underworld through which Orpheus, king of the Thracian tribe of the Cicones, traveled to save his lover, Eurydice, from the oblivion of Hades. In Greek mythology Orpheus was reputed to have given humanity music, writing, and medicine and is often thought to have promoted the cult of Dionysus. Apollo gave Orpheus a golden lyre and taught him to play music that had the power to tame animals, make inanimate objects come to life, and soothe all of creation, including the dwellers of the underworld. Many archaeologists and historians claim that he promoted ecstatic and mystical practices to the common people. Indeed, it is speculated that the Thracians performed human sacrifices during ecstatic Dionysian rituals, leaving dismembered bodies to decompose in the karst-filled gorge of the Devil's Throat.

Evangeline had become engrossed in reading about the history of Orpheus and his place in ancient mythology, yet the information was not in keeping with Celestine's account. She had made no mention of Orpheus or the Dionysian cultists he had allegedly inspired. Therefore it came as quite a surprise to find her attention completely diverted upon reading the next paragraph:

In the Christian era, the Devil's Throat cavern was believed to be the location where the rebel angels fell after their expulsion from heaven. Christians living in the area believed that the sharp vertical descent at the cave's opening was carved by Lucifer's fiery body as it plummeted through the earth to hell — hence the cavern's name. In addition, the cave was long believed to be the prison not only of the original contingent of fallen angels but also the prison of the "Sons of God," the oft-contested creatures of the pseudoepigraphical Book of Enoch. Known as the "Watchers" by Enoch and the "Sons of Heaven" in the Bible, this group of disobedient angels earned God's disfavor after consorting with human women and producing the species of angelic-human ʰrids called the Nephilim (see Genesis

6). The Watchers were imprisoned below the earth after their crime. Their underground prison is referenced throughout the Bible. See Jude 1:6.

Leaving the book open, she stood and walked to the New American Bible lying on an oak pedestal table at the center of the library. Paging through, she skimmed past the Creation, the Fall, and the murder of Abel by Cain. Stopping at Genesis 6, she read:

1 When men began to multiply on earth and daughters were born to them, 2 the sons of heaven saw how beautiful the daughters of man were, and so they took for their wives as many of them as they chose. 3 Then the LORD said: "My spirit shall not remain in man forever, since he is but flesh. His days shall comprise one hundred and twenty years." 4 At that time the Nephilim appeared on earth (as well as later), after the sons of heaven had intercourse with the daughters of man, who bore them sons. They were the heroes of old, the men of renown. 5 When the LORD saw how great was man's wickedness on earth, and how no desire that his heart conceived was ever anything but evil, 6 he regretted that he had made man on the earth, and his heart was grieved. So the LORD said: "I will wipe out from the

earth the men whom I have created, and not only the men, but also the beasts and the creeping things and the birds of the air, for I am sorry that I made them."

This was the passage from which Celestine had quoted earlier that afternoon. Although Evangeline had read through that section of Genesis hundreds of times before — as a girl, when her mother read Genesis aloud to her, it had been her first great narrative infatuation, the most dramatic, cataclysmic, awe-inspiring story she'd ever heard — she had never paused to think about these odd details: the birth of strange creatures called Nephilim, the condemnation of men to live only 120 years, the disappointment the Creator felt in his creation, the maliciousness of the Deluge. In all her studies, in all her preparations as a novice, in all the hours of biblical discussion she had participated in with the other sisters at St. Rose, this passage had never once been analyzed. She read the passage again, pausing to consider the phrase *At that time the Nephilim appeared on earth (as well as later), after the sons of heaven had intercourse with the daughters of man, who bore them sons. They were the heroes of old, the men of renown.* Then she turned to Jude and read: *The angels too, who did not keep to their own domain but deserted their proper dwelling, he has kept in eternal chains, in gloom, for the judgment of the great day.*

Feeling the onset of a headache, Evangeline closed the Bible. Her father's voice filled her mind, and once again she climbed the stairs of a cold, dusty warehouse, her Mary Janes soft upon the metal steps. The sharp shearing of a wing, the luminosity of a body, the strange and beautiful presence of the caged creatures looming overhead — these were visions she had long suspected were the inventions of her own imagination. The thought that these beasts were real — and that they were the reason her father had brought her to St. Rose — was more than she could bear to think about.

Standing, Evangeline went to the back of the room, where a row of nineteenth-century books lined the shelves of a locked glass case. Although the books were the oldest in their library, brought to St. Rose Convent the year it was founded, they were modern compared to the texts analyzed and discussed in their pages. Taking the key from a hook on the wall, she opened the case and removed one, cradling it in her arms carefully as she walked to the wide oak table near the fireplace. She examined the book — *Anatomy of the Dark Angels* — and ran her fingers over the soft leather binding with great tenderness, afraid she might, in her haste to open it, damage the spine.

After slipping on a pair of thin cotton gloves,

she delicately opened the cover and looked inside, finding hundreds of pages of facts about the shadow side of angels at her disposal. Each page, each diagram, each etching related in some way to the transgressions of angelic creatures who had defied the natural order. The book brought together everything from biblical exegesis to the Franciscan position on exorcism. Evangeline flipped through the pages, pausing at an examination of demons in church history. Although never discussed among the sisters, and an enigma to Evangeline, the demonic had once been a source of much theological discussion in the church. St. Thomas Aquinas, for example, had asserted that it was a dogma of faith that demons had the power to produce wind, storms, and a rain of fire from heaven. The demonic population — 7,405,926 divided into seventy-two companies, according to Talmudic accounts — was not directly accounted for in Christian works, and she doubted that this number could be anything more than numeric speculation, but the figure struck Evangeline as astonishing. The first chapters of the book contained historical information about angelic rebellion. Christians, Jews, and Muslims had been arguing over the existence of the dark angels for thousands of years. The most concrete reference to the disobedient angels could be found in Genesis, but there were apocryphal and pseudepigraphical texts circulated throughout the centuries after Christ that had shaped the Judeo-Christian conception of angels. Stories of angelic visitation abounded, and misinformation about the nature of angels was as prevalent in the ancient world as it was in the present era. It was a common mistake, for example, to confuse the Watchers — who were thought to have been sent to earth by God for the specific purpose of spying on humanity — with the rebel angels, those angelic beings rendered popular by *Paradise Lost* who followed Lucifer and were banished from heaven. The Watchers were of the tenth order of bene Elohim, whereas Lucifer and the rebel angels — the devil and his demons — were from the Malakim, which included the more perfect orders of angels. Whereas the devil had been condemned to eternal fire, the Watchers were merely imprisoned for an indeterminate period of time. Contained in what was variously translated as a pit, a hole, a cave, and hell, they awaited freedom.

After reading for some time, Evangeline found that she had unwittingly pushed the pages of the book flat against the oak table. Her gaze drifted from the book to the doorway of the library, where, only a few hours before, she had looked upon Verlaine for the first time. It had been such a profoundly odd day, the progression from her morning ablutions to her present state of anxiety more dream than reality. Verlaine had burst into her life with such force that he seemed to be — like the memories of her family — a creation of her mind, both real and unreal at the same time.

Taking his letter from her pocket and straightening it upon the table, she read it once again. There had been something in his manner — his directness, his familiarity, his intelligence — that had cracked through the shell in which she'd lived these past years. His appearance had reminded her that another world existed outside, beyond the convent grounds. He had given her his telephone number on a scrap of paper. Evangeline knew that despite her duty to her sisters and the danger of being discovered, she must speak with him again.

A sense of urgency overtook her as she walked through the busy hallways of the first floor. She hurried past a Prayer Partner informational meeting under way in the Perpetual Peace Lounge and a crafts class in the St. Rose of Viterbo Art Center. She did not pause in the communal cloakroom to find her jacket, and she did not stop by the Mission and Recruitment Office to see about the day's mail. She did not even pause to be sure the Adoration Prayer Schedule was in order. She simply marched out of the main entrance to the great brick garage on the south side of the grounds, where she lifted a ring of keys from a gray metal box on the wall and started the convent car. Evangeline knew from experience that the only truly secluded place for a Franciscan Sister of Perpetual Adoration at St. Rose Convent was to be found inside the brown four-door sedan.

She was certain that no one would object to her taking the convent car. The task of driving to the post office was a chore she usually looked forward to performing. Every afternoon she packed the St. Rose correspondence into a cotton bag and turned onto Route 9W, a two-lane highway snaking along the Hudson River. Only a handful of the sisters had a driver's license, and so Evangeline volunteered to do most errands above and beyond her mail duties: retrieving prescription medicines, restocking office supplies, and picking up gifts for sisters' birthday celebrations.

Some afternoons Evangeline drove across the river, taking the metalwork Kingston-Rhinecliff Bridge into Dutchess County. Slowing as she crossed the bridge, she would roll down the window and gaze at the estates scattered like overgrown mushrooms along both sides of the water — the monastic grounds of various religious communities, including the towers of St. Rose Convent and, somewhere around a bend, the Vanderbilt Mansion, protected by acres of land. From that height she could see for miles. She felt the car veer slightly in the wind, sending a shiver of panic

189

through her. How very high above the water she had driven, so high that, looking down, she understood for a second how it might feel to fly. Evangeline had always loved the feeling of freedom she felt going over water, a fondness she had developed on her many walks across the Brooklyn Bridge with her father. When she reached the end of the bridge, she would make a U-turn and drive back to the other side again, letting her eye drift to the purple-blue spine of the Catskills rising in the western sky. Snow had begun to fall, rising and scattering in the wind. Once more, as the bridge carried her higher and higher above the earth, the pilings bearing her up, she felt a pleasant sense of disembodiment, a sensation of vertigo similar to what she felt some mornings in the Adoration Chapel — a pure reverence for the immensity of creation.

Evangeline relied upon her afternoon drives to clear her mind. Before that day her thoughts had invariably turned to the future, which seemed to stretch before her like an endless, dimmed corridor through which she might walk forever without finding a destination. Now, as she turned onto 9W, she thought of little else but Celestine's bizarre tale and Verlaine's unsolicited entry into her life. She wished her father were alive so she might ask him what he, in all his experience and all his wisdom, would have her do in such a situation.

Rolling the window down, she let the car fill with icy air. Despite the fact that it was the dead of winter and she had left the convent without a jacket, her skin burned. Sweat soaked her clothing, making her feel clammy. She caught sight of herself in the rearview mirror and saw that her neck had broken out into splotches of red hives, amoeba-shaped blotches staining her pale flesh crimson. The last time this had occurred had been the year her mother died, when she had developed a list of inexplicable allergies, all of which had disappeared after her arrival at St. Rose. The years of contemplative life may have created a bubble of ease and comfort around her, but they had done little to prepare her to face her past.

Turning off the main highway, Evangeline drove onto the narrow, winding road that led into Milton. Soon the dense trees diminished, the forest cutting sharply away to reveal an expanse of vaulted sky awash with snow. On Main Street the sidewalks were empty, as if the snow and cold had driven everyone indoors. Evangeline pulled into a gas station, filled the car with unleaded, and headed inside to use the pay phone. Her fingers trembling, she deposited a quarter, dialed the number Verlaine had given her, and waited, her heart beating loud in her chest. The phone rang five, seven, nine times before the answering machine picked up. She listened to Verlaine's voice on the message, but replaced the receiver without speaking, losing her quarter. Verlaine wasn't there.

Starting the car, she glanced at the clock embedded next to the speedometer. It was nearly seven. She had missed afternoon chores and dinner. Sister Philomena would surely be waiting for her to return, expecting an explanation for her absence. Chagrined, she wondered what was wrong with her, driving to town to call a man she didn't know to discuss a subject that he would surely find absurd, if not completely insane. Evangeline was about to turn around and return to St. Rose when she saw him. Across the street, framed by a large, frosty picture window, was Verlaine.

Milton Bar and Grill, Milton, New York

How Evangeline had known that he needed
her — that he was bloodied and stranded
and, by now, significantly drunk on Mexi-
can beer — was an act Verlaine considered
both miraculous and intuitive, perhaps even a
trick she'd learned in her years in the cloister,
something altogether beyond his powers of
understanding. Nevertheless, there she was,
walking slowly toward the tavern door, her
posture too perfect, her bobbed hair tucked
behind her ears, her black clothes resembling,
if he stretched his imagination, the moody
attire of the girls he'd dated in college, those
dark, artistic, mysterious girls he made laugh
but could never convince to sleep with him.
In a matter of seconds, she'd walked through
the barroom and taken a seat across from
him, an elfin woman with large green eyes
who had clearly never been in a place like the
Milton Bar and Grill before.

He watched as she gazed over his shoulder,
taking in the scene, glancing at the pool table

and jukebox and dartboard. Evangeline didn't appear to notice or to care that she appeared significantly out of place among the crowd. Looking him over in the way one examines an injured bird, she furrowed her eyebrows and waited for Verlaine to tell her what had happened to him in the hours since their meeting.

"There was a problem with my car," Verlaine said, avoiding the more complicated version of his plight. "I walked here."

Genuinely astonished, Evangeline said, "In this storm?"

"I followed the highway for the most part but got a little lost."

"That is a long way to walk," she said, a hint of skepticism in her voice. "I'm surprised you didn't get frostbitten."

"I got a lift about halfway here. It's a good thing, too, or I'd still be out there, freezing my ass off."

Evangeline scrutinized him a bit too long, and he wondered if she objected to his language. She was a nun, after all, and he should try to behave with a certain restraint, but he found it impossible to read her. She was too different from his — admittedly stereotypical — vision of what a nun should be. She was young and wry and too pretty to fit into the profile he had drawn in his mind of the severe and humorless Sisters of Perpetual Adoration. He didn't know how she did it, but there was something about Evangeline that made him feel as if he could say anything at all.

"And why are you here?" he asked her, hoping his humor would come off the right way. "Aren't you supposed to be praying or doing good works or something?"

Smiling at his joke, she said, "As a matter of fact, I came to Milton to call you."

It was his turn to be astonished. He wouldn't have guessed that she would want to see him again. "You're kidding."

"Not at all," Evangeline replied, brushing a strand of dark hair from her eyes. Her manner had turned serious. "There is no privacy at St. Rose. I couldn't risk calling you from there. And I knew I needed to ask you something that must remain between us. It is a very delicate matter, a matter upon which I hope you can give me guidance. It is about the correspondence you've found."

Verlaine took a drink of his Corona, struck by how vulnerable she looked, perched at the edge of her bar chair, her eyes reddening from the thick cigarette smoke, her long, thin, ringless fingers chapped from the winter cold. "There's nothing I'd like to talk about more," he said.

"Then you won't mind," she said, leaning forward against the table, "telling me where you found these letters?"

"In an archive of Abigail Aldrich Rockefeller's personal papers," Verlaine said. "The letters were not cataloged. They had been overlooked entirely."

"You stole them?" Evangeline asked.

Verlaine felt his cheeks flush at Evangeline's reprimand. "Borrowed. I will return them once I understand their meaning."

"And how many do you have?"

"Five. They were written over a period of five weeks in 1943."

"All of them from Innocenta?"

"Not a Rockefeller in the bunch."

Evangeline held Verlaine's eyes, waiting for him to say more. The intensity of her gaze startled him. Perhaps it was the interest she showed in his work — his research had been underappreciated, even by Grigori — or maybe it was the sincerity of her manner, but he found himself anxious to please her. All his fear, his frustration, the sense of futility he'd been carrying with him washed away.

"I need to know if there is anything at all in the letters about the sisters at St. Rose," Evangeline said, disturbing his thoughts.

"I can't be sure," Verlaine said, sitting back in his chair. "But I don't think so."

"Was there anything at all about a collaborator in Abigail Rockefeller's work? Anything about the convent or the church or the nuns?"

Verlaine was perplexed by the direction in which Evangeline was going. "I don't have the letters memorized, but from what I recall, there isn't anything about the nuns at St. Rose."

"But in Abigail Rockefeller's letter to Innocenta," Evangeline said, raising her voice over the jukebox, her composure slipping, "she specifically mentioned Sister Celestine — 'Celestine Clochette will be arriving in New York early February.'"

"Celestine Clochette was a nun? I've been trying all afternoon to figure out who Celestine was."

"*Is,*" Evangeline said, lowering her voice so that it was barely audible over the music. "Celestine *is* a nun. She is very much alive. I went to see her after you left. She is elderly, and not very well, but she knew about the correspondence between Innocenta and Abigail Rockefeller. She knew about the expedition mentioned in the letter. She said a number of rather frightening things about —"

"About what?" Verlaine asked, growing more concerned by the second. "What did she say?"

"I don't understand it exactly," Evangeline said. "It was as though she were speaking in riddles. When I tried to puzzle out their meaning, it made even less sense."

Verlaine was torn between an impulse to embrace Evangeline, whose complexion had gone completely pale, and wanting to shake her. Instead he ordered two more Coronas and slid his handwritten copy of the Rockefeller letter across the table. "Read this again. Maybe Celestine Clochette was carrying an artifact from the Rhodope Mountains to St. Rose Convent? Did she tell you anything about this expedition?" Forgetting that he hardly knew Evangeline, he reached across the table and touched her hand. "I want to help you."

Evangeline pulled her hand away from his, glanced at him suspiciously, and looked at her watch. "I can't stay. I've been gone too long already. You obviously don't know much more about these letters than I do."

As the waitress set two beers before them, Verlaine said, "There must be more letters — at least four more. Innocenta was clearly responding to Abigail Rockefeller. You could look for them. Or perhaps Celestine Clochette knows where we can find them."

"Mr. Verlaine," Evangeline said in an imperious tone that struck Verlaine as forced, "I am sympathetic to your search and to your desire to fulfill the wishes of your client, but I cannot participate in something like that."

"This has nothing to do with my client," Verlaine said, taking a long drink of his beer. "His name is Percival Grigori. He's unbelievably awful; I should have never agreed to work for him. In fact, he just had some thugs break into my car and take all my research papers. Clearly, he's after something, and if this something is the correspondence we've found — which I haven't told him about, by the way — then we should find the other half before he does."

"Broke into your car?" Evangeline said, incredulous. "Is that why you're stranded here?"

"It doesn't matter," Verlaine said, hoping to appear unconcerned. "Well, actually, yes, it does matter. I need to ask you for a ride to a train station. And I need to know what Celestine Clochette brought with her to America. St. Rose Convent is the only possible place it could be. If you could find it — or at least look for the letters — we would be on our way to understanding what this is all about."

Evangeline's expression softened slightly, as if weighing his request with care. Finally she said, "I can't promise you anything, but I'll look."

Verlaine wanted to hug her, to tell her how happy it made him to have met her, to beg her to come back to New York with him and begin their work that very night. But seeing how anxious his attention made her, he decided against it.

"Come on," Evangeline said, picking up a set of car keys from the table. "I'll give you a ride to the train station."

St. Rose Convent, Milton, New York

Evangeline had missed the communal meal in the cafeteria, just as she had missed lunch, leaving her ravenous. She knew that she could find something to eat in the kitchen if she chose to look — the industrial-size refrigerators were always filled with trays of leftovers — but the thought of food made her feel ill. Ignoring her hunger, she walked past the stairway leading to the cafeteria and continued toward the library.

When she opened the library door and turned on the lights, she saw that the room had been cleaned in her absence: the leather registry (left open on the wooden table that afternoon) had been closed; the books piled on the couch had been returned; a meticulous hand had vacuumed the rugs plush. Obviously one of the sisters had covered for her. Feeling guilty, she vowed to do twice as much cleaning the next afternoon, perhaps volunteer for laundry duty, even though, with the abundance of veils to hand-wash, it was a much-hated chore. It had been wrong to leave her work to the others. When one is absent, the rest must carry the load.

Evangeline placed her bag on the couch and squatted before the hearth to kindle a fire. Soon a diffuse light folded over the floor. Evangeline sank into the soft cushions of the couch, crossed one leg over the other, and tried to arrange the cluttered pieces of her day. It was such an extraordinary tangle of information that she struggled to keep it orderly in her mind. The fire was so comforting and the day had been so trying that Evangeline stretched out on the couch and soon fell asleep.

A hand on her shoulder startled her awake. Sitting upright, she found Sister Philomena standing over her, looking at her with some severity. "Sister Evangeline," Philomena said, still touching Evangeline's shoulder. "Whatever are you doing?"

Evangeline blinked. She had been so soundly asleep that she could hardly gain her bearings. It seemed to her as though she were seeing the library — with its shelves of books and flickering fireplace — from deep underwater. Quickly, she shifted her feet to the floor and sat.

"As I'm sure you are aware," Philomena said, sitting on the couch next to Evangeline, "Sister Celestine is one of our community's oldest members. I do not know what happened this afternoon but she is quite upset.

I have spent the entire afternoon with her. It has not been easy to calm her."

"I'm very sorry," Evangeline said, feeling her senses click into focus at the mention of Celestine. "I went to see her to ask her about something I found in the archives."

"She was in quite a state when I found her this evening," Philomena said. "Exactly what did you say to her?"

"It was never my intention to distress her," Evangeline said. The folly of attempting to speak to Celestine about the letters struck her. It had been naïve to think that she could keep such a volatile conversation secret.

Sister Philomena gazed at Evangeline as if gauging her willingness to cooperate. "I am here to tell you that Celestine would like to speak with you again," she said finally. "And to ask that you report back to me about all that transpires in Celestine's cell."

Evangeline found her manner odd and could not discern what Philomena's motives might be, but she nodded in assent.

"We must not allow her to become so over-wrought again. Please be cautious in what you say to her."

"Very well," Evangeline replied, standing and brushing lint from the couch off her turtleneck and skirt. "I'll go immediately."

"Give me your word," Philomena said severely as she led Evangeline to the library door, "that you will inform me of everything

Celestine tells you."

"But why?" Evangeline asked, startled by Philomena's brusque manner.

At this, Philomena paused, as if chastened. "Celestine is not as strong as she appears, my child. We do not want to put her in danger."

In the hours since Evangeline's last visit, Sister Celestine had been moved into her bed. Her dinner — chicken broth, crackers, and water — sat untouched on a tray by the bedside table. A humidifier spewed steam into the air, blanketing the room in a moist haze. The wheelchair had been rolled into the corner of the room, near the window, and abandoned. The drawn curtains gave the chamber the aspect of a sanitary, somber hospital room, an effect that heightened as Evangeline closed the door softly behind her, shutting out the sound of the sisters gathering in the hallways.

"Come in, come in," Celestine said, gesturing for Evangeline to approach the bed.

Celestine folded her hands upon her chest. Evangeline felt a sudden urge to cover the old woman's white, fragile fingers with her hand, to protect them — although from what, she could not say. Philomena had been right: Celestine was painfully frail.

"You asked to see me, Sister," Evangeline said.

With great effort Celestine pushed herself up against a bank of pillows. "I must ask you to excuse my behavior earlier this afternoon," she said, meeting Evangeline's eye. "I do not know how to explain myself. It is only that I have not spoken of these things for many, many years. It was quite a surprise to find that, despite the time, the events of my youth are still so vivid and so upsetting to me. The body may age, but the soul remains young, as God made it."

"There is no need to apologize," Evangeline said as she placed her hand upon Celestine's arm, thin as a twig under the tissue of her nightgown. "I was at fault for upsetting you."

"Truthfully," Celestine said, her voice hardening, as if she were drawing upon a reserve of anger, "I was simply taken by surprise. I have not been confronted with these events for many, many years. I knew there would be a time when I would tell you. But I expected that it would be later."

Once again Celestine had confounded her. She had a way of tipping Evangeline off balance, upsetting Evangeline's delicate sense of equilibrium in a most disturbing fashion.

"Come," Celestine said, looking about the room. "Pull that chair over here and sit with me. There is much to tell."

Evangeline lifted a wooden chair from a corner and brought it to Celestine's bedside where she sat listening carefully to Sister Celestine's faint voice.

"I think you know," Celestine began, "that

I was born and educated in France and that I came to St. Rose Convent during the Second World War."

"Yes," Evangeline said lightly. "I was aware of this."

"You might also know . . ." Celestine paused, meeting Evangeline's eyes, as if to find judgment in them ". . . that I left everything — my work and my country — in the hands of the Nazis."

"I imagine that the war forced many to seek refuge in the United States."

"I did not seek refuge," Celestine said, emphasizing each word. "The war's deprivations were serious, but I believe I could have survived them had I stayed. You may not know this, but I was not a professed sister in France." She coughed into a handkerchief. "I took my vows in Portugal, en route to the United States. Before this I was a member of another order, one with many of the same goals as ours. Only" — Celestine held her thought for a moment — "we had a different approach to attaining them. I ran away from this group in December of 1943."

Evangeline watched as Celestine edged herself higher up in the bed and took a sip of water.

"I left this group," Celestine said at last. "But they were not quite done with me. Before I could leave them, I had one final duty to perform. The members of this group instructed me to carry a case to America and present it to a contact in New York."

"Abby Rockefeller," Evangeline ventured.

"In the beginning Mrs. Rockefeller was no more than a rich patron attending New York meetings. Like so many other society women, she participated in a purely observational capacity. It's my guess that she dabbled in angels the way the wealthy dabble in orchids — with great enthusiasm and little real knowledge. Honestly, I cannot say where her real interests lay before the war. When war struck, however, she became very sincere in her involvement. She kept our work alive. Mrs. Rockefeller sent equipment, vehicles, and money to assist us in Europe. Our scholars were not overtly affiliated with either side of the war — we were at heart pacifists, privately funded, just as we had been from the beginning."

Celestine blinked, as if a mote of dust had irritated her eyes, then continued.

"And so, as you can guess, private donors were essential to our survival. Mrs. Rockefeller sheltered our members in New York City, arranging their passage from Europe, meeting them at the docks, giving them refuge. It was through her support that we were able to undertake our greatest mission — an expedition to the depths of the earth, the very center of evil. The journey had been in the planning for many years, since the discovery of a written account outlining a previous expedition to the gorge. This account was brought to light in 1919. A second expedition was undertaken in 1943. It was risky driving into the mountains as bombs were falling over the Balkans, but — due to the excellent provisions Mrs. Rockefeller donated — we were well equipped. You might say that Mrs. Rockefeller was our guardian angel during the war, although many would be unwilling to go that far."

"But you left," Evangeline said quietly.

"Yes, I left," she replied. "I will not go into the details of my motivations, but suffice it to say that I no longer wanted to participate in our mission. I knew that I was finished even before I arrived in America."

A fit of coughing overtook Celestine. Evangeline helped her to sit up and gave her a sip of water. "On the night we returned from the mountains," Celestine continued, "we experienced a terrible tragedy. Seraphina, my mentor, the woman who had recruited me when I was fifteen years old and trained me, was compromised. I loved Dr. Seraphina dearly. She gave me the opportunity for study and advancement that few girls my age had attained. Dr. Seraphina believed I could be one of their finest. Traditionally our members have been monks and scholars, and so my academic skills — I was quite precocious in school, having a working knowledge of many ancient languages — were especially attractive to them. Dr. Seraphina promised that they would admit me as a full member, giving me access to their vast resources, both spiritual and intellectual, after the expedition. Dr. Seraphina was very dear to me. After that night all of my work suddenly meant nothing. I blame myself for what happened to her."

Evangeline could see that Celestine was deeply upset, but she was at a loss for how to comfort her. "Surely you did all that you could have done."

"There was much to grieve for in those days. It may be difficult for you to imagine, but millions were dying in Europe. At the time I felt that our mission to the Rhodopes was the most vital mission at hand. I did not understand the extent of what was happening in the world at large. I cared only for my work, my goals, my personal advancement, my cause. I hoped to impress the council members, who decided the fate of young scholars like myself. Of course, I was wrong to be so blind."

"Forgive me, Sister," Evangeline said, "but I still don't understand — what mission? What council?"

Evangeline could see the tension growing in Celestine's expression as she contemplated the question. She ran her desiccated fingers over the bright colors of the crocheted blanket.

"I will tell you directly, just as my teachers told me," Celestine said at last. "Only my teachers had the advantage of being able to introduce me to others like myself and to show me the Angelological Society's holdings in Paris. Whereas I was presented with solid, incontrovertible proof that I could see and touch, you must believe me at my word. My teachers were able to guide me gently into the world I am about to reveal to you, something I am unable to do for you, my child."

Evangeline began to speak, but a look from Celestine stopped her cold.

"To put it simply," Celestine said, "we are at war."

Unable to respond, Evangeline held the gaze of the woman before her.

"It is a spiritual warfare that plays out upon the stage of human civilization," Celestine said. "We are continuing what began long before, when the Giants were born. They lived on the earth then, and they live today. Humanity fought them then, and we fight them now."

Evangeline said, "You extrapolate this from Genesis."

"Do you believe the literal word of the Bible, Sister?" Celestine asked sharply.

"My vows are based upon it," Evangeline said, startled by the alacrity with which Celestine struck out at her, the note of chastisement in her voice.

"There have been those who interpret Genesis 6 as metaphorical, as a kind of parable. This is not my interpretation or my experience."

"But we do not ever speak of these creatures, these Giants. Not once have I heard them mentioned by the sisters of St. Rose."

"Giants, Nephilim, the Famous Ones — these were the ancient names for the children of the angels. Early Christian scholars argued that angels were free of matter. They characterized them as luminous, spectral, illuminated, evanescent, incorporeal, sublime. Angels were the messengers of God, infinite in number, made to carry His will from one realm to the next. Humans, created less perfect — created in God's image, but from clay — could only watch in awe at the fiery disembodiment of the angels. They were superior creatures characterized by lustrous bodies, speed, and holy purpose, their beauty befitting their roles as the intermediaries between God and creation. And then some of them, a rebellious few, mixed with humanity. The Giants were the unhappy result."

"Mixed with humanity?" Evangeline said.

"Women bore the children of angels." Celestine paused, searching Evangeline's eyes to be sure the young woman had understood her. "The technical details of the mingling have long been an object of intense scrutiny. For centuries the church denied that reproduction had occurred at all. The passage in Genesis is an embarrassment to those who believe that angels have no physical attributes. To explain the phenomenon, the church asserted that

210

the reproductive process between angels and humans had been asexual, a mixing of spirits that left women with child, a kind of inverse Virgin Birth where the offspring were evil rather than holy. My teacher, the same Dr. Seraphina I spoke of earlier, believed this to be utter nonsense. By reproducing with women, she asserted, the angels proved that they were physical beings, capable of sexual intercourse. She believed that the angelic body is closer to the human body than one might expect. During the course of our work, we documented the genitalia of an angel, taking photographs meant to prove once and for all that angelic beings are — how shall I say it? — endowed with the same equipment as humans."

"You have photographs of an angel?" Evangeline asked, her curiosity getting the better of her.

"Photographs of an angel killed in the tenth century, a male. The angels that fell in love with human women were, by all accounts, male. But this does not preclude the possibility of female members of the heavenly host. It has been said that one-third of the Watchers did not fall in love. These obedient creatures returned to heaven, to their celestial home, where they remain to this day. I suspect they were the female angels, who were not tempted in the same manner as the male angels."

Celestine took a deep, labored breath and adjusted herself in bed before continuing.

"The angels who remained on earth were extraordinary in many respects. It has always struck me as wondrous how human they seem. Their disobedience was an act of free will — a very human quality reminiscent of Adam and Eve's ill-conceived choice in the Garden. The disobedient angels were also capable of a uniquely human variety of love — they loved wholly, blindly, recklessly. Indeed, they traded heaven for passion, a trade that is difficult to fully comprehend, especially because you and I have given up all hope of such love."

Celestine smiled at Evangeline, as if in sympathy for the loveless life that lay ahead of her.

"They are fascinating in this respect, wouldn't you say? Their ability to feel and suffer for love allows one to feel empathy for their misguided actions. Heaven, however, did not demonstrate such empathy. The Watchers were punished without mercy. The offspring of the unions between the angels and women were monstrous creatures who brought great suffering to the world."

"And you believe they are still among us," Evangeline said.

"I know they are still among us," Celestine replied. "But they have evolved over the centuries. In modern times these creatures have taken cover under new and different names. They hide under the auspices of ancient families, extreme wealth, and untraceable corporations. It is hard for one to imagine that they live in our world among us, but I promise you: Once you open your eyes to their presence, you find that they are everywhere."

Celestine looked carefully at Evangeline, as if to gauge her reception of the information.

"If we were in Paris, it would be possible to present you with concrete and insurmountable proof — you would read testimonies from witnesses, perhaps even see the photographs from the expedition. I would explain the vast and wonderful contributions angelological thinkers have made over the centuries — St. Augustine, Aquinas, Milton, Dante — until our cause would appear clear and sparkling before you. I would lead you through the marble halls to a room where the historical records are preserved. We kept the most elaborate, intricately drawn schemas called angelologies that placed each and every angel exactly in its place. Such works give the universe order. The French mind is extremely tidy — Descartes' work is evidence of this, not the origin — and something about these systems was extremely soothing to me. I wonder if you, too, would find them so?"

Evangeline did not know how to respond, and so she waited for further explanation.

"But of course times have changed," Celestine said. "Once angelology was one of the greatest branches of theology. Once kings and popes sanctioned the work of theologians and paid great artists to paint the angels. Once the orders and purposes of the heavenly host were debated among the most brilliant scholars of Europe. Now angels have no place in our universe."

Celestine leaned close to Evangeline, as if relaying the information gave her new strength.

"Whereas angels were once the epitome of beauty and goodness, now, in our time, they are irrelevant. Materialism and science have banished them to nonexistence, a sphere as indeterminate as purgatory. It used to be that humanity believed in angels implicitly, intuitively, not with our minds but with our very souls. Now we need proof. We need material, scientific data that will verify without a doubt their reality. Yet what a crisis would occur if the proof existed! What would happen, do you suppose, if the material existence of angels could be verified?"

Celestine lapsed into silence. Perhaps she was tiring herself, or perhaps she had simply become lost in thought. Conversely, Evangeline was beginning to be alarmed. The turn Celestine's tale was taking was frightfully concurrent with the mythology Evangeline had schooled herself in earlier that afternoon. She had hoped to find reason to dismiss the existence of these monstrous creatures, not confirm them. Celestine appeared to be slipping into the kind of agitation she had displayed earlier that afternoon.

"Sister," Evangeline said, hoping Celestine would confess that all she'd said was an illusion, a metaphor for something practical and innocuous, "tell me that you are not serious."

"It is time for my pills," Celestine said, gesturing to her night table. "Can you bring them?"

Turning to the night table, Evangeline stopped short. Where earlier in the afternoon there had been a stack of books, now there stood bottles and bottles of medication, enough to suggest that Celestine suffered from a serious and protracted illness. Evangeline picked up one of the orange plastic bottles to examine it. The label gave Celestine's name, the dosage, and the drug name — strings of unpronounceable syllables that Evangeline had never heard before. She herself had always been healthy, her recent problem with chest colds being the only experience she'd had with illness. Her father had been hale until the minute he died, and her mother had disappeared in her prime. Certainly Evangeline had never witnessed someone so ruined by illness. It struck her that she had not thought about the complex combinations of remedies needed to maintain and soothe a damaged body. Her lack of sensitivity filled her with shame.

Evangeline opened the drawer below the

night table. There she found a pamphlet explaining the possible side effects of cancer medications and, clipped to it, a neat column of medicine names and dosage schedules. She caught her breath. Why hadn't she been informed that Celestine had cancer? Had she been so selfishly absorbed with her own curiosity that the condition had escaped her? She sat at Celestine's side and counted out the correct dosage.

"Thank you," Celestine said, taking the pills and swallowing them with water.

Evangeline was consumed by regret at her blindness. She had resisted asking too many questions of Celestine, and yet she had been desperate to be enlightened about all the old nun had said earlier in the day. Even now, watching Celestine struggle to swallow the tablets, she felt a terrible yearning for the gaps to be filled in. She wanted to know the connection between the convent, their rich patron, and the study of angels. Even more, she needed to know how she was a part of this strange web of associations.

"Forgive me for pressing you," Evangeline said, feeling guilty for her persistence even as she pressed onward. "But how did Mrs. Rockefeller come to help us?"

"Of course," Celestine said, smiling slightly. "You still want to know about Mrs. Rockefeller. Very well. But you may be surprised to learn that you have had the answer all along."

"How can that be?" Evangeline replied. "I learned only today of her interest in St. Rose."

Celestine sighed deeply. "Permit me to start from the beginning," she said. "In the 1920s one of the leading scholars in our group — Dr. Raphael Valko, the husband of my teacher, Dr. Seraphina Valko —"

"My grandmother married a man named Raphael Valko," Evangeline said, interrupting.

Celestine regarded Evangeline coolly. "Yes, I know, although their marriage happened after I left Paris. Long before this, Dr. Raphael uncovered historical records proving that an ancient lyre had been discovered in a cavern by one of our founding fathers, a man named Father Clematis. The lyre had until that time been a source of great study and speculation among our scholars. We knew the legend of the lyre, but we did not know if the lyre itself indeed existed. Until Dr. Raphael's discovery, the cave had simply been associated with the myth of Orpheus. I'm not sure if you are aware, but Orpheus was in fact an actual living man, one who rose to prominence and power due to his charisma and artistry and, of course, his music. Like many such men, he became a symbol after his death. Mrs. Rockefeller learned of the lyre through her contacts within our group. She funded our expedition with the belief that we could take possession of the lyre."

"Her interest was artistic?"

"She had wonderful taste in art, but she also understood the value of artifacts. I believe she came to care about our cause, but her initial assistance arose from financial concerns."

"She was a business partner?"

"Such involvement does not diminish the importance of the expedition. We had been planning the expedition to uncover the lyre for many years. Her assistance was used only as a means to an end. We always had our own agenda. But without Mrs. Rockefeller's assistance, we would not have made it. With the dangers of the war and the ruthlessness and power of our enemies, it is remarkable that we undertook the journey to the cavern at all. I can only credit our success to assistance and protection from a higher place."

As Celestine struggled for breath, Evangeline could see that she was growing tired. And yet the old nun continued.

"Once I arrived at St. Rose, I gave the case that contained our discoveries in the Rhodopes to Mother Innocenta, who in turn entrusted the lyre to Mrs. Rockefeller. The Rockefeller family had such vast sums of money — those of us in Paris could hardly imagine such fortune — and I felt a great sense of relief that Mrs. Rockefeller would care for the instrument."

Celestine paused, as if contemplating the

dangers of the lyre. Finally she said, "My part in the saga of the treasure was finished, or so I thought. I believed that the instrument would be protected. I did not realize that Abigail Rockefeller would betray us."

"Betray you?" Evangeline asked, breathless with wonder. "How?"

"Mrs. Rockefeller agreed to shield the Rhodope artifacts. She did an excellent job. She died on April fifth, 1948, four years after they came into her possession. In fact, she did not disclose her hiding place to anyone. The location of the instrument died with her."

Evangeline's feet had grown numb from sitting. She stood, walked to the window, and drew back the curtain. There'd been a full moon two days before, but that night the sky was black with clouds. "Is it so precious?" she asked at last.

"Beyond reckoning," Celestine said. "Over one thousand years of research built to our findings in the cavern. The creatures, who have thrived on human toil for so long, flourishing from the labor of mankind, mimicked our efforts with equal vigor. They watched us, studied our movements, planted spies among our numbers, and occasionally — just to maintain a level of terror among us — kidnapped and killed our agents."

Evangeline thought immediately of her mother. She had long suspected that something more had happened to her than her father had disclosed, but the thought that the creatures Celestine described could be responsible was too horrible to imagine. Determined to understand, Evangeline asked, "But why only a few? If they were so powerful, why didn't they kill all of you? Why not simply destroy the entire organization?"

"It is true that they could have exterminated us with ease. They certainly have the strength and the means to do so. But it would not be in their best interests to cleanse the world of angelology."

"Why is that?" Evangeline said, surprised.

"With all their power, they have a remarkable flaw: They are sensual creatures, wholly blinded by the pleasures of the body. They have wealth, strength, physical beauty, and a ruthlessness that is hardly believable. They have ancient family connections that buoy them during the tumultuous periods of history. They have developed financial strongholds in nearly every corner of the globe. They are the winners of a power system they themselves have created. But what they do not have is the intellectual prowess, or the vast store of academic and historical resources, that we do. Essentially, they need us to do their thinking for them." Celestine sighed once again, as if the topic caused her pain. Struggling to continue, she said, "This tactic nearly worked in 1943. They killed my mentor, and when they learned that I had escaped to the United

States, they destroyed our convent and dozens of others in search of me and the object I'd brought with me."

"The lyre," Evangeline said, the pieces of the puzzle coming together suddenly.

"Yes," Celestine said. "They want the lyre, not because they know what it can do but because they know we prize it — and that we fear their possession of it. Of course, it was a hazardous endeavor to unearth the treasure at all. We had to find someone who could protect it. And so we entrusted it to one of our most illustrious contacts in New York City, a powerful and wealthy woman who vowed to serve our cause."

A look of pain flickered in Celestine's expression.

"Mrs. Rockefeller was our last great hope in New York. I have no doubt she took her role seriously. Indeed, she was so adept that her secret has remained hidden to this day. The creatures would kill every last one of us in order to discover it."

Evangeline touched the lyre pendant, the gold warm against her fingertips. At last she understood the significance of her grandmother's gift.

Celestine smiled. "I see you understand me. The pendant marks you as one of us. Your grandmother was right to give it to you."

"You know my grandmother?" Evangeline asked, astonished and confused that Celestine should know the precise provenance of her necklace.

"I knew Gabriella many years ago," Celestine said, the faintest hint of sadness in her voice. "And even then I did not truly know her. Gabriella was my friend, she was a brilliant scholar and a dedicated fighter for our cause, but to me she has always been a mystery. Gabriella's heart was one thing nobody, not even her closest friend, could discern."

It had been ages since Evangeline had last spoken with her grandmother. As the years had passed, she began to believe that Gabriella had died. "Then she is alive?" Evangeline asked.

"Very much alive," Celestine said. "She would be proud to see you now."

"Where is she?" Evangeline asked. "France? New York?"

"That I cannot tell you," Celestine said. "But if your grandmother were here, I know that she would explain everything to you. As she is not, I can only try, in my own way, to help you to understand."

Pulling herself up in her bed, Celestine gestured for Evangeline to go to the opposite side of the room, where an antique trunk sat in a corner, its leather trim scuffed. A brass-plated catch gleamed in the light, a padlock hanging from it like a piece of fruit. Evangeline walked to it and held the cool lock in her hand. A tiny key protruded from the keyhole.

Checking to be sure that Celestine approved, Evangeline twisted the key. The lock popped open. She unhooked it, set it lightly upon the wooden floorboard, and pushed open the trunk's heavy wooden top. The brass hinges, without oil for many decades, creaked with a sharp feline whine and gave way to the earthy smell of stale sweat and dust mixed with the more refined, musky smell of perfume that has begun to soften with age. Inside, she found a layer of yellowed tissue paper placed neatly over the surface, so light it seemed to hover above the edges of the trunk. Evangeline lifted the paper, careful not to crease it, and found pressed stacks of clothing beneath. Taking them from the trunk, she examined them one by one: a black cotton pinafore, brown jodhpurs stained black at the knees, a pair of women's lace-up leather boots with the wooden soles worn down. Evangeline unfolded a pair of wide-legged wool trousers that seemed better suited to a young man than to Celestine. Running her hand over the trousers, her nails catching upon the rough fabric, Evangeline could smell the dust trapped in the material.

Digging deeper, Evangeline's fingers brushed against something velvety soft at the bottom of the trunk. A mass of satin lay crumpled in a corner. When Evangeline unfurled it with a flick of the wrist, it opened into a fluid sheet of glossy scarlet fabric. She draped the dress over her arm, examining it closely. She had never touched material quite so soft; it fell across her skin like water. The style of the dress was like something in a black-and-white film — bias cut, with a plunging neckline, a tapered waist, and a narrow skirt that fell to the floor. A series of tiny satin-covered buttons climbed up the left side of the gown. Evangeline found a tag sewn into a seam. It read CHANEL. A series of numbers were stamped below it. Holding the dress close, she tried to imagine the woman who wore such a dress. What would it be like, she wondered, to wear this beautiful gown?

Evangeline was returning the dress to the trunk when, nestled in a fold of old clothing, she found a bundle of envelopes. Green, red, and white — the envelopes were the colors of Christmas. They had been fastened together by a thick black satin band, which Evangeline slid her finger over, the slick track soft and smooth.

"Bring them to me," Celestine said softly, the extent of her weariness beginning to weigh upon her.

Leaving the trunk open, Evangeline carried the envelopes to Celestine. With trembling fingers Celestine untied the ribbon and returned the envelopes to Evangeline. Flipping through them, Evangeline found that the cancellation dates corresponded with the Christmas season of each year, beginning in

1988, the year she became a ward of St. Rose Convent, and ending with Christmas 1998. To her amazement the name on the return address read "Gabriella Lévi-Franche Valko." The letters had been sent to Celestine by Evangeline's grandmother.

"She sent them for you," Celestine said, her voice tremulous. "I have been collecting and saving them for many years — eleven, to be precise. The time has come for you to have them. I wish I could explain more, but I am afraid that I have already pushed myself beyond my strength this evening. Speaking of the past has been more difficult for me than you can imagine. Explaining the complicated history between Gabriella and me would be even more so. Take the letters. I believe that they will answer many of your questions. When you have read them, come to me again. There is much we must discuss."

With great care Evangeline tied the letters together with the black satin ribbon, securing the knot in a tight bow. Celestine's appearance had changed dramatically over the course of their discussion — her skin had become ashen and pale, and she could hardly keep her eyes open. For a moment Evangeline wondered if she should call for assistance, but it was clear that Celestine needed nothing more than to rest. Evangeline straightened the crocheted blanket, tucking the edges over Celestine's frail arms and shoulders, making

225

sure she was warm and comfortable. With
the pack of letters in hand, she left Celestine
to sleep.

Sister Celestine's cell, St. Rose Convent, Milton, New York

Celestine folded her hands across her chest beneath the crocheted blanket, straining to see beyond the bright colors of her bedspread. The room was little more than a haze of shadow. Although she had looked upon the contours of her bedroom each day for over fifty years and knew the placement of each object in her possession, the room had a formless unfamiliarity that confused her. Her senses had dimmed. The clanking of the steam radiators was distant and muted. Try as she might, she could not make out the trunk at the far end of the room. She knew it was there, holding her past like a time capsule. She had recognized the clothing Sister Evangeline had lifted from its hold: the scuffed boots Celestine had kept from the expedition, the uncomfortable pinafore that had so tortured her as a schoolgirl, and the marvelous red dress that had made her — for one precious evening — beautiful. Celestine could even detect the scent of perfume mingling with the mustiness, proof that the cut-crystal bottle

227

she'd brought with her from Paris — one of the few treasures she allowed herself in the frantic minutes before her flight from France — was still there, buried in dust but potent. If she had the strength, she would have gone to the trunk, taken the cold bottle in her hand. She would have eased the crystal stopper from the glass and allowed herself to inhale the scent of her past, a sensation so delicious and forbidden that she could hardly bring herself to think of it. For the first time in many years, her heart ached for the time of her girlhood.

Sister Evangeline's resemblance to Gabriella had been so pronounced that there were moments when Celestine's mind — weakened from exhaustion and illness — had fallen into confusion. The years dropped away, and, to her dismay, she could not discern time or place or the reason for her confinement. As she drifted asleep, images of the past lifted through the evanescent layers of her mind, emerging and fading like colors upon a screen, each one dissolving into the next. The expedition, the war, the school, the days of lessons and study — these events of her youth seemed to Celestine as clear and vibrant as those of the present. Gabriella Lévi-Franche, her friend and rival, the girl whose friendship had so changed the course of her life, appeared before her. As Celestine drifted in and out of sleep, the barriers of time fell away, allowing her to see the past once again.

THE SECOND SPHERE

*Praise him with the sound of the trumpet:
Praise him with the psaltery and harp.
Praise him with the timbrel and dance:
Praise him with stringed instruments and
  organs.
Praise him upon the loud cymbals:
Praise him upon the high sounding cym-
  bals.*

— Psalm 150

*Angelological Academy of Paris,
Montparnasse*

Autumn 1939

It was less than a week after the invasion of
Poland, an afternoon in my second year as
a student of angelology, when Dr. Seraphina
Valko sent me to locate my errant classmate,
Gabriella, and bring her to the Athenaeum.
Gabriella was late for our tutorial, a habit she'd
developed over the summer months and had
continued, to our professor's dismay, into the
cooler days of September. She was nowhere
to be found in the school — not in the courtyard where she often went to be alone during
breaks, nor in any of the classrooms where
she often studied — and so I guessed her to
be in her bed, sleeping. My bedroom being
next to hers, I knew that she had not come
in until well after three o'clock that morning,
when she put a record on the phonograph and
listened to a recording of *Manon Lescaut,* her
favorite opera, until dawn.

I walked through the narrow streets off the
cemetery, passing a café filled with men listening to news of the war on a radio, and cut

231

through an alleyway to our shared apartment on the rue Gassendi. We lived on the third floor, our windows opening over the tops of the chestnut trees, a height that removed us from the noise of the street and filled the rooms with light. I climbed the wide staircase, unlocked the door, and stepped into a quiet, sunny apartment. We had an abundance of space — two large bedrooms, a narrow dining room, a servant's chamber with an entrance to the kitchen, and a grand bathroom with a porcelain bathtub. The apartment was far too luxurious for schoolgirls, this I knew from the moment I set foot upon its polished parquet. Gabriella's family connections had assured her the best of everything our school could offer. How I had been assigned to live with Gabriella in such quarters was a mystery to me.

Our Montparnasse apartment was a great change in my circumstances. In the months after I had moved in, I basked in its luxury, taking care to keep everything in perfect order. Before I'd come to Paris, I had never seen such an apartment, while Gabriella had lived well all her life. We were opposites in many ways, and even our appearance seemed to confirm our differences. I was tall and pale, with big hazel eyes, thin lips, and the foreshortened chin I had always considered the hallmark of my northern heritage. Gabriella, by contrast, was dark and classically beautiful. She had a way about her that caused others to take her seriously, despite her weakness for fashion and the Claudine novels. Whereas I came to Paris on scholarship, my fees and board paid entirely through donations, Gabriella came from one of the oldest and most prestigious of the Parisian angelological families. Whereas I felt lucky to be allowed to study with the best minds of our field, Gabriella had grown up in their presence, absorbing their brilliance as if it were sunlight. Whereas I plodded through texts, memorizing and categorizing in the meticulous manner of an ox plowing a field, Gabriella had an elegant, dazzling, effortless intellect. I systemized each piece of minutia into notebooks, making charts and graphs to better retain information, while to my knowledge Gabriella never took notes. And yet she could answer a theological question or elaborate upon a mythological or historical point with an ease that escaped me. Together we were at the top of our class, and yet I always felt that I had stolen my way into the elite circles that were Gabriella's birthright.

Walking through our apartment, I found it much as I had left it that morning. A thick, leather-bound book written by St. Augustine lay open upon the dining table alongside a plate with the remains of my breakfast, a crust of bread and strawberry preserves. I cleared the table, bringing my book to my room and placing it amid the mess of loose papers on my desk. There were books waiting to be read, jars of ink, and any number of my half-filled notebooks. A yellowed photograph of my parents — two sturdy, weatherworn farmers surrounded by the rising hills of our vineyard — sat next to a faded photograph of my grandmother, Baba Slavka, her hair tied in a head scarf in the way of her foreign village. My studies had occupied me so completely that I'd not been home in over a year.

I was the daughter of winemakers, a sheltered, shy girl from the countryside, with academic talent and strong, unwavering religious beliefs. My mother came from a line of *vignerons* whose ancestors had quietly survived through hard work and tenacity, harvesting auxerrois blanc and pinot gris all the while bricking the family savings in the walls of the farmhouse, preparing for the days when war would return. My father was a foreigner. He had immigrated to France from eastern Europe after the First World War, married my mother, and took her family name before assuming responsibility of managing the vineyard.

While my father was no scholar, he recognized the gift in me. From the time I was old enough to walk, he put books in my hands, many of them theological. When I was fourteen, he arranged for my studies in Paris, bringing me to the school by train for testing and then, once my scholarship had been secured, to my new school. Together we had packed all my belongings in a wooden trunk that had belonged to his mother. Later, when I discovered that my grandmother had aspired to study at the very school I would attend, I understood that my destiny as an angelologist had been many years in the making. As I set about locating my well-connected and tardy friend, I wondered at my willingness to trade the life I'd led with my family. If Gabriella were not at our apartment, I would simply meet Dr. Seraphina at the Athenaeum alone.

As I left my room, something in the large bathroom at the end of the hallway caught my eye. The door was closed, but movement behind the frosted glass alerted me to a presence beyond. Gabriella must have run a bath, an odd thing to do when she should have been at school. I could see the outline of our large bathtub, which must have been filled to the top with hot water. Waves of steam rose through the room, coating the glass of the door in a thick, milky fog. I heard Gabriella's voice, and although I found it odd that she would speak to herself, I believed her to be alone. I raised my hand to knock, ready to alert Gabriella to my presence, when I saw a flash of scintillating gold. An enormous figure passed behind the glass. I could not trust my vision, yet it seemed to me that the room was filled with a soft light.

I drew closer and, endeavoring to understand the scene before me, pushed the door ajar. A mélange of clothes had been scattered about the tile floor — a white linen skirt and a patterned rayon blouse that I recognized as belonging to Gabriella. Twisted alongside my friend's clothing I discerned a pair of trousers, crumpled as a flour sack, clearly thrown aside in haste. It was obvious that Gabriella was not alone. And yet I did not turn away. Instead I stepped even closer. Peering deeper into the room, I exposed myself to a scene that shocked my senses so thoroughly that I could do nothing but watch in a state of horrified awe.

At the far side of the bathroom, draped in a mist of steam, stood Gabriella, entwined in the arms of a man. His skin was luminous white and appeared to me — so startled by his presence — to have an unearthly glow. He had pressed Gabriella against the wall, as if he meant to crush her under his weight, an act of domination that she did not attempt to repel. Indeed, her pale arms were wrapped about his body, holding him.

I stole away from the bathroom, careful to mask my presence from Gabriella, and fled the apartment. Upon returning to the academy, I spent some time wandering through the warren of halls, attempting to recover my bearings before reporting to Dr. Seraphina Valko. The buildings filled many blocks and were strung together by narrow corridors and underground passageways that gave the school a shadowy irregularity that I found strangely soothing, as if the asymmetry echoed my state of mind. There was little grandeur to the dwellings, and although our quarters were often unsuited to our needs — the lecture halls were too small and the classrooms without proper heat — my absorption in my work did much to distract me from these discomforts.

Walking past the dimmed, abandoned offices of the scholars who had already left the city, I tried to understand the shock I felt at finding Gabriella with her lover. Aside from the fact that male guests were restricted from visiting our apartments, there had been something disturbing about the man himself, something eerie and abnormal that I could not fully identify. My inability to understand what I had seen and the chaotic mix of loyalty and rivalry I felt toward Gabriella made it impossible to tell Dr. Seraphina, although I knew in my heart that this was the correct path. Instead I pondered the meaning of Gabriella's actions. I speculated upon the moral dilemma her affair thrust upon me. I must give Dr. Seraphina an account of what kept me, but what would I say? I could not very well betray Gabriella's secret. While she was my only friend, Gabriella Lévi-Franche was also my most ardent rival.

In reality my anxieties were pointless. By the time I returned to Dr. Seraphina's office, Gabriella had arrived. She sat upon a Louis XIV chair, her appearance fresh, her demeanor calm, as if she had spent the morning lounging in a shaded park reading Voltaire. She wore a bright green crepe de chine dress, white silk stockings, and a heavy scent of Shalimar, her favorite perfume. When she greeted me in her usual terse manner, kissing me perfunctorily on each cheek, I understood with relief that she was unaware of what I had seen.

Dr. Seraphina welcomed me with warmth and concern, asking what had kept *me*. Dr. Seraphina's reputation rested not just upon her own accomplishments but on the achievements and caliber of the students she took on, and I was mortified that my search for Gabriella would be construed as tardiness on my part. I harbored no illusions about the security of my stature at the academy. I, unlike Gabriella with her family connections, was expendable, although Dr. Seraphina would never say so overtly.

The Valkos' popularity among their students at large was no mystery. Seraphina Valko was married to the equally brilliant Dr. Raphael Valko and often conducted joint lectures with her husband. Their lectures filled to capacity each autumn, the crowds of young and eager scholars in attendance expanding well beyond those first-year students required to take it. Our two most distinguished professors specialized in the field of antediluvian geography, a small but vital branch of angelic archaeology. The Valkos' lectures encompassed more than their specialization, however, outlining the history of angelology from its theological origins to its modern practice. Their lectures made the past come alive, so much so that the texture of ancient alliances and battles — and their role in the maladies of the modern world — became plain before all in attendance. Indeed, in their courses Dr. Seraphina and Dr. Raphael had the power to lead one to understand that the past was not a far-off place of myths and fairy tales, not merely a compendium of lives crushed by wars and pestilences and misfortune, but that history lived and breathed in the present, existing among us each day, offering a window into the misty landscape of the future. The Valkos' ability to make the past tangible to their students ensured their popularity and their position at our school.

Dr. Seraphina glanced at her wristwatch. "We had better be going," she said, straightening some papers on her desk as she prepared to leave. "We're already late."

Walking quickly, the stacked heels of her shoes clicking upon the floor, Dr. Seraphina led us through the narrow, darkened hallways to the

Athenaeum. Although the name suggested a noble library studded with Corinthian columns and high, sun-filled windows, the Athenaeum was as lightless as a dungeon, its limestone walls and marble floors barely discernible in the perpetual haze of a windowless twilight. Indeed, many of the rooms used for instruction were located in similar chambers tucked away in the narrow buildings throughout Montparnasse, scattered apartments acquired over the years and connected with haphazard corridors. I learned soon after my arrival in Paris that our safety depended upon remaining hidden. The labyrinthine nature of the rooms ensured that we could continue our work unmolested, a tranquillity threatened by the impending war. Many of the scholars had already left the city.

Still, despite its dour environs, the Athenaeum had offered me much solace in my first year of study. It contained a large collection of books, many of which had been left undisturbed upon their shelves for decades. Dr. Seraphina had introduced our Angelological Library to me the year before by remarking that we had resources that even the Vatican would envy, with texts dating back to the first years of the postdiluvian era, although I had never examined such ancient texts, as they were locked in a vault out of the reach of students. Often I would come in the middle of the night, light a small oil lamp, and sit in a corner nook, a stack of books at my side, the sweet, dusty smell of aging paper around me. I didn't think of my hours of study as a sign of ambition, although it surely must have seemed that way to the students who found me studying at dawn. To me the endless supply of books served as a bridge into my new life — it was as though, upon my walking into the Athenaeum, the history of the world lifted out of a fog, giving me the sense that I was not alone in my labors but part of the vast network of scholars who had studied similar texts many centuries before my birth. To me, the Athenaeum represented everything that was civilized and orderly in the world.

It was thus all the more painful to see the rooms of the library in a state of total dismemberment. As Dr. Seraphina led us deeper into the space, I saw that a crew of assistants had been assigned to disassemble the collection. The procedure was being carried out in a systematic fashion — with such a vast and valuable collection, it was the only way to go about such a move — and yet it appeared to me that the Athenaeum had descended into pure chaos. Books were piled high on the library tables, and large wooden crates, many filled to the top, were scattered across the room. Only months before, students had sat quietly at the tables preparing for exams, carrying on their work as generations of students had done before them. Now it felt to me that all had been lost. What would be left once our texts were hidden away? I averted my eyes, unable to look at the undoing of my sanctuary.

In reality, the impending move was no great surprise. As the Germans drew closer, it was unsafe to remain in such vulnerable quarters. I knew that we would soon be suspending classes and beginning private lessons in small, well-hidden groups outside the city. Over the past weeks, most of our lectures had been canceled. Interpretations of Creation and Angelic Physiology, my two favorite courses, had been suspended indefinitely. Only the Valkos' lectures had continued, and we were aware that they would soon be disbanded. Yet the danger of invasion had not felt real until the moment I found the Athenaeum in shambles.

Dr. Seraphina's manner was tense and hurried as she brought us into a chamber at the back of the library. Her mood reflected my own: I could not calm myself after what I had witnessed that morning. I stole glances at Gabriella, as if her appearance might have been altered by her actions, but she was as cool as ever. Dr. Seraphina paused, tucked a stray hair behind her ear, and straightened her dress, her anxiety plain. At the time I believed that my delayed arrival had upset her and that she was concerned that we would be late to her lecture, but when we arrived at the back of the Athenaeum and found an altogether different sort of meeting under way, I understood that there was more to Dr. Seraphina's manner than this.

A group of prestigious angelologists sat arrayed about a table, deep in heated debate. I knew the council members by reputation — many had been visiting lecturers during the previous year — but I had never seen them all gathered together in such an intimate setting. The council was composed of great men and women stationed in positions of power throughout Europe — politicians and diplomats and social leaders whose influence extended well beyond our school. These were the scholars whose books had once lined the shelves of the Athenaeum, scientists whose research on the physical properties and chemistry of angelic bodies made our discipline modern. A nun dressed in a habit of heavy black serge — an angelologist who divided her time between theological study and fieldwork — sat near Gabriella's uncle, Dr. Lévi-Franche, an elderly angelologist who specialized in the art of angelic summoning, a dangerous and intriguing field I longed to study. The greatest angelologists of our time were there, watching as Dr. Seraphina brought us into their presence.

She gestured for us to sit at the back of the room, at a remove from the council members. Deeply curious about the subject of such an extraordinary meeting, I found that it took all my efforts to keep from staring impolitely, and so I focused my attention upon a series of large maps of Europe that had been posted upon the wall. Red dots marked cities of interest — Paris, London, Berlin, Rome. But what truly piqued my interest was that a number of obscure cities had been singled out: There were marks upon cities along the border of Greece and Bulgaria, creating a line of red between Sofia and Athens. The area held particular interest to me, as it was in that obscure location at the farthest reaches of Europe where my father was born.

Dr. Raphael stood by the maps waiting to speak. He was a serious man, one of the few completely secular members to rise to the level of council chair while retaining a teaching post at the academy. Dr. Seraphina had once mentioned that Dr. Raphael held the same dual position of administrator and scholar as Roger Bacon, the English angelologist of the thirteenth century who had taught Aristotle at Oxford and Franciscan theology in Paris. Bacon's balance of intellectual rigor and spiritual humility was an accomplishment regarded with great respect throughout the society, and I could not help but see Dr. Raphael as his successor. As Dr. Seraphina took her place at the table, Dr. Raphael began to speak, resuming where he had left off.

"As I was saying," Dr. Raphael said, gesturing to the half-empty shelves and the assistants wrapping and packing the books into boxes scattered throughout the Athenaeum, "our time has grown short. Soon all of our resources will be packed up and stored in secure locations throughout the countryside. Of course it is the only way — we are protecting ourselves from the contingencies of the future. But the move comes at the worst possible time. Our work cannot be postponed during the war. There is no question that we have to make a decision now."

His voice was grave as he continued.

"I don't believe our defenses will fail — there is every indication that we are ready for whatever battles lie ahead — but we must prepare for the worst. If we wait any longer, we face being surrounded."

"Look at the map, Professor," said a council member named Vladimir, a young scholar sent to Paris from the underground Angelological Academy in Leningrad, of whom I knew only by reputation. Boyish and handsome, he had pale blue eyes and a lithe build. The quiet, certain manner with which he conducted himself gave him the presence of an older man, although he could not have been more than nineteen years old. "It seems we are surrounded already," he said.

"There is a marked difference between the machinations of the Axis powers and our enemies," Dr. Lévi-Franche said. "Earthly danger is nothing in comparison to that of our spiritual enemies."

"We must be ready to defy both," said Vladimir.

"Exactly," Dr. Seraphina said. "And to do this we must increase our efforts to find and destroy the lyre."

Dr. Seraphina's assertion was met with silence. The council members were not quite certain how to react to such a bold statement.

"You know my feelings about this," Dr. Raphael said. "Sending a team to the mountains is our best hope."

The nun's veil cast a shadow over her features as she looked about the table at the council. "The area Dr. Raphael proposes is far too large for anyone — including our teams — to cover without exact coordinates. The precise location of the gorge must be mapped before such an expedition takes place."

"With the right resources," Dr. Seraphina said, "nothing is impossible. We have been given generous assistance from our American benefactress."

"And the equipment supplied by the Curie family estate will be more than adequate," Dr. Raphael added.

"Let's look at the realities at hand, shall we?" said Dr. Lévi-Franche, clearly skeptical of the project. "How large is the area we are discussing?"

"Thrace was part of the eastern Roman

Empire, later to be called Byzantium, whose territory consisted of land from present-day Turkey, Greece, and Bulgaria," Dr. Raphael said. "The tenth century was a time of great territorial changes for the Thracians, but from the Venerable Clematis's account of his expedition we can narrow our search somewhat. We know Clematis was born in the city of Smolyan at the heart of the Rhodope mountain chain of Bulgaria. Clematis wrote that he had traveled to the land of his birth during his expedition. Thus, we can narrow the area to northern Thrace."

"This, as my colleague so correctly pointed out, is an immense area," Dr. Lévi-Franche said. "Do you suppose that we can explore a fraction of this terrain without being detected? Even with vast resources and a thousand agents, it would take years, perhaps decades, to scratch the surface, let alone go underground. We do not have the funding or the manpower for such an endeavor."

"There will be no shortage of volunteers for the mission," Vladimir said.

"It is important to remember," Dr. Seraphina said, "that the danger the war poses is not merely the destruction of our texts and the physical structures of our school. We stand to lose much more if the details of the cavern, and the treasure hidden there, are made public."

"Perhaps," the nun said. "But our enemies are watching the mountains at every moment."

"It is true," said Vladimir, whose field of study was ethereal musicology. "And that is precisely why we must go after it now."

"Why now?" Dr. Lévi-Franche countered, lowering his voice. "We have hunted down and protected lesser celestial instruments while leaving the most dangerous one at large. Why not wait until the threat of war has passed?"

Dr. Seraphina said, "The Nazis have positioned teams throughout the area. They adore antiquities — especially those of mythological significance to their regime — and the Nephilim will use this opportunity to gain a powerful tool."

"The lyre's powers are notorious," Vladimir said. "Of all the celestial instruments, it is the one that might be used to disastrous ends. It may be that its destructive force is more insidious than anything the Nazis might do. But then again, the instrument is too precious to leave. You know as well as I that the Nephilim have always coveted the lyre."

"But it is obvious," Dr. Lévi-Franche said, growing perturbed, "that the Nephilim will follow our party on whatever recovery effort we make. If we have the miraculous luck of finding the lyre, we have no idea what happens to those who possess it. It may not be safe. And even worse, it could be taken from us. Any effort we make may simply assist our enemies. We would then be responsible for the horrors that the lyre's music could bring."

"Perhaps," the nun said, stiffening in her chair, "it is not as powerful as you believe. No one has ever seen the instrument. Much of the terror it has caused arises from pagan legends. There is every possibility that the evil the lyre can inflict is merely the stuff of legend."

As the angelologists considered this, Dr. Raphael said, "And so we are faced with the choice to act or to do nothing."

"Reckless action is worse than wise restraint," Dr. Lévi-Franche said, and I could not help but dislike the smugness of his response, so much in contrast to my professors' earnest attempts at persuasion.

"In our case," Dr. Raphael said, growing more and more agitated, "inaction is the more reckless course. Our passivity will have terrible consequences."

"That is exactly why we must act now," Vladimir said. "It is up to us to find and protect the lyre."

"If I may interrupt," Dr. Seraphina said gently. "I would like to make a proposal." Walking to where Gabriella and I sat and drawing the attention of the council members upon us, Dr. Seraphina continued, "Many of you are acquainted with them already, but for those of you who are not, I would like to present two of our brightest young angelologists. Gabriella and Celestine have been working with me to put order to our holdings during the transition. They have been busy at work cataloging texts and transcribing notes. I have found their work to be very useful. In fact, it is the attention that they have brought to the minutiae of our collection and the information they have carefully extracted from our historical papers that has given Dr. Raphael and me an idea of how to proceed at this very important juncture."

"As many of you are aware," Dr. Raphael said, "in addition to our duties here at the academy, Dr. Seraphina and I have been working on a number of private projects, including trying to bring more precision to the location of the cavern. In the process we have accumulated a plethora of addenda and field notes previously overlooked."

I glanced at Gabriella, hoping to find some sort of commiseration in our position, but she only turned away, supercilious as ever. Suddenly I wondered if she understood the details of what the council members were discussing. There was the chance that she had been given inside information while I had been excluded. Dr. Seraphina had never spoken to me of a lyre, nor the need to keep it from our enemies. That Gabriella had been taken into her confidence filled me with jealousy.

"When we understood that the impending war could disrupt our work," Dr. Seraphina said, "we decided to make certain that our papers would be well preserved, whatever happens. With this in mind, we asked Gabriella and Celestine to assist us in sorting and filing research notes. They began some months ago. The labor of their efforts has been taxing, the menial work of collecting facts, but they have shown ingenuity and determination to complete the project before the move. We have been thrilled with their progress. Their youth affords them a certain patience with what might seem to most of us simple clerical work, but their diligence has yielded excellent results. The data have been incredibly useful, allowing us to review a massive amount of information that has been hidden for decades."

Dr. Seraphina walked to the maps and, taking a pen from the pocket of her cardigan, drew a triangle over the Rhodope Mountains from Greece into Bulgaria.

"We know that the site we seek is located within these boundaries. We know that it has been explored previously and that there have been many scholarly attempts to describe the geology and landscape surrounding the gorge. Our scholars have been intellectually scrupulous in their work, but our organizational methods have been, perhaps, less than perfect. While we do not have the exact coordinates, I believe that if we comb all of the texts at our disposal — including accounts that have not been examined previously for this purpose — we will shed a new light upon the location."

"And you believe," the nun said, "that

through this method you will discover the co-ordinates of the cave?"

"Our proposal is this," Dr. Raphael said, taking over for his wife. "If we are able to narrow our search to a radius of one hundred kilometers, we want full approval for the Second Expedition."

"If we fail to narrow the search," Dr. Seraphina said, "we hide the information as best we can, go into exile as planned, and pray that our maps do not fall into the hands of our enemies."

I was shocked to see how readily the council members approved the plan after so much heated debate had already taken place. Perhaps Dr. Seraphina knew that Gabriella's advancement was a card she could play to win Dr. Lévi-Franche's approval. Whatever her strategy, it had worked. Although I was confused about the nature of the treasure we sought, my ambition had been flattered. I was overjoyed. Gabriella and I had been placed at the very center of the Valkos' search for the cave of the imprisoned angels.

The next morning I arrived at Dr. Seraphina's office an hour earlier than our scheduled meeting time of nine o'clock. I had slept very badly the previous night, while in the next room Gabriella had moved about, opening her window, smoking cigarettes, playing her favorite recording of Debussy's *Douze Études* as she paced from one end of her chamber to the next. I imagined that her secret relationship contributed to her sleeplessness, as it did mine, although in truth Gabriella's feelings were a mystery to me. I knew her better than anyone else I knew in Paris, and yet I did not know her at all.

I was so unmoored by the events of that afternoon that I did not have a moment to consider the magnitude of the role the Valkos had assigned us in hunting for the cavern. That I could think of little other than Gabriella with her arms wrapped about a strange man only heightened my wariness toward my friend. As a result, I left my bed before the sun rose, collected my books, and set out to study through the early-morning hours in my corner of the Athenaeum.

Being alone among our texts gave me the opportunity to consider the council meeting of the previous day. It was difficult for me to believe that an expedition of such consequence could be conducted without knowing the exact location of the gorge. The map — the most essential component of any mission — was missing. Even a first-year student of average intelligence would know that an expedition could not be considered a success without complete cartographic evidence. Lacking the precise geographical location of the journey, future scholars had no way to replicate the mission. In short, absent a map there was no solid proof.

I would not have been sensitive to the relevance of a map if it were not for my years with the Valkos, whose examination of cartography and geological formations bordered upon the obsessive. Much as a scientist relies on replication to verify experiments, the Valkos' work in antediluvian geology arose from their passion for precise, concrete reproduction of past expeditions. Their clinical discussions of mineral and rock formations, volcanic activity, the development of mantles, soil varieties, and karst topography left no room for doubt that they were scientific in their methods. There could be no mistake. If there had been a map to be found, Dr. Raphael would have seized upon it. He would have reconstructed the journey step-by-step, rock by rock.

After the sun rose, I knocked softly upon Dr. Seraphina's door and, hearing her voice, pushed it open. To my surprise, Gabriella sat with our teacher on a settee upholstered in vermilion silk, a coffee service before them. I could see that they were deep in discussion. Gone was the anxious Gabriella of the night before. Instead I found Gabriella the aristocrat, perfumed and powdered and immaculately dressed, her hair combed glossy black. I had been defeated once again by Gabriella, and, unable to hide my consternation, I stood in the doorway as if confused about my place. "What are you doing, Celestine?" Dr. Seraphina said, a hint of irritation in her voice. "Come in and join us."

I had visited Dr. Seraphina's office many times in the past and knew it to be one of the finest rooms in the school. Located on the top floor of a Haussmann-style building, it commanded a grand view of the neighborhood — the square before the school, with its fountain and endlessly circling pigeons, dominating all else. The morning sun illuminated a wall of French windows, one of which was open to the crisp morning air, washing the room with the smell of earth and water, as if it had rained all night, leaving a dredge of silt behind. The room itself was large and elegant, with built-in bookshelves, fluted moldings, and a marble-topped escritoire. It was an office that one might expect to find on the Right Bank rather than its location on *la rive gauche*. Dr. Raphael's office, a dusty, tobacco smoke-stained room stacked high with books, was more representative of our school. Dr. Raphael could often be found lounging in the sunny depths of his wife's polished office, discussing the finer points of a lecture or — as Gabriella was doing that morning — drinking coffee from Dr. Seraphina's Sèvres service.

That Gabriella had beaten me to Seraphina's office upset me more than I revealed. I could not know her motives, but it appeared to me that she had arranged a private conference, excluding me to her advantage. At the very least, Gabriella had taken the opportunity to speak with Dr. Seraphina about the work we would be undertaking, perhaps requesting the choice tasks. I knew that the outcome of our efforts could change our individual standing in the school. If the Valkos were pleased with the results, there would be a place on the expedition team. Only one of us would attain this.

We had been assigned work suited to our scholarly strengths, which were as opposite as our appearances. Whereas I loved the technical components of our coursework — the physiology of angelic bodies, the composition ratios of matter to spirit in created beings, and the mathematical perfection of early taxonomies — Gabriella was attracted to the more artistic elements of angelology. She liked to read the grand epic histories of battles between angelologists and the Nephilim; she could gaze at religious paintings and find symbolism that surely would have been lost upon me; she parsed ancient texts with such care that one believed that the meaning of a single word had the power to change the course of the future. She had faith in the progress of good, and over our first year of studies she made me believe that such progress was possible, too. Accordingly, Dr. Seraphina assigned Gabriella to work through the mythical texts, leaving me the more systematic task of sorting the empirical data of previous attempts to find the gorge, sifting geological information of various epochs, and collating outdated maps.

From the look of satisfaction upon Gabriella's face, they must have been chatting for some time. A series of wooden crates sat at the center of the office, their rough-hewn edges pressing upon the red and gold Oriental carpet. Each crate had been stuffed with field notebooks and loose papers, as if they had been packed in haste.

My astonishment at Gabriella's presence, not to mention my curiosity regarding the crates of notebooks, did not go unnoticed. Dr. Seraphina waved me into the room, asking me to close the door and join them. "Come in, Celestine," she said again as she gestured for me to sit on a divan near the bookshelves. "I was wondering when you might arrive."

As if to second Dr. Seraphina's remark, a grandfather clock at the far end of the office chimed eight o'clock. I was an hour early. "I thought we began at nine," I said.

"Gabriella wanted to get a head start," Dr. Seraphina said. "We have been looking through some of the new materials that you will catalog. These boxes are Raphael's papers. He brought them from his office last night."

Walking to her desk, Dr. Seraphina took a key and unlocked a cupboard. The shelves were filled with notebooks, each shelf ordered and meticulous. "And these are my papers.

I have arranged them by subject and date, the years of my schooling are on the lower shelves, and my most recent notes — mostly quotations and outlines for articles — are on the top. I have refrained from cataloging my work for years. Secrecy has been a large factor, but, more important, I have been waiting for the right assistants. You are both bright students with exposure to the basic fields of angelology — teleology, transcendental frequencies, theories of morphistic angelology, taxonomy. While you have studied these at an introductory level, you have also learned a bit about our field of antediluvian geology. You are hardworking and meticulous, knowledgeable and talented in different ways, but not specialized. I am hoping that you will come to the task with fresh eyes. If there is anything in the boxes that we've missed, I know that you girls will catch it. I am also going to require that you sit in on my lectures. I realize that you completed my introductory course last year, but the subject matter is of special significance to our task."

Running her fingers along a row of journals, she extracted a number of volumes and placed them on the coffee table between us. Although my first instinct was to take one of the journals, I waited, endeavoring to follow Gabriella's lead. I did not want to appear too anxious.

"You may want to begin with these," Seraphina said, settling lightly upon the settee. "I think you will find Raphael's files to be a bit of a challenge to put in order."

"There are so many," I said, enthralled by the sheer amount of papers to go through and curious as to how we would document such a mass of information.

"I have already given Gabriella precise instructions about our methodology for cataloging the papers," Seraphina said. "She will pass those instructions on to you. There is only one directive I will repeat: You must remember that these notebooks are exceptionally precious. They form the bulk of our original research. Although we have excerpted some of the material for publication, none of these has been copied in its entirety. I ask that you take special care to preserve the more delicate notebooks, particularly the texts outlining our expeditions. These papers cannot leave my office, I'm afraid. But as long as you work through the material in a timely fashion, you may read them as you wish. I believe that there is much to learn, however disorderly the papers may be. Indeed, I am hoping that our work will help you to understand the history of our struggle and, if we are very lucky, help us discover what we are seeking."

Taking a leather notebook and giving it to me, she said, "These are some of my writings from my student years. There are notes from lectures, some conjectures about angelology and its historical development. It's been so long since I've looked at it that I cannot fully account for what you might find. I was once an ambitious student myself and, like you, Celestine, spent many, many hours in the Athenaeum. With so much information about the history of angelology, I felt that I needed to make it all a bit more compact. I'm afraid some of my rather naïve speculations may be included, which you should take with a grain of salt."

I struggled to imagine Dr. Seraphina as a student, learning the very things we were learning. It was difficult to imagine her ever having been naïve about anything.

Dr. Seraphina said, "The notes from later years might be more engrossing. I rewrote the material from this journal into a more — how shall I say it? — succinct account of the history of our work. One objective that our scholars and agents have tried to adhere to is that angelology is purely functional — we use our study as a concrete tool. Theory is only as good as its execution, and in our case historical research plays a large role in our ability to fight the Nephilim. Personally, I have a rather empirical mind. I am not at all adept at understanding abstractions, and so I used narrative to make angelological theories more tangible to me. It is much the same way that I order my lectures. While the use of narrative is commonplace in many aspects of theology — allegories and the like — the church eschewed such an approach when speaking of angelological systems. As you perhaps know, hierarchical systems were often constructed as a kind of argument by the church fathers. They believed that as God created hierarchies of angels, so He made hierarchies on earth. Explaining one would illuminate the other. For example: As the seraphim are superior angelic intelligences to the cherubim, so, too, is the archbishop of Paris to the farmer. You see how it might work: God created hierarchies, and everyone must remain in their God-appointed place. And pay their taxes, *bien sûr.* The church's angelic hierarchies reinforced the social and political structures. They also offered a narrative of the universe, a cosmology that gave order to the seeming chaos of ordinary people's lives. Angelologists, of course, diverged from this path. We observe a horizontal structure, one that allows intellectual freedom and advancement through merit. Our system is quite unique."

"How could such a system survive?" Gabriella asked. "Surely the church would not have allowed it."

Startled by Gabriella's brazen question, I looked down at my hands. Never would I be able to question the church in such a forthright manner. Perhaps it was a detriment, my belief in the soundness of the church.

"I believe that this question has been asked

many times before," Dr. Seraphina said. "The founding fathers of angelology developed the perimeters of our work at a grand meeting of angelologists in the tenth century. There is a wonderful account of the meeting, written by one of the fathers in attendance." Dr. Seraphina returned to the cupboard and removed a book. Turning through the pages, she said, "I suggest that you read it when you have the chance, which will not be now, as you have more than your share of work ahead of you this morning."

Seraphina placed the book on the table. "Once you begin reading the history of our group, you will see that there is more to angelology than study and debate. Our work grew from the wise decisions of a band of serious, spiritual men. The First Angelological Expedition, the very first physical attempt made by angelologists to uncover the prison of the angels, arose when the Venerable Fathers, at the invitation of their Thracian brothers, organized the Council of Sozopol. It was the founding meeting of our discipline, and according to the Venerable Father Bogomil, one of the greatest of the founding fathers, the council was a huge success, not only in forging the standards of our work, but in bringing together the foremost religious thinkers of the time — not since the Council of Nicea had such a large assembly of extradenominational representatives gathered. Priests, deacons, acolytes, rabbis, and Manichaean holy men participated in a flurry of debate over dogma in the main hall. But a secret gathering was taking place elsewhere. An old priest called Clematis, a bishop of Thracian birth who lived in Rome, had called together a select group of sympathetic fathers who shared his great passion for finding the cavern of the Watchers. As a matter of fact, he had developed a theory of the location of the cave, positing that it, like the remnants of Noah's Ark, were to be found in proximity to the Black Sea coast. Eventually Clematis went to the mountains to test this theory. Dr. Raphael and I have assumed — although we have no proof to bear out our assumptions — that Clematis had drafted a map."

"But how can you be so certain that there is anything there?" Gabriella said. "What evidence do we have? What if there is no cavern and it is just a legend?"

"There must be a basis of truth in it," I said, feeling that Gabriella was too quick in her desire to challenge our teacher.

"Clematis found the cavern," Dr. Seraphina said. "The Venerable Father and his team are the only ones to have discerned the actual location of the pit, the only ones to have descended into it, and the only people in many thousands of years to have seen the disobedient angels. Clematis died for the privilege. Thankfully, he dictated a brief account of the expedition before his death. Dr. Raphael and I have used this account as our primary text in our search."

"Surely the account points to the location," I said, anxious to understand the details of Clematis's expedition.

"Yes, there is a location mentioned in Clematis's account," Dr. Seraphina said. Taking a piece of paper and a fountain pen, she wrote a series of letters in Cyrillic and presented them to us.

Гяурското Бърло

"The name given in Clematis's account is Gyaurskoto Burlo, which means "Infidels' Prison" in Old Bulgarian or, more loosely, "The Hiding Place of the Infidels" — an accurate description of the Watchers, who were called disobedient or unfaithful by Christians of the era. The Turks occupied the region around the Rhodope Mountains from the fourteenth century until the Russians assisted the Bulgarians in driving them out in 1878, and this serves to complicate the modern hunt: The Muslims referred to the Bulgarian Christians as infidels, placing another layer of meaning over the original description of the cave. We made a number of trips to Greece and Bulgaria in the twenties, but to our great disappointment we found no caves matching this name. When questioned, the villagers associate the name with the Turks or say they have never heard of the cave at all. After years of cartographic hunting, we have been unable to find the name on any map of the region. Whether by carelessness or design, the cave does not exist on paper."

"Perhaps it is more correct to conclude," Gabriella said, "that Clematis erred and that there is no such cave."

"There you are wrong," Dr. Seraphina said, the quickness of her response giving evidence of her passion for the subject. "The prison of the disobedient angels exists. I have wagered my career upon it."

"Then there must be a way to find it," I said, understanding for the first time the full extent of the Valkos' desire to solve the riddle. "We need to study Clematis's account."

"That," Seraphina said, going to her cupboard once again, "is for another time, after you have completed the work at hand."

I opened the volume before me, curious about what lay under its covers. I could not help but feel satisfied that my ideas were so aligned with Dr. Seraphina's work and that Gabriella — who usually won the Valkos' admiration — had clashed with our teacher. Yet, to my dismay, Gabriella was utterly untouched by Dr. Seraphina's disapproval. In fact, she appeared to be thinking of something else entirely. It was clear to me that Gabriella did not harbor the same sense of rivalry that I did.

She felt no need to prove herself.

Seeing how eager I was to begin, Dr. Seraphina stood. "I will leave you to your work," she said. "Perhaps you will see something in these papers that has eluded me. I have found that our texts will speak deeply to someone or they will say nothing whatsoever. It depends upon your sensitivity toward the subject. The mind and spirit become ripe in their own fashion and at their own pace. Beautiful music plays, but not everyone with ears can hear it."

From my first days as a student, it was my habit to arrive at the Valkos' lectures early, so as to secure a spot among the multitude of students. Despite the fact that Gabriella and I had sat through the Valkos' lectures the previous year, we continued to attend them each week. I was drawn to the ambience of passionate inquiry and the illusion of scholarly unity that the lectures presented, while Gabriella appeared to revel in her status as a second-year student from a well-known family. The younger students stared at her throughout the lecture as if gauging her reaction to the Valkos' assertations. The lectures were conducted in a small limestone chapel built on the fortifications of a Roman temple, its walls thick and calcified, as if they had risen from the quarries that stretched below. The chapel's ceilings were composed of crumbling brick buttressed by wooden beams, which appeared so rickety that when the rumbling of cars outside became strong, I believed the noise might send the whole edifice tumbling down upon us.

Gabriella and I found seats in the back of the chapel as Dr. Seraphina arranged her papers and began her lecture.

"Today I will share a story familiar to most of you in some form or other. As the founding story of our discipline, its central position in history is indisputable, its poetic beauty unassailable. We begin in the years before the Great Flood, when heaven dispatched a fleet of two hundred angels called the Watchers to monitor the activities of creation. The chief Watcher, according to these accounts, was named Semjaza. Semjaza was beautiful and commanding, the very image of angelic bearing. His chalk-white skin, pale eyes, and golden hair marked the ideal of heavenly beauty. Leading two hundred angels through the vault of the heavens, Semjaza came to rest in the material world. Among his charges were Araklba, Rameel, Tamlel, Ramlel, Danel, Ezeqeel, Baraqijal, Asael, Armaros, Batarel, Ananel, Zaqiel, Samsapeel, Satarel, Turel, Jomjael, Kokabiel, Araqiel, Shamsiel, and Sariel.

"The angels moved among the children of Adam and Eve unseen, living quietly in the shadows, hiding in mountains, taking shelter where humanity would not find them. They traveled from region to region, following the movements of men. In this fashion they discovered the populous civilizations along the Ganges, the Nile, the Jordan, and the Amazon. They lived quietly in the outer regions of human activity, dutifully observing the ways of man.

"One afternoon, in the era of Jared, when the Watchers were stationed on Mount Hermon, Semjaza saw a woman bathing in a lake, her brown hair twisting about her. He called the Watchers to the edge of the mountain, and together the majestic beings looked upon the woman. According to numerous doctrinal sources, it was then that Semjaza suggested the Watchers choose wives from among the children of men.

"No sooner had he spoken these words than Semjaza grew anxious. Aware of the penalty for disobedience — he had witnessed the fall of the rebel angels — he reasserted his plan. He said, 'The Daughters of Men should be ours. But if you do not follow me, I will suffer the penalty of this great sin alone.'

"The Watchers made a pact with Semjaza, swearing to suffer the penalties with their leader. They knew that the union was forbidden and that their pact broke every law in heaven and earth. Nonetheless, the Watchers descended Mount Hermon and presented themselves to human women. The women took these strange creatures as their husbands and soon became pregnant. After some time children were born to the Watchers and their wives. These creatures were called Nephilim.

"The Watchers observed their children as they grew. They saw that they were different from their mothers and also different from the angels. Their daughters grew to be taller and more elegant than human women; they were intuitive and psychic; they possessed the physical beauty of the angels. The boys grew to be taller and stronger than normal men; they reasoned with shrewdness; they possessed the intelligence of the spiritual world. As a gift, the Watchers brought their sons together and taught them the art of warfare. They taught the boys the secrets of fire — how to kindle and keep it, how to harness it for cooking and energy. This was a gift so precious that the Watchers would be mythologized in human legend, most notably in the story of Prometheus. The Watchers taught their sons metallurgy, an art the angels had perfected but kept hidden from humanity. The Watchers demonstrated the art of working precious metals into bracelets and rings and necklaces. Gold and gemstones were pried from the ground, polished and made into objects, and assigned value. The Nephilim stored their wealth, hoarding gold and grain. The Watchers showed their daughters how to use dyes for cloth and how to color their eyelids with glittering minerals ground into powder. They adorned their daughters, causing jealousy among the human women.

"The Watchers taught their children how to fashion tools that would make them stronger than men, instructing them to melt metal and fashion swords, knives, shields, breastplates, and arrowheads. Understanding the power the tools gave them, the Nephilim made caches of fine, sharp weapons. They hunted and stored meat. They protected their belongings with violence.

"And there were other gifts the Watchers gave their children. They taught their wives and daughters secrets even more powerful than fire or metallurgy. They separated the women from the men, taking them away from the city and traveling deep into the mountains, where they showed the women how to cast spells and to use herbs and roots in medicines. They gave them the secret of the magical arts, teaching them a system of symbols to record their spells. Soon scrolls were passed among them. The women — who had until then been at the mercy of men's strength — became powerful and dangerous.

"The Watchers divulged more and more of these heavenly secrets to their wives and daughters:

Baraqijal taught astrology.
Kokabiel taught them to read portents in
    the constellations.

Ezeqeel gave them a working knowledge
 of the clouds.
Araqiel instructed in signs of the earth.
Shamsiel mapped the course of the sun.
Sariel mapped the signs of the moon.
Aramos taught counterspells.

"With these gifts the Nephilim organized
into a tribe, arming themselves and taking
control of land and resources. They perfected
the art of warfare. They began to amass more
and more power over humanity. They identi-
fied themselves as lords of the earth, cutting
out huge domains of land and claiming the
kingdoms as their own. They took slaves and
made flags to represent their armies. They
divided their realms, assigning men to be
soldiers, merchants, and laborers to serve
them. Equipped with the eternal secrets and
a hunger for power, the Nephilim dominated
mankind.

"As the Nephilim ruled over the earth and
men perished, mankind cried to heaven for
help. Michael, Uriel, Raphael, and Gabriel,
the archangels who had observed the Watchers from their first descent to the world, also
monitored the progress of the Nephilim.

"When commanded, the archangels confronted the Watchers, surrounding them in
a ring of fire. They disarmed their brothers.
Once defeated, the Watchers were shackled
and transported to a remote, unpopulated

cavern high in the mountains. At the lip of the abyss, their chains heavy upon them, the Watchers were ordered to descend. Through a crevice in the earth's crust they fell, plummeting deeper and deeper until they came to rest in a prison of darkness. From the depths they grieved for air and light and their lost freedom. Separated from heaven and earth, awaiting the day of their release, they prayed for heaven's forgiveness. They called out for their children to save them. God ignored their pleas. The Nephilim did not come.

"The angel Gabriel, messenger of good news, could not abide the Watchers' anguish. In a moment of pity, he threw his lyre to his fallen brothers so that they might diminish their suffering with music. Even as the lyre fell, Gabriel realized his mistake: The lyre's music was seductive and powerful. The lyre could be used to the Watchers' benefit.

"Over time the Watchers' granite prison came to be called the underworld, the land of the dead where heroes descended to find eternal life and wisdom. Tartarus, Hades, Kurnugia, Annwn, hell — the legends grew as the Watchers, chained to the pit, cried for their release. Even today, somewhere in the depths of the earth, they cry to be saved.

"It has been a source of speculation as to why the Nephilim did not rescue their fathers," Dr. Seraphina said in conclusion. "Surely the Nephilim would have been stronger with the assistance of the Watchers, and surely they would have assisted in their release if they had the power to do so. But the Watchers' prison remains unknown. It is in this mystery that our work takes root."

Dr. Seraphina was a gifted speaker, with a dramatic ability to animate her point for first-year students, a talent that not many of our professors possessed. As a result of her efforts, she often appeared exhausted by the end of an hour's lecture, and that day was no exception. Looking up from her notes, she announced a short break. Gabriella gestured for me to follow her, and, leaving the chapel by a side exit, we walked through a series of narrow hallways until we reached an empty courtyard. Dusk had fallen, and a warm autumn evening settled over us, scattering shadows on the flagstones. A great beech tree towered above the courtyard, its skin strangely mottled, as if it suffered from leprosy. The Valkos' lectures could last for hours, often bleeding into the night, and I was keen to take in the outdoor air. I wanted to ask Gabriella's opinion about the lecture — indeed, I had grown to be her friend through such analysis — but saw that she was in no mood.

Taking a cigarette case from the pocket of her jacket, Gabriella offered one to me. When I refused, as I always did, she merely shrugged. It was a shrug I had come to recognize, a slight but insouciant gesture that made it clear how much she disapproved of my inability to enjoy myself. *Celestine the naïf,* the shrug seemed to say; *Celestine, child of the provinces.* Gabriella had taught me much by her small rejections and silences, and I had always watched her with particular care, noticing the way she dressed, what she read, the way she wore her hair. In the past weeks, her clothes had become prettier, more revealing. Her makeup, which had always been distinct, had become darker and more pronounced. The spectacle I had witnessed the previous morning suggested the reason for this change, but still her manner captured my interest. Despite everything, I looked up to her as one does to an older sister.

Gabriella lit her cigarette with a lovely gold lighter and inhaled deeply, as if to demonstrate all that I was missing.

"How beautiful," I said, taking the lighter from her and turning it in my hand, the gold burnishing to a roseate hue in the evening light. I was tempted to ask Gabriella to tell me how such an expensive lighter had come into her possession, but I stopped myself. Gabriella discouraged even the most superficial questions. Even after a year of seeing each other every day, we spoke very little about our personal lives. I settled, therefore, upon a simple statement of fact. "I haven't seen it before."

"It belongs to a friend," she said without

meeting my eye. Gabriella had no friends but me — she ate with me, studied with me, and if I happened to be occupied, she preferred solitude to forming new friendships — and so I knew at once it belonged to her lover. Surely she must have discerned that her secrecy would make me curious. I could not restrain myself from asking her a direct question.

"What sort of friend?" I said. "I ask because you have seemed so distracted from our work lately."

"Angelology is more than studying old texts," Gabriella said. Her look of reproach suggested that my vision of our endeavor at the school was deeply flawed. "I have given everything to my work."

Unable to mask my feelings, I said, "Your attention has been overwhelmed by something else, Gabriella."

"You don't know the first thing about the powers that control me," Gabriella said. Although she had meant to respond with her typical haughtiness, I detected a crack of desperation in her manner. My questions had surprised and hurt her.

"I know more than you think," I said, hoping that a direct confrontation would lead her to confess everything. I'd never before taken such a strident tone with her. The error of my approach was evident before I had finished speaking.

Snatching the lighter from me and tucking it into the pocket of her jacket, Gabriella tossed her cigarette onto the slate flagstones and walked away.

When I returned to the chapel, I found my seat next to Gabriella. She had placed her jacket upon my chair, saving it for me, but she refused even to glance my way as I sat. I could see that she had been crying — a faint ring of black smudged the edges of her eyes where tears had mixed with the kohl. I wanted to speak with her. I was desperate for her to open her heart to me, and I longed to help her overcome whatever error in judgment had befallen her. But there was no time to talk. Dr. Raphael Valko took his wife's place behind the podium, arranging a sheaf of papers as he prepared to give a portion of the lecture. And so I placed my hand upon her arm and smiled, to let her know that I was sorry. My gesture was met with hostility. Gabriella pulled away, refusing even to look at me. Leaning back in the hard wooden chair, she crossed her legs and waited for Dr. Raphael to begin.

During my first months of study, I learned that there were two distinct sets of opinions regarding the Valkos. Most students adored them. Drawn in by the Valkos' wit, their arcane knowledge, and their dedication to pedagogy, these students hung upon their every word. I, along with the majority, belonged to this group. A minority of our peers remained less adoring. They found the Valkos' methods suspect and their joint lectures pretentious. Although Gabriella would never allow herself to be categorized with either lot, and had never confessed how she felt about Dr. Raphael and Dr. Seraphina's lectures, I suspected that she was critical of the Valkos, just as her uncle had been in the assembly gathered at the Athenaeum. The Valkos were outsiders who had worked their way to the top of the academy, while Gabriella's family position gave her instant rank. I had often listened to Gabriella's opinions about our teachers, and I knew that her ideas often diverged from the Valkos'.

Dr. Raphael tapped the edge of the podium to quiet the room and began his lecture.

"The origins of the First Angelic Cataclysm are often contested," he began. "In fact, looking over the various accounts of this cataclysmic battle in our own collection, I found thirty-nine conflicting theories about just how it began and how it ended. As most of you know, scholarly methods for dissecting historical events of this nature have changed, evolved — some would say devolved — and so I will be frank with you: My method, like that of my wife, has changed over time to include multiple historical perspectives. Our readings of texts, and the narratives we create from fragmentary material, reflect our larger goals. Of course, as future scholars, you will draw your own theories about the First Angelic

Cataclysm. If we have succeeded, you will leave this lecture with the kernel of doubt that inspires individual and original research. Listen carefully, then. Believe and doubt, accept and dismiss, transcribe and revise all that you learn here today. In this way the future of angelological scholarship will be sound.'"

Dr. Raphael held a leather-bound volume in his hands. He opened it and, his voice steady and serious, began his lecture:

"High in the mountains, under a ledge that sheltered them from the rain, the Nephilim stood together, begging guidance from the daughters of Semjaza and the sons of Azazel, whom they considered to be their leaders after the Watchers had been taken below the earth. Azazel's eldest son stepped forward and addressed the endless crowd of pale giants filling the valley below.

"He said, 'My father taught us the secrets of warfare. He taught us to use a sword and knife, to fashion arrows, to wage war upon our enemies. He did not teach us to protect ourselves from heaven. Soon we will be trapped on all sides by water. Even with our strength and our numbers, it is impossible to build a vessel like Noah's. It is equally impossible to directly attack Noah and take his craft. The archangels are watching over Noah and his family.'

"It was well known that Noah had three sons and that these sons had been chosen to assist in maintaining his Ark. Azazel's son announced that he would go to the seashore where Noah was loading his boat with animals and plants, and there he would discern a way to infiltrate the Ark. Bringing along their most powerful sorceress, the eldest daughter of Semjaza, he left the Nephilim, saying, 'My brothers and sisters, you must remain here, at the highest point of the mountain. It is possible that the waters will not rise to this height.'

"Together the son of Azazel and the daughter of Semjaza walked down the steep mountain path through the relentless rain, making their way to the shore. At the Black Sea, all was chaos. Noah had warned of the Flood for many months, but his countrymen did not pay attention in the least. They carried on with feasting and dancing and sleeping, happy in the face of utter destruction. They laughed at Noah, and some of them even stood near Noah's Ark, jeering as he brought food and water aboard.

"For some days Azazel's son and Semjaza's daughter watched the comings and goings of Noah's sons. They were called Shem, Ham, and Japheth, each very different from the others. Shem, the eldest, was dark-haired and green-eyed, with elegant hands and a brilliant way of speaking; Ham was darker than Shem, with large brown eyes, great strength, and good sense; Japheth had fair skin, blond hair, and blue eyes, the most frail and thin of the three. While Shem and Ham did not tire as they helped their father load animals, satchels of food, and jars of water, Japheth worked slowly. Shem and Ham and Japheth had been long married, and between them Noah had many grandchildren.

"Semjaza's daughter saw that Japheth's appearance was close to their own and decided that this was the brother her companion should take. The Nephilim waited for many days, watching, until Noah had loaded the final animals onto the Ark. The son of Azazel stole to the great boat. Its massive shadow fell upon him, blanketing him in shadow as he called for Japheth.

"Noah's youngest leaned over the edge of the Ark, his blond curls falling into his eyes. Azazel's son summoned Japheth to accompany him away from the seashore, along a footpath that led deep into a forest. The archangels, who stood guard at the boat's prow and hull, inspecting every object that entered and exited the Ark so that it fit God's dictate, paid no attention to Japheth as he left the ship and trailed the luminous stranger into the woods.

"As Japheth followed Azazel's son deeper and deeper into the forest, the rain began to fall, pounding the canopy of leaves above his head and echoing loud as thunder. Japheth was out of breath when he caught up to the majestic stranger. Hardly able to speak, he asked, 'What do you want of me?'

"Azazel's son did not reply but wrapped his fingers around the neck of Noah's son and squeezed until he felt the brittle bones of the throat collapse. In that moment, even before the Flood wiped out the wicked creatures of the earth, God's plan of a purified world faltered. The future of the Nephilim race solidified, and the new world came into being.

"Semjaza's daughter stepped from the forest and placed her hands over the face of Azazel's son. She had memorized the spells her father had taught her. As she touched Azazel's son, his appearance changed: His lustrous beauty dimmed, and his angelic features faded. She whispered words into his ear, and he transformed into the image of Japheth. Weakened by the transformation, he stumbled away from Semjaza's daughter, making his way through the forest to the Ark.

"Noah's wife took one look at her son and knew in an instant that he had changed. His face was the same and his bearing the same, but something about his manner was strange, and so she asked him where he had been and what had happened to him. He could not speak in human language, and so Azazel's son remained quiet, further terrifying his mother. She sent for Japheth's wife, a lovely woman who had known Japheth from his childhood. She, too, discerned the corruption of her Japheth, but as his physical characteristics were identical to those of the man she had married, she could not say what had changed. Japheth's brothers recoiled, fearful of Japheth's presence. Nevertheless, Japheth remained on board the Ark as the water began to sweep the ground from below. It was the seventeenth day of the second month. The Flood had begun.

"The rain poured over the Ark, filling the valleys and the cities. Water rose to the base of the mountains and then to the peaks. The Nephilim watched as the water lifted higher and higher, until they could not see land any longer. Terrified cheetahs and leopards clung to trees; the terrible howling of dying wolves echoed through the air. A giraffe stood on a lone hilltop, water gushing over its body as it angled its nose up and up and up until the water overwhelmed it. The bodies of humans and animals and Nephilim floated like dragonflies over the surface of the world, undulating with the tides, rotting and sinking to the ocean floor. Tangles of hair and limbs sloshed against the prow of Noah's boat, rising and sinking in the soup of water. The air became sweet with the smell of sun-baked flesh.

"The Ark floated adrift over the earth until the twenty-seventh day of the second month of the following year, a total of three hundred seventy days. Noah and his family encountered nothing but endless death and endless water, an ever-moving gray sheet of rain, a wave-tossed horizon for as far as one could see, water and more water, a shoreless world bereft of solidity. They floated upon the surface of the sea for so long that they exhausted their store of wine and grain and lived on chicken eggs and water.

"When the Ark grounded and the waters receded, Noah and his family released the animals from the belly of the boat, took their bags of seed, and planted them. Before long the sons of Noah began to repopulate the world. The archangels, acting out the will of God, came to their aid, bestowing great fertility upon the animals, the soil, and the women. The crops had sun and rain; the animals found sufficient food; the women did not die in childbirth. Everything grew. Nothing perished. The world began again.

"The sons of Noah claimed everything that they saw as their own. They became patriarchs, each founding a race of humanity. They migrated to far-off regions of the planet, establishing dynasties that we recognize even today as distinct. Shem, Noah's oldest son, traveled to the Middle East, founding the Semitic tribe; Ham, Noah's second son, moved below the equator, into Africa, forming the Hamitic tribe; and Japheth — or rather, the creature disguised as Japheth — took over the area between the Mediterranean and the Atlantic, founding what would one day be called Europe. Japheth's progeny have plagued us

283

ever since. As Europeans, we must contemplate our relation to our ancestral origins. Are we free of such devilish associations? Or are we in some way connected to the children of Japheth?"

Dr. Raphael's lecture ended abruptly. He stopped speaking, closed his notebook, and urged us to return to his next lecture. I knew from experience that Dr. Raphael halted his lectures in this manner on purpose, leaving his students expecting more. It was a pedagogical tool that I came to respect after having attended his lectures as a first-year student — I had not missed one of them. The rustling of papers and the shuffling of feet filled the room as students gathered in groups, preparing for dinner or evening study. Like the others, I collected my belongings. Dr. Raphael's tale had left me in something of a trance, and I found it particularly difficult to come to my senses in a group of people, many of whom were complete strangers to me. Gabriella's familiar presence at my side was comforting. I turned to ask her if she would like to walk to our apartment to prepare dinner.

Once I saw her, however, I stopped cold. Gabriella's appearance had changed. Her hair was matted with sweat, her skin pallid and clammy. The thick black kohl she wore about her eyes — a flourish of cosmetics that I had come to think of as Gabriella's morbid trademark — had smeared even farther below her eyes, whether from perspiration or tears, I could not say. Her large green eyes gazed ahead but appeared to see nothing at all. Her disposition gave her a most frightening appearance, as if she were in the grip of tubercular devastation. It was then that I noticed the bloodied burns that had eaten the flesh of her forearm and the lovely golden lighter clutched in her hand. I tried to speak, to ask her for an explanation for such strange behavior, but a look from Gabriella stopped me before I could speak. In her eyes I saw a strength and determination that I myself did not possess. I knew that she would remain inscrutable. Whatever dark and terrible secrets she held would never be opened to me. For some reason, although I could not understand why, this knowledge both comforted and horrified me at once.

Later, when I returned to our apartment, Gabriella sat in the kitchen. A pair of scissors and some white bandages lay on the table before her. Seeing that she might need my assistance, I went to her. In the sunny atmosphere of our apartment, the burn took on a ghastly color — her flesh had been blackened by the flame and oozed a clear substance. I measured out a length of bandage.

Gabriella said, "Thank you, but I can take care of myself."

My frustration grew as she took the bandage

from me and proceeded to dress the wound. I watched her for a moment, then said, "How could you do such a thing? What is wrong with you?"

She smiled as if I had said something that amused her. Indeed, I thought for a moment she might laugh at me. But she simply returned to dressing her arm and said, "You wouldn't understand, Celestine. You are too good, too pure, to understand what is wrong with me."

In the days that followed, the more I tried to understand the mystery of Gabriella's actions, the more secretive she became. She began to spend her nights away from our shared apartment on the rue Gassendi, leaving me to wonder at her whereabouts and her safety. She returned to our quarters only when I myself was away, and I detected her comings and goings by the clothes she left behind or removed from her closet. I would step through the apartment and find a drinking glass, its rim imprinted with a smudge of red lipstick; a strand of black hair; the scent of Shalimar lingering upon her clothing; and I understood that Gabriella was avoiding me. It was only during the daytime, when we worked together in the Athenaeum, boxes of notebooks and papers spread before us, that I was in the company of my friend, but even then it was as if I weren't there at all.

Worse, I had begun to believe that Gabriella examined my papers in my absence, reading my notebooks and checking my place in various books we'd been assigned, as if gauging my advancement and measuring it against her own. She was too cunning to leave evidence of her intrusions, and I had never found proof of her presence in my room, so I took extra care of what I left lying about my desk. I had no doubt that she would steal anything she found useful, even as she maintained her disposition of blithe apathy toward our shared work at the Athenaeum.

As the days went by, I began to lose myself in daily routine. Our tasks were tedious in the beginning, consisting of little more than reading notebooks and making reports of potentially useful information. Gabriella had been given work that suited her interest in the mythological and historical aspects of angelology, while I had been assigned the more mathematical task of categorizing caves and gorges, working to isolate the location of the lyre.

One afternoon in October, as Gabriella sat across from me, her black hair curling at her chin, I drew a notebook from one of the many boxes before us and examined it with care. It was an unusual notebook, short and rather thick, with a hard, scuffed binding. A leather strap — fastened by a golden clasp — bound the covers together. Examining the clasp more closely, I saw that it had been fashioned into the likeness of a golden angel no bigger in size than my smallest finger. It was long and narrow, with a stylized face containing two inlaid blue sapphire eyes, a flowing tunic, and a pair of sickle-shaped wings. I ran my fingers over the cold metal. Pressing the wings between my fingers, I felt resistance and then a satisfying pop as the mechanism gave. The notebook fell open, and I placed it flat upon my lap, straightening the pages under my fingers. I glanced at Gabriella to see if she had noticed my discovery, but she was engrossed in her reading and did not, to my relief, see the beautiful notebook in my hands.

I understood at once that this was one of the journals Seraphina had mentioned having kept in her later years of study, her observations consolidated and distilled into a succinct primer. Indeed, the journal contained much more than simple lecture notes. Flipping to the beginning of the book, I found the word ANGELOLOGY stamped into the first page in golden ink. The pages had been cluttered with consolidated notes, speculations, questions jotted down during lectures or in preparation for an exam. As I read, I detected Dr. Seraphina's burgeoning love for antediluvian geology: Maps of Greece, Macedonia, Bulgaria, and Turkey had been drawn meticulously over the pages, as if she had traced the exact contours of each country's border, sketching every mountain range and lake. The names of caves and mountain passes and gorges appeared in Greek, Latin, or Cyrillic, depending upon the alphabet native to the region. Tiny notations appeared in the margins, and it soon became apparent that these drawings had been created in preparation for an expedition. Dr. Seraphina had had her heart set on a second expedition since she was a student. I realize that by resuming Dr. Seraphina's work with these maps, there was a chance that I myself could uncover the geographical mystery of Clematis's expedition.

Reading further, I found Dr. Seraphina's sketches scattered like treasures among the narrow columns of words. There were halos, trumpets, wings, harps, and lyres — the thirty-year-old doodlings of a dreamy student distracted during lectures. There were pages filled with drawings and quotations excerpted from early works of angelology. At the center of the notebook, I came across some pages of numerical squares, or magic squares as they were commonly known. The squares consisted of a series of numbers that equaled a constant sum in each row, diagonal, and column: a magic constant. Of course, I knew the history of magic squares — their presence in Persia, India, and China and their earliest advent in Europe in the engravings of Albrecht Dürer, an artist whose work I admired — but

I had never had the opportunity to examine one.

Dr. Seraphina's words were written across the page in faded red ink:

One of the most famous squares — and the most commonly used for our purposes — is the Sator-Rotas Square, the oldest example of which was discovered in Herculaneum, or Ercolano as it is called today, an Italian city partially destroyed by the explosion of Mount Vesuvius in year 79 of the present era. The Sator-Rotas is a Latin palindrome, an acrostic that can be read in a number of ways. Traditionally, the square has been used in angelology to signify that a pattern is present. The square is not a code, as it is often mistaken to be, but a symbol to alert the angelologist that a larger schematic importance is at hand. In certain cases the square alerts us that something is hidden nearby — a missive or communication, perhaps. Magical squares have always played a part in religious ceremonies, and this square is no exception. The use of such squares is ancient, and our group does not take credit for their development in this regard. Indeed, the squares have been found in China, Arabia, India, and Europe and were even constructed by Benjamin Franklin in the United States in the eighteenth century.

S	A	T	O	R
A	R	E	P	0
T	E	N	E	T
O	P	E	R	A
R	O	T	A	S

The next page contained the Square of Mars, the numbers of which drew my eye into it with an almost magnetic pull.

11	24	7	20	3
4	12	25	8	16
17	5	13	21	9
10	18	1	14	22
23	6	19	2	15

Below the square Seraphina had written:

The Sigil of Michael. Sigil derives from the Latin *sigilum,* which means "seal," or the Hebrew *segulah* meaning "word of spiritual effect." In ceremony each sigil represents a spiritual being — either white or black — whose presence can be summoned by the angelologist, most prominently the higher orders of angels and demons. Summoning occurs through incantations, sigils, and a series of sympathetic interchanges between spirit and summoning agent. Nota bene: Incantatory summoning is an extraordinarily dangerous undertaking, often proving fatal to the medium, and must be used only as a last and final effort to bring forth angelic beings.

Turning to another page, I found numerous sketches of musical instruments — a lute and a lyre and a beautifully rendered harp, similar to the drawings that filled earlier pages of the notebook. Such instruments meant little to me. I could not imagine the sounds the instruments would make when played, nor did I know how to read musical notation. My strengths had always been numerical, and as a result I had studied mathematics and the sciences and knew next to nothing about music. Ethereal musicology — which Vladimir, the angelologist from Russia, knew so well — had thus far completely baffled me, the modes and scales clouding my mind.

Occupied with these thoughts for some time, I at last looked up from my reading. Gabriella had moved next to me on the settee, her chin resting in her hand, her eyes moving languidly over the pages of a bound text. She wore clothing I had not noticed before, a silk twill blouse and wide-legged trousers that appeared custom-tailored to her figure. The hint of a bandage could be seen under the diaphanous silk sleeve of her left arm, the only remaining evidence of the trauma I had witnessed after Dr. Raphael's lecture weeks earlier. She seemed to be another person entirely from the frightened girl who had burned her arm.

Examining the book in her hands, I discerned the title *The Book of Enoch* stamped upon the spine. Much as I wanted to share my discovery with Gabriella, I knew better than to interrupt her reading, and so instead I refastened the golden clasp of the journal, pressing the delicate sickle-shaped wings together until they caught and clicked. Then, resolving to forge ahead in our cataloging duties, I braided my hair — long, unruly blond hair that I wished to cut into a severe bob, as Gabriella had done — and began the tedious task of sorting through the Valkos' papers alone.

Dr. Seraphina came to check on us each day at noon, bringing a basket of bread and cheese, a pot of mustard, and a bottle of cold water for our lunch. Usually I could hardly wait for her arrival, but that morning I had been so engrossed in my work that I did not realize it was nearly time for a break until she swept into the room and deposited the basket on the table before us. In the hours that had passed, I had barely noticed anything at all but the seemingly endless accretion of data, especially the Valkos' field notes from their earliest expedition, a grueling journey through the Pyrenees, with measurements of caves, their gradations and densities of granites filling ten field journals. It was only as Dr. Seraphina sat with us and I was able to pull myself away from my work did I realize that I was extremely hungry. Clearing the table, I gathered the papers and closed the notebooks. I made myself comfortable on the settee, my gabardine skirt slipping on the textured vermilion silk, and prepared for lunch.

After arranging the basket on the table before us, Dr. Seraphina turned to Gabriella. "How are you progressing?"

"I have been reading Enoch's account of the Watchers," Gabriella replied.

"Ah," Dr. Seraphina said. "I should have known you would be attracted to Enoch. It is one of the most interesting texts in our canon. And one of the strangest."

"Strangest?" I said, glancing at Gabriella. If Enoch was so brilliant, why hadn't Gabriella shared his work with me?

"It is a fascinating text," Gabriella said, her face brimming with intelligence, the very passionate brilliance that I usually admired. "I had no idea that it existed."

"When was it written?" I asked, not a little jealous that Gabriella was once again ahead of the game. "Is it modern?"

"It is an apocryphal prophecy written by a direct descendant of Noah," Gabriella said. "Enoch claimed to have been taken into heaven and given direct access to the angels."

"In the modern era, *The Book of Enoch* has been dismissed as the dream vision of a mad patriarch," Dr. Seraphina said. "But it is our primary reference to the story of the Watchers."

I had discovered a similar story in our professor's journal and began to wonder if I had read the same text. As if detecting my thoughts, Dr. Seraphina said, "I copied some sections of Enoch into the journal you have been reading, Celestine." Picking up the journal with the angel clasp, she turned it over in her hand. "Surely you came across the passages. But *The Book of Enoch* is so elaborate, so filled with wonderful information, that I recommend you read it in its entirety. In fact, Dr. Raphael will require you to read it in your third year. If, that is, we will be conducting courses next year at all."

Gabriella said, "There is a passage that particularly struck me."

"Yes?" Dr. Seraphina said, looking delighted. "Do you recall it?"

Gabriella recited the passage. " 'And there appeared to me two men very tall, such as I have never seen on earth. And their faces shone like the sun, and their eyes were like burning lamps, and fire came forth from their lips. Their dress had the appearance of feathers: their feet were purple, their wings brighter than gold; their hands were whiter than snow.'"

I felt my cheeks grow hot. Gabriella's talents, which had once made me love her, now had the opposite effect.

"Excellent," Dr. Seraphina said, looking both pleased and circumspect at once. "And why did that passage strike you?"

"These angels are not the sweet cherubs standing at heaven's gate, not the luminous figures we see in Renaissance paintings," Gabriella said. "They are fearsome, frightening creatures. I found, as I read Enoch's account of the angels, that they are horrible, almost monstrous. To be honest, they terrify me."

I stared at Gabriella in disbelief. Gabriella returned my gaze, and I sensed — for the briefest moment — that she was trying to tell me something but could not. I longed for her to say more, to explain herself to me, but she merely turned a cold eye on me once more.

Dr. Seraphina thought Gabriella's statement over for a moment, and I wondered if she might know more about my friend than I. Standing, she walked to her cupboard, opened a drawer, and removed a hammered-copper cylinder. After slipping on a pair of white gloves, she twisted it, popped off a wafer-thin copper lid, and tapped out a scroll. Flattening it on the coffee table before us, she lifted a leaded-crystal paperweight and anchored one end of the scroll upon the tabletop. The other she held with the palm of her long, thin hand. I stared at the yellow, crinkled scroll as Dr. Seraphina unfolded it.

Gabriella leaned over and touched the edge of the scroll. "That is Enoch's vision?" she asked.

"A copy," Dr. Seraphina said. "There were hundreds of such manuscripts circulating during the second century B.C. According to our chief archivist, we have a number of the originals, all slightly different, as these things usually were. We became interested in preserving them when the Vatican began to destroy them. This one is not nearly as precious as those in the vault."

The scroll was made of thick, leathery paper, the rubric in Latin and the words drawn in precisely articulated calligraphy. The margins were illuminated with slender golden angels, their silver robes curling against folded golden wings.

Dr. Seraphina turned to us. "Can you read it?"

I had studied Latin as well as Greek and Aramaic, but the calligraphy was difficult to make out and the Latin seemed strange and unfamiliar.

Gabriella asked, "When was the scroll copied?"

"The seventeenth century or so," Dr. Seraphina said. "It is a modern reproduction of a much older manuscript, one that predates the texts that became the Bible. The original is locked up in our vault, as are hundreds of other manuscripts, where they are safe. We have been scavengers of texts since our work began. It is our greatest strength — we are the holders of the truth, and this information protects us. In fact, you would find that many of the fragments collected in the Bible itself — and many that should have been included but were not — reside in our possession."

Leaning closer to the scroll, I said, "It is difficult to read. Is it Vulgate?"

"Let me read it for you," Dr. Seraphina said, smoothing the scroll once again with her gloved hand. " 'And the men took me and brought me to the second heaven, and showed me the darkness, and there I saw the prisoners suspended, reserved for and waiting the eternal judgment. And these angels were gloomy in appearance, more than the darkness of the earth. And they unceasingly wept every hour, and I said to the men who were with me: "Why are these men continually tortured?" ' "

I turned the words over in my mind. Although I had spent years reading the old texts, I had never heard anything like it before. "What is it?"

"Enoch," Gabriella said, instantly. "He has just entered the second heaven."

"The second?" I asked, confused.

"There are seven," Gabriella said authoritatively. "Enoch visited each one and wrote of what he found there."

"Go," Dr. Seraphina said, gesturing to a bookshelf that spanned the entire wall of the room. "On the farthest shelf, you will find the Bibles."

I followed Dr. Seraphina's directions. After choosing a Bible I found to be particularly lovely — with a thick leather cover and a hand-stitched binding, a book that was heavy and difficult to carry — I brought it back to the table and placed it before my professor.

"You've chosen my favorite," Dr. Seraphina said, as if my choice confirmed her faith in my judgment. "I saw this same Bible as a girl, when I first announced to the council that I would be an angelologist. It was at their famous conference of 1919, after Europe had been ravaged by the war. I had an instinctual attraction to the profession. There hadn't been an angelologist in my family before, which is rather strange — angelology runs in families. Yet at sixteen years old, I knew exactly what I would be and was not in the least shy about it!" Dr. Seraphina paused, collected herself, and said, "Now, come closer. I have something to show you."

She placed the Bible on the table and opened the pages slowly, carefully. "Here is Genesis 6. Read it."

We read the passage, taken from the 1297 translation of Guyart des Moulins:

And it came to pass when the children of men had multiplied that in those days were born to them beautiful and fair daughters. And the angels, the sons of heaven, saw and lusted after them, and said to one another: "Come, let us choose wives from among the children of men and have children with them."

"I read that this afternoon," Gabriella said.

"No," Dr. Seraphina corrected. "This is not Enoch. Although there is a very similar version in *The Book of Enoch,* this is different. It is from Genesis and is the single point where the accepted version of events — those that contemporary religious scholars accept as true — meets the apocryphal. Of course, the apocryphal works are the richest source of angelic history. Once Enoch was studied extensively, but as is often the case with a dogmatic institution like the church, they found it threatening and began to remove Enoch from the canon."

Gabriella seemed distressed. "But why?" she asked. "This material could be so helpful, especially to scholars."

"Helpful? I don't see how. It was only natural that the church would suppress such information," Dr. Seraphina responded brusquely. "*The Book of Enoch* was dangerous to their version of history. This version," she said, uncapping the cylinder and tapping out another scroll, "was written after many years of oral legend. It does in fact come from the same source. The author wrote it at the time of many of the texts in the Old Testament of the Bible — in other words, at the time the Talmudic texts were composed."

"But that doesn't explain the church's reason for suppressing it," Gabriella said.

"Their reason is obvious. Enoch's version of the story is laced with all sorts of ecstatic language — religious and visionary extremes that conservative scholars thought to be exaggerations, or worse: madness. Enoch's personal reflections about what he calls 'the elect' were particularly disturbing. There are many passages of Enoch's personal conversations with God. As you can imagine, most theologians found the work blasphemous. To be frank, Enoch was considered controversial throughout the earliest years of Christianity. Nonetheless, *The Book of Enoch* is the most significant angelological text we have. It is the only record of the true origin of evil on earth that was written by a man and passed among men."

My envy of Gabriella disappeared, replaced

301

by an intense curiosity about what Dr. Seraphina would tell us.

"When religious scholars became interested in restoring *The Book of Enoch*, a Scottish explorer named James Bruce found a version of this text in Ethiopia. Another copy was found in Belgrade. As you can imagine, these discoveries were at cross purposes to the church's attempt to wipe out the text completely. But it may surprise you to know that we have helped them along the way, taking copies of Enoch out of circulation and storing them in our library. The Vatican's desire to pretend that Nephilim and angelologists do not exist is equal to our desire to remain hidden. It all works out quite well, I suppose, our mutual agreement to pretend the other does not exist."

"It is surprising that we don't work together," I said.

"Not at all," Dr. Seraphina replied. "Once angelology was the center of attention in religious circles, one of the most revered branches of theology. That quickly changed. After the Crusades and the outrages of the Inquisition, we knew that it was time to distance ourselves from the church. Even before this, however, we had moved the majority of our efforts underground, hunting the Famous Ones alone. We have always been a force of resistance — a partisan group, if you will — fighting them from a safe distance. The less visible we became, the better, especially because the Nephilim themselves had contrived to create an almost perfect secrecy. The Vatican is aware of our activities, of course, but has chosen to leave us in peace, at least for the time being. The advancements the Nephilim made under the cover of businesses and government operations made them anonymous. Their greatest achievement in the past three hundred years has been hiding themselves in plain sight. They have put us under constant surveillance, emerging only to attack us, to benefit from wars or shady business dealings, and then they quietly disappear. Of course, they have also done a marvelous job separating the intellectuals from the religious. They have made sure that humanity will not have another Newton or Copernicus, thinkers who revere both Science and God. Atheism was their greatest invention. Darwin's work, despite the man's extreme dependence upon religion, was twisted and propagated by them. The Nephilim have succeeded in making people believe that humanity is self-generated, self-sufficient, free of the divine, sui generis. It is an illusion that makes our work much more difficult and their detection nearly impossible."

Carefully, Dr. Seraphina rolled the scroll and slid it into the copper cylinder. Turning to the woven basket containing our lunch, she opened it and placed a baguette and cheese before us, encouraging us to eat. I was famished. The bread was warm and soft in my hands, leaving the slightest slick of butter on my fingers as I tore off a piece.

"Father Bogomil, one of our founding fathers, compiled our first independent angelology in the tenth century as a pedagogical tool. Later angelologies included taxonomies of the Nephilim. As the majority of our people resided in monasteries throughout Europe, the angelologies were copied by hand and guarded by the monastic community, usually within the monastery itself. It was a fruitful period in our history. Outside the exclusive group of angelologists, whose mission was narrowly focused upon our enemies, scholarship on the general properties, powers, and purposes of angels flourished. For the angelologist the Middle Ages were a time of great advances. Awareness of angelic powers, both good and evil, rose to its prime. Shrines, statues, and paintings gave pervasive awareness of the basic principles of angelic presence to the masses of people. A sense of beauty and hope became a part of everyday life, in spite of the illnesses that ravaged the population. Although there were magicians and Gnostics and Cathars — various sects that exalted or distorted angelic reality — we were able to defend ourselves from the machinations of the hybrid creatures, or Giants, as we often refer to them. The church, for all the harm

304

it was capable of doing, protected civilization under the aegis of belief. Frankly, although my husband would say otherwise, this was the last time we had the upper hand against the Nephilim."

Dr. Seraphina paused to watch me finish my lunch, perhaps concluding that my studies had left me starved, although Gabriella — who had not eaten a thing — seemed to have lost her appetite completely. Embarrassed by my lack of manners, I wiped my hands on the linen napkin in my lap.

"How did the Nephilim attain this?" I asked.

"Their dominance?" Dr. Seraphina asked. "It is very simple. After the Middle Ages, the balance of power changed. The Nephilim began to recover lost pagan texts — the work of Greek philosophers, Sumerian mythologies, Persian scientific and medical texts — and circulate them through the intellectual centers of Europe. The result, of course, was a disaster for the church. And this was only the beginning. The Nephilim made certain that materialism became fashionable among the elite families. The Hapsburgs were just one example of how the Giants infiltrated and overwhelmed a family, the Tudors another. Although we agree with the principles of the Enlightenment, it was a major victory for the Nephilim. The French Revolution — where the separation of church and state and the illusion that humans should rely upon rationalism in lieu of the spiritual world — was another. As time passed, the Nephilistic program unfolded on earth. They promoted atheism, secular humanism, Darwinism, and the extremes of materialism. They engineered the idea of progress. They created a new religion for the masses: science.

"By the twentieth century, our geniuses were atheists and our artists relativists. The faithful had fractured into a thousand bickering denominations. Divided, we have been easy to manipulate. Unfortunately, our enemies have fully integrated into human society, developing networks of influence in government, industry, the newspapers. For hundreds of years, they have simply fed off the labor of humanity, giving nothing back, taking and taking and building their empire. Their greatest victory, however, has been to hide their presence from us. They have made us believe we are free."

"And we are not?" I asked.

"Look around you, Celestine," Dr. Seraphina said, growing irritated by my naïve questions. "Our entire academy is being disbanded and forced underground. We are utterly helpless in the face of their advances. The Nephilim seek out human weaknesses, latching on to the most power-hungry and ambitious; then they advance their causes through these figures. Luckily, the Nephilim are limited in their power. They can be out-smarted."

"How are you so certain?" Gabriella asked. "Perhaps it is humanity who will be out-smarted."

"It is entirely possible," Dr. Seraphina said, studying Gabriella. "But Raphael and I will do everything in our power to prevent it from happening. The First Angelological Expedition marked the beginning of the effort. Father Clematis, the erudite and brave man who led the expedition, dictated his account of his efforts to find the lyre. The account of this journey was lost for many centuries. Raphael, as you surely know, recovered it. We will use it to find the location of the gorge."

The momentous discovery of the account of Clematis's expedition was legendary among those students who adored the Valkos. Dr. Raphael Valko had recovered Father Clematis's journal in 1919, in a village in northern Greece, where it had been buried among papers for many centuries. He'd been a young scholar at the time, with no distinction. The discovery catapulted him to the highest levels of angelological circles. The text was a valuable account of the expedition, but, most important, it offered the hope that the Valkos might reenact Clematis's journey. If the precise coordinates of the cavern could have been discerned in the text, the Valkos would certainly have embarked upon their own expedition years ago.

"I thought Raphael's translation fell out of favor," Gabriella said, an observation that, no matter how true, struck me as insolent. Dr. Seraphina, however, appeared unfazed.

"The society has studied this text extensively, trying to understand exactly what happened during the expedition. But you are right, Gabriella. Ultimately, we have found Clematis's account to be barren."

"Why?" I asked, astonished that such a significant text could be disregarded.

"Because it is an imprecise document. The most important portion of the account was taken down during the final hours of Clematis's life, when he was half mad from the travails of his journey to the cave. Father Deopus, the man who transcribed Clematis's account, could not have captured every detail accurately. He did not draw a map, and the original that brought Clematis to the gorge was not found with his papers. After many attempts we have accepted the sad truth that the map must have been lost in the cave itself."

"What I do not understand," Gabriella said, "is how Clematis could fail to create a copy. It is the most basic procedure in any expedition."

"Clearly something went terribly wrong," Dr. Seraphina said. "Father Clematis returned to Greece in a state of distress and fell into severe confusion for the remaining weeks of his life. His entire expedition party had perished, his supplies were gone, even the donkeys had been lost or stolen. According to the accounts of contemporaries, particularly Father Deopus, Clematis seemed like a man awoken from a dream. He ranted and prayed in a most horrible fashion, as if touched by madness. So, to answer your question, Gabriella, we understand that something happened, but we are not sure exactly what."

"But you have a theory?" Gabriella asked.

"Of course," Dr. Seraphina said, smiling. "It is all there in his account, dictated at his deathbed. My husband took great pains to translate the text precisely. I believe Clematis found exactly what he was looking for in the cavern. It was Clematis's discovery of the angels in their prison that drove the poor man mad."

I could not say why Dr. Seraphina's words caused me such agitation. I had read many secondary sources surrounding the First Angelological Expedition, and yet I was utterly terrified by the image of Clematis trapped in the depths of the earth, surrounded by otherworldly creatures.

Dr. Seraphina continued, "Some say that the First Angelological Expedition was foolhardy and unnecessary. I, as you both know, believe that the expedition was essential. It was our duty to verify that the legends surrounding the Watchers and the generation of the Nephilim were, in fact, true. The First Expedition was primarily a mission to discern the truth: Were the Watchers imprisoned in the cave of Orpheus, and, if so, were they still in possession of the lyre?"

"It is confounding that they were imprisoned for simple disobedience," Gabriella said.

"There is nothing simple about disobedience," Dr. Seraphina said sharply. "Remember that Satan was once one of the most majestic of the angels — a noble seraph until he disobeyed God's command. Not only did the Watchers disobey their orders, they brought divine technologies to earth, teaching the art of warfare to their children, who in turn imparted it to humanity. The Greek legend of Prometheus illustrates the ancient perception of this transgression. This was thought to be the most damnable of sins, as such knowledge upset the balance of postlapsarian human society. Since we have *The Book of Enoch* before us, let me read what they did to poor Azazel. It was quite awful."

Dr. Seraphina took the book Gabriella had been studying and began to read:

" 'The Archangel Raphael was told: Bind Azazel hand and foot and cast him into the darkness and split open the desert, which is in Dundael, and cast him in it. And fill the hole by covering him with rough and jagged rocks, and cover him with darkness, and let him live there forever, and cover his face that he may not see the light. And on the day of the great judgment, he shall be hurled into the fire.' "

"They can never be freed?" Gabriella asked.

"In truth, we have no idea when or if they can be set free. Our scholars' interest in the Watchers pertains only to what they can tell us about our earthly, mortal enemies," she said, removing the white gloves. "The Nephilim will stop at nothing to reclaim what was lost in the Flood. This is the catastrophe we have been trying to prevent. The Venerable Father Clematis, the most intrepid of the founding members, took it upon himself to initiate the battle against our vile enemies. His methods were flawed, and yet there is much to be learned from studying Clematis's account of his journey. I find it most fascinating, despite the mystery it leaves behind. I only hope you will read it with care one day."

Gabriella stared intently at her teacher, eyes narrowed. "Perhaps there is something in Clematis you've overlooked?" she said.

"Something new in Clematis?" Dr. Seraphina replied, amused. "It is an ambitious goal, but rather unlikely. Dr. Raphael is the preeminent scholar on the First Angelological Expedition. He and I have gone over every word of Clematis's account a thousand times and have found nothing new."

"But it *is* possible," I said, not to be outdone by Gabriella once again. "There is always a chance that new information will emerge about the location of the cave."

"Frankly, it will be a much greater use of your time if you focus upon the smaller details of our work," Dr. Seraphina said, dismissing our hopes with a wave of her hand. "Thus far the data you have collected and organized has offered the best hope for finding the cavern. Of course, you may try your luck with Clematis. However, I must warn you that he can be a great puzzle. He beckons one forward, promising to answer the mysteries of the Watchers, and then remains eerily silent. He is an angelological sphinx. If you are capable of bringing something new to light from Clematis, my dear, you will be the first to accompany me on the Second Angelic Expedition."

Throughout the remaining weeks of October, Gabriella and I spent our days in Dr. Seraphina's office, working with quiet determination as we cataloged and organized the mountains of information. The intensity of our schedule and the passion with which I strove to understand the materials before me left me too exhausted to ponder Gabriella's increasingly strange behavior. She spent little time at our apartment and no longer attended the Valkos' lectures. Her work on cataloging had fallen off so that she came to Dr. Seraphina's office only a few days a week, while I was there every day. It was a relief to be so occupied as to forget the rift that had developed between us. For a month I charted mathematical data relating to the depth of Balkan geologic formations, a task that was so tedious I began to wonder at its benefit. Yet despite the seemingly endless stream of facts the Valkos had collected, I carried on without complaint, knowing that there was a larger purpose at hand. The pressure of our impending move from our school buildings and the dangers of the war only added urgency to my task.

On a sleepy afternoon in early November, the gray sky pressing upon the large windows of Dr. Seraphina's office, our professor arrived and announced that she had something of interest to show us. There was so much work before us, and Gabriella and I were so buried in papers, that we began to object to the interruption.

"Come," Dr. Seraphina said, smiling slightly, "you have worked hard all day. A short break will clear your minds."

It was an odd request to make — Dr. Seraphina had warned us often that time was running out — but a relief nonetheless. I welcomed the recess, and Gabriella, who had been agitated most of the day for reasons I could only guess, appeared to need a respite as well.

Dr. Seraphina led us away from her office, through a winding hallway and into the farthest reaches of the school, where a series of long-abandoned offices opened upon a darkened gallery. Inside, under the dim light of electric bulbs, hired assistants were fitting paintings and statues and other works of fine art into wooden boxes. Sawdust littered the marble floor so that in the waning afternoon light the room had the aspect of the ruins of an exhibition. Gabriella's characteristic appreciation of such precious works drew her to wander from object to object, looking carefully upon each, as if memorizing it before its departure. I turned to Dr. Seraphina, hoping she would explain the nature of our visit, but she was wholly absorbed in studying Gabriella. She watched her every move, weighing her reactions.

On the tables, waiting to be packed away, uncountable manuscripts lay open for view. The sight of so many precious objects collected in one place made me wish that I were with the Gabriella I had known the year before. Then our friendship had been one of intense scholarship and mutual respect. A year ago Gabriella and I would have stopped to discuss the exotic beasts leering down from the paintings — the manticore with its human face and lion's body, the harpy, the dragonlike amphisbaena, and the lascivious centaur. Gabriella would have explained everything in precise detail — how these representations were artistic depictions of evil, each one a manifestation of the devil's grotesqueries. I used to marvel at her ability to retain an encyclopedic catalog of angelology and demonology, the academic and religious symbolism that so often eluded my more mathematical mind. But now, even if Dr. Seraphina were not present, Gabriella would have kept her observations to herself. She had withdrawn from me entirely, and my longing for her insights was the desire for a friendship that had ceased to exist.

Seraphina stayed close by, watching our reactions to the objects that surrounded us, paying particular attention to Gabriella.

"This is the point of departure for all treasures this side of the Maginot Line," Dr. Seraphina finally said. "Once properly boxed and cataloged, they will be moved to safe locations throughout the country. My only worry," she said, pausing before a carved ivory diptych laid out upon a bed of blue velvet, a fan of pale tissue paper crinkled about its edges, "is that we won't get them out in time."

The anxiety Dr. Seraphina felt at the possible invasion by the Germans was evident in her manner — she had aged considerably in the past months, her beauty tempered with fatigue and worry.

"These," she said, gesturing to a number of wooden crates, each one nailed shut, "are being sent to a safe house in the Pyrenees. And this lovely depiction of Michael," she said, bringing us before a glossy Baroque painting

of an angel in Roman armor, his sword raised
and his silver breastplate gleaming, "will be
smuggled through Spain and sent to private
collectors in America, along with a number of
other precious pieces."

"You have sold them?" Gabriella asked.

"In times like these," Dr. Seraphina said,
"ownership matters less than that they are
protected."

"But won't they spare Paris?" I asked, recognizing the moment I spoke how silly the question was. "Are we really in such danger?"

"My dear," Dr. Seraphina said, her wonder
at my statement clear, "if they have their way,
there will be nothing left of Europe, let alone
Paris. Come, there are some objects I would
like to show you. It may be many years before
we see them again."

Pausing at a partially filled wooden crate,
Dr. Seraphina removed a parchment pressed
between sheets of glass and brushed its surface
free of sawdust. Drawing us close, she placed
the manuscript on the surface of a table.

"This is a medieval angelology," she said,
her image reflected in the protective glass. "It
is extensive and meticulously researched, like
our best modern angelologies, but its design
is a bit more ornate, as was the fashion of
the era."

I recognized the medieval markings of the
manuscript — the strict, orderly hierarchy of
choirs and spheres; the beautiful renderings

of golden wings, musical instruments, and halos; the careful calligraphy.

"And this tiny treasure," Dr. Seraphina said, stopping before a painting the size of an outstretched hand, "dates from the turn of the century. Quite lovely, I think, as it is painted in a modern style and focuses solely upon the representation of the Thrones — a class of angels that has been the focus of interest for angelologists for many centuries. The Thrones are of the first sphere of angels, along with the Seraphim and Cherubim. They are conduits between the physical worlds and have great powers of movement."

"Incredible," I said, gazing at the painting in what must have been obvious awe.

Dr. Seraphina began to laugh. "Yes, it is," she said. "Our collections are immense. We're building a network of libraries throughout the world — Oslo, Budapest, Barcelona — simply to house them. We are hoping to one day have a reading room in Asia. Such manuscripts remind us of the historical basis of our work. All of our efforts are rooted in these texts. We depend upon the written word. It is the light that created the universe and the light that guides us through it. Without the Word, we would not know from where we came or where we are going."

"Is that why we are so interested in preserving these angelologies?" I asked. "They are guides to the future?"

"Without them we would be lost," Seraphina said. "John said that in the Beginning there was the Word and the Word was with God. What he did not say is that in order to be meaningful the Word requires interpretation. That is our role."

"Are we here to interpret our texts?" Gabriella asked lightly. "Or to protect them?"

Dr. Seraphina gazed at Gabriella with a cool, assessing eye. "What do you believe, Gabriella?"

"I believe that if we do not protect our traditions from those who would destroy them, soon there will be nothing left to interpret."

"Ah, so you are a warrior, then," Dr. Seraphina said, challenging Gabriella. "There are always those who would put on armor and go to battle. But the real genius is in finding a way to get what you desire without dying for it."

"In times like these," Gabriella said, walking ahead, "one has no choice."

We examined a number of objects in silence until we came to a thick book placed at the center of a table. Dr. Seraphina called Gabriella over, watching her intently, as if she were reading her gestures for something, although I could not say what.

"Is it a genealogy?" I asked, examining the rows of charts drafted upon the surface. "It is filled with human names."

"Not all human," Gabriella said, stepping closer to read the text. "There are Tzaphkiel and Sandalphon and Raziel."

Squinting at the manuscript, I saw that she was correct: Angels were mixed into the human lines. "The names aren't arranged in a vertical hierarchy of spheres and choirs, but in another kind of schema."

"These diagrams are the speculative charts," Dr. Seraphina said, a gravity to her voice that made me believe she had brought us through the maze of treasures so that we might at last come to this very place. "Over the course of time, we have had Jewish, Christian, and Muslim angelologists — all three religions reserve a central place in their cosmology for angels — and we have had more unusual scholars: Gnostics, Sufis, a number of representatives from Asian religions. As you might imagine, our agents' works have deviated in crucial ways. The speculative angelologies are the work of a band of brilliant Jewish scholars from the seventeenth century who became engrossed in tracing the genealogies of Nephilistic families."

I came from a traditional Catholic family and, having been educated in a strict fashion, knew very little about the doctrines of other religions. I did know, however, that my fellow students were from many different backgrounds. Gabriella, for example, was Jewish, and Dr. Seraphina — perhaps the most empirically minded and skeptical of all my teachers aside from her husband — claimed to be agnostic, to the chagrin of many of the professors. This, however, was the first time I fully understood the range of religious affiliations incorporated into the history and canon of our discipline.

Dr. Seraphina continued, "Our angelologists studied Jewish genealogies with great care. Historically, Jewish scholars kept meticulous genealogical records due to inheritance laws, but also because they understood the essential importance of tracing one's history to the very root, so accounts can be cross-referenced and verified. When I was your age and intent upon researching the finer points of angelology, I studied Jewish genealogical practices. As a matter of fact, I recommend that all serious students learn these methods. They are marvelously precise."

Dr. Seraphina turned the pages of the book, stopping before a beautifully drawn document framed in gold leaf. "This is a genealogy of Jesus's family trees drawn in the twelfth century by one of our scholars. According to the Christian schema, Jesus was a direct descendant of Adam. Here we have Mary's family tree, as it was written by Luke — Adam, Noah, Shem, Abraham, David." Dr. Seraphina's finger traced the line down the chart. "And here is the family history of Joseph written by Matthew — Solomon, Jehoshaphat, Zerubbabel, and so on."

"Such genealogies are rather common, aren't

they?" Gabriella said. Clearly she had seen a hundred such genealogies. Since I'd had no previous exposure to such a text, my reaction could not have been more different.

"Of course," Dr. Seraphina said, "there have been many genealogies tracing how bloodlines matched Old Testament prophecies — the promises made to Adam and Abraham and Judah and Jesse and David. This one, however, is a bit different."

The names branched one to the next, creating a vast net of relations. I found it profoundly humbling to imagine how each name corresponded to a person who had lived and died, had worshipped and struggled, perhaps without ever knowing his or her purpose in the greater web of history.

Dr. Seraphina touched the page, her nail gleaming in the soft overhead light. Hundreds of names were written in colored inks, so many thin branches lifting from a slight stalk. "After the Flood, Noah's son Shem founded the Semitic race. Jesus, of course, emerged from that line. Ham founded the races of Africa. Japheth — or, as you learned in Raphael's lecture last week, the creature posing as Japheth — has been credited with the propagation of the European race, including the Nephilim. What Raphael did not emphasize in his lecture, and something I believe to be of great importance for more advanced students to understand, is that the genetic dispersion of humankind and Nephilim is much more complex than it first appears. Japheth went on to father many children with his human wife, resulting in an array of descendants. Some of these children were fully Nephilistic, some were hybrids. The children whom Japheth — the human Japheth, killed by the Nephilistic creature who posed as Japheth, that is — had fathered before his death were fully human. And so the descendants of Japheth were human, Nephilistic, and hybrid. Their intermarrying brought forth the population of Europe."

"It is so complicated," I said, trying to work out the various groups. "I can hardly sort through it."

"Now you've hit upon the very reason for keeping these genealogical charts," Dr. Seraphina said. "We would be in something of a mess without them."

"I have read that a number of scholars believe that Japheth's bloodline mixed with Shem's," Gabriella said, pointing to a branch of the speculative genealogy and isolating three names: Eber, Nathan, and Amon. "Here and here and here."

I leaned in close to read the names. "How can they be sure?"

Gabriella smiled, something cruel in her manner, as if anticipating my question. "I believe there is documentation of some sort but in all truth they cannot be one hundred percent sure."

"That is why this is called *speculative* angelology," Dr. Seraphina said.

"But many scholars believe it," Gabriella said. "It is a valid and ongoing part of angelological work."

"Surely modern angelologists do not believe this," I said, trying to hide my intense reaction to this information. My religious beliefs were strong even then, and such crude speculation about Christ's paternity was not accepted doctrine. The chart, which only seconds before had seemed wonderful, now upset me a great deal. "The idea that Jesus had the blood of the Watchers is absurd."

"Perhaps," Dr. Seraphina said, "but there is a whole area of angelological study about this very subject. It is called angelmorphism, and it deals strictly with the idea that Jesus Christ was not even human, but an angel. After all, the Virgin Birth occurred after the Angel Gabriel's visit."

Gabriella said, "I believe I've read something about that. The Gnostics believed in Jesus's angelic origins as well."

"There are — or there were, I should say — hundreds of books in our library about it," Dr. Seraphina said. "Personally, I don't care who Jesus's ancestors were. My concern is entirely elsewhere. This, for example, is something I find utterly fascinating, speculative or not," Dr. Seraphina said, leading us to the next table, where a book lay open as if waiting for our examination. "It is a Nephilistic angelology that begins with the Watchers, moves through Noah's family, and branches out with great detail throughout the ruling families of Europe. It is called *The Book of Generations*."

I glanced over the page, reading the descending ladder of names as the angelology moved through the generations. Although I understood the power and the influence the Nephilim had upon human activity, I was taken aback to discover that the family lines moved through nearly every royal bloodline in Europe — the Capetians, the Hapsburgs, the Stuarts, the Carolingians. It was like reading the history of Europe dynasty by dynasty.

Dr. Seraphina said, "We cannot be completely certain that these lines were infiltrated, but there is enough proof to convince most of us that the great families of Europe have been — and still are — deeply infected with the blood of the Nephilim."

Gabriella hung upon all that Seraphina said as if she were memorizing a timeline of dates for an examination or — and this was more apt to be at the heart of it — studying our teacher to discover her motivation for bringing us to this strange text. At last Gabriella said, "But the names of nearly all the noble families are listed. Are they all implicated in the terrors they have perpetuated?"

"Indeed. The Nephilim were the kings

and queens of Europe, their desires shaping the lives of millions of people. They kept their stronghold through intermarriage, primogeniture, and brute military force," Dr. Seraphina said. "Their kingdoms collected taxes, slaves, properties, and all kinds of mineral and agricultural wealth, attacking any group that acquired even the smallest degree of independence. Their influence was so unrivaled during the medieval period that they did not even bother to hide themselves as they once had. According to accounts of angelologists of the thirteenth century, there were cults dedicated to fallen angels that were fully orchestrated by the Nephilim. Many of the evils attributed to witches — the accused were nearly always women — were actually part of Nephilistic rituals. They believed in ancestor worship and celebrated the return of the Watchers. These families still exist today. In fact," Dr. Seraphina said, looking at Gabriella with a strange, almost accusatory look, "we are keeping very close watch on them. These families in particular are under surveillance."

While I glanced at the page and saw a number of names, none of which meant anything in particular to me, the effect of Seraphina's words upon Gabriella was intense. As she read the names, she stepped back in fright. Her manner reminded me of the trance of horror I had witnessed come over her during Dr. Raphael's lecture, only now she seemed on the verge of hysteria.

"You are wrong," Gabriella said, her voice rising with each word. "We are not watching them. They are watching us."

With this, she turned and ran from the room. I stared after her, wondering what could have caused such an emotional outburst. It seemed to me that she had gone mad. Turning to the manuscript once again, I saw nothing more than a page filled with family names, most of them unknown to me, some of prestigious ancient families. It was as unremarkable as any page from any of the history books we had studied together, none of which had caused Gabriella any measure of distress.

Dr. Seraphina, however, appeared to understand Gabriella's reaction exactly. In fact, from the sanguine manner in which she had assessed Gabriella's reactions, it was as if Dr. Seraphina had not only expected her to recoil from the book but had planned it. Seeing my confusion, Dr. Seraphina closed the book and tucked it under her arm.

"What happened?" I asked, as astonished by her manner as by Gabriella's inexplicable behavior.

"It pains me to tell you," Dr. Seraphina said, leading me from the room, "but I believe that our Gabriella has gotten herself into terrible trouble."

My first impulse was to confess everything to Dr. Seraphina. The burden of Gabriella's double life and the pall it had cast over my days had become nearly too much for me to bear. But just as I was about to speak, I was startled into silence. A dark figure swept before us, stepping from a shadowy corridor like a black-cloaked demon. I caught my breath, momentarily unbalanced by the interruption. After a brief examination, I saw that it was the heavily veiled nun — the council member I had met in the Athenaeum months before. She blocked our path.

"May I speak with you a moment, Dr. Seraphina?" The nun spoke in a low, lisping manner that I found, to my embarrassment, instantly repulsive. "There are some questions we have regarding the shipment to the United States."

It comforted me to see that Dr. Seraphina took the nun's presence in stride, speaking to her with her usual authority. "What questions could there be at this late hour? All has been arranged."

"Quite correct," the nun said. "But I wish to make certain that the paintings in the gallery are to be shipped to the United States along with the icons."

"Yes, of course," Dr. Seraphina said, following the nun into the hallway, where a large gallery of crates and boxes awaited shipment. "They are to be received by our contact in New York."

Looking over the crates, I saw that many of

them had been marked for shipping.

Dr. Seraphina said, "The shipment will leave tomorrow. We need only to be sure that everything is here and that it gets to the port."

As the nun and Dr. Seraphina continued their discussion of the shipment and how they had, in the increasingly tightened schedule of vessels leaving France's harbors, secured the evacuation of our most priceless objects, I returned to the hallway. Holding back the words I'd wished to speak, I walked away in silence.

Moving through the dark, stone corridors, I passed empty classrooms and abandoned lecture halls, my footsteps echoing through the pervasive silence that had fallen over the rooms months before. The Athenaeum proved equally still. The librarians had left for the evening, turning out the lights and locking the doors. I used my key — given by Dr. Seraphina at the outset of my studies — to let myself in. As I opened the doors and examined the long, shadowy room, I felt utterly relieved to be alone. It was not the first time I'd felt thankful that the library was empty — I often found myself there after midnight, continuing my work after everyone else had left the school — but it was the first time that I had come in desperation.

Empty shelves lined the walls, the occasional volumes tipped and stacked at random. On every side I found boxes of books waiting to be moved from our school to secure locations throughout France. Where these locations might be, I did not know, but I could see that we would need many cellars to hide such a large collection. My hands shook as I went through one of the boxes. The books were in such a state of disarray that I began to worry that I might never find the one I had come for. After some minutes of searching, my panic growing at each disappointment, I at last located a box of Dr. Raphael Valko's original works and translations. In keeping with Dr. Raphael's disposition, the contents were arranged in no discernible order. I found a folio containing detailed maps of various caves and gorges, sketches made during exploratory expeditions through the mountain ranges of Europe — the Pyrenees in 1923, the Balkans in 1925, the Urals in 1930, and the Alps in 1936 — along with pages of script relating to the history of each mountain chain. I examined annotated texts and bundles of lecture notes, commentaries and pedagogical guides. I looked at the title and date of each of the works Dr. Raphael had produced, finding that he'd written even more books and folios than I had imagined. And yet after I had opened and closed every one of Dr. Raphael's texts, I had not found the only one I hoped to read: The translation of Clematis's journey to the cave of disobedient angels was not in the Athenaeum.

Leaving the books scattered upon the table, I collapsed into the hard seat of a chair and tried to pull myself out of the fog of disappointment that had fallen over me. As if defying my efforts, tears welled up in my eyes, dissolving the dim Athenaeum into a wash of pale color. My ambition for advancement consumed me. Uncertainty about my abilities, about my place in our school, and about the future weighed heavily upon my mind. I wished my fate to be known, contracted, sealed, and set down so that I might follow it dutifully. Above all else I wished for purpose and utility. The very notion that I was not worthy of my calling, that I might be sent back to my parents in the countryside, or that I might fail to secure a place among the scholars I admired filled me with dread.

Leaning upon the wooden table, I buried my face in my arms, closing my eyes and lapsing into a momentary state of despair. I do not know how long I remained thus, but soon I sensed a movement in the room, the slightest change in the texture of the air. My friend's distinct perfume — an Oriental scent of vanilla and labdanum — alerted me to Gabriella's presence. I lifted my eyes and saw, through the wash of tears, a blur of scarlet fabric so shiny it appeared a swath of inlaid rubies.

"What is the matter?" Gabriella said. The

sheet of jeweled fabric transformed, once my vision cleared, into a sleeveless bias-cut satin dress of such liquid beauty that I could do nothing but gape at it. My obvious astonishment only irritated Gabriella. She slid into a chair opposite me, tossing a beaded bag onto the table. A necklace of cut gemstones encircled her throat, and a pair of long black opera gloves rose to her elbows, covering the scar on her forearm. The air in the Athenaeum had grown cold, but Gabriella appeared unaffected by the chill — even with her thin, sleeveless gown and transparent silk stockings her skin retained a glow of warmth while I had begun to shiver.

"Tell me, Celestine," Gabriella said. "What has happened? Are you ill?"

"I am quite well," I replied, composing myself as best I could. I was not used to being the object of her scrutiny — in fact, she had taken no interest in me at all in the past weeks — and so, hoping to divert attention from myself, I said, "You are going somewhere?"

"A party," she said without meeting my eye, a clear indication that she would be meeting with her lover.

"What kind of party?" I asked.

"It has nothing to do with our studies and would not interest you," she said, ending all possibility of further questioning. "But tell me: What are you doing here? Why are you so distraught?"

"I have been looking for a text."

"Which one?"

"Something to help me with the geological tables I have been creating," I said, knowing even as I spoke that I sounded unconvincing.

Gabriella glanced beyond me at the books I had left upon the table and, seeing that they were all written by Dr. Raphael Valko, guessed my objective. "Clematis's journal isn't circulated, Celestine."

"I have just discovered this fact," I said, wishing I had returned Dr. Raphael's books to the crates.

"You should know that they would never keep such a text here in the open."

"Then where is it?" I asked, my agitation growing by the second. "In Dr. Seraphina's office? In the vault?"

"Clematis's account of the First Angelological Expedition contains very important information," Gabriella said, smiling with pleasure at her advantage. "Its location is a secret that only a very few are allowed to know."

"So *you* have read it?" I said, my jealousy at Gabriella's access to restricted texts causing me to lose all sense of caution. "How is it that you, who seem to care so little for our studies, have read Clematis and I, who have dedicated everything to our cause, cannot so much as touch it?"

I immediately regretted what I'd said. The silence we had forged was an uncomfortable truce, but the artifice had allowed me to progress with my work.

Gabriella stood, took her beaded bag from the table and, her voice unnaturally calm, said, "You think that you understand what you have seen, but it is more complicated than it appears."

"I should think it rather obvious that you are involved with an older man," I said. "And I suspect that Dr. Seraphina believes as much, too."

For a moment I believed that Gabriella would turn and leave, as had become her habit when she felt cornered. Instead she stood before me, defiant. "I wouldn't speak of it to Dr. Seraphina, or to anyone else, if I were you."

Feeling I was in a position of power at last, I pressed my point. "And why not?"

"If anyone were to discover what you think you know," Gabriella said, "the greatest harm would befall all of us."

Although I could not fully understand the meaning of her threat, the urgency in her voice and the genuine terror of her expression stopped me cold. We had come to an impasse, neither one knowing how to proceed.

At last Gabriella broke the silence. "It is not impossible to gain access to Clematis's account," she said. "If one wishes to read it, one only need know where to look."

"I thought the text wasn't circulated," I said.

"It isn't," Gabriella answered. "And I should not help you to find it, especially when it is clearly not in my best interest. But you look as though you might be willing to help me, too."

I met her gaze, wondering exactly what she could mean by this.

"My proposal is this," Gabriella said, leading me from the Athenaeum and into the dark hallway of the school. "I will tell you how to find the text, and you, in turn, will remain silent. You will not mention a word to Seraphina about me or your speculations about my activities. You will not speak of my comings and goings from the apartment. Tonight I will be out for some time. If anyone comes to the apartment for me, you will say that you don't know where I am."

"You are asking me to lie to our teachers."

"No," she said. "I am asking that you tell the truth. You *don't* know where I will be this evening."

"But why?" I asked. "Why are you doing this?"

The faintest look of weariness appeared in Gabriella's features, a hint of desperation that made me believe that she would open herself to me and confess everything, a hope that was crushed the moment it emerged. "I don't have time for this," she said, impatient. "Do you agree or not?"

I did not need to say a word. Gabriella understood me perfectly. I would do anything to gain access to Clematis's text.

A series of exposed electric bulbs illuminated our passage to the medieval wing of the school. Gabriella moved quickly, her platform shoes tapping the quick, erratic rhythm of her footfall, and when she stopped, halting abruptly midstep, I stumbled against her, breathless.

Although clearly annoyed by my clumsiness, Gabriella didn't utter a sound. Instead she turned toward a door, one of hundreds of identical doors throughout the building, each one the same size and color, without numbers or nameplates to indicate where it led.

"Come," she said, looking to the arch above the door, an assemblage of crumbling limestone blocks that rose to a peak. "You are taller than I am. Perhaps you can reach the keystone."

Stretching as best I could, I brushed my fingers against the grainy stone. To my surprise, the block moved under the pressure of my touch and, with a bit of wiggling, slid from its place, leaving a wedge of open space. At Gabriella's instruction I reached inside and removed a cold metal object the size of a penknife.

"It is a key," I said, holding it before me, astonished. "How did you know it was here?"

"It will get you into the school's underground storage," Gabriella said, gesturing for me to replace the stone. "Through this door there is a set of stairs. Follow it down and you will find a second door. The key will unlock that door. It is the entrance to the Valkos' private chambers — Dr. Raphael's translation of Clematis's account is kept here."

I tried to recall hearing anything about such a space and could not. It made sense, of course, that we would create a secure location for our treasures, and it answered the question of where the books from the Athenaeum were being stored. I wanted to ask more — to demand that she explain the details of this hidden space. But Gabriella raised a hand to cut off all questioning. "I am late and haven't the time to explain. I cannot lead you to the book myself, but I'm certain your curiosity will assist you in finding what you are looking for. Go. And remember when you are finished to return the key to its hiding place and do not speak of this evening to anyone."

With this, Gabriella turned and walked down the hall, her red satin dress catching the weak light. I wanted to call for her to come back, to guide me into the subterranean chambers, but she was gone. Only the slightest odor of her perfume remained.

Following Gabriella's instructions, I opened the door and peered into the darkness. A kerosene lamp hung from a hook at the top of the stairs, its fluted glass chimney charred black from smoke. I lit the wick and held it before me. A set of rough-hewn stone steps fell downward at a steep angle. Each lozenge of stone was frosted in moss, making the passage dangerously slippery. From the dampness of the air and the smell of mold, it felt to me as though I were descending step-by-step into the cellar of my family's stone farmhouse, a vast, dank underground bunker stockpiled with thousands of bottles of aging wine.

At the bottom of the staircase, I found an iron door, barred like the entrance to a prison cell. To either side of it, brick passageways opened and receded into an almost pure darkness. I raised the lamp so that I might see the spaces beyond. Where the brick had crumbled, I could make out patches of pale, unquarried limestone, the very rock that formed the foundation of our city. The key unfastened the lock with ease, so the only obstacle that remained to me was the overpowering urge to turn, walk up the steps, and go back to the familiar world above.

It did not take long before I came upon a series of rooms. Although my lamp did not allow me to see with great clarity, I found that the first room had been filled with crates of weapons — Lugers and Colt .45s and M1 Garands. There were boxes of medical supplies, blankets, and clothing — the items we would surely need in an extended conflict. In another room I discovered many of the very crates I had observed being packed in the

Athenaeum weeks before, only now they had been nailed shut. Prying them open without tools would be next to impossible.

Continuing through the darkness of the brick passage, the lamp growing heavier with each step, I began to understand the enormous scale of the angelologists' move underground. I had not imagined how elaborate and calculated our resistance would be. We had transferred all the necessities of life to below the city. There were beds and makeshift toilets and water pipes and a number of small kerosene stoves. Weapons, food, medicines — everything of value resided under Montparnasse, hidden in burrows and tunnels carved from the limestone. For the first time, I realized that, once the battle began, many would not flee the city but move into these chambers and fight.

After examining a number of these cells, I stepped into another chiseled, damp space, less a storage area than a warren delved into the soft limestone. Here I found many objects, some of which I recognized from visits to Dr. Raphael's office, and I knew at once that I had found the Valkos' private chamber. In the corner, under a heavy cotton tarpaulin, there was a table stacked with books. Light from the kerosene lamp fell over the dusty room.

I discovered the text without much trouble, though to my surprise it appeared to be less a book than a sheaf of notes bound together. The volume was no bigger than a pamphlet, with a hand-stitched binding and a plain cover. It was light as a crêpe in my hand, too insubstantial, I thought, to contain anything important. Opening it, I saw that the text had been handwritten on transparent foolscap in blotched ink, each letter scratched into the paper by the uneven pressure of a careless hand. Running my finger over the letters, feeling the indentations on the paper and brushing the dust from its pages, I read: *Notes on the First Angelological Expedition of A.D. 925 by the Venerable Father Clematis of Thrace, Translated from the Latin and Annotated by Dr. Raphael Valko.*

Below these words, pressed into the pulpy surface of the page, was a golden seal containing the image of a lyre, a symbol I had not seen before but would from that day forth understand to be at the heart of our mission.

Holding the pamphlet close to my chest, suddenly afraid that it might dissolve before I had the chance to read its contents, I placed the lamp on a smooth stretch of the limestone floor and sat beside it. The light fell over my fingers, and when I opened the pamphlet once more, Dr. Raphael's handwriting became distinct. Clematis's account of his expedition captivated me from the first word.

Notes on The First Angelological Expedition of A.D. 925 by The Venerable Father Clematis of Thrace

Translated from the Latin and Annotated by Dr. Raphael Valko

I*

Blessed be the servants of His Divine vision on Earth! May the Lord, who planted the seed of our mission, bring it to fruition!

II

Our mules heavy with provisions and our

*While the original manuscript of the Venerable Clematis' expedition was not organized in discrete sections, the translator has imposed a system of numbered entries for this edition. Such divisions have been created for the purpose of clarity. The original fragments — for the recovered notebook cannot be designated anything other than the roughest of personal writings, scraps of thoughts and reflections jotted down during the course of the journey perhaps intended as a mnemonic device for the eventual composition of a book about the first quest to locate the fallen angels — were without system. The imposed divisions attempt to divide the notebook chronologically and offer a semblance of cohesion to the manuscript. — R.V.

souls light with expectation, we began our journey through the provinces of the Hellenes, below the mighty Moesia and into Thracia. The roads, well-maintained and regular thoroughfares built by Rome, signaled our arrival in Christendom. Yet, despite the gilding of civilization, the threat of thievery remains. It has been many years since I last set foot in the mountainous homeland of my father and his father's father. My native tongue will surely ring strange, accustomed as I am to the language of Rome. As we begin our ascent into the mountains, I fear that even my robes and the seals of the church will do little to protect us once we leave the larger settlements. I pray that we meet few villagers on our journey to the mountain paths. We have no weapons and will have little recourse but to depend upon the goodwill of strangers.

III

As we paused by the roadside on our way up the mountain, Brother Francis, a most ardent scholar, spoke to me of the distress that has come to haunt him regarding our mission. Taking me aside, he confessed that he believes our mission to be the work of dark spirits, a seduction of the disobedient angels upon our minds. His unrest is not uncommon. Indeed, many of our brothers have expressed reservations about the expedition, but Francis' assertion chilled me to my very soul. Rather than question him about this sentiment, I listened to his fears, understanding that his words were another sign of the growing fatigue in the search. In opening my ear to his cares, I took them upon myself, lightening his heavy spirit. This is the burden and the responsibility of an elder brother, but my role is even more crucial now, as we prepare for what will surely be our most difficult journey. Shaking away the temptation to remonstrate with Brother Francis, I labored through the remaining hours of travel in silence.

Later, in my solitude, I strove to understand Brother Francis' distress, praying for guidance and wisdom so that I might help him overcome his doubts. It is well known that scholars have missed the mark entirely in past expeditions. I am certain that this will soon change. Yet, Francis' phrase "brotherhood of dreamers" plagues my thoughts. The faintest breeze of doubt begins to shake my insuperable faith in our mission. What, I wonder to myself, if we have been foolhardy in our efforts? How are we to be certain that our mission is one with God's? The kernel of disbelief growing in my mind is easily ground down, however, when I think of the necessity of our work. The battle has been fought for generations before us and will continue for generations after. We must encourage our young men, despite the recent losses. Fear is to be expected. It is natural that the incident at Roncesvalles,* which all have studied, is on their minds. And still, my faith does not allow me to doubt that God moves behind our actions, animating our bodies and spirits as we move up the mountain. I will persist in my belief that hope will soon revive among us. We must have faith that this journey, unlike

*The incident at the pass at Roncesvalles occurred during an exploratory mission to the Pyrenees in A.D. 778. Little is known about the journey, except that the mission lost the majority of its men due to an ambush. Witnesses described the attackers as giants with extrahuman strength, superior weaponry, and astonishing physical beauty — descriptions perfectly in line with contemporary portraits of the Nephilim. One testimony claims that winged figures descended upon the giants in a blaze of fire, suggesting a counterattack by archangels, a claim that scholars have studied with some fascination, as this would signal only the third angelophony for the purpose of battle. An alternate version is recorded in *La Chanson de Roland,* an account that differs significantly from angelological records.

our recent miscalculations, will end in success.*

IV

On the fourth night of the journey, as the fire burnt to embers and our humble party sat together after our meal, discussion turned to the history of our enemy. One of the young brothers asked how it had come to pass that our land, from the tip of Iberia to the Ural Mountains,† came to be so colonized by the dark spawn of angels and women. How did we, humble servants of God, come to be charged with the cleansing of the Lord's Earth? Brother Francis, whose melancholy has so affected my thoughts of late, wondered aloud how God would allow the evil ones to infest His dominion with their presence. How, he asked, can pure good exist in the presence of pure evil? And so, as the evening air grew colder and the frozen moon hung in the night sky, I related to our party how these evil seeds were sowed in holy soil:

*The Venerable Fathers' search for artifacts and relics throughout Europe is well documented in Frederic Bonn's *The Sacred Missions of the Venerable Fathers: A.D. 925–954,* which includes copies of the maps, omens, and oracles used in such journeys.
†Modern place-names have been substituted for those of the tenth century wherever applicable.

In the decades after the Flood ceased, Japheth's sons and daughters of purely human provenance separated from the false Japheth's sons and daughters of angelic provenance, forming two branches of one tree, one pure and the other poisoned, one weak and the other strong. Along the great north and south sea lanes they scattered, taking root in the rich alluvial gulfs. They swept over the alpine mountains in tremendous flocks, settling like bats at the highest reaches of Europa. Along the rocky coasts and the vast fertile plains they moored, sinking into the shores of river passages — the Danube, the Volga, the Rhine, the Dniester, the Ebro, the Seine — until every region had become filled with the spawn of Japheth. Where they rested, settlements grew. Despite common ancestry, there remained a deep distrust between the two groups. The cruelty, avarice, and physical power of the Nephilim led to the gradual enslavement of their human brothers. Europe, the Giants claimed, was their birthright.

The first generations of Japheth's tainted heirs lived in great health and happiness, dominating every river, mountain, and plain of the continent, their power over their weaker brothers secure. Within decades, however, a flaw appeared in their race, as sharp as a fissure across the gleaming surface of a mirror. A baby was born that appeared weaker than the others — tiny, mewling, it was unable to gather enough air in its weak lungs to cry. As the baby grew, they saw that it was smaller than the others, slower, and had a susceptibility to illness unknown in their race. This child was human, born in the likeness of their great-great-grandmothers, the Daughters of Men.* It took noth-

*The recent recovery and systemization of the work of Gregor Mendel, Augustinian monk and member of the Angelological Scholars of Vienna from 1857 to 1866, has done much to shed light upon what had been a millennial mystery to historians of Nephilistic and human growth in Europe. One can see that, according to the Mendelian chromosome theory of heredity, recessive human traits from the Daughters of Men were carried through Japheth's Nephilistic line, waiting to reemerge in future generations. Although the chromosomal repercussions of the human-Nephilistic cross strike modern investigators as an obvious result of such breeding, the emergence of human beings into the pool of Nephilim most surely came as a great shock to the population and was considered to be the work of God. In earlier writings, the Venerable Clematis himself had written that human children were insinuated into the Nephilistic line of Japheth by God Himself. The Nephilim, of course, had quite a different interpretation of such genetic calamity.

ing — not beauty or strength or angelic form — from the Watchers. When the child reached manhood, he was stoned to death.

For many generations, this baby was an anomaly. Then, God desired to populate the dominions of Japheth with his own children. He sent a multitude of human babies to the Nephilim, revivifying the Holy Spirit upon the fallow earth. In their first appearances, these beings often died in infancy. With time, they learned to care for the weak children, nursing them to their third year before allowing them to join with the other, stronger children.* If they survived into adulthood, they grew to be four heads shorter than their parents. They began to age and decline in the third decade of life, and die before the eighth. Human women died in childbirth. Sickness and disease required the development of medicines, and even when treated, humans lived for only a fraction of the years of their Nephilistic brothers. The inviolate dominion of

*There are various documents pertaining to the superior physical strength of Nephilistic offspring and the genetic inevitability of the emergence of humans in the children of Watchers and women, particularly Dr. G. D. Holland's survey of Nephilistic demographics in *Human and Angelic Bodies: A Medical Inquiry* (Gallimard, 1926).

the Nephilim had been corrupted.*

Over time, human children married others of their kind and the human race grew alongside the Nephilistic. Despite their physical inferiority, Japheth's pure children persevered under the rule of their Nephilistic brothers. The occasional intermarriage occurred between the groups, bringing further hybridization to the race, but these unions were discouraged. When a human child was born to Nephilim, it was sent outside the walls of the city, where it died in the elements among humans. When a Nephilistic child was born to human civilization, it would be taken from its parents and assimilated into the master race.†

*Among certain tribes of Nephilim, the practice of sacrificing human children became popular. It is speculated that this was both a means of controlling the growing human population — which was a threat to Nephilistic society — and an appeal to God to forgive the sins of the Watchers, still imprisoned deep below the earth.

†Although this is not the first appearance of the term "master race" in discussion of the Nephilim, as there are numerous instances of Nephilistic creatures labeled as belonging to a "master race" or "super race," it was certainly the most famous and oft-quoted source. Ironically, Clematis' notion of a super race or superman — held by angelologists to

Soon, the Nephilim receded to castles and manor houses. They built fortifications of granite, mountaintop retreats, sanctuaries of luxury and power. Although subservient, God's children were graced with divine protection. Their minds were sharp, their souls blessed, and their wills strong. As the two races lived side by side, the Nephilim receded behind wealth and fortifications. Human beings, left to suffer under the strains of poverty and illness, became slaves to invisible, powerful masters.

V

At dawn, we rose and walked many hours along the precipitous path to the top of the mountain, the sun rising from behind the towering stone pinnacles, casting a glorious golden emanation over creation. Provided with sturdy mules, thick leather sandals, and pristine weather, we carried forth. By midmorning, a village filled with stone mountain houses arose over a crag,

---

be the mark of Nephilistic self-mythology — was appropriated and reinvented in more modern times by scholars such as Count Arthur de Gobineau, Friedrich Nietzsche, and Arthur Schopenhauer as a component of human philosophical thought, which in turn was used in Nephilistic circles to support the racial theory of die Herrenrasse, a notion that has grown in popularity in contemporary Europe.

the orange clay tiles layered above the slate. After we'd consulted our map, it was apparent that we had arrived at the highest reach of the mountain in proximity to the gorge the locals call Gyaurskoto Burlo. Taking refuge in the home of a villager, we bathed, ate, and rested before inquiring after a guide to the cavern. Straightaway a shepherd was brought before me. Short and thick in the way of Thracian mountain people, his beard flecked white but his body strong, the shepherd listened intently as I described our mission into the gorge. I found him intelligent, articulate, and willing, although he made it plain that he would take us to the floor of the gorge but no farther. After some discussion, we agreed upon a price. The shepherd promised to supply equipment, saying he would lead us there the next morning.

We discussed our prospects over a meal of klin and dried meat, a simple but hearty repast to give us strength for the next day's journey. I placed a parchment on the surface of the table, opening it for the others to see. My brothers leaned close to the table, straining to discern the light shadings of the ink drawing.

"The site is here," I said, dragging a finger over the map, along a wedge of mountains signified by dark blue ink. "We should have no trouble crossing."

"Yet," one of my brothers said, his unkempt beard brushing the table as he reached across it, "how can we be certain this is the correct location?"

"There have been sightings," I attested.

"There have been sightings in the past," Brother Francis said. "Peasants see with different eyes. Their visions most often lead to nothing."

"Villagers claim to have seen the creatures."

"If we follow the fantastic stories of mountain peasants, we will be traveling to every village in Anatolia."

"In my humble opinion, it is worth our attention," I replied. "According to our brothers in Thrace, the mouth of the cave cuts away sharply into an abyss. Deep below, there flows an underground river, much as it is described by legend. Villagers claim to have heard emanations at the edge of the abyss."

"Emanations?"

"Music," I said, striving to remain cautious in my assertions. "The villagers hold feasts at the mouth of the cave so that they might hear the sound, however faint, rising from the cavern. They say the music has an unusual power over the villagers. The sick are made well. The blind see. The crippled walk."

"This is most wondrous," Brother Francis said.

"The music rises from the depths of the earth, and it will lead us forth."

Despite my confidence in our cause, my hand trembles at the dangers of the abyss. Years of preparation have bolstered my will, and still I fear the prospect of failure looming over me. How past failures haunt my memory! How my lost brothers visit my thoughts! My enduring faith drives me forward, and the balm of God's grace soothes my troubled soul.* Tomorrow, we descend the gorge at sunrise.

VI

As the world turns back to the sun, so the corrupted earth returns to the light of Grace. As the stars illumine the dark sky, so the children of God will one day rise through the haze of injustice, free at last of evil masters.

*It is at this juncture that Clematis' handwriting gives way to a faltering scribble. This corruption is due, no doubt, to the extreme pressure of the mission at hand, but also, perhaps, to a growing fatigue. The Venerable Father was nearly sixty years old in the year A.D. 925, and his strength must surely have been compromised by the journey up the mountain. The translator has taken great care in his attempt to decipher the text and render it accessible to the modern reader.

VII

In the darkness of my despair, I turn to
Boethius as an eye turns to a flame — my
Lord, my excellence hath been lost to the
Tartarean Cave.*

VIII†

I am a man forsaken. Through burned

---

*Here Clematis refers to the famous line of *The Con-
solation of Philosophy*, 3.55, associated with the myth
of Orpheus and Eurydice: *For he who overcomes
should turn back his gaze toward the Tartarean cave,
Whatever excellence he takes with him he loses when
he looks below.*

†Hereafter, the remaining sections of Clematis' account are written in the hand of a monk, Father
Deopus, who was assigned to care for Clematis in the
immediate aftermath of the expedition. At Clematis'
request, Deopus sat at his side for the purpose of
dictation. According to Deopus' personal account
of the days he spent at Clematis' deathbed, when he
was not occupied as a scribe, he made tinctures and
compresses he placed over Clematis' body, to ease
the pain of his charred skin. That Deopus was able
to capture so thorough an account of the disastrous
First Angelological Expedition under such conditions, when the Venerable Father's injuries surely
prevented communication, is a great benefit to scholars. The discovery of Father Deopus' transcription
in 1919 opened the door to further scholarly inquiry
into the First Angelological Expedition.

lips I speak, my voice ringing hollow in my ears. My body lies broken; my charred flesh oozes with gaping sores. Hope, that ethereal and airy angel upon whose wings I rose to meet my wretched fate, is crushed evermore. Only my will to relate the horror I have seen drives me to open my cankered, scorched lips. For you, future seeker of freedom, future acolyte of justice, I tell of my misfortune.

The morning of our journey broke cold and clear. As is my custom, I woke many hours before sunrise and, leaving the others to their slumber, found my way to the hearth of the small house. The mistress of the house busied herself about the humble space, breaking twigs for the fire. A pot of barley bubbled above the flames. Endeavoring to make myself useful, I offered to stir the mixture, warming myself over the fire as I did so. How the memories of my childhood flooded upon me as I stood over the hearth. Fifty years ago, I was a boy with arms as thin as saplings, assisting my mother in this same domestic task, listening to her hum as she wrung clothing in basins of clean water. My mother — how long had it been since I had thought of her goodness? And my father, with his love of the Book and his devotion to our Lord — how had I lived so many years without recalling his gentleness?

These thoughts dissipated as my brothers, perhaps smelling their breakfast cooking, descended to the hearth. Together, we ate. In the light of the fire, we packed our sacks: rope, chisel, and hammer, vellum and ink, a sharp knife made of a fine alloy, and a roll of cotton cloth, for bandages. With the sun's rising, we bade our hosts good-bye and set out to meet our guide.

At the far end of the village, where the path wound into an ever-rising stairway of stony crags, the shepherd waited, a large woven sack over his shoulder and a polished walking stick in his hand. Nodding good morning, he turned and walked up the mountain, his body compact and solid as a goat's. His manner struck me as exceedingly terse, and his expression remained so somber that I expected him to forfeit his duties and abandon us upon the path. Yet, he walked on, slow and steady, leading our party to the gorge.

Perhaps because the morning had grown warm and our breakfast had been pleasant, we commenced our journey in good spirits. The brothers talked among themselves, cataloging the wildflowers growing along the path and commenting upon the strange variety of trees — birch and spruce and towering cypress. Their pleasant humor was a relief, lifting the clouds of doubt from our mission. The melancholy of the previous days had weighed upon us all. We began the morning with renewed spirits. My own anxieties were considerable, although I kept them hidden. The brothers' boisterous laughter inspired my own merriment, and soon we were joyous and light of heart. We could not foresee that this would be the last time any of us would hear the sound of laughter again.

Our shepherd walked for half an hour farther up the mountain before cutting into a copse of birch trees. Through the foliage, I saw the mouth of a cave, a deep cut into a wall of solid granite. Inside the cave, the air was cool and moist. Tracks of colorful fungus grew over the walls. Brother Francis pointed to a series of painted amphorae lined against the far wall of the cave, thin-necked jars with bulbous bodies perched elegantly as swans on the dirt floor. The larger jars contained water, the smaller oil, which led me to believe that this cavern was used as a rough and makeshift shelter. The shepherd confirmed my speculation, although he could not say who would endeavor to rest so far above civilization and what necessity would drive one to do so.

Without hesitating further, the shepherd unloaded his sack. He placed two thick iron spikes, a mallet, and a rope ladder upon the cave's floor. The ladder was impressive and caused the younger brothers to gather around to examine it. Two long strips of woven hemp formed the vertical axis of the ladder, while metal rods, fastened with bolts into the hemp, formed the horizontal crossbars. The artistry of the ladder was unmistakable. It was both strong and easily portable. My admiration of our guide's industry grew at the sight of it.

The shepherd used the mallet to pound the iron spikes into the rock. He then fastened the rope ladder to the iron spikes with metal clasps. These small devices, no bigger than coins, ensured the ladder's stability. When the shepherd had finished, he flung the ladder over the edge and stepped away, as if to marvel at the distance it fell. Beyond, the roar of water crashed upon the rocks.

Our guide explained that the river flowed under the surface of the mountain, its course cutting through rock, feeding upon reservoirs and streams before bursting in a rush of pressure into the gorge. From the waterfall, the river twisted through the gorge, descending once again into a maze of underground caverns before emerging upon the surface of the earth. The villagers, our guide informed us, called it the river Styx and believed that the bodies of the dead littered the stone floor of the gorge. They believed the cave shaft to be the entrance to hell and had named it the Infidels' Prison. As he spoke, his face filled with apprehension, the first sign that he might be afraid to continue. In haste, I declared it time to descend into the pit.*

IX

One can hardly imagine our delight upon gaining passage into the abyss. Only Jacob in his vision of the mighty procession of Holy Messengers might have beheld a ladder more welcome and majestic. To our divine purpose, we proceeded into the terrible blackness of the forsaken pit, filled with expectation of His protection and Grace.

As I lowered myself down the frigid rungs of the ladder, the roar of water rang in my ears. I moved quickly, surrendering myself to the forceful pull of the deep, hands slipping on the moist, cold metal, knees slamming against the sheer surface of the rock. Fear filled my heart. I whispered a

*According to an account by Father Deopus, Clematis spent a number of agonized hours raving these words before, in a fit of madness, he tore at his burned flesh, ripping the bandages and compresses from his charred skin. Clematis' act of self-mutilation left flecks of blood upon the pages of the notebook, stains that are clearly visible even now, at the time of translation.

prayer, asking for protection and strength and guidance against the unknown. My voice disappeared in the whirling, deafening noise of the waterfall.

The shepherd was the last to descend, arriving some minutes after. Opening his sack, he removed a cache of beeswax candles and a flint and tinder with which to light them. In a matter of minutes, a glowing circle encompassed us. Despite the chill in the air, sweat fell into my eyes. We joined hands and prayed, believing that even in that deepest, darkest crevice of hell our voices would be heard.

Gathering my robes, I set off toward the edge of the river. The others followed, leaving our guide at the ladder. The waterfall fell in the distance, sheets of torrid, endless water. The river itself flowed in a thick artery through the center of the cavern as if Styx, Phlegethon, Acheron, and Cocytus — the forking rivers of hell — had converged into one. Brother Francis was the first to discern the boat, a small wooden craft tied to the river's edge, floating in a swirling haze of fog. We soon stood around the prow, contemplating our course. Behind, a stretch of flat stone separated us from the ladder. Ahead, across the river, a honeycomb of caves awaited our inspection. The choice was clear: We set out to discover what lay beyond the treacherous river.

Being five in number, and all of healthy weight, my first concern was that we would not fit into the cavity of the narrow boat. I stepped inside, holding myself upright against the violent rocking beneath my feet. I had no doubt that if the craft should tip, the merciless current would drag me down into a labyrinth of rocks. With some maneuvering, I achieved equilibrium and sat securely at the helm. The others followed, and soon we set off into the current, Brother Francis pushing the boat slowly toward the far shore with a wooden pole oar, the river sweeping us away from the entrance of the cavern and on to our doom.

X*

The creatures hissed from their rocky cells as we approached, venomous as snakes,

*The narrative leap one encounters in this section may be the result of a gap in Father Deopus' transcription but is more likely an accurate reflection of Clematis' incoherent state of mind. One must remember that the Venerable Father was in no condition to relate his experiences in the cavern with clarity. That Father Deopus went to such lengths to fashion a narrative from Clematis' desperate ranting is a testament to his resourcefulness.

their startling blue eyes fixing upon us, their mighty wings beating against the bars of their prison, hundreds of impenitent dark angels tearing at their glowing white robes, crying out for salvation, beseeching us, the emissaries of God, to set them free.

XI

My brothers fell to their knees, transfixed by the horrible spectacle before us. Deep in the hollow of the mountain, stretching as far as the eye could see, were innumerable prison cells containing hundreds of majestic creatures. I stepped closer, trying to comprehend what I saw. The creatures were otherworldly, so infused with light that I could not look into the depths of the cave without averting my eyes. Yet, as one longs to look into the center of a flame, burning one's vision upon the palest blue core of the fire, so I desired to see the heavenly creatures before me. At last I discerned that each narrow cell contained a single bound angel. Brother Francis clutched my arm in terror, begging me to return to the boat. But in my fervor, I did not listen. I turned to the others and ordered them to rise and follow me inside.

The moaning ceased as we entered the prison. The creatures peered from behind thick iron bars, their bulging eyes following our every movement. Their desire for liberation could be no surprise: They had been chained inside the mountain for thousands of years, waiting to be released. Yet, there was nothing wretched about them. Their bodies radiated an intense luminosity, a golden light that rose from their transparent skin, creating a golden nimbus around them. Physically, they were far superior to humankind — tall and elegant, with wings that folded about them from shoulder to ankle, shrouding their tapering bodies like pure white cloaks. Such beauty was like nothing I had seen or imagined before. At last I understood how these celestial creatures had seduced the Daughters of Men and why the Nephilim so admired their patrimony. As I stepped deeper into their midst, my anticipation growing with each step, it struck me that we had made our way to the abyss to fulfill a purpose we had not anticipated. I had believed our mission to be the recovery of the angelic treasure, but I now gleaned the terrible truth: We had come to the pit to set the Disobedient Angels free.

From the recesses of a dingy cell, an angel with masses of golden hair stepped forward. He held a polished lyre in his hands, its belly rotund.* Lifting the lyre into his arms, he plucked the strings until a fine, ethereal music echoed through the cavern. I cannot say whether it was the particular resonance of the cave or the quality of the instrument, but the sound was rich and full, an enchanting music that worked upon my senses until I thought I would go mad from bliss. Soon,

---

*The reference to the Archangel Gabriel's golden lyre is the most tantalizing and frustrating passage to be found in the Venerable Clematis' account of his journey to Hades. According to a communication written by Father Deopus, the Venerable Father had a small metal disk in his possession upon escaping the cavern which, after Clematis' death, was sent to Paris for examination. Under the scrutiny of ethereal musicologists, it was discovered that Clematis had discovered a plectrum — a metal pick used to play stringed instruments, most commonly the lyre. As a plectrum is traditionally fastened to the instrument by a silk cord, one can infer that Clematis did, in fact, have contact with the lyre, or an instrument that employs a similar plectrum. This leaves the whereabouts of the lyre itself open to speculation. If Clematis had brought the instrument from the gorge, he might have dropped it at the mouth of the pit or perhaps lost hold of it as he fled the mountain. The plectrum rules out the possibility that the lyre was a figment of Clematis' delusional state, a mythological creation of his beleaguered mind.

the angel began to sing, its voice climbing and falling with the lyre. As if taking cue from this divine progression, the others joined the chorus, each voice rising to create the music of heaven, a confluence akin to the congregation described by Daniel, ten thousand times ten thousand angels. We stood, transfixed, utterly disarmed by the celestial choir. The melody has been burned upon my mind. Even now I hear it.*

From where I stood, I watched the angel. Gently, it lifted its long thin arms and stretched its immense wings. Going to the door of its cell, I unlatched a heavily calcified hook, and in a burst of force that knocked me upon the floor, the angel pushed open the door to its cell and stepped free. I discerned the pleasure the creature took in its liberty. The imprisoned angels roared from their cells, jealous of their brother's victory, vicious and hungry creatures demanding freedom.

In my fascination with the angels themselves, I had failed to notice the effect the

*It is generally believed that Deopus, at the bequest of the Venerable Clematis, transcribed the melody of the angels' heavenly chorus. Although the score has never been located, there is great hope a full score of this harmonic progression exists.

music had upon my brothers. Suddenly, before I could perceive that a spell had been cast upon his mind by this demonic production, Brother Francis rushed to the angelic choir. In what appeared to be a state of insanity, Brother Francis knelt before the creatures in supplication. The angel dropped the lyre, instantly halting the chorus of sublime music, and touched Brother Francis, casting a light so thick over the bewildered man that he appeared to have been dipped in bronze. Gasping, Francis fell to the ground, covering his eyes as the intense light burned his flesh. To my horror, I watched as his garments dissolved from his body and his flesh melted away, leaving charred muscle and bone. Brother Francis, who minutes before had clutched my arm, beseeching me to return to the boat, had died of the angel's poisoned light.*

*After careful examination of Clematis' account of Brother Francis' death, and the wounds that led to Clematis' own death, the general conclusion of angelological scholars has been that Brother Francis died from the effects of extreme exposure to radiation. Studies on the radioactive properties of angels were initiated after a generous donation from the family of Marie Curie and are currently being undertaken by a group of angelological scholars in Hungary.

XII

The minutes after Brother Francis' death are all confusion. I recall the sound of the angels hissing from their cells. I remember Francis' horrid corpse, blackened and misshapen before me. But all else is lost in darkness. Somehow the angel's lyre, the very treasure that had brought me to the pit, was within my grasp. With all haste, I collected the treasure from the fallen creature, cradling the object in my charred hands and placing it in my satchel, safe from harm.

I found myself sitting at the prow of the wooden boat, my robes ripped and tattered. My entire being pained me. The flesh peeled from my arms, curling away in bloody, blackened sheets. Clumps of hair from my beard had burned to the roots. It was then I realized that I, like Brother Francis, had fallen under the horrid light of the angel.

As had the other brothers. Two stood together in the boat, pushing desperately against the current with the pole, their robes singed, their skin badly burned. The remaining member of our party lay dead at my feet, his hands pressed over his face, as if he had died of terror. As the boat came to the opposite bank of the river, we blessed our martyred brother and disembarked, leaving the boat to spin down the river.

To our dismay, the murderous angel stood at the riverbank awaiting our arrival. Its beautiful face was serene, as if it had just woken from a restful slumber. Upon seeing the creature, my brothers fell to the earth in prayer and supplication, undone by terror, for the angel was formed of gold. Their fear was justified. The angel turned its poisonous light upon them, killing them just as it had killed Francis. I fell to my knees, praying for their salvation, knowing they had died in worthy service. Looking about me, I saw that there was no hope of assistance. The shepherd had abandoned his post, deserting us in the gorge, leaving only his woven satchel and the ladder, a betrayal I felt bitterly. We had required his assistance.

The angel examined me, its expression one of vapidity, as if it were little more than a medium of the wind. With a voice more lovely than any music, it spoke. Although I could not make out the language, somehow I understood its message clearly. The angel said: *Our freedom has come at great cost. For this, your reward will be great in heaven and earth.*

The sacrilege of the angel's words affected me more than I would have imagined. I could not fathom that such a fiend would dare promise a heavenly reward.

In a terrible burst of fury, I lurched at the angel, wrestling it to the ground. The celestial creature was taken off guard by my anger, lending me a superiority I used to my advantage. Despite its brilliance, it was a physical being composed of substance not unlike my own, and in an instant I tore at its mighty wings, grasping for the naked, delicate flesh where the appendages met the creature's back.

Clutching the warm bone at the base of the wings, I threw the luminous creature to the cold, hard rock. Passion overwhelmed me, for I do not recall the exact measures I took to achieve my ends. I know only that in my struggle to keep hold of the creature and my desperation to escape the pit, the Lord blessed me with an unnatural strength against the beast. Wrenching the wings with a ferocity I could scarce believe came from my own aged hands, I felled the creature. I felt a crack under my hands, as if I had broken the thin glass of an ampoule. A sudden exhalation of air escaped the angel's body, a soft sigh that left the creature helpless at my feet.

I assessed the broken body before me. I had torn a wing from its mooring, ripping the pink flesh so that the pure white feathers folded at an asymmetric angle against the body. The angel writhed in agony, and a pale blue fluid poured from the wounds

I had opened on its back. A disquieting sound emanated from its chest, as if the humors, once released from their internal vessels, had mixed in a disastrous alchemy. I soon understood that the wretched creature was choking to death, and that its horrid suffocating had resulted from the injury to its wing.* It is thus that the

*The physical properties of angelic wing structure have been shown most definitively in the influential 1907 study *Physiology of Angelic Flight,* a work whose superiority in mapping the skeletal and pulmonary properties of wings has become a touchstone in all discussions of the Watchers. Whereas it was once believed that wing appendages were exterior attachments to the body, held in place entirely via musculature, it is now believed that the wings of angels are themselves an outgrowth of the lungs, each wing serving a dual purpose as a means of flight and an external organ of great delicacy. From further modeling, it has been determined that the wing appendages originate in the capillaries of the lung tissue, gaining mass and strength as they blossom forth from the muscles of the back. A mature wing acts as an anatomically complex system of external aspiration in which oxygen is absorbed and carbon dioxide is released through minuscule alveoli-like sacs on the wing shafts. It is estimated that only 10 percent of all respiratory function occurs via the mouth and windpipe, making the wing essential for respiratory function. This is perhaps the single physical flaw in breath dies. The violence of my actions against a celestial creature tormented me beyond all fathoming, and at last I fell to my knees and begged the Lord's mercy and forgiveness, for I had laid waste to one of heaven's most sublime creations.

It was then that I heard a faint cry — the shepherd, crouching against the rocks, called my name. Only after he had made numerous gestures for me to follow him did I understand that he meant to help me up the ladder. Creeping as quickly as my deformed body would allow, I abandoned myself to the shepherd, who, by the grace of God, was strong and able-bodied. He lifted me onto his trembling back and carried me from the pit.*

I closed the pages of Clematis's account of confusion. I could not fully assess my conflicting feelings upon finishing Dr. Raphael's translation of the Venerable Clematis's account of the First Angelological Expedition. My hands trembled with excitement, or fear, or anticipation — I could not identify which

the angelic structure, an Achilles' heel in an otherwise perfect organism, a weakness Clematis hit upon to great effect.

*According to notes left by Deopus, Clematis died before finishing his tale, cutting his narrative to an abrupt end.

emotion took control of me. And yet I knew one thing for certain: The Venerable Clematis had overwhelmed me with the story of his journey. I was both reverent at the audacity of his mission and terrified by the horror of his encounter with the Watchers. That a man had gazed upon these heavenly creatures, that he had touched their luminous flesh and had heard their celestial music was a truth I could not fathom.

Perhaps the oxygen in our school's quarters below the earth was too thin, because soon after setting the pamphlet aside I began to feel short of breath. The air in the chamber felt heavier, thicker, and more oppressive than it had only minutes before. The small, airless rooms of brick and weeping limestone turned, for a moment, into the depths of the angels' subterranean prison. I half expected to hear the crashing of the river or strains of the Watchers' celestial music. Although I knew this to be a morbid fantasy, I could not remain one minute longer belowground. Rather than leave Dr. Raphael's translation in its original place, I folded the pamphlet into the pocket of my skirt, carrying it with me out of the subterranean storage chambers and into the delicious cool air of the school.

Although it was well after midnight and I knew the school to be deserted, I could not risk being detected. Quickly, I unwedged the stone from its secure place in the archway over the door and, standing on tiptoes, slid the key into the narrow recess. After I had fitted the stone in its place, smoothing its edges to the flat of the wall, I stood back and assessed my work. The door looked like any one of the hundreds of such doors throughout the school. No one would suspect what lay hidden behind the stones.

I left the school and walked into a chill autumnal night, following my usual path from the school to my apartment on the rue Gassendi, hoping to find Gabriella in her bedroom so that I might question her. The apartment was utterly dark. After knocking at Gabriella's bedroom door and getting no response, I retreated to the privacy of my bedroom, where I might read through the pages of Dr. Raphael's translation a second time. The text pulled me into it, and before I knew it, I had read Clematis's account a third time and then a fourth. With each reading I found that the Venerable Clematis caused me more and more confusion. My unease began as an inchoate feeling, a subtle but persistent sense of discomfort that I could not identify, but as the night progressed, I was driven to a state of terrible anxiety. There was something in the manuscript that did not fit with my preconceptions of the First Angelological Expedition, an element to the tale that grated against the lessons I had absorbed. Although weary from the extraordinary strain of the day, I did not sleep. Instead I dissected each stage of the journey, looking for the precise reason for my anxiety. At last, after reliving Clematis's ordeal many times over, I understood the thorn of my distress: In all my hours of study, in all the lectures I had attended, in my months of work in the Athenaeum, the Valkos had not once mentioned the role of the musical instrument Clematis had discovered in the cavern. It was the object of our expedition, a source of fear in the face of Nazi advancement, and yet Dr. Seraphina had refused to explain the precise nature of its significance.

Yet as Clematis's account made clear, the lyre had been at the very heart of the first expedition. I recalled the tale of the Archangel Gabriel's gift of the lyre to the Watchers, mentioned in one of the Valkos' lectures, but even in that cursory account they had avoided mentioning the significance of the instrument. How they could keep such an important detail a secret filled me with wonder. My frustration only grew when I realized that Gabriella must have read Clematis's account long before and therefore had been aware of the lyre's importance. Yet she, like the Valkos, had remained silent on the subject. Why had I been excluded from their confidence? I began to review my time in Montparnasse with suspicion. Clematis had spoken of "an enchanting music that worked upon my senses until I thought I would go mad from bliss," but what consequences did such celestial music pose? I could not help but wonder why those I had trusted most, those to whom I had given my complete loyalty, had deceived me. If they'd failed to tell me the truth about the lyre, surely there were other pieces of information they'd kept from me as well.

These were the doubts filling my mind when I heard the rumbling of a car below my bedroom window. Drawing aside the curtain, I was astonished to discover that the sky had brightened to a pale gray hue, tinting the street with a hazy presentiment of dawn. The night was gone, and I had not slept at all. But I was not the only one who had endured a sleepless night. Through the murky light, I saw Gabriella emerge from the car, a white Citroën Traction Avant. Although she wore the same dress she had worn in the Athenaeum, its satin still giving off all its liquid luster, Gabriella had changed dramatically in the hours that had passed. Her hair was in disarray, and her shoulders hung heavy with exhaustion. She had removed the black opera gloves, revealing her pale hands. Gabriella turned from the car to the apartment building, as if contemplating what she might do, and then, leaning against the car, buried her head in her arms and began to sob. The car's driver, a man whose face I could not make out, emerged, and although I could not know his intentions, it appeared to me that he intended to further harm Gabriella.

Despite the anger I had felt toward her, my first instinct was to help my friend. I rushed from the apartment and down the successive flights of stairs, hoping that Gabriella would not leave before I made it to the street. When I arrived at the entrance of our building, however, I saw that I had been wrong. Rather than harm Gabriella, the man had embraced her, holding her in his arms as she cried. I stood at the doorway, watching in confusion. The man stroked her hair with tenderness, speaking to her in what appeared to me to be the manners of a lover, although at fifteen years of age I had never been touched in such a way. Pushing the door open slowly, so that my presence would not be detected, I listened to Gabriella. Through her sobs she repeated, "I can't, I can't, I can't," her voice filled with despair. Although I had some idea of what inspired Gabriella's remorse — perhaps her actions had at last registered upon her conscience — my astonishment was truly great at the words the man spoke. "But you must," he said, holding her closer. "We have no choice but to continue."

I recognized the voice. It was then that I saw, in the growing light of dawn, that the man comforting Gabriella was none other than Dr. Raphael Valko.

After returning to the apartment, I sat in

my room waiting to hear Gabriella's footsteps upon the stairs. Her keys rattled as she unlocked the door and walked into the hallway. Rather than go to her room, as I would have expected, she went to the kitchen, where a clattering of pans told me that she was making herself coffee. Fighting an urge to join her, I waited in the shadows of my bedroom, listening, as if the noises she made would help me to understand what had happened in the street and what was the nature of her relationship with Dr. Raphael Valko.

Some hours later I knocked upon the door to Dr. Seraphina's office. It was still early in the morning, not yet seven o'clock, although I knew she would be there working in her usual manner. She sat at her escritoire, her hair tied back in a severe bun, her pen poised above an open notebook as if I had caught her mid-sentence. Although my visits to her office had become routine — indeed, I had worked upon the vermilion settee each day for many weeks cataloging the Valkos' papers — my fatigue and anxiety over Clematis's journal must have been apparent. Dr. Seraphina knew that this was no ordinary visit. She came to the settee in an instant, sat across from me, and demanded to know what had brought me to her at such an early hour.

I placed Dr. Raphael's translation between us. Startled, Seraphina picked up the pamphlet and turned the thin pages, taking in the words her husband had translated so long before. As she read, I saw — or imagined that I saw — a glimmer of youth and happiness return to her features, as if time peeled away as she turned each page.

Finally Dr. Seraphina said, "My husband discovered the Venerable Clematis's notebook nearly twenty-five years ago. We were conducting research in Greece, in a small village at the base of the Rhodope mountain chain, a place Raphael had tracked down after coming across a letter from a monk named Deopus. The letter had been written from a mountain village of only a few thousand people, where Clematis died not long after the expedition, and hinted that Deopus had transcribed Clematis's last account of his expedition. There was only the vaguest promise of discovery in the letter, and yet Raphael believed his intuition and undertook what many believed to be a quixotic mission to Greece. It was a momentous time in his career — in both of our careers, actually. The discovery had tremendous consequences for us, bringing recognition and invitations to speak at every major institute in Europe. The translation cemented his reputation and secured our place here in Paris. I remember how happy he was to come here, how much optimism we possessed."

Dr. Seraphina stopped suddenly, as if she had said more than she wished. "I am very curious to know where you found this."

"In the storage chambers below the school," I replied, without a moment of hesitation. I would not have been able to lie to my teacher even if I wished to do so.

"Our subterranean storage areas are restricted," Dr. Seraphina said. "The doors are locked. You must have a key to enter."

"Gabriella showed me how to find the key," I said. "I returned it to its hiding place in the keystone."

"Gabriella?" Dr. Seraphina said, astonished. "But how is Gabriella aware of the hiding place?"

"I thought you might know. Or," I said, measuring my words, anxious not to reveal more than would be prudent, "perhaps Dr. Raphael knows."

"I certainly do not know, and I am sure my husband knows nothing about it either," Dr. Seraphina said. "Tell me, Celestine, have you noticed anything strange about Gabriella's behavior?"

"What do you mean?" I asked, leaning back into the cool silk of the settee, waiting with great anticipation for Dr. Seraphina to help me understand the puzzle Gabriella presented.

"Let me tell you what I have observed," Dr. Seraphina said, standing and walking to the window, where the pale morning light fell over her. "In the past months, Gabriella

378

has become unrecognizable to me. She has fallen behind in her coursework. Her past two essays were written significantly below her abilities — although she is so advanced that only a teacher who knows her as well as I do would notice. She has been spending quite a lot of time outside the school, especially at night. She has changed her appearance to match that of the girls one sees in the quartier Pigalle. And, perhaps worst of all, she has begun to harm herself."

Dr. Seraphina turned to me as if expecting me to disagree with her assessment. When I did not, she continued.

"Some weeks ago I watched her burn herself during my husband's lecture. You know the episode I am referring to. It was the most unsettling experience of my career, and believe me, I have had many. Gabriella brought the flame to her bare wrist, impassive as her skin charred. She knew that I was watching her, and as if to defy me she stared at me, daring me to interrupt the class to save her from herself. There was more than desperation in her behavior, more than the usual childish desire for attention. She had lost control of her actions."

I wanted to object, to tell Dr. Seraphina that she was wrong, that I had not noticed the disturbing characteristics she described. I wanted to tell her that Gabriella had burned herself through some accident, but I could not.

"Needless to say, Gabriella shocked me," Dr. Seraphina said. "I considered confronting her immediately — the girl needed medical attention, after all — but thought better of it. Her behavior pointed to a number of maladies, all psychological, and if this were the case, I did not want to exacerbate the problem. However, I feared another cause, one that had nothing to do with Gabriella's mental state but another force entirely."

Dr. Seraphina bit her lip, as if contemplating how to go on, but I urged her to continue. My curiosity about Gabriella was as strong as Dr. Seraphina's, perhaps stronger.

"Yesterday, as you recall, I planted *The Book of Generations* among the treasures we are sending away for safekeeping. In fact, *The Book of Generations* is not going to be shipped off to the United States — it is too important for that and will remain with me or another high-level scholar — but I placed it there, with the other treasures, so that Gabriella would come across it. I left the book open to a certain page, one with the family name Grigori in plain sight. It was essential for me to catch Gabriella by surprise. She had to see the book and read the names written upon the pages without any time to mask her feelings. Equally important: I wanted to witness her reaction. Did you notice it?"

"Of course," I said, recalling her violent outburst, her physical distress at the names she had read. "It was frightening and bizarre."

"Bizarre," Dr. Seraphina said, "but predictable."

"Predictable?" I asked, growing even more confused. Gabriella's behavior was a complete mystery to me. "I don't understand."

"At first the book made her simply uncomfortable. Then, when Gabriella recognized the name Grigori, and perhaps other names, her discomfort transformed to hysteria, to pure animal fright."

"Yes, it is true," I said. "But why?"

"Gabriella displayed all the characteristics of someone who has been discovered in a devious plot. She reacted like one tormented by guilt. I have seen it before, only the others were much more adept at hiding their shame."

"You believe that Gabriella is working against us?" I asked, my voice betraying my astonishment.

"I cannot know for certain," Dr. Seraphina said. "It is likely she is caught up in an unfortunate relationship, one that has gotten the better of her. Any way one looks at it, however, she has been compromised. Once one begins a life of duplicity, it is very difficult to escape. It is a pity that Gabriella has made an example of herself, but it *is* an example, one I want you to heed."

Too stunned to respond, I stared at Dr. Seraphina, hoping she would say something to ease my anxiety. Although she did not have proof of her suspicions, I did.

"The rooms below the school are completely off-limits, their entrances sealed for the safety of us all. You must not reveal to anyone what you found there." Seraphina went to her desk, opened a drawer, and held up a second key. "There are only two keys to the cellar. I have one. The other was hidden by Raphael."

"Perhaps Dr. Raphael showed her the location of the key," I ventured. I remembered the words that had passed between Dr. Raphael and Gabriella that morning, and I knew that this was indeed the answer, one that I did not have the heart to relate to Dr. Seraphina.

"Impossible," Dr. Seraphina said. "My husband would never reveal such important information to a student."

I was deeply uncomfortable by what I now suspected to be Dr. Raphael's intimate relationship with Gabriella, and I was equally uncertain about the nature of Gabriella's crimes, and yet, to my chagrin, I felt a perverse pleasure at having gained Seraphina's confidence. Never before had my teacher spoken to me with such seriousness and camaraderie, as if I were not merely her assistant but a colleague.

Therefore it was all the more difficult to contemplate Gabriella's deceptions. If the impressions I had formed were correct, not only was Gabriella working against the angelologists, but in her involvement with Dr. Raphael she had betrayed Dr. Seraphina personally. Whereas I'd believed that Gabriella had been distracted by a man outside our school, I now knew that her affair was more insidious than I had previously expected. In fact, Dr. Raphael might even be working with Gabriella against our interests. I knew that I must tell Dr. Seraphina, but I could not bring myself to do so. I needed time to understand my own feelings before revealing what I knew to anyone.

Finding it necessary to talk of other matters, I broached the topic that had brought me to her office.

"Forgive me for changing the subject," I said softly, gauging her reaction. "There is something that I must ask you about the First Angelological Expedition."

"That is why you came to me this morning?"

"I spent most of the night studying Clematis's text," I said. "I read it many times, and each time it left me more uncertain. I couldn't understand why the account bothered me, and then I realized why: You have never spoken to me of the lyre."

Dr. Seraphina smiled, her professorial serenity returning to her manner. "It is why my husband gave up on Clematis," she said. "He spent over a decade trying to find information about the lyre — searching libraries and antique stores throughout Greece, writing letters to scholars, even hunting down the relations of Brother Deopus. But it was no use. If Clematis found the lyre in the cavern — as we believe he did — it was either lost or destroyed. Having no means to come into possession of it ourselves, we have agreed to keep silent about the lyre."

"And if you had the means?"

"There would be no more need for silence," Dr. Seraphina said. "With the map we would be in a different position."

"But you do not need a map," I said. All my worries about Gabriella and Dr. Raphael and Dr. Seraphina's suspicions evaporated in light of my anticipation, and I took the pamphlet in my hands and opened it to the page that I had been puzzling over. "You do not need a map. Everything is written here, in Clematis's account."

"Whatever do you mean?" Seraphina said, eyeing me as if I had just confessed to a murder. "We have gone over every word of every sentence of the text. There is no mention of the cave's precise location. There is only a nonexistent mountain somewhere near Greece, and Greece is a very big place, my dear."

"You may have gone over every word," I said, "but those words have misled you. Does the original manuscript still exist?"

"Brother Deopus's original transcription?" Dr. Seraphina said. "Yes, of course. It is locked in our vaults."

"If you give me access to the original text," I said, "I am certain that I can show you the location of the cave."

Devil's Throat Cavern, Rhodope Mountains, Bulgaria

November 1943

We drove through the narrow mountain roads, climbing through mist and tall, clipped canyons. I had studied the geology of the region before embarking upon the expedition, and still the landscape of the Rhodope Mountains was not as I had pictured it. From my grandmother's descriptions and my father's childhood stories, I had envisioned villages enclosed in an endless summer of fruit trees and vines and sun-baked stone. In my childish imaginings, I had believed the mountains to be like sand castles in the onslaught of the sea — blocks of crumbling sandstone with flutes and runnels bitten from their pale, soft surfaces. But as we ascended through sheets of fog, I found a solid and forbidding mountain range of granite peaks, one layering upon the last like decaying teeth against the gray sky. In the distance, ice-capped pinnacles rose over snowy valleys; fingerling crags grasped at the pale blue sky. The Rhodope Mountains loomed dark and majestic before me.

Dr. Raphael had remained in Paris, making preparations for our return, a delicate procedure in light of the occupation, one that left Dr. Seraphina to head the expedition. To my astonishment, nothing whatsoever appeared to have changed in their marriage in the aftermath of my conversation with Dr. Seraphina, or so it seemed to me, who studied them with avid attention until the war descended upon Paris. Although I had prepared myself for the disruptions the war would bring, I could not have known how quickly my life would change once the Germans occupied France. At Dr. Raphael's request, I lived with my family in Alsace, where I studied the few books I had carried with me and awaited news. Communication was difficult, and for months at a time I heard nothing at all of angelology. Despite the urgency of the mission, all plans of our expedition had been suspended until the end of 1943.

Dr. Seraphina rode in the front of the van, speaking with Vladimir — the young Russian angelologist I had admired from our first meeting — in a mixture of broken Russian and French. Vladimir drove fast, riding so close to the edge of the precipice that it seemed we might follow the swift slide of the van's reflection, slipping down the glassy surface never to be seen again. As we ascended, the road narrowed into a sinuous path through slate and thick forest. Every so often a village appeared below the road. Clusters of mountain houses sprouted in pockets of vale like hardy mushrooms. Beyond, in the distance, the stone ruins of Roman walls grew from the mountain, half buried in snow. The stark, foreboding beauty of the scene filled me with awe for the country of my grandmother and father.

Every so often, when the tires fell into a snowy rut, we unloaded and dug ourselves out. With our thick wool coats and rugged sheepskin boots, we could have been mistaken for mountain villagers stranded in the snowstorm. Only the quality of our vehicle — an expensive American K-51 radio van with chains wrapped about its tires, a gift from the Valkos' generous patron in the United States — and the equipment we placed inside, carefully secured with burlap and rope, might give us away.

The Venerable Clematis of Thrace would have envied our halting pace. He had made the journey on foot, his supplies carried by mules. I had always believed the First Angelological Expedition to have been much less hazardous than the Second Expedition — we were endeavoring to enter the cavern in the dead of winter, during a war. And yet Clematis faced dangers we did not. The founders of angelology had been under greater pressure to mask their efforts and conceal their work. They lived in an era of conformity, and their actions would have been under constant scrutiny. As a result, advances came slowly, without the great breakthroughs of modern angelology. Their studies brought them laborious progress that, over the centuries, created the foundation for all I had learned. If they had been discovered, they would have been declared heretics, excommunicated from the church, perhaps imprisoned. I knew that persecution would not have stopped their mission — the founding members of angelology had sacrificed much to further their cause — but it would have caused severe setbacks. They believed that their orders came from a higher authority, just as I believed that I had been called to my mission.

While Clematis's expedition had faced the threat of theft and the ill will of villagers, our greatest fear was that we would be intercepted by our enemies. After the occupation of Paris in June 1940, we had been forced to go into hiding, a move that postponed the expedition. For years we'd prepared for the journey in secret, collecting supplies and gathering information about the terrain, sealing ourselves in a tight network of trusted scholars and council members, angelologists whose many years of dedication and sacrifice assured loyalty. Security measures changed, however, when Dr. Raphael found a patron — a wealthy American woman whose reverence for our work drove her to assist us. Accepting the support of an outsider, we opened ourselves to detection. With our benefactress's money and influence, our plans moved forward even as our fears grew. We could never know for certain if the Nephilim had detected our intentions. We could not know if they were in the mountains, following us each step of the way.

I shivered inside the van, feeling ill from the violent lurching as we made our way over ice and uneven roads. I was aware that I should have been frozen from the lack of heat, but my entire body tingled with anticipation. The other members of our party — three well-seasoned angelologists — sat nearby, speaking of the mission ahead with a confidence I could hardly believe. These men were much older than I and had worked together for as long as I'd been alive, but it was I who had solved the mystery of the location, and this gave me special status among them. Gabriella, who had once been my only rival for this position, had left the school in 1940, disappearing without so much as saying good-bye. She had simply taken her belongings from our apartment and vanished. At the time I believed that she had been reprimanded in some fashion, perhaps even expelled, and that her silent departure was one of shame. Whether she had gone into exile or gone underground, I did not know. Although I understood that my efforts had earned me my place on the expedition, I was left with doubts. Secretly I wondered if her absence was why I had been selected for the mission.

Dr. Seraphina and Vladimir analyzed the detail of our descent into the gorge. I did not join their discussion however, so lost was I in my own nervous thoughts about our journey. I was acutely aware that anything at all could happen. Suddenly every possibility arrayed itself before me. We might complete our work in the gorge with ease, or we might never return to civilization. One thing was certain. In the next hours, we would win everything or lose everything.

With the wind howling in the distance and the faint roar of an airplane droning overhead, I could not help but think of the terrible end Clematis had met. I thought of the doubt that Brother Francis had expressed. He had called the expedition party a "brotherhood of dreamers," and I had to wonder, as we emerged at last at the peak of the mountain, driving past a crag of ice-covered granite, if Francis's assessment did not hold for us so many centuries later. Were we chasing a phantom treasure? Would we lose our lives to a fruitless fantasy? Our journey could be, as Dr. Seraphina believed, the culmination of all that our scholars had striven for. Or it could be the very thing Brother Francis had so feared: the delusion of a group of dreamers who had lost their way.

In their great passion to understand the details of the Venerable Clematis's account, Dr. Raphael and Dr. Seraphina had overlooked a most subtle fact: Brother Deopus was a Bulgarian monk of the Thracian region who, although trained in the language of the church and fully capable of taking down Clematis's words in Latin, was also most certainly a native speaker of the local language, a variation of early Bulgarian forged in the ancient Cyrillic of St. Cyril and St. Methodius in the ninth century. The Venerable Clematis was also a native speaker of early Bulgarian, having been born and educated in the Rhodope Mountains. As I read and reread Dr. Raphael's translation that fateful night four years before, it had crossed my mind that in Clematis's maddened retelling of his descent into the cave, he had perhaps reverted to the comfort and ease of his native tongue. Clematis and Brother Deopus surely would have communicated in their common language, especially when speaking of traditions that would not translate easily into Latin. Perhaps Brother Deopus had written these words in Cyrillic, his native script, riddling the manuscript with early Bulgarian words. If he had felt ashamed of such inelegant literary execution as this — for Latin was the educated language of the time — he may have recopied his transcription into proper Latin. Assuming that this had occurred, it was my hope that the original version had been preserved. If Dr. Raphael had used this copy to assist in his translation of Brother Deopus's transcription, I could check the words to be sure that no errors had occurred in rendering the Latin into modern French.

After coming to this conclusion, I recalled reading in one of Dr. Raphael's numerous footnotes that the manuscript had contained the stains of faded blood, presumably from Clematis's injuries in the cave. If this were indeed the case, Deopus's original manuscript had not in fact been destroyed. Given the opportunity to look upon it, I would doubtless comprehend the markings of Cyrillic scattered through the text, a script I had learned from my grandmother, Baba Slavka, a bookish woman who read Russian novels in their original and wrote volumes of poetry in her native Bulgarian. With the original manuscript, I could extract the Cyrillic words and, with the assistance of my grandmother, find the correct translation from early Bulgarian into Latin and then, of course, French. It was simply a game of working backward from the modern to the ancient languages. The secret of the cave's location could be discerned, but only if I could study the original manuscript.

Once I'd explained the circuitous path my mind had taken in coming to this conclusion, Dr. Seraphina — whose excitement over my speculations grew as I spoke — brought me straightaway to Dr. Raphael and asked me to explain my theory again. Like Dr. Seraphina, Dr. Raphael approved the logic of the idea, but he warned that he had taken great care in translating Brother Deopus's words and had found no Cyrillic in the manuscript. Nonetheless the Valkos brought me to the Athenaeum vault, where the original manuscript was kept. They both slipped on white cotton gloves and gave me a pair so I could do the same. Dr. Raphael lifted the manuscript from a shelf. After unwrapping it from a thick white cotton cloth, Dr. Raphael placed it before me so that I might examine it. As he stepped away, our eyes met, and I could not help but remember his early-morning encounter with Gabriella, nor could I help but wonder of the secrets he had kept from everyone, including his wife. Yet Dr. Raphael appeared as he always did: charming, erudite, and utterly inscrutable.

The manuscript before me soon absorbed my attention. The paper was so delicate that I feared damaging it. Sweat had streaked the ink, and flecks of blackened blood marred a number of pages. As I had expected, Brother Deopus's Latin was imperfect — his spelling was not always accurate, and he tended to muddle his declensions — but to my great disappointment Dr. Raphael was correct: No Cyrillic letters were to be found in the transcription. Deopus had written the entire document in Latin.

My frustration might have been overwhelming — I had hoped to impress my teachers and secure my place on any future expedition — had it not been for Dr. Raphael's genius. Even as I began to give up hope, his expression filled with exuberance. He explained that in the months that he had translated Deopus's section of the manuscript from Latin to French, he had come across a number of words that were unfamiliar to him. He had speculated that Deopus, under extraordinary pressure to reproduce Clematis's words, which must have been spoken at a maddening pace, had Latinized a number of words from his native tongue. It would be only natural, Dr. Raphael explained, as Cyrillic was a rather recent development, having emerged with systemization merely a century before Deopus's birth. Dr. Raphael remembered the words well, and their place in the account. Taking a paper from his pocket, he uncapped a fountain pen and began to write. He copied a series of Latinized Bulgarian words from the manuscript — "gold," "world," "spirit" — forming a list of fifteen or so.

Dr. Raphael explained that it had been necessary to rely upon dictionaries to render the list of words from Bulgarian into Latin, which he then translated into French. He had searched a number of early Slavonic reference texts and found that there were indeed correspondences to the sounds represented in Latin. Endeavoring to smooth the inconsistencies over, he supplied what he believed to be the correct terms, checking each one with the surrounding context to assure that it made sense. At the time the lack of precision had struck Dr. Raphael as unfortunate but routine, the kind of guesswork one must make in any ancient manuscript. Now he saw that his method had corrupted the integrity of the language at the very least and, at worst, had led him to egregious errors in the translation.

Examining the list together, we soon isolated the early Bulgarian words that had been misrepresented. As the words were fairly elementary, I picked up Dr. Raphael's fountain pen and demonstrated the errors. Deopus had written the word Злото (evil), which Dr. Raphael thought to be Злато (gold), and had translated the phrase "for the angel was formed of evil" as "for the angel was formed of gold." Similarly, Deopus had written the word Дух (spirit), which Dr. Raphael had mistranslated as Дъх (breath), rendering the sentence "It is thus that the spirit dies" as "It is thus that the breath dies." For our purposes, however, the most intriguing question became whether Gyaurskoto Burlo, the name Clematis gave for the cavern, was an early Bulgarian place-name or if it had been corrupted in some fashion. With Dr. Raphael's fountain pen, I transcribed Gyaurskoto Burlo in my remedial Cyrillic and then in

Latin letters.

Гяурското Бърло

GYAURSKOTO BURLO

I stared at the paper as if the exterior form of the letters might break open, seeping the essence of meaning upon the page. For all my efforts, I could not see how the words could have been misconstrued. While the question of the etymology of Gyaurskoto Burlo was well beyond my capabilities, I knew that there was one person who would understand the history of the name and the misrepresentations it had suffered at the hands of its translators. Dr. Raphael packed the manuscript into his leather case, wrapping it in its cotton cloth to protect it, and by nightfall the Valkos and I had arrived in my native village to speak with my grandmother.

The privilege of my access to the Valkos' thoughts — not to mention their manuscripts — was something that I had long wished for. Only months before, I had been outside their notice, a mere student who wished to prove herself. Now the three of us were standing in the foyer of my family's farmhouse, hanging our coats and wiping our shoes as my mother and father introduced themselves. Dr. Raphael was as polite and affable as ever, exemplifying the very embodiment of decorum, and I had to wonder if my image of him with Gabriella had been correct. I could not quite reconcile the perfect gentleman before me with the rapscallion I had witnessed holding his fifteen-year-old student in his arms.

We sat at the smooth wooden table in the kitchen of my parents' stone house as Baba Slavka examined the manuscript. Although she had lived in our French village for many years, she had never come to resemble the women born there. She wore a bright cotton scarf tied over her hair, large silver earrings, and heavy eye makeup. Her fingers flashed with gold and gemstones. Dr. Raphael explained our questions and presented her with the manuscript and the list of words he had extracted from Deopus's account. Baba Slavka read the list and, after considering the manuscript for some time stood, went to her room, and returned with a collection of loose sheets I soon understood to be maps. Opening a page, she showed us a map of the Rhodopes. I read the village names written in Cyrillic: Smolyan, Kesten, Zhrebevo, Trigrad. The names were those near the place of my grandmother's birth.

Gyaurskoto Burlo, she explained, meant "Hiding Place of the Infidels," or "Infidels' Prison," as Dr. Raphael had rightly translated it from Latin. "It was no wonder," my grandmother continued, "that a place called Gyaurskoto Burlo has never been found, as it does not exist." Placing her finger near the town of Trigrad, Baba Slavka pointed out a cavern that fit the description of the one we sought, a cavern that had long been held to be a mystical site, the place of Orpheus's journey to the underworld, a geological marvel and a source of great wonder to the villagers. "This cave has the qualities that you describe, but it is not called Gyaurskoto Burlo," Baba Slavka said. "It is called Dyavolskoto Gurlo, the Devil's Throat." Gesturing to the map, my grandmother said, "The name is not written there, or on any other map, and yet I have walked to the opening in the mountain myself. I have heard the music that emanates from the gorge. It is what made me wish for you to pursue your studies, Celestine."

"You have been to the cavern?" I asked, astonished that the answer to the Valkos' search had been so close at hand all along.

My grandmother gave a strange and mysterious smile. "It is near the ancient village of Trigrad that I met your grandfather, and it was in Trigrad that your father was born."

After my part in locating the cavern, I had expected to return to Paris to assist the Valkos in preparations for the expedition. But with the danger of invasion looming, Dr. Raphael would hear nothing of it. He spoke with my parents, arranging for my belongings to be sent to me by train, and then the Valkos left. Watching them go, I felt that all my dreams and all my work had been for naught. Abandoned in Alsace, I waited for news of our impending journey.

At long last we were approaching the Devil's Throat. Vladimir stopped the van at a dull wooden sign with a scattering of black Cyrillic letters painted upon it. At Dr. Seraphina's instruction, he followed the sign toward the village, driving along a narrow, snow-covered road that lifted sharply up into the mountain. The incline was icy and steep. When the van slid backward, Vladimir downshifted, grinding the gears against gravity. The van's tires spun on the packed snow, gained traction, and carried us lurching ahead into the shadows.

When we reached the top of the road, Vladimir parked the van at the ledge of the mountain, a vast snowy wasteland opening before us. Dr. Seraphina turned to address us. "You've all read the Venerable Clematis's account of his journey. And we have all been through the logistics of entering the cavern. You are aware that the dangers we're facing ahead are unlike any we've encountered before. The physical process of descending the gorge will take all of our strength. We must go in with precision and speed. We have no margin for error. Our equipment will be of great use, but there are more than the physical challenges. Once we are inside the cavern itself, we must be prepared to face the Watchers."

"Whose strength is formidable," Vladimir added.

Looking carefully at us, the full gravity of the mission etched into her expression, Dr. Seraphina said, " 'Formidable' doesn't adequately describe what we may find. Generations of angelologists have dreamed that we would one day have the capability to confront the imprisoned angels. If we succeed, we will have accomplished something no other group has before."

"And if we fail?" I asked, hardly allowing myself to think of the possibility.

"The powers they hold," Vladimir said, "and the destruction and suffering they could bring to humanity are unimaginable."

Dr. Seraphina buttoned her wool coat and pulled on a pair of leather military gloves, preparing to face the cold mountain wind. "If I'm right, the gorge is at the top of this pass," she said, stepping out of the van.

I walked from the van to the mountain ledge and looked over the strange, crystalline world that had materialized around me. Above, a wall of black rock rose to the sky, casting a shadow over our party, while ahead a snow-covered valley fell steeply away. Without delay, Dr. Seraphina trekked toward the mountain. Following close behind, I climbed through drifts of snow, my heavy leather boots breaking my path. Clutching a case filled with medical equipment tightly in my hand, I tried to bring my thoughts to focus upon what lay ahead. I knew we would need to be precise in our efforts. Not only were we to face the rugged descent into the gorge, it might be necessary to navigate the spaces beyond the river, the honeycomb of caverns in which Clematis had encountered the angels. There would be no room for mistakes.

As we entered the mouth of the cave, a heavy darkness descended upon us. The interior space was barren and chill, filled with the ominous echoing rush of the underground waterfall Clematis had described. The flat rock at the entrance had none of the pockmarks and vertical shafts I had expected from my studies of Balkan geology but had been mantled with a thick, even layer of glacial deposit. The amount of snow and ice packed into the rock made it next to impossible to know what lay beneath.

Dr. Seraphina turned on a flashlight and brought the beam over the craggy interior. Ice clung to the rock face and, high in the dome of the cave, bats clung to the stone in tight mounds. The light fell over the razor-shorn walls, flickering upon mineral folds, along the rough-hewn stone floor, and then, with the slightest adjustment, the beam dissolved into blackness as it disappeared over the edge of the gorge. Looking about the cavern, I wondered what had become of the objects Clematis had described. The clay amphorae would have crumbled in the moisture long ago if they had not been taken by villagers to store olive oil and wine. But the cave contained no amphorae. Only rock and thick ice remained.

Holding the case of medical equipment with both hands, I walked toward the ledge, the rush of water growing more distinct with each step. As Dr. Seraphina moved the beam of the flashlight before her, something small and bright caught my eye. I squatted to the ground and, placing my hand upon the freezing rock, felt the icy metal of an iron stake, its head hammered flush with the cave's floor. "This is a remnant of the First Expedition," Dr. Seraphina said as she knelt at my side to examine my discovery. As I traced the cold iron stake with the tip of my finger, a great sense of wonder came over me: Everything I had studied, including the iron ladder that Father Clematis had described, was real.

And yet there was no time to ponder this truth. In haste Dr. Seraphina knelt at the precipice and examined the steep drop. The shaft plunged in a straight, lightless verticality. As she removed a rope ladder from her pack, my heart began to beat faster at the idea of stepping away from the ledge and relinquishing myself to the dark insubstantiality of air and gravity. The crossbars of the ladder were fastened to two strips of synthetic rope the likes of which I had never seen before, most likely the very newest technology developed for the war effort. I crouched at her side as Dr. Seraphina dropped the rope into the gorge.

Using a hammer, Vladimir secured the iron spikes into the rock, pinching the rope under iron clasps. Dr. Seraphina stood over him, watching his movements with great attention. She gave the ladder a hard shake, a test to determine that it would hold. When satisfied with its strength, she instructed the men — who carried the sacks of equipment, heavy burlap bags of twenty kilograms each — to secure their packs and follow us down.

I listened to the depths, trying to determine what lay beyond. In the stomach of the cavern, water pounded against rock. Looking over the ledge, I could not be sure if the earth below me remained stable or if it was I who had begun to tremble. I placed my hand upon Dr. Seraphina's shoulder, to hold myself steady against the nauseating spell the cavern had cast upon me.

She took me by the hand and, seeing my distress, said, "You must calm yourself before you proceed. Breathe deeply and do not think of how far you have to go. I'll lead you. Keep one hand on the crossbar and the other on the rope. If you somehow slip, you won't lose your footing completely, and if you should fall, I will be directly below to catch you." Then, without another word, she descended.

Gripping the cold metal with my bare hands, I followed. Trying to find comfort,

I recalled the joyous account Clematis had written about the ladder. The simplicity of his pleasure had inspired me to memorize the words he'd written: *"One can hardly imagine our delight upon gaining passage into the abyss. Only Jacob in his vision of the mighty procession of Holy Messengers might have beheld a ladder more welcome and majestic. To our divine purpose we proceeded into the terrible blackness of the forsaken pit, filled with expectation of His protection and Grace."*

We formed a line, each angelologist moving slowly down the rock face into the darkness, the sound of crashing water growing louder as we descended. The air became frigid as we moved deeper and deeper into the earth. A startling heaviness began to spread through my limbs, as if a vial of mercury had been released in my blood. It seemed that no matter how often I blinked, my eyes were filled with tears. In my panic I imagined that the narrow walls of the gorge would pinch together and I would be trapped in a granite vise, fixed in a stifling darkness. Clutching the cold, wet iron, the rush of the waterfall in my ears, I felt as if I were moving into the heart of a whirlpool.

Quickly I went, letting gravity take me. As the shaft deepened, the darkness thickened to a cool, opaque soup. I could see no farther than the whites of my knuckles wrapped around the ladder's rung. The wooden soles of my boots slipped on the metal, knocking me ever so slightly off balance. Clutching the case tightly to my side, so as to regain balance, I slowed my pace. Measuring each step, I positioned my feet carefully, delicately, one after the other. The blood rushed in my ears as I looked up at the dissolving track of the ladder. Poised at the center of the void, I had no choice but to continue into the watery darkness. A biblical passage rushed into my thoughts, and I could not help but whisper it, knowing that the crashing waterfall would wash away my voice the moment I spoke the words: " 'And God said unto Noah, The end of all flesh is come before me; for the earth is filled with violence through them; and, behold, I will destroy them with the earth.' "

As I reached the bottom of the descent, the soles of my boots leaving the last swinging rung of the rope ladder and brushing the solid earth, I knew that Dr. Seraphina had discovered something momentous. The angelologists quickly unpacked the burlap sacks and lit our battery-operated lanterns, placing them at intervals across the flat rock floor of the cavern so that a fitful, oily light opened the darkness. The river, described in Clematis's account as the boundary of the angels' prison, coursed by in the distance, a glimmering black ribbon of movement. I could see Dr. Seraphina ahead, shouting orders, but the sound of the waterfall consumed her words.

When I reached her, she stood over the body

of the angel. Upon taking my place at her side, I, too, fell under the trance of the creature. It was even more beautiful than I had imagined it to be, and I could do nothing for some time but stare, so overwhelmed was I by its perfection. The creature's physical properties were identical to the description I had read in the literature at the Athenaeum: elongated torso, gaunt features, massive hands and feet. Its cheeks retained the vivacity of a living being's. Its robes were pristine white, woven of a metallic material that wrapped about the body in luxurious folds.

"The First Angelological Expedition occurred in the tenth century, and still the body has the appearance of vitality," Vladimir said. He bent before the creature and lifted the white metallic gown, rubbing the fabric between his fingers.

"Be careful," Dr. Seraphina said. "The level of radioactivity is very high."

Vladimir considered the angel. "I've always believed that they could not die."

"Immortality is a gift that can be taken as easily as it is bequeathed," Dr. Seraphina said. "Clematis believed that the Lord struck the angel down as vengeance."

"Is that what you believe?" I asked.

"After its role in bringing the Nephilim into the world, killing this devilish creature seems perfectly justified," Dr. Seraphina said.

"Its beauty is incomprehensible," I said,

struggling to reconcile the fact that beauty and evil could be so intertwined in one body.

"What remains a mystery to me," Vladimir said, looking beyond the body of the angel to the far side of the cavern, "is that the others were allowed to live."

The party split into groups. Half stayed to document the body — extracting cameras and lenses and the aluminum case filled with biological testing apparatus from the heavy burlap bags holding them — and the other half set off to search for the lyre. Vladimir led the latter group, while Dr. Seraphina and I stayed with the angel. At our side, the remaining members of our party examined the half-buried bones of two human skeletons. The bodies of Clematis's brothers had remained exactly as they fell one thousand years before.

At Dr. Seraphina's orders, I put on protective gloves and lifted the angel's head in my hands. Running my fingers through the creature's glossy hair, I brushed the forehead, as if comforting a sick child. My touch was blunted by the gloves, but it seemed to me that the angel was warm with life. Smoothing the metallic gown, I unfastened two brass buttons at the clavicle and tugged at the fabric. It fell away, revealing a flat chest, smooth, without nipples. A clutch of ribs pressed against taut, translucent skin.

From head to foot, the creature looked to

be over two meters tall, a length that, in the ancient system of measurement the founding fathers had used, translated to 4.8 Roman cubits. Other than the golden ringlets falling about the shoulders, the body was completely hairless, and, to Dr. Seraphina's delight — she had staked her professional reputation upon the very question — the creature had distinct sexual organs. The angel was male, as all the imprisoned Watchers had been. As Clematis's account attested, one of the wings had been torn away and hung at an odd angle to the body. There could be no doubt that this was the very creature the Venerable Clematis had killed.

Together we lifted the creature and turned it on its side. We removed the robe entirely, exposing the skin to the harsh light of the lantern. The body was pliable, the joints limber. Under Dr. Seraphina's direction, we began photographing it with care. It was important to capture small details. Developments in photographic technology, especially multilayered color film, gave us hope that we would achieve great accuracy, perhaps even capture the color of the eyes — too blue to be real, as if someone had ground lapis in oil and brushed it over a sun-filled windowpane. These attributes would be documented in our field notes and duly added to the appropriate accounts of the journey, but photographic evidence was essential.

After we had completed the first series of photographs, Dr. Seraphina removed a measuring tape from a burlap camera bag and squatted at the creature's side. Placing the tape along the body, she took its measurements and converted the results to cubits, to better compare them with ancient documentation of the giants. As she calculated the measurement into cubits, she shouted the numbers aloud so that I might record them. The measurements were as follows:

Arms = 2.01 cubits
Legs = 2.88 cubits
Head Circumference = 1.85 cubits
Chest Circumference = 2.81 cubits
Feet = 0.76 cubits
Hands = 0.68 cubits

My own hands shook as I jotted the findings in a notebook, leaving a track of nearly illegible markings that I retraced, reading the numbers back to Dr. Seraphina to make certain each measurement was correct. From the numbers, I estimated the creature to be 30 percent larger than the average human being. Seven feet was an impressive height, awe-inspiring even in our modern era, but in ancient times such height would have seemed nothing short of miraculous. Such extreme height explained the terror that ancient cultures associated with the Giants and the dread that had surrounded such Nephilim as Goliath, one of the most famous of their race.

A sound rose from the cavern, but when I turned to Dr. Seraphina, she didn't seem to notice anything except me. She was observing me as I executed the field notes, perhaps worried that the task had overwhelmed me. My distress had grown more visible. I had started to shake and could only imagine how I must appear to her. I began to wonder if perhaps I had taken ill on the journey through the mountains — the ride had been cold and damp, and none of us were dressed well enough to protect us from the mountain winds. My pencil trembled in my hand, and my teeth chattered. Occasionally I stopped writing and turned to the darkness that stretched in a seemingly endless cavity beyond. Again I heard something in the distance. A terrifying sound echoed from the depths.

"Are you all right?" she asked, her gaze falling upon my shaking hands.

"Don't you hear it?" I asked.

Dr. Seraphina halted her work and walked away from the body, to the edge of the river. After listening for some minutes, she returned to me and said, "It's nothing but the sound of water."

"There is something else," I said. "They are here, waiting. They expect us to free them."

"They have been waiting for thousands of years, Celestine," she said. "And if we are successful, they will wait for thousands more."

Dr. Seraphina turned back to the angel and commanded me to do the same. Despite my fear I was drawn in by the angel's strange beauty — its translucent skin, its soft and continual light, the sculptural poise of its repose. There was much speculation about angelic luminosity, the predominant theory being that angelic bodies contained a radioactive material that accounted for their endless brightness. Our protective clothing only minimized exposure. Radioactivity also explained the horrid death suffered by Brother Francis during the First Angelological Expedition and the sickness that claimed Clematis.

I knew that I should have as little contact with the body as possible — it was one of the first things one learned when preparing for the expedition — and yet I could not restrain myself from drawing nearer to the creature's body. I peeled away my gloves and knelt at its side, placing my hands upon its forehead. I felt the skin, cold and wet against my palm, retaining the elasticity of living cells. It was like touching the smooth, iridescent skin of a serpent. Although it had been submerged in the depths of the cavern for over a thousand years, the white-blond hair shone. The shocking blue eyes, so disconcerting at first glace, now had the opposite effect upon me. Looking into them, I felt that the angel sat by my side, calming me with its presence, lifting all my fears away, and granting me an eerie opiate comfort.

"Come here," I said to Dr. Seraphina. "Quickly."

My teacher's eyes widened at the sight of my hands on the creature — even an angelologist as young and inexperienced as I should have known that physical contact broke our safety protocol. Yet, perhaps she was drawn to the angel as I had been. Dr. Seraphina sat next to me and placed her palms upon the forehead, resting her fingertips in the roots of its hair. I saw the change in Dr. Seraphina in an instant. She closed her eyes, and a sensation of bliss appeared to wash over her. The tension in her body eased into pure serenity.

Suddenly a hot, sticky substance seeped over the skin of my palms. Lifting my hands, I squinted, trying to determine what had happened. A gummy golden film, transparent and glistening as honey, coated my hands, and when I held them in the light of the angel's skin, the substance refracted, scattering a reflective dust over the cavern floor, as if my palms were coated in millions of microscopic crystals.

Quickly, before the other angelologists saw what we had done, we wiped our hands against the rocky surface of the cavern wall and slipped them back into our gloves. "Come, Celestine," Dr. Seraphina said. "Let's finish with the body."

I opened the medical kit and placed it at her side. Everything — scalpels, swabs, a packet of straight blades, tiny glass vials with screw caps — had been strapped inside with elastic bands. I lifted the creature's arm over my lap, steadying it at the elbow and wrist as Dr. Seraphina scraped the grain of a fingernail with the edge of the razor blade. Flakes broke from the nails, collecting at the bottom of a glass vial, chunky and mineral as sea salt. Turning the blade at an angle, Dr. Seraphina made two parallel incisions along the inner surface of the forearm and, careful not to rip the skin, pulled. A layer of skin peeled away, leaving exposed musculature. Pressed between plates of glass, the swath of skin glittered golden, brilliant and reflective in the weak light.

A wave of nausea passed over me at the sight of the exposed muscle. Afraid that I might be sick, I excused myself, apologizing as I left. At some distance from the expedition party, I took a deep breath, trying to calm myself. The air was bitter cold, filled with a thick moisture that hung in my chest. The cavern opened before me, a series of endless, dark concavities that pulled me into them. As the feeling of nausea dissipated, a sense of wonder took its place. What lay beyond, hidden in darkness?

I took a small metal flashlight from my pocket and turned it toward the cavern's depths. The light grew fainter as I moved deeper into the cavern, as if eaten by the sticky, ravenous fog. I could see only one meter, perhaps two, in front. Behind me, Dr. Seraphina's strong, impatient voice directed the others as they worked. Ahead, another voice — a soft, insistent, melodic voice — called me forth. I paused, letting the darkness settle around me. The river was before me, separating me from the Watchers. I had ventured too far from the others, putting myself at risk. Something awaited me in the granite heart of the gorge. I needed only to discover it.

I stood at the edge of the river. The black water rushed by, sweeping into the darkness beyond. As I stepped along its bank, a wobbling rowboat materialized, the twin of the boat Clematis had used to navigate across the river. His image, or perhaps a shade of his voice, beckoned me to follow his path. The edge of my trousers skimmed the water as I pushed the boat from the riverbank, the heavy wool darkening as it brushed the surface. The boat had been fastened by rope to a pulley — evidence that others, perhaps local historians, had ventured to the river — so that in tugging the rope I was able to pull myself across without the assistance of oars. From my perch I saw a waterfall at the head of the river, the thick mist rising before the endless hollow of cave, and I understood why legend designated the river as Styx, the river of the dead: Pulling the boat across the water, I felt a deathly presence descend, a dark emptiness so complete that it seemed to me that my life would be pressed away.

The waters brought me swiftly to the opposite shore. I left the boat, which was securely fixed to the rope pulley, and climbed onto the bank. The cave's mineral formations grew dramatic the farther I moved from the water: There were spires of rock, clusters of minerals, crystal formations, and a comb of caves opening on all sides. The indecipherable summons that had drawn me away from Dr. Seraphina grew clear. I could hear the distinct sound of a voice, rising and falling, as if in time with my footfall. If only I could reach the source of the music, I knew that I would see the creatures that had lived in my imagination for so long.

Suddenly the rock floor dropped from underfoot, and before I could catch my balance, I fell headlong onto the wet, smooth granite. Training my flashlight over the floor, I saw that I had tripped upon a small leather satchel. I picked myself up, took the satchel in my hands, and unbound it. The worn material felt as if it might disintegrate at my touch. Passing the flashlight over the interior of the sack, I saw a brilliant metallic glimmer. I peeled away a layer of tattered calfskin and held the lyre, its gold shining as if freshly polished. I had found the very object we'd prayed we would discover.

I could think only of bringing the lyre to Dr. Seraphina. Quickly, I wrapped the treasure in the satchel and began to make my way through the darkness, taking care not to fall again upon the wet granite. The river was near, and I could see the boat lifting and falling upon the black water, when a flickering of light from within the depths of a cave caught my attention. At first the source of the illumination remained obscure. I believed that I had found the members of our expedition party, their flashlights trailing over the rocky cavern walls. Walking nearer so that I might look closer, I sensed that the light had an altogether different quality from the harsh bulbs we'd brought into the gorge. Hoping to better understand what I saw, I ventured even closer to the mouth of the cave. A being of wondrous appearance stood within it, its great wings open, as if preparing for flight. The angel was so brilliant I could hardly bear to look at it directly. To soothe my eyes, I glanced beyond. In the distance stood a choir of angles, their skin emitting a tempered, diaphanous light that illuminated the gloom of their cells.

I could not take my eyes from the creatures. There were between fifty and one hundred angels, each one as majestic and lovely as the last. Their skin appeared molded of liquid gold, their wings of carved ivory, their eyes composed of chips of bright blue glass. Luminous nebulae of milky light floated about them, ringing their masses of blond curls. Although I had read of their sublime appearance and had tried to envision them, I'd never believed that the creatures would have such a seductive effect upon me. Despite my terror, they drew me to them with an almost magnetic force. I wanted to turn and flee, and yet I was unable to move.

The beings sang out in joyous harmony. The chorus thrumming through the cavern was so unlike the demonic nature I had long associated with the imprisoned angels that my fear all but melted. Their music was unearthly and beautiful. In their voices I understood the promise of paradise. As the music drew me under its spell, I found myself unable to walk away. To my astonishment, I wanted to pluck the strings of the lyre.

Holding the base of the lyre upon my knees, I ran my fingers over the taut metal strings. I had never played such an instrument — my musical training had been limited to a chapter in *Ethereal Musicology* — and yet the sound that emerged from the lyre was lush and melodious, as if the instrument played itself.

At the sound of the lyre, the Watchers left off their singing. They looked about the cave, and the horror I felt as the creatures fixed their attention on me was tempered with awe — the Watchers were among God's most perfect creatures, physically luminous, weightless as flower petals. Paralyzed, I held the lyre close to my body, as if it might give me strength against the creatures.

As the angels pressed themselves against the metal bars of their prisons, blinding light dizzied me, throwing me off balance. An intense heat came over me, hot and sticky, as if I had been drenched in boiling oil. I cried out in pain, although my voice did not seem my own. Collapsing upon the ground, I covered my face with the satchel as a second blast of searing heat seized me, more intensely painful than the first. It felt to me that my thick wool clothing — meant to protect me from the cold — would melt away, as Brother Francis's robes had dissolved. In the distance the voices of the angels rose once again in sweet harmony. It was under the spell of the angels that I fell unconscious, the lyre wrapped in my arms.

Some minutes passed before I rose from the depths of oblivion to find Dr. Seraphina hovering above me, an expression of concern upon her face. She whispered my name, and for a moment I believed that I had died and emerged upon the other side of existence, falling asleep in our world and waking in another, as if Charon had in fact taken me across the deathly river Styx. But then a seizure of pain overwhelmed my senses, and I knew that I had been hurt. My body felt stiff and hot, and it was then I recalled how I had been injured. Dr. Seraphina took the lyre from my hands and, too stunned to speak, examined it. Helping me to sit, she tucked the instrument under her arm and, with a surefootedness that I longed to emulate, led me back to the boat.

She pulled us across the waters, gripping the rope attached to the pulley. As the prow lifted and fell with the current, Dr. Seraphina removed wax plugs from her ears. Prepared as usual, my teacher had been able to protect herself from the sound of the angels' music.

"What in the name of God were you doing?" she demanded without turning to me. "You should know better than to have wandered off alone."

"The others?" I asked, thinking that I had somehow put the expedition party in danger. "Where are they?"

"They've ascended to the cave and will be waiting for us," she said. "We searched three hours for you. I was beginning to think we'd lost you. Surely the others will want to know what happened to you. You must not under any circumstances tell them. Promise me this, Celestine: You must not speak of what you saw on the other side of the river."

As we reached the shore, Dr. Seraphina helped me from the boat. When she saw that I was in pain, her manner softened. "Remember, our work has never been with the Watchers, my dear Celestine," she said. "Our duties lie with the world we live in and must return to. There is much to be done. Although I am terribly disappointed in your choice to cross the river, you have discovered the object that fulfills our mission here. Well done."

My body aching with each step, we returned to the ladder, passing the remains of the angel. Its robe had been cast aside and the body carefully dissected. Although it was little more than a shell of its former self, the ruins of its body gave off a dim, phosphorescent glow.

Aboveground all was dark. We carried the burlap bags filled with our precious samples through the snow. After packing the equipment carefully in the van, we climbed inside and began our descent down the mountain. We were exhausted, covered in mud, and injured — Vladimir had a gouge over his eye, a deep and bloody cut from a rock ledge he had hit on his ascent, and I had been exposed to a sickening light.

As we made our way through the mountains, moving swiftly along the icy roads, it was clear that snow had been falling for some time. Drifts piled heavy on crags and new snow fell thick against the sky. Ice coated the road ahead and behind, determining our meandering pace. I looked at my wristwatch and was surprised to learn that it was nearly four o'clock in the morning. We had been in the Devil's Throat for over fifteen hours. We were so behind schedule that we could not stop for sleep. We would only pause to refuel with petrol packed in canisters at the back of the van.

Despite Vladimir's efforts we arrived many hours late to meet the plane, just as the sun was rising. A Model 12 Electra Junior, twin-engined and ready for flight, sat on the runway, just as we'd left it the day before. Ice hung from the wings like fangs, proof of the bitter cold. It had been difficult to fly to our destination but it would have been utterly impossible to have driven. We had been forced to take a number of detours in our flight to Greece — we had flown first to Tunisia and then to Turkey to avoid detection — and our return would be no less difficult. The plane was large enough for six passengers, our equipment and supplies. We loaded our materials on board, and soon the plane climbed through the snow-filled air, rising into the sky in a flurry of noise.

Twelve hours later, as we landed at the airfield outside of Paris, I saw that a Panhard et Levassor Dynamic waited in the distance, a luxurious vehicle with a polished grille and sweeping running boards, an object of wonder among the intense deprivations of the war. I could only guess how we had acquired such a treasure but suspected that it, like the Model 12 and the K-51, had been arranged through foreign patrons. Donations had kept us alive in the past years, and I was grateful to see the car, but how we had managed to keep such a treasure from the Germans was another question altogether, one I dared not ask.

I sat in silence as the car sped through the night. Despite hours of sleep on the plane, I was still exhausted from the trip down the gorge. I closed my eyes. Before I knew it, I had fallen into a deep sleep. The tires bumped over the battered roads, and the others whispered at the edge of my hearing, but all meaning of their words was lost. My dreams were a mélange of images of everything that I had seen in the cave. Dr. Seraphina and Vladimir and the other party members appeared before me; the deep and terrifying cavern opened below; and the legion of luminous angels, their brilliant pallor radiating about them, danced before me.

When I woke, I recognized the deserted cobblestone streets of Montparnasse, an area of resistance and utter poverty during the occupation. We drove past apartment buildings and darkened cafés, barren trees rising on each side, snow frosting their branches. The driver slowed and turned into the Cimetière du Montparnasse, stopping before a great iron gate. He gave a short honk from the horn, and the gate opened, rattling aside as the car crawled forward. The interior of the cemetery was still and frozen, coated in ice that glimmered in the headlights, and I felt for a moment that this one shimmering place had been spared the ugliness and depravity of the war. The driver cut the engine before a statue of an angel perched upon a stone pedestal — *Le Génie du Sommeil Éternel, The Spirit of Eternal Sleep,* a bronze guardian gazing over the dead.

I stepped out of the car, still groggy with exhaustion. Although the night was clear, the stars glowing above in the sky, the air hung wet upon the tombstones, giving the faintest aura of fog. A man stepped from behind the statue, clearly assigned to meet the car, but all the same I started with fright. He wore the clothing of a priest. I had never seen the man before, not at any of our meetings or assemblies, and I had been trained to be suspicious of everyone. Only the month before, the Nephilim had tracked down and killed one of our senior council members, a professor of ethereal musicology named Dr. Michael, taking his entire collection of musicological writings. It was one instance of a senior-level scholar's losing priceless information. The enemy waited for such chances.

Dr. Seraphina appeared to know the priest and followed him readily. Urging the group to come with him, the priest led us to a dilapidated stone structure in a far corner of the cemetery, one of the remaining buildings of a long-abandoned monastery. Years before, the building had served as the Valkos' lecture hall. Now it remained empty. The priest unlocked a swollen wooden door and led us inside.

None of us, not even Dr. Seraphina, who had close ties to the most senior council members — indeed, Dr. Raphael Valko led the resistance in Paris — knew exactly where we would meet during the war. We had no regular schedule, and all messages were delivered by word of mouth or — like this one — in silence. Assemblies convened in impromptu locations — out-of-the-way cafés, small towns beyond Paris, abandoned churches. Even with these extreme precautions, I knew that we were most likely being monitored every moment.

The priest brought us into a hallway off the sanctuary, stopped before a door, and gave three sharp raps. The door opened, revealing a stone room lit by exposed bulbs — more precious supplies bought on the black market with dollars from America. The narrow windows were covered by heavy black cloth, to block out the light. The meeting appeared to be under way — members of the council sat at a round wooden table. As the priest ushered us inside, the council members stood, examining us with great interest. I was not allowed to attend the council meetings and had no method of gauging their usual proceedings, but clearly the council had been waiting for the expedition party to arrive.

Dr. Raphael Valko, acting chair of the council, sat at the head of the table. The last I had seen him had been as he drove away from my farmhouse in Alsace, leaving me in exile, an abandonment for which I could not forgive him, even though I was aware that it had been for the best. He had changed significantly since then. His hair had grayed about the temples, and his manner had taken on a new level of gravity. I would have taken him for a stranger if I'd met him in the street.

Greeting us tersely, Dr. Raphael gestured to a number of empty chairs and began what I knew would be the first of many rounds of questioning about the expedition. "You have much to report," he said, folding his hands upon the table. "Begin as you wish."

Dr. Seraphina gave a detailed description of the gorge: the steep vertical drop, the rock shelves that studded the lower regions of the cavern, and the distinct sound of the waterfall in the distance. She described the body of the angel, giving a list of precise measurements and outlining the characteristics she had recorded in her field notebook, mentioning with obvious pride the distinct genitalia. She reported that the photographs would reveal new truths about the physicality of the angels. The expedition had been a great success.

As the other members of the party spoke, each giving an elaborate account of the journey, I felt myself turn inward. I stared at my hands in the dim light. They were eaten raw from the cold and ice of the gorge and burned from the angel. I wondered at the sense of dislocation that had overtaken me. Had we been in the mountains only hours before? My fingers trembled so severely that I tucked them into the pockets of my thick wool coat, to hide them. In my mind the aquamarine eyes of the angel stared up at me, bright and polished as colored glass. I recalled how Seraphina had lifted the creature's long arms and legs, weighing each limb as if it were a piece of wood. The creature seemed so vital, so filled with life that I could not help but believe that it had been living only minutes before we'd arrived. I realized that I had never quite believed that the body would be there, that despite all my study I had not expected to actually see it, to touch it, to puncture its skin with needles and draw fluid. Perhaps at the back of my mind I'd hoped that we were wrong. When the skin had been cut from the arm and the sample of flesh held into the light, I had been overcome with horror. I saw it again and again: the razor edging under the white skin, slicing, lifting. The glimmering of the membrane in the weak light. As the youngest among them, I felt that it was imperative I perform well, carrying more than my share. Always I had pushed myself to spend more hours working and studying than the others. The past years were spent proving myself worthy of the expedition — reading texts, attending lectures, equipping myself with information for the journey — and yet this had not helped to prepare me for the gorge. To my chagrin, I had reacted like a neophyte.

"Celestine?" Dr. Raphael said, jarring me from my thoughts. I was startled to see the others looking intently at me, as if expecting me to speak. Apparently Dr. Raphael had asked me a question.

"I'm sorry," I whispered, feeling my face burn. "Did you ask me something?"

"Dr. Seraphina was explaining to the council that you made a crucial discovery in the cavern," Dr. Raphael said, examining me carefully. "Would you care to elaborate?"

Fearful that I would give away the secret promise I had made Dr. Seraphina, and equally terrified of exposing how foolhardy I had been to cross the river, I said nothing at all.

"It is obvious that Celestine isn't feeling well," Dr. Seraphina said, interceding on my behalf. "If you don't mind, I would like her to rest for the moment. Allow me to describe the discovery."

Dr. Seraphina explained the discovery to the council members. She said, "I found Celestine near the riverbank, the careworn sack in her arms. I knew at once by the worn leather that it must have been very old. There is, if you recall, mention of a satchel in the Venerable Father's account of the First Angelological Expedition."

"Yes," Dr. Raphael said. "You are correct.

I recall the line exactly: 'With all haste, I collected the treasure from the fallen creature, cradling the object in my charred hands and placing it in my satchel, safe from harm.'"

"Only after opening the satchel and examining the lyre did I know for certain that it had belonged to Clematis. The Venerable Clematis must have been too stricken to carry the sack to the surface of the gorge," Dr. Seraphina said. "It is this very satchel that Celestine discovered."

The council members were awestruck at this news. They turned to me, clearly expecting that I would give the account in greater detail, but I could not speak. Indeed, I could hardly believe that I, of all the members of their party, had made such a long-awaited discovery.

Dr. Raphael remained silent for a moment, as if contemplating the magnitude of the expedition's success. Then, with a sudden burst of energy, he stood and turned to the council members.

"You may go," Dr. Raphael said, dismissing the group. "There is food in our rooms below. Seraphina and Celestine, would you please stay a moment?"

As the others left, Dr. Seraphina caught my eye, giving me a kind look, as if to assure me that everything would be fine. Dr. Raphael guided the others from the room, radiating a confident serenity that I admired, for his strength of character to contain his emotions was a virtue I wished to emulate. He said, "Tell me, Seraphina — did the party members perform to your expectations?"

"It was, in my opinion, a great success," Dr. Seraphina said.

"And Celestine?" he inquired.

I felt my stomach twist: Had the expedition been some kind of test?

"For a young angelologist," Dr. Seraphina said, "she impressed me. The discovery alone should be enough to prove her skill."

"Fine," Dr. Raphael said, turning to me. "You are pleased with your work?"

I glanced from Dr. Seraphina to Dr. Raphael, unsure of how to respond. To say that I was satisfied with my work would be a lie, but to speak in detail of what I had done would be to break the promise I had made to Dr. Seraphina. Finally I whispered, "I wish that I had been more prepared."

"We prepare all of our lives for such moments," Dr. Raphael said, crossing his arms and looking at me with a critical gaze. "When the time comes, we can only expect that we have learned enough to succeed."

"You were quite capable," Dr. Seraphina added. "Your work was superb."

"I cannot account for my reaction to the gorge," I said simply. "I found the mission deeply troubling. Even now I have not recovered."

Dr. Raphael put his arm around his wife, kissing her on the cheek. "Go to the others, Seraphina. There is something I would like to show Celestine."

Dr. Seraphina turned to me and took my hand. "You were very brave, Celestine, and one day you will make an excellent angelologist." With this she kissed my cheek and departed. I would never see her again.

Dr. Raphael ushered me from the meeting room and into a corridor smelling of earth and fungus. "Follow me," he said, stepping quickly down the steps and into darkness. At the bottom of the stairs, there was another passageway, this one longer than the first. I felt the sharp decline in the floor as we walked and adjusted my weight to bolster myself. As we hurried onward, the air grew cooler and the smell became intensely rancid. The damp air moved through my clothes, penetrating the thick wool jacket I had worn into the cavern. Brushing my hands against the wet stone walls, I realized that the uneven fragments were not stone but bones piled into the cavity in the wall. At once I understood their location: We were moving below Montparnasse by way of the catacombs.

We climbed through a second corridor, up a stairway, and into another building. Dr. Raphael unlocked a series of doors, the last of which opened to the crisp, cold air of an alleyway. Rats scattered in all directions, leaving half-eaten scraps — rotting potato peels and chicory, a wartime substitute for coffee. Dr. Raphael took me by the arm and led me around another corner and into the street. We soon found ourselves a number of blocks from the cemetery, where the Panhard et Levassor idled, waiting for us. As we approached the car, I noticed that a square of paper written entirely in German had been fastened in the window. Although I could not make out what it said, I guessed it to be a German permit or license that would allow us to pass checkpoints throughout the city. Now I understood how we managed to keep such a luxurious car and obtain fuel: The Panhard et Levassor belonged to the Germans. Dr. Valko, who oversaw our undercover operations in the German ranks, had managed to obtain use of it — at least for the evening.

The driver opened the door, and I slid into the warm backseat, Dr. Raphael moving in next to me. Turning, he took my face between his cold hands and gazed at me dispassionately. "Look at me," he said, examining my features, as if searching for something particular. I returned his gaze, seeing him up close for the first time. He was at least fifty, his skin lined and his hair even more flecked with gray than I had noticed earlier. Our proximity startled me. I had never been so close to a man before.

"Your eyes are blue?" he asked.

"Hazel," I responded, confused by the strange question.

"Good enough," he said, opening a small travel suitcase between us. He lifted a satin evening gown, silk stockings and garter belt, and a pair of shoes. I recognized the dress instantly. It was the same red satin dress Gabriella had worn years before.

"Put these on," Dr. Raphael said. My astonishment must have been apparent, for he added, "You will soon see why this is necessary."

"But they are Gabriella's," I said, objecting before I could stop myself. I could not bring myself to touch the dress, knowing all that I did about her activities. I recalled Dr. Raphael and Gabriella together, and I wished that I had said nothing.

"What of it?" Dr. Raphael demanded.

"The night she wore this dress," I said, unable to look him in the eye, "I saw the two of you together. You were in the street below our apartment."

"And you believe that you understand what you saw," Dr. Raphael said.

"How could I misinterpret it?" I whispered, glancing out the window at the dull gray buildings, the progression of streetlamps, the dismal face of Paris in winter. "It was very clear what was happening."

"Put the dress on," Dr. Raphael said, his voice stern. "You must place more faith in

Gabriella's motives. Friendship should be stronger than idle suspicions. In times like this, trust is all we have. There is much you do not know. Very soon you will understand the dangers Gabriella has faced."

Slowly, I unbound myself from my thick woolen clothing. I unbuttoned my trousers and slid the heavy sweater — worn for protection against the icy mountain wind — over my head and wiggled into the gown, careful not to tear it. The dress was too big; I felt it immediately. Four years ago, when Gabriella had worn it, the dress would have been too small for me, but I had lost ten kilos during the war and was little more than skin and bones.

Dr. Raphael Valko went through a similar costume change. As I dressed, he withdrew the black jacket and trousers of an Allgemeine SS Nazi uniform from his case, pulling a pair of stiff, glossy black riding boots from under the seat. The uniform was in perfect condition, without the wear or smell of black-market hand-me-downs. I supposed it to be another useful acquisition from one of our double agents in the SS, one with Nazi connections. The uniform sent chills through me — it transformed Dr. Raphael completely. When he had finished dressing, he brushed a clear liquid onto his upper lip and pressed a thin mustache upon it. Then he slicked back his hair with pomade and attached an SS pin to his lapel, a small but precise addition that filled me with repulsion.

Dr. Raphael narrowed his eyes and examined me, checking my appearance with care. I crossed my arms over my chest, as if I might hide myself from him. Clearly I had not metamorphosed to his satisfaction. To my great embarrassment, he straightened the dress and fussed over my hair in the way my mother used to do before bringing me to church as a child.

The car sped through the streets, stopping at the Seine. A soldier at the bridge tapped the glass with the butt of a Luger. The driver unrolled the window and spoke to the soldier in German, showing a packet of papers. The soldier glanced into the back of the car, resting his gaze upon Dr. Raphael.

"Guten Abend," Dr. Raphael said with what sounded to me to be a perfect German accent.

"Guten Abend," the soldier muttered, examining the papers before he waved us across the bridge.

As we climbed the wide stone steps of a municipal banquet hall featuring a series of columns rising before a classical façade, we passed men in evening attire and beautiful women on their arms. German soldiers stood guard at the door. Compared to the elegant women, I knew I must appear sickly and exhausted, too thin and pale. I had pulled my hair back in a chignon and applied a bit of rouge from Dr. Raphael's case, but how unlike them — with their styled hair and fresh complexions — I was. Warm baths, powders, perfumes, and fresh clothing did not exist for me, or for any of us in occupied France. Gabriella had left behind a cut crystal bottle of Shailmar, a precious reminder of happier times that I had kept with me since her disappearance, but I dared not use a drop of the scent for fear that I might waste it. I remembered comfort as something of my childhood, something I had experienced once and never again, like loose teeth. There was little chance I would be mistaken for one of these women. Still, I clung to Dr. Raphael's arm, trying to remain calm. He walked swiftly, with confidence, and, to my surprise, the soldiers let us pass without incident. All at once we stood in the warm, noisy, lush interior of the banquet hall.

Dr. Raphael led me to the far side of the hall and up a set of stairs to a private table on the balcony. It took a moment to adjust to the noise and odd lighting, but as I did, I saw that the dining room was long and deep, with a high ceiling and mirrored walls that reflected the crowd, capturing the nape of a woman's neck here, the glistening of a watch fob there. Red banners stamped with black swastikas hung at intervals throughout the room. The tables were covered in white linen, matching china, bouquets of flowers blooming at the center — roses in the dead of a wartime winter, a minor miracle. Crystal chandeliers threw wavering light upon the dark tiled floor, catching upon satin shoes. Champagne, jewels, and beautiful people gathered in the candlelight. The room was aflutter with hands raising wineglasses — *Zum Wohl! Zum Wohl!* The abundance of wine being served from one end of the room to the other took me by surprise. While food was difficult to acquire in general, good wine was nearly impossible for those unconnected with the occupation forces. I had heard that the Germans requisitioned bottles of champagne by the thousands, and my family's cellar had been drunk dry. To me even one bottle was an extreme luxury. Yet here it was, flowing like water. At once I understood how very different the lives of the victorious were from the lives of the conquered.

From the height of the balcony, I examined the revelers up close. At first glance the crowd appeared to be like any other attending an elegant gathering. But with further inspection, I found a number of guests to have an odd appearance. They were thin and angular, with high cheekbones and wide, feline eyes, as if they had been cut from a pattern. Their blond hair, translucent skin, and unusual height marked them as Nephilistic guests.

Voices lifted to the balcony as waiters moved through the crowd, distributing glasses of champagne.

"This," Dr. Raphael said, gesturing to the hundreds of revelers below, "is what I wanted you to see."

I looked over the crowd once again, feeling as if I might be sick. "Such merriment while France starves."

"While Europe starves," Dr. Raphael corrected.

"How do they have so much food?" I asked. "So much wine, such fine clothing, so many pairs of shoes?"

"Now you see," Dr. Raphael said, smiling slightly. "I wanted you to understand what we are working for, what is at stake. You are young. Perhaps it is difficult for you to fully realize what we are up against."

I leaned against the reflective brass railing, my bare arms burning against the cold metal.

"Angelology is not just some theoretical chess game," Dr. Raphael said. "I know that in the early years of study, when one is mired in Bonaventure and Augustine, it seems that way. But your work is not solely winning debates about hylomorphism and drawing up the taxonomies of guardian angels." He gestured to the crowd below. "Your work is happening here, in the real world."

I noticed the passion with which Dr. Raphael spoke and how closely his words echoed Seraphina's warning to me as I came to in the

Devil's Throat. *Our duties lie with the world we live in and must return to.*

"You realize," he said, "that this is not just a battle between a handful of resistance fighters and an occupying army. This has been a war of attrition. It has been one continuous struggle from the very beginning. St. Thomas Aquinas believed that the dark angels fell within twenty seconds of creation — their evil nature cracked the perfection of the universe almost instantly, leaving a terrible fissure between good and evil. For twenty seconds the universe was pure, perfect, unbroken. Imagine what it was like to exist in those twenty seconds — to live without fear of death, without pain, without the doubt that we live with. Imagine."

I closed my eyes and tried to picture such a universe. I could not.

"There were twenty seconds of perfection," Dr. Raphael said, accepting a glass of champagne from a waiter and another for me. "We get the rest."

I took a sip of the cold, dry champagne. The taste was so wonderful that my tongue recoiled as if in pain.

Dr. Raphael continued, "In our time evil has overcome. Yet we continue the fight. There are thousands of us in every part of the world. And thousands — hundreds of thousands, perhaps — of them."

"They have grown so powerful," I said, examining the wealth on display in the ballroom below. "I have to believe that it wasn't always this way."

"The founding fathers of angelology took special delight in planning the extermination of their enemy. However, it was a much-studied fact that the fathers overestimated their abilities: They believed that the battle would be swift. They did not understand how petulant the Watchers and their children could be, how they reveled in subterfuge, violence, and destruction. Whereas the Watchers were angelic creatures, retaining the celestial beauty of their origins, their children were tainted with violence. They, in turn, tainted all they touched."

Dr. Raphael paused, as if thinking over a riddle.

"Consider," he said at last, "the desperation the Creator must have felt at destroying us, the sorrow of a father killing his children, the extremity of his actions. The millions of creatures drowned and the civilizations lost — and still the Nephilim prevailed. Economic greed, social injustice, war — these are the manifestations of evil in our world. Clearly, destroying life on the planet did not eliminate evil. For all their wisdom, the Venerable Fathers had not examined such things. They had not been fully prepared for the fight. They are an example of how even the most dedicated angelologists might err by ignoring history.

"Our work took quite a blow during the Inquisition, although we made up lost ground soon after," Dr. Raphael said. "The nineteenth century was equally worrisome, when the theories of Spencer and Darwin and Marx were twisted into systems of social manipulation. But in the past we've *always* recovered lost ground. Now, however, I'm growing worried. Our strength is diminishing. Death camps overflow with our kind. The Nephilim have scored a major victory with the Germans. They have been waiting for quite a while for this kind of platform."

I found that I had the opportunity to ask a question that had been at the back of my mind for some time. "You believe the Nazis are Nephilistic?"

"Not exactly," Dr. Raphael said. "Nephilim are parasitic, feeding off human society. They are mixed, after all — part angel, part human. This gives them a certain flexibility to move in and out of civilizations. Through history they have attached themselves to groups like the Nazis, promoted them, assisted them financially and militarily, and made way for their successes. It is a very old, and very successful, practice. Once they find victory, the Nephilim absorb the rewards, quietly dividing the spoils, and go back to their private existences."

"But they are called the Famous Ones," I said.

"Yes, and many of them *are* famous. But their riches buy them protection and privacy." Dr. Raphael continued, "There are a number of them here. As a matter of fact, there is one very influential gentleman I should like to introduce you to."

Dr. Raphael stood and shook hands with a tall, blond gentleman in a gorgeous silk tuxedo, who — although I could not say how — was exceedingly familiar to me. Perhaps we had met before, because he examined me with equal interest, eyeing my dress with care.

"Herr Reimer," the man said. The familiarity of his address, coupled with Dr. Raphael's false name, signaled to me that the man had no idea who we really were. Indeed, he spoke to Dr. Raphael as if they were colleagues. "Haven't seen you about Paris much this month — the war biting into your leisure?"

Dr. Raphael laughed, his voice measured. "No," he said, "just spending time with this lovely young lady. This is my niece, Christina. Christina," Dr. Raphael said, "this is Percival Grigori."

I stood and offered my hand to the man. He kissed it, his freezing lips pressing my warm skin.

"Lovely girl," the man said, although he had hardly glanced at me, so taken was he with my dress.

With that he removed a cigarette case from his pocket, offered one to Dr. Raphael, and, to my astonishment, lifted the very lighter that Gabriella had carried in her possession four years before. In an instant of horrid recognition, the man's identity was revealed to me. Percival Grigori was Gabriella's lover, the man I had found in her arms. I watched, stunned, as Dr. Raphael spoke lightly of politics and theater, touching upon the most noteworthy events of the war. Then, with a nod, Percival Grigori left us.

I sat in my chair, unable to understand how Dr. Raphael might know this man, or how Gabriella had come to be involved with him. In my confusion I chose the more prudent course: I remained silent.

"Are you feeling better?" Dr. Raphael asked.

"Better?"

"You were ill on the journey."

"Yes," I said, looking over my arms, which were redder than ever, as if I had been severely sunburned. "I believe I will be fine. My skin is fair. It will need some days to heal." Wishing to change the subject, I said, "But you didn't finish telling me about the Nazis. Are they completely under Nephilistic control? If so, how could we possibly win against them?"

"The Nephilim are very strong, but when they are defeated — and until now they have always been defeated — they disappear quickly, leaving their human hosts to face punishment alone, as if the evil actions were their own. The Nazi Party is rife with Nephilim, but those in power are one hundred percent human. That is why they are so hard to exterminate. Humanity understands, even desires, evil. There is something in our nature that is seduced by evil. We are easily convinced."

"Manipulated," I said.

"Yes, perhaps 'manipulated' is the better word. It is the more generous word."

I sank into my velvet chair, the soft fabric soothing the skin on my back. It seemed to me that I had not felt so warm in years. Music began to play in the hall, and couples began to dance, filling the floor.

"Dr. Raphael," I asked, the champagne making me feel bold, "can I ask you something?"

"Of course," he replied.

"Why did you ask if my eyes were blue?"

Dr. Raphael looked at me, and for a moment I thought that he might tell me something about himself, something that would reveal the inner life he kept hidden from his students. His voice softened as he said, "It is something you should have learned in my classes, my dear. The appearance of the Giants? Their genetic makeup?"

I recalled his lectures and flushed, embarrassed. *Of course,* I thought. *The Nephilim have luminous blue eyes, blond hair, and above-average height.* "Oh, yes," I said. "I remember now."

"You are quite tall," he observed. "And thin. I thought I could get you by the guards easier if your eyes were blue."

I finished the rest of the champagne in one quick sip. I did not like to be wrong, especially in the presence of Dr. Raphael.

"Tell me," Dr. Raphael said, "do you understand why we sent you to the gorge?"

"Scientific purposes," I replied. "To observe the angel and collect empirical evidence. To preserve the body for our records. To find the treasure Clematis left behind."

"Of course, the lyre *was* at the heart of the journey," Dr. Raphael said. "But did you wonder why an inexperienced angelologist such as yourself would be sent on a mission of this caliber? Why did Seraphina, who is only forty, lead the party and not one of the older council members?"

I shook my head. I knew that Dr. Seraphina had her own professional ambitions, but I had found it odd that Dr. Raphael had not gone to the mountain himself, especially after his early work on Clematis. I understood that my inclusion had been a reward for uncovering the location of the gorge, but perhaps there had been more to it.

"Seraphina and I wanted to send a young angelologist to the cave," Dr. Raphael said, meeting my eye. "You have not been overexposed to our professional practices. You would not color the expedition with preconceptions."

"I'm not sure what you mean," I said, placing the empty crystal flute upon the table.

"If I had gone," Dr. Raphael said, "I would have seen only what I expected to see. You, on the other hand, saw what was there. Indeed, you discovered something the others did not. Tell me the truth: How did you find it? What happened in the gorge?"

"I believe that Dr. Seraphina gave you our report," I replied, suddenly anxious about Dr. Raphael's intentions in taking me here.

"She described the physical details, the number of photographic records you made, the time it took to climb from top to bottom. Logistically, she was very thorough. But that isn't all, is it? There was something more, something that frightened you."

"I'm sorry, but I don't understand what you mean."

Dr. Raphael lit a cigarette and leaned back into his chair, amusement illuminating his features. I was unsettled still more by how handsome I found him. He said, "Even now, safe in Paris, you are frightened."

Arranging the satin fabric of the bias-cut dress, I said, "I don't know how to describe it, exactly. There was something deeply horrifying about the cavern. As we descended into the gorge, everything grew so very . . . dark."

"That seems quite natural," Dr. Raphael

said. "The gorge is deep below the surface of the mountain."

"Not physical darkness," I said, unsure of whether even in this I was giving too much away. "It was another quality altogether. An elemental darkness, a pure darkness, the kind of darkness one feels in the middle of the night after waking in a cold, empty room, the sound of bombs falling in the distance, a nightmare in the back of one's mind. It is the kind of darkness that proves the fallen nature of our world."

Dr. Raphael stared at me, waiting for me to continue.

"We were not alone in the Devil's Throat," I said. "The Watchers were there, waiting for us."

Dr. Raphael continued to assess me, and I could not tell if it was an expression of amazement or fear or — I secretly hoped — admiration. He said, "Surely the others would have mentioned this."

"I was alone," I said, breaking my promise to Dr. Seraphina. "I left the party and crossed the river. I was disoriented and cannot recall the exact details of what transpired. What I do know for certain is that I saw them. They stood in darkened cells, just as they had when Clematis encountered them. There was an angel who looked upon me. I felt its desire to be free, to be in the company of humanity, to be favored. The angel had been there for thousands of years, waiting for our arrival."

Dr. Raphael Valko and I got to the emergency council meeting in the early-morning hours. The location had been set hastily, and everyone had relocated from the previous meeting space to the center of our buildings in Montparnasse, the Athenaeum. The imposing and noble Athenaeum had fallen into disuse in the years of the occupation. Where once it had been filled with books and students, with the rustle of pages and the whisper of librarians, now the shelves were bare and the corners filled with cobwebs. I had not set foot in our library for many years, and the transformation made me long for a time when I had no worries greater than my studies.

The change of location had been made as a simple safety measure, but the precaution had cost us time. Leaving the ball, we had been given a message by a young soldier on a bicycle that told of the meeting and requested our presence immediately. Once we arrived at the designated point, we were given a second message, with a series of clues meant to bring us to the location undetected. It was nearly two o'clock in the morning before we took our seats at high-backed chairs on both sides of a narrow table in the Athenaeum.

Two small lamps lit at the center of the meeting table threw a dim, watery light upon all who sat there. There was a sense of tension and energy in the room that gave me the distinct feeling that something momentous had occurred. This perception was verified by the sobriety with which the members of the council greeted us. It appeared to me that we had interrupted a funeral.

Dr. Raphael took the seat at the head of the table, gesturing for me to sit on a bench at his side. To my great surprise, Gabriella Lévi-Franche sat at the far end of the table. It had been four years since I had last seen her. In appearance Gabriella was much the same as I remembered her. She wore her black hair in a short bob, her lips were painted bright red, and her expression was one of placid watchfulness. Yet while most of us had fallen into an anemic state of exhaustion during the war, Gabriella had the look of a pampered and well-protected woman. She was better clothed and better fed than any of the angelologists in the Athenaeum.

Noticing that I had arrived with Dr. Raphael, Gabriella raised an eyebrow, a hint of accusation forming in her green eyes. It was plain that our rivalry had not ended. Gabriella was as wary of me as I was of her.

"Tell me everything," Dr. Raphael said, his voice cracking with emotion. "I want to know exactly how it happened."

"The car was stopped for inspection at the Pont Saint-Michel," replied an elderly angelologist, the nun I had met some years before. The nun's heavy black veil and the lack of light made her appear to be an extension of the shadowy room. I could see nothing but her gnarled fingers folded upon the glossy tabletop. "The guards forced them from the car and searched them. They were taken."

"Taken?" Dr. Raphael said. "Where?"

"We have no way of knowing," said Dr. Lévi-Franche, Gabriella's uncle, his small round spectacles perched upon his nose. "We've alerted our cells in every arrondissement in the city. No one has seen them. I'm sorry to say they could be anywhere."

Dr. Raphael said, "And what of their cargo?"

Gabriella stood and placed a heavy leather case on the table. "I kept the lyre with me," she said, resting her small fingers over the brown leather case. "I was traveling in the car behind Dr. Seraphina. When we saw that our agents were being arrested, I ordered my driver to turn around and drive back to Montparnasse. Fortunately, the case holding the discoveries was with me."

Dr. Raphael's shoulders sank in a clear sign of relief. "The case is safe," he said. "But they are holding our agents."

"Of course," the nun said. "They would never let such valuable prisoners go free without asking for something equally valuable in return."

"What are the terms?" Dr. Raphael asked.

"A trade — the treasures for the angelologists," the nun replied.

"And what exactly did they mean by 'treasures'?" Dr. Raphael asked quietly.

"They were not specific," the nun said. "But somehow they know we have recovered something precious from the Rhodopes. I believe we should comply with their wishes."

"Impossible," Dr. Lévi-Franche said. "It is simply out of the question."

"It is my opinion that they do not know what the group actually found in the mountains, only that it is prized," Gabriella said, straightening in her chair.

"Perhaps the captured agents have told them what they extracted from the cavern," suggested the nun. "Under such duress it would be the natural outcome."

"I believe that our angelologists will honor our codes," Dr. Raphael answered, a hint of anger in his response. "If I know Seraphina at all, she won't allow the others to speak." He turned away, and I could see the faintest glistening of sweat forming upon his forehead. "She will endure their questions, although we all know that their methods can be horribly cruel."

The atmosphere turned grim. We all understood how brutal the Nephilim could be to our agents, especially if they wanted something. I had heard tales of the methods

451

of torture they used, and I could only imagine what they would do to my colleagues to extract information. Closing my eyes, I whispered a prayer. I could not foresee what would happen, but I understood how important the evening had become: If we lost what we had recovered from the cavern, our work would have been for nothing. The discoveries were precious, but would we willingly sacrifice an entire team of angelologists for them?

"One thing is certain," the nun said, looking at her wristwatch. "They are still alive. We received the call approximately twenty minutes ago. I myself spoke with Seraphina."

"Could she speak freely?" Dr. Raphael said.

"She urged us to make the trade," the nun said. "She specifically asked Dr. Raphael to go forward."

Dr. Raphael folded his hands before him. He seemed to be examining something minute on the surface of the table. "What are your thoughts about such a trade?" he asked, addressing the council.

"We don't have much choice in the matter," Dr. Lévi-Franche said. "Such a trade is against our protocol. We have never made such trades in the past, and I believe we should not make an exception, no matter how we value Dr. Seraphina. We cannot possibly give them the materials recovered from the gorge. Retrieving them has been hundreds of years in the planning."

I was horrified to hear Gabriella's uncle speak of my teacher in such cold terms. My indignation was assuaged slightly as I caught Gabriella glaring at him with annoyance, the very look she had once reserved for me.

"And yet," said the nun, "Dr. Seraphina's expertise has brought us the treasure. If we lose her, how will we progress?"

"It is impossible to make the trade," Dr. Lévi-Franche insisted. "We have not had the opportunity to examine the field notes or develop the photographs. The expedition would be an utter waste."

Vladimir said, "And the lyre — I cannot possibly imagine what the consequences of their possession of it would hold for all of us. For all the world, for that matter."

"I agree," Dr. Raphael said. "The instrument must be kept away from them at all costs. Surely there must be some alternative."

"I am aware that my views are not popular among you," the nun said. "But this instrument is not worth the cost of human life. We must certainly make the trade."

"But the treasure we have found today is the culmination of great efforts," Vladimir objected, his Russian accent thick. The cut over his eye had been sutured and cleaned and had the appearance of raw and gruesome embroidery. "Surely you do not mean that we destroy something we have worked so hard to recover?"

"It is exactly what I mean," the nun said. "There is a point when we must realize that we have no power in these matters. It is out of our hands. We must leave it to God."

"Ridiculous," Vladimir said.

As the arguments erupted between the members of the council, I studied Dr. Raphael, who sat so close by that I could smell the sour-sweet aroma of the champagne we'd been drinking only hours before. I could see that he was quietly formulating his thoughts, waiting for the others to exhaust their arguments. Finally he rose, gestured for the group to be silent. "Quiet!" he said, with more force than I had ever heard him use before.

The council members turned to him, surprised at the sudden authority in his voice. Although he was the head of the council and our most prestigious scholar, he rarely displayed his power.

Dr. Raphael said, "Earlier this evening I took this young angelologist to a gathering. It was a ball, thrown by our enemies. I think that I can say it was quite a brilliant affair, wouldn't you agree, Celestine?"

At a loss for words, I simply nodded.

Dr. Raphael continued, "My reasons for doing this were practical. I wanted to show her the enemy up close. I wanted her to understand that the forces we are fighting against are here, living next to us in our cities, stealing and killing and pillaging as we watch, helpless. I think the lesson made an impression upon her. Yet I see now that many of you might have benefited from such an educational episode. It is obvious to me that we have forgotten what we are doing here."

He gestured to the leather case sitting between them.

"This is not our fight to lose. The Venerable Fathers who risked heresy in founding our work, who preserved texts during the purges and burnings of the church, who copied the prophecies of Enoch and risked their lives to pass down information and resources — this is their fight we are carrying out. Bonaventure, whose *Commentary on the Sentences* so eloquently proved our founding metaphysics of angelology, that angels are both material and spiritual in substance. The scholastic fathers. Duns Scotus. The hundreds of thousands of those who have striven to defeat the machinations of the evil ones. How many have sacrificed their lives for our cause? How many would gladly do so again? This is their fight. And yet all of these hundreds of years have led to this singular moment of choice. Somehow the burden is on our shoulders. We are entrusted with the power to decide the future. We can continue the struggle, or we can give in." He stood, walked to the case, and took it in his hands. "But we must decide immediately. Each member will vote."

As Dr. Raphael called for the council to vote, the members raised their hands. To my utter amazement, Gabriella — who had never been allowed to attend a meeting, let alone help make decisions — had gained full voting privileges, while I, who had spent years working to prepare for the expedition and risked my life in the cavern, was not asked to participate. Gabriella was an angelologist, and I was still a novice. Tears of anger and defeat filled my eyes, blurring the room so that I could only just make out the voting. Gabriella raised her hand in favor of the trade, as did Dr. Raphael and the nun. Many of the others, however, wished to remain faithful to our codes. After the votes were counted, it was plain that many were in favor of making the trade and an equal number were against it.

"We are evenly divided," Dr. Raphael said.

The council members looked from one to another, wondering who might change his or her vote to break the tie.

"I suggest," Gabriella said at last, giving me a look that seemed laced with hope, "that we allow Celestine the opportunity to vote. She was a member of the expedition. Hasn't she earned the right to participate?"

All eyes turned to me, sitting quietly behind Dr. Raphael. The council members agreed. My vote would decide the matter. I considered the choice before me, knowing that my decision put me at last among the other angelologists.

The council waited for me to make my choice.

After I cast my vote, I begged the pardon of the council, stepped into the empty hallway, and ran as fast as I could. Through the corridors, down a flight of wide stone steps, out the door, and into the night I ran, my shoes striking the rhythm of my heart on the flagstones. I knew that I might find solitude in the back courtyard, a place Gabriella and I had gone often, the very place I'd first glimpsed the gold lighter that Nephilistic monster had used in my presence earlier that night. The courtyard was always empty, even during the daylight hours, and I needed to be alone. Tears softened the edges of my vision — the iron fence surrounding the ancient structure melted, the majestic elephant-skinned beech tree in the courtyard dissolved, even the sharpened sickle of the crescent moon suspended in the sky blurred into an indistinct halo above me.

Checking to be sure that I had not been followed, I crouched against the wall of the building, hid my face in my hands, and sobbed. I cried for Dr. Seraphina and for the other members of the expedition party whom I had betrayed. I cried for the burden my vote had placed upon my conscience. I understood that my decision had been the correct one, but the sacrifice cracked through me, shattering my belief in myself, my colleagues, and our work. I had betrayed my teacher, my mentor. I had washed my hands of a woman I loved as deeply as I loved my own mother. I had been given the privilege to vote, but upon casting it I had lost my faith in angelology.

Although I wore a thick wool jacket — the same heavy coat I'd used to stave off the wet winds of the cavern — I had nothing underneath it but the thin dress Dr. Raphael had given me to wear to the party. I wiped my eyes with the back of my hand and shivered. The night was freezing, utterly still and quiet, colder than it had been only a few hours earlier. Regaining control of my emotions, I took a deep breath and prepared to return to the council room when, from somewhere near the side entrance of the building, there came the soft whisper of voices.

Stepping back into the shadows, I waited, wondering who would have left the building by that odd exit, the usual course being through the portico at the front entrance. In a matter of seconds, Gabriella stepped into the courtyard, speaking in a low, nearly inaudible voice to Vladimir, who listened to her as if she were telling him something of great importance.

I struggled to see them better. Gabriella was particularly striking in the moonlight — her black hair shone, and her red lipstick defined her lips dramatically against the whiteness of her skin. She wore a luxurious camel-colored overcoat, fitted snugly and belted at the waist, clearly tailored for her figure. I could not imagine where she had found such clothing and how she could have paid for it. Gabriella had always dressed beautifully, but for me clothes like Gabriella's existed only in films.

Even after years apart, I knew her expressions well. The furrow in her brow meant she was pondering some question Vladimir had asked her. A sudden flash of brightness in her eyes, accompanied by a perfunctory smile, signified that she had answered him with her customary aplomb, a witticism, an aphorism, something biting. He listened with all his attention. His gaze did not leave her for even a moment.

As Gabriella and Vladimir spoke, I could hardly breathe. Given the events of the evening, Gabriella should have been as distressed as I. The loss of four angelologists and the threat of losing our discoveries from the expedition should have been enough to kill all merriment, even if the relationship between Dr. Seraphina and Gabriella had been superficial. But despite everything, the two had been exceptionally close once, and I knew that Gabriella had loved our teacher. Yet in the courtyard Gabriella appeared — I could hardly bear to think of the word — "joyous." She had an air of triumph, as if she'd won a hard-fought victory.

A burst of light scattered over the courtyard as a car stopped, its headlights streaming through the iron gates and illuminating the great beech tree, whose branches stretched into the watery air like tentacles. A man stepped from the car. Gabriella glanced over her shoulder, her black hair framing her face like a bell. The man was striking, tall, with a beautiful double-breasted jacket and shoes that gleamed from polish. His appearance struck me as extraordinarily refined. Such wealth was an exotic sight during the war, and that evening I had been surrounded by it. As he stepped closer, I saw that it was Percival Grigori, the Nephilim I'd met earlier that evening. Gabriella recognized him at once. She gestured that he wait at the car and, kissing Vladimir quickly on each cheek, she turned and strode over the flagstones to her lover.

I crouched farther into the shadows, hoping that my presence would not be discovered. Gabriella was only meters away, so close I could have whispered to her as she passed. It was at that proximity that I saw it: the case containing our treasure from the mountain. Gabriella was delivering it to Percival Grigori.

This discovery had such an effect upon me that I momentarily lost my composure. I stepped into the plain light of the moon. Gabriella stopped short, taken by surprise to find me there. As our eyes met, I realized that it would not have mattered what the council had voted to do: All along, Gabriella had planned to give the case to her lover. In that moment the years of Gabriella's strange behavior — her disappearances, her unaccountable rise in the angelological ranks, her falling-out with Dr. Seraphina, the money that seemed to come to her from out of the blue — all of it made sense to me. Dr. Seraphina had been correct. Gabriella was working with our enemies.

"What are you doing?" I said, hearing my own voice as if it belonged to another woman.

"Go back inside," Gabriella answered, clearly startled by my appearance, her voice very low, as if she were afraid we would be overheard.

"You cannot do this," I whispered. "Not now, after all we've suffered."

"I am sparing you from further suffering," Gabriella said, and, breaking free of my gaze, she walked to the car and climbed into the backseat, Percival Grigori following close behind.

The shock of Gabriella's actions held me momentarily paralyzed, but as the car drove into the tangled obscurity of the narrow streets, I awoke. I ran through the courtyard and into the building, fear pushing me faster and faster through the vast, cold hallway.

Suddenly a voice called out to me from the end of the corridor. "Celestine!" Dr. Raphael said, stepping in my path. "Thank God you

461

haven't been hurt."

"No," I said, struggling to catch my breath. "But Gabriella has left with the case. I have just come from the courtyard. She's stolen it."

"Follow me," Dr. Raphael said. Without further explanation he led me along a neglected hallway back to the Athenaeum, where the council had convened their meeting only half an hour before. Vladimir had also returned. He greeted me tersely, his expression grave. Looking past him, I saw that the windows at the far end of the room had been shattered and a cold, harsh breeze fell over the mutilated bodies of the council members, their corpses lying in pools of blood upon the floor.

The sight struck me with such force that I was unable to muster any response but disbelief. I supported myself upon the table where we had voted away my teacher's life, unable to tell if the sight before me was real or if an evil fantasy had taken hold of my imagination. The brutality of the killings was horrifying. The nun had been shot point-blank in the head, leaving her habit soaked in blood. Gabriella's uncle, Dr. Lévi-Franche, lay on the marble floor, equally bloody, his glasses crushed. Two other council members slumped upon the table itself.

I closed my eyes and turned from the awful sight. My only relief came when Dr. Raphael, whose arm encircled my shoulders, held me steady. I leaned against him, the scent of his body giving bittersweet comfort. I imagined that I would open my eyes and everything would be just as it had been years before — the Athenaeum would be filled with crates and papers and busy assistants packing our texts away. The council members would be arrayed about the table, studying Dr. Raphael's maps of wartime Europe. Our school would be open, the council members would be alive. But upon opening my eyes, I was hit by the horror of the massacre again. There was no way to escape its reality.

"Come, now," Dr. Raphael said, leading me from the room, steering me forcefully through the hallway and to the front entrance. "Breathe. You are in shock."

Looking about as if in a dream, I said, "What has happened? I don't understand. Did Gabriella do this?"

"Gabriella?" Vladimir said, joining us in the corridor. "No, of course not."

"Gabriella had nothing to do with it," Dr. Raphael said. "They were spies. We had known for some time that they were monitoring the council. It was part of the plan to kill them this way."

"You did this?" I said, astonished. "How could you?"

Dr. Raphael looked at me, and I saw the faintest shadow of sadness register in his expression, as if it hurt him to bear witness to my disillusionment. "It's my job, Celestine," he said at last as he took me by the arm and guided me through the hall. "One day you will understand. Come, we must get you out of here."

As we approached the main entrance of the Athenaeum, the numbness brought on by the scene had begun to wear away, and I was overcome by nausea. Dr. Raphael led me into the cold night air, where the Panhard et Levassor waited to chauffer us away. As we walked down the wide stone steps, he pressed a case into my hand. The case was identical to the one Gabriella had held in the courtyard — the same brown leather, the same gleaming clasps.

"Take this," Dr. Raphael said. "Everything is ready. You will be driven to the border tonight. Then, I'm afraid, we'll have to rely upon our friends in Spain and Portugal to get you through."

"Through to where?"

"To America," Dr. Raphael said. "You will take this case with you. You — and the treasure from the gorge — will be safe there."

"But I saw Gabriella leave," I said, examining the case as if it were an illusion. "She took the instrument. It is gone."

"It was a replica, dear Celestine, a decoy," Dr. Raphael said. "Gabriella is diverting the enemy so that you can escape and Seraphina can be freed. You owe her much, including your presence on the expedition. The lyre is now in your care. You and Gabriella have gone your separate ways, but you must always remember that your work is for a single cause. Hers will be here, and yours will be in America."

THE THIRD SPHERE

*And there appeared to me two men very
tall, such as I have never seen on earth.
And their faces shone like the sun, and their
eyes were like burning lamps; and fire came
forth from their lips. Their dress had the appearance of feathers: their feet were purple,
their wings brighter than gold; their hands
whiter than snow.*

— The Book of Enoch

Sister Evangeline's cell, St. Rose Convent,
Milton, New York

December 24, 1999, 12:01 A.M.

Evangeline went to the window, pushed back
the heavy curtains, and gazed into the darkness. From the fourth floor, she could see
clear across the river. At scheduled times
each night, the passenger train cut through
the dark, slicing a bright trail against the
landscape. The presence of the night train
comforted Evangeline — it was as reliable as
the workings of St. Rose Convent. The train
passed, the sisters walked to prayer, the heat
seeped from steam radiators, the wind rattled
the windowpanes. The universe moved in
regular cycles. The sun would rise in a few
hours, and when it did, Evangeline would
begin another day, following the rigid schedule she had followed every other day: prayer,
breakfast, Mass, library work, lunch, prayer,
chores, library work, Mass, dinner. Her life
moved in spheres as regular as the beads on
a rosary.

Sometimes Evangeline would watch the
train and imagine the shadowy outline of a

traveler making his precarious way through the aisle. The train and the man would flash by and then, in a clatter of metal and neon light, move off to some unknown destination. Gazing into the darkness, she longed for the train carrying Verlaine to pass while she watched.

Evangeline's room was the size of a linen closet and, appropriately, smelled of freshly laundered linens. She had recently waxed the pine floor, cleaned the corners of spiderwebs, and dusted the room from floor to ceiling and wainscoting to sill. The stiff white sheets on her bed seemed to call out to her to take her shoes off and lie down to sleep. Instead she poured water from a pitcher into a glass on the bureau and drank. Then she opened the window and took a deep breath. The air was cold and thick in her lungs, soothing as ice on a wound. She was so tired she could hardly think. The clock's electric digits gave the hour. It was just after midnight. A new day was beginning.

Sitting upon her bed, Evangeline closed her eyes and let all thoughts of the previous day's encounter settle. She took the pack of letters Sister Celestine had given her and counted. There were eleven envelopes, one sent each year, the return address — a New York City address she did not recognize — the same on each one. Her grandmother had posted letters with remarkable consistency, the cancel-

470

lation on the stamp dating the twenty-first of December. A card had arrived annually, from 1988 until 1998. Only the present year's card was not among them.

Careful, so as not to rip the faces of the envelopes, Evangeline removed the cards and examined them, arranging them in chronological order across the surface of the bed, from the first card to arrive to the last. The cards were covered in pen-and-ink sketches, bold blue lines that did not appear to form any specific image. The designs had been executed by hand, although Evangeline could not understand the purpose or meaning of the images. One of the cards contained a sketch of an angel climbing a ladder, an elegant, modern depiction that had none of the excesses of the angelic images in Maria Angelorum.

Although many sisters did not agree with her, Evangeline much preferred artistic depictions of angels to the biblical descriptions, which she found frightening to imagine. Ezekiel's wheels, for example, were described in the Bible as beryl-plated and circular, with hundreds of eyes lining their outer rims. The cherubim were said to have four faces — a man, an ox, a lion, and an eagle. This ancient vision of God's messengers was unnerving, almost grotesque, when compared with the Renaissance painters' work, which forever changed the visual representation of angels. Angels blowing trumpets, carrying harps, and hiding behind delicate wings — these were the angels Evangeline cherished, no matter how removed from biblical reality they were.

Evangeline examined the cards one by one. On the first card, dated December 1988, there was the image of an angel blowing a golden trumpet, its white robes traced in gold. When she opened it, she found a piece of creamy paper fastened inside. A message, written with crimson ink in her grandmother's elegant hand, read:

Be forewarned, dear Evangeline: Understanding the significance of Orpheus's lyre has proved to be a trial. Legend surrounds Orpheus so heavily that we cannot discern the precise outline of his mortal life. We do not know the year of his birth, his true lineage, or the real measure of his talents with the lyre. He was reputed to have been born of the muse Calliope and the river god Oeagrus, but this, of course, is mythology, and it is our work to separate the mythological from the historical, disentangle legend from fact, magic from truth. Did he give humanity poetry? Did he discover the lyre on his legendary journey to the underworld? Was he as influential in his own lifetime as history claims? By the sixth century B.C., he was known through the Greek world as the master of songs and music, but how he came upon the instrument of the angels has been widely debated among historians. Your mother's work only gave confirmation to long-held theories of the lyre's importance.

Evangeline turned the paper over in her hand, hoping the red ink would continue. Surely the message was a fragment of a larger communication. But she found nothing.

She glanced about her bedroom — the solid edges of which had gone soft as her exhaustion grew — then turned back to the cards. She opened another card and then another. There were identical creamy pages fastened inside each card, all of which had been filled with lines of writing that began and ended without any discernible logic whatsoever. Of the eleven cards, only the one addressed to her contained a definite starting or ending point. There were no numbers on the pages, and the order could not be discerned from the chronology in which they'd been mailed. In fact, it appeared to Evangeline that the pages had been simply filled up with an endless stream of words. To make matters worse, the words were so small it strained her eyes to read them.

After examining the pages for some time, Evangeline returned each card to its envelope, being sure to keep the envelopes in the order of cancellation date. The effort of trying to understand the tangled pages of her grandmother's writing made her head throb. She could not think clearly, and the pain in her temples was acute. She should have gone to sleep hours before. Bundling the cards together, she placed them under her pillow, careful not to bend or crease the edges. She could do nothing more until she had some sleep.

Without pausing to put on her pajamas, she stepped out of her shoes and fell into bed. The sheets were wonderfully cool and soft against her skin. Pulling her comforter to her chin and wiggling her nylon-encased toes, she dropped into the bottomless free fall of sleep.

Metro-North Hudson Line train, somewhere between Poughkeepsie and Harlem–125th Street station, New York

Verlaine had caught the last southbound train of the night. To his right, the Hudson River ran alongside the tracks; to his left, the snow-covered hills rose to meet the night sky. The train was warm, well lit, and empty. The Coronas he had drunk at the bar in Milton and the slow, rocking rhythm of the train had combined to calm him to the point of resignation, if not contentment. Although he hated the thought of leaving his Renault behind, the reality was that he would probably never get his car back in working order. It was a model with a boxy body whose simple design gestured to the early Renaults of the postwar era, cars that — because they had never been imported to the United States and he had never been to France — Verlaine had seen only in photographs. Now it was smashed up and gutted.

Even worse than losing his car, however, was the loss of his entire body of research. In addition to the meticulously organized material he'd used to support his doctoral thesis — a binder of colored plates, notes, and general information regarding Abigail Rockefeller's work with the Museum of Modern Art — there were hundreds of pages of photocopies and further notes he'd made in the past year of his work for Percival Grigori. While his formulations were not exactly original, they were all he had. Everything had been in the backseat, in the bag Grigori's men had stolen. He had made copies of much of his work but with Grigori riding him he'd been more disorganized than usual. He could not recall how much of the St. Rose/Rockefeller material he'd actually duplicated, nor was he completely certain of what he'd thrown in his bag and what he'd left behind. He would need to stop by his office and check his files. For now he had to hold out hope that he'd been assiduous enough to keep a reserve of the most important documents. In spite of all that had happened in the past hours, there was some reassurance: First, the original letters from Innocenta to Abigail Rockefeller were locked in his office, and second, he had kept the architectural drawings of St. Rose Convent with him.

Sliding his injured hand deep into the inside pocket of his overcoat, he removed the bundle of plans. After Grigori's dismissive attitude toward them in Central Park, he had almost thought them worthless. Why, then, would Grigori send thugs to break into his car if they

476

weren't valuable?

Verlaine spread the plans out on his lap, his eye falling upon the seal of the lyre. The coincidence of the icon seal matching Evangeline's pendant was an oddity Verlaine was keen to explain. In fact, everything about the lyre — from its presence on the Thracian coin he'd found to its prominence on St. Rose's insignia — felt larger than life, almost mythological. It was as though his personal experiences had taken on the properties of symbolism and layered historical meaning that he was used to applying to his art-history research. Perhaps he was imposing his own scholarly training upon a situation, drawing connections where none existed, romanticizing his work and blowing the whole thing out of proportion. Now that he'd settled into his seat on the train and had the peace of mind to think it all through, Verlaine began to wonder if he hadn't overreacted a bit to the lyre necklace. Indeed, there was the chance that the men who had broken into his Renault had nothing to do with Grigori. Perhaps there was another, completely logical explanation for the bizarre events that had happened that day.

Verlaine took the sheets of blank St. Rose Convent stationery and pressed them over the top of the architectural drawings. The paper was thick cotton bond, pink, with an elaborately woven heading of roses and angels executed in a lush Victorian-era style that, to his surprise,

Verlaine quite liked, despite his preference for modernism. He had not said so at the time, but Evangeline had been wrong that their founding mother had designed the stationery two hundred years before: The invention of a chemical method for making paper from wood pulp, a technological revolution that bolstered the postal service and allowed individuals and groups to create individualized stationery, did not occur until the mid-1850s. The St. Rose stationery was most likely created in the late nineteenth century, using their founding mother's artwork for the heading. The practice had in fact become extraordinarily popular during the Gilded Era. Luminaries like his very own Abigail Rockefeller had put great effort into making dinner-party menus, calling cards, invitations, and personalized envelopes and stationery, each with family symbols and crests pressed into the highest-quality paper available. He'd sold a number of pristine sets of such custom-printed bond at auction over the years.

He had not corrected Evangeline's error, he realized now, because she'd thrown him off guard. If she had been an old bulldog of a woman, ill-tempered and overprotective of the archives, he would have been perfectly prepared to handle her. In his years of begging access to libraries, he'd learned how to win over librarians, or at least gain their sympathy. But he'd been helpless upon seeing Evangeline. Evangeline was beautiful, she was intelligent, she was strangely comforting, and — as a nun — completely off-limits. Perhaps she liked him, just a little. Even as she was about to kick him out of the convent, he'd felt a strange connection between them. Closing his eyes, he tried to remember exactly how she'd looked sitting in the bar in Milton. She'd looked — aside from that funky black nun outfit — like a normal person having a normal night out. He didn't think he would be able to forget the way she'd smiled, just slightly, when he touched her hand.

Verlaine let the rocking of the train car lull him into a state of reverie, thoughts of Evangeline playing through his mind, when a crack against the windowpane jarred him awake. An immense white hand, its fingers spread apart like the points of a starfish, had pressed against the window. Startled, Verlaine sat back, trying to examine it from a different angle. Another hand appeared on the glass, slapping against it as if it might push the thick square of plastic inward, popping it from its frame. A swift, fibrous, red feather brushed against the window. Verlaine blinked, trying to decide if he had somehow fallen asleep, if this bizarre show was a dream. But upon looking more closely, he saw something that chilled his blood: Two immense creatures hovered outside the train, their great red eyes staring at him with menace, their large wings carrying them along in tandem with the car. He stared at them in fright, unable to pull his gaze away. Was he going crazy or did these bizarre beings resemble the thugs he had watched trash his car? To his amazement and consternation, he concluded that they did.

Verlaine jumped up, grabbed his jacket, and ran to the train's restroom, a small, windowless compartment that smelled of chemicals. Breathing deeply, he tried to calm himself down. His clothes were soaked in sweat, and there was a lightness in his chest that made him feel as though he might faint. He had felt this way only once, in high school, when he'd drunk too much at his prom.

As the train hit upon the edges of the city, Verlaine tucked the maps and stationery deep into his pocket. He left the bathroom and walked quickly to the front of the train. There were only a few passengers to get off the midnight train in Harlem. The stark depopulated midnight station gave him the eerie sensation, as he stepped onto the platform, that he'd made some kind of mistake, perhaps missed his stop or, worse, had taken the wrong train entirely. He walked the length of the platform and down a set of iron stairs to the dark, cold, city street below. He felt as if some cataclysm had hit New York in his absence, and, through some trick of destiny, he had returned to a ravaged and empty city.

Upper East Side, New York City

Sneja had ordered Percival to stay indoors, but after pacing the billiard room for hours waiting for Otterley to call with news, he could not tolerate being alone any longer. When his mother's entourage had left for the night and he was certain that Sneja had gone to sleep, Percival dressed with care — putting on a tuxedo and a black overcoat, as if he'd just been to a gala — and took the elevator down to Fifth Avenue.

It used to be that contact with the outside world left him indifferent. As a young man, when he'd lived in Paris and could not help but be confronted with the stench of humanity, he had learned to ignore people entirely. He had no need for the ceaseless scurrying of human activity — the tireless toil, the festivities, the amusements. It had bored him. Yet his illness had transformed him. He had begun to watch human beings, examining their odd habits with interest. He had begun to sympathize with them.

He knew that this was symptomatic of the larger changes — those he'd been warned would occur, and that he had been prepared to accept as the natural progression of his metamorphosis. He was told that he would begin to feel new and startling sensations, and indeed he found that he recoiled in discomfort at the sight of these pitiful creatures' suffering. At first these odd sentiments had poisoned him with absurd bouts of emotion. He knew very well that human beings were inferior and that their suffering was in direct proportion to their position in the order of the universe. It was just so with animals, whose wretchedness seemed only slightly more pronounced than that of humans. Yet Percival began to see beauty in their rituals, their love of family, their dedication to worship, their defiance in the face of physical weakness. Despite his contempt for them, he had begun to understand the tragedy of their plight: They lived and died as if their existence mattered. If he were to mention these thoughts to Otterley or Sneja, he would be ridiculed without mercy.

Slowly, painfully, Percival Grigori made his way past the majestic apartment buildings of his neighborhood, his breathing labored, his cane aiding his progress along the icy sidewalks. The cold wind did not hinder him — he felt nothing but the creaking of the harness about his rib cage, the burning in his chest as he breathed, and the crunching of his knees and hips as the bones ground to powder. He wished he could remove his jacket and unbind his body, let the cold air soothe the burns on his skin. The mangled, decaying wings on his back pressed against his clothes, giving him the appearance of a hunchback, a beast, a deformed being shunned by the world. He wished, on late-night walks like this one, that he could trade places with the carefree, healthy people walking past him. He would almost consent to be human if it would free him of pain.

After some time the strain of the walk overwhelmed him. Percival stopped at a wine bar, a sleek space of polished brass and red velvet. Inside, it was crowded and warm. Percival ordered a glass of Macallan scotch and chose a secluded corner table from where he could watch the revelry of the living.

He had just finished his first glass of whiskey when he noticed a woman at the far end of the room. The woman was young, with glossy black hair cut in the style of the 1930s. She sat at a table, a group of friends encircling her. Although she wore trashy modern clothing — tight jeans and a lacy, low-cut blouse — her beauty had the classical purity Percival associated with women of another era. The young woman was the twin of his beloved Gabriella Lévi-Franche.

For an hour Percival did not take his eyes

from her. He composed a profile of her gestures and expressions, noting that she was like Gabriella in more than appearance. Perhaps, Percival reasoned, he wanted to see Gabriella's features too desperately: In the young woman's silence, Percival detected Gabriella's analytic intelligence; in the young woman's impassive stare, he saw Gabriella's propensity to hoard secrets. The woman was reserved among her friends, just as Gabriella had always been reserved in a crowd. Percival guessed that his prey preferred to listen, letting her friends carry on with whatever amusing nonsense filled their lives, while she privately assessed their habits, cataloging their strengths and faults with clinical ruthlessness. He determined to wait until she was alone so that he might speak to her.

After he had ordered many more glasses of Macallan, the young woman finally gathered her coat and made her way to the door. As she walked by, Percival blocked her path with his cane, the polished ebony brushing her leg. "Forgive me for accosting you in such a forthright fashion," he said, standing so that he rose above her. "But I insist upon buying you a drink."

The young woman looked at him, startled. He could not tell what surprised her more — the cane blocking her way or his unusual approach to asking her to stay with him.

"You're awfully dressed up," she said, eyeing his tuxedo. Her voice was high-pitched and emotional, the exact opposite of Gabriella's cold, uninflected manner of expression, an inversion that damaged Percival's fantasy in an instant. He had wanted to believe he'd discovered Gabriella, but it was clear that this person was not as similar to Gabriella as he'd hoped. Nevertheless, he yearned to speak to her, to look at her, to re-create the past.

He gestured for her to sit across from him. She hesitated just a moment, glanced once again at his expensive clothing, and sat. To his disappointment, her physical resemblance to Gabriella diminished even further when he examined her at close proximity. Her skin was peppered with fine freckles; Gabriella's had been creamy and unblemished. Her eyes were brown; Gabriella's had been brilliant green. Yet the curve of her shoulders and the way her blunt-cut black hair rested upon her cheeks was similar enough to hold his fascination. He ordered a bottle of champagne — the most expensive bottle available — and began to regale her with stories of his adventures in Europe, altering the tales to mask his age or, rather, his agelessness. While he had lived in Paris in the thirties, he told her he'd lived there in the eighties. While his business interests had been entirely directed by his father, he claimed to run his own enterprise. Not that she noticed the finer points or details of what he told her. It seemed to matter little what he said — she drank the champagne and listened, utterly unaware that she caused him such utter discomfort. It didn't matter if she were as mute as a mannequin, so long as he could keep her there before him, silent and wide-eyed, half amused and half adoring, her hand draped carelessly over the table, her fleeting similarities to Gabriella intact. All that mattered was the illusion that time had fallen away.

The fantasy allowed him to recall the blind fury Gabriella's betrayal had caused him. The two of them had planned the theft of the Rhodope treasure together. Their plan had been precisely calibrated and, to Percival's mind, brilliant. Their relationship had been one of passion, but also of mutual advantage. Gabriella had brought him information about angelological work — detailed reports on the holdings and whereabouts of angelologists — and Percival gave Gabriella information that allowed her to advance through the hierarchy of the society with ease. Their business interactions — there could be no other word for these worldly exchanges — had only served to make him admire Gabriella. Her hunger to succeed made her all the more precious to him.

With Gabriella's guidance the Grigori family learned of the Second Angelological Expedition. Their plan had been brilliant. Percival and Gabriella had set up the abduction of Seraphina Valko together, designating the route the caravan would take through Paris, making certain that the leather case remained in Gabriella's hands. They had wagered that a trade — releasing the angelologists in exchange for the case containing the treasure — would be instantly approved by the Angelological Council. Dr. Seraphina Valko was not only an angelologist of world renown, she was the wife of the council leader, Raphael Valko. There was no possibility that the council would let her die, no matter how precious the object in question. Gabriella had assured him that their plan would work. He had believed her. Yet it soon became clear that something had gone terribly wrong. When he realized that there would be no trade, Percival killed Seraphina Valko himself. She had died in silence, although they'd done all they could to encourage her to divulge information about the object she'd recovered. But worst of all, Gabriella had betrayed him.

The night she had given him the leather case containing the lyre he would have married her. He would have brought her into their circle, even against the objections of his parents, who long suspected that she was a spy working to infiltrate the Grigori family. Percival had defended her. But when his mother had taken the lyre to be examined by a German specialist in the history of musical instruments, a man often called upon to verify Nazi treasures, they found that the lyre was nothing more than a well-rendered replica, an ancient Syrian specimen made of cattle bone. Gabriella had lied to him. He had been humiliated and ridiculed for his faith in Gabriella, whom Sneja had never trusted.

After the betrayal he'd washed his hands of Gabriella, leaving her to the others, a decision he found painful. He learned sometime later that her punishment had been exceptionally severe. It had been his intention that she die — indeed, he had instructed that she be killed rather than tortured — but through some combination of luck and extraordinary planning on the part of her colleagues she had been rescued. She recovered and went on to marry Raphael Valko, a match that assisted her career advancement. Percival would be the first to admit that Gabriella was the best in her field, one of the few angelologists to fully penetrate their world.

In reality he had not spoken to Gabriella for more than fifty years. Like the others, she had been kept under continual surveillance, her professional and personal activities monitored at all times of the day and night. He knew that she was living in New York City and that she continued her work against him and his family. But Percival knew very little about the details of her personal life. After their affair his family had made sure that all information about Gabriella Lévi-Franche Valko be kept from him.

The last he'd heard, Gabriella was still struggling against the inevitable decline of angelology, fighting against the hopelessness of their cause. He imagined that she would be old now, her face still beautiful but fallen. She would look nothing at all like the frivolous, silly young woman now sitting across from him. Percival leaned back in his chair and examined the woman — her ridiculously low-cut blouse and her uncouth jewelry. She had become drunk — in fact, she had more than likely been so even before he'd ordered the champagne. The tawdry woman before him was nothing at all like Gabriella.

"Come with me," Percival said, throwing a stack of bills on the table. He put on his overcoat, took up his cane, and walked out into the night, his arm about the young woman. She was tall and thin, larger-boned than Gabriella. Percival could feel the pure sexual attraction between them — since the beginning it had been thus, human women falling prey to angelic charm.

This one was no different from the others. She went along with Percival willingly, and for some blocks they walked in silence until, finding a secluded alley, he took her by the hand and led her into the shadows. The unbearable, almost animal desire he felt for her fueled his anger. He kissed her, made love to her, and then, in a rage, he encircled her delicate, warm throat with his long, cold fingers and pressed the bones until they began to snap. The young woman grunted and pushed him away, struggling to free herself from his grip, but it was too late: Percival Grigori was caught up in the kill. The ecstasy of her pain, the sheer bliss of her struggle, sent shudders of desire through him. Imagining that it was Gabriella in his grasp only made the pleasure more acute.

St. Rose Convent, Milton, New York

Evangeline woke at three in the morning in a panic. After years of abiding a rigorously strict routine, she had the tendency to become disoriented when she deviated from her schedule. Glancing about her room and feeling the pull of sleep weighing upon her senses, she decided that what she saw was not her chamber at all but a small, orderly room with immaculate windowpanes and dusted shelves that existed in a dream, and she went back to sleep.

The fleeting image of her mother and father appeared before her. They stood together in the apartment in Paris, her childhood home. In the dream her father was young and handsome, happier than Evangeline had seen him after her mother's death. Her mother — even in the midst of dreaming, Evangeline struggled to see her — stood in the distance, a shadowy figure, her face obscured by a sun hat. Evangeline reached for her, desperate to touch her mother's hand. From the depths of her dream, she called for her mother to come closer. But as she strained to be near to her, Angela receded, dissolving like a diaphanous, insubstantial fog.

Evangeline woke for a second time, startled by the intensity of the dream. The bright red light of her alarm clock illuminated three numbers — 4:55. A shot of electricity sparked through her: She was about to be late for her scheduled hour of adoration. As she blinked and looked about the room, she realized that she had left the drapes open, and her chamber absorbed the night sky. Her white sheets were tinted grayish purple, as if covered in ash. Standing at her bedside, she stepped into her black skirt, buttoned her white blouse, and fitted her veil over her hair.

As she recalled her dream, a wave of longing enveloped her. No matter how much time passed, Evangeline felt her parents' absence as acutely as she had as a child. Her father had died suddenly three years before, his heart stopping in his sleep. Though she observed the date of his death each year, performing a novena in his honor, it was difficult to reconcile herself to the fact that he would not know how she'd grown and changed since taking vows, how she'd become more like him than either of them would have thought possible. He'd told her many times that in temperament she was like her mother — both were ambitious and single-minded, eyes trained blindly upon the end rather than the means. But in truth, it was the stamp of his personality that had been impressed upon Evangeline.

Evangeline was about to leave when she remembered the cards from her grandmother that had so frustrated her the night before. She reached under her pillow, sorted through them, and, despite the fact that she was late for adoration, decided to try one more time to understand the tangled words her grandmother had sent to her.

She removed the cards from the envelopes and placed them upon the bed. One of the images caught her attention. In her exhaustion, she had overlooked it the previous night. It was a pale sketch of an angel, its hands upon the rungs of a ladder. She was certain she had seen the image before, although she could not recall where she'd come across it or why it seemed so familiar. The hint of recognition compelled her to move another card next to it, and as she did so, something clicked in her mind. Suddenly the images made sense: The sketches of angels on the cards were fragments of a larger picture.

Evangeline rearranged the pieces, moving them into various shapes, matching colors and borders as if constructing a jigsaw puzzle until a whole panorama emerged — swarms of brilliant angels stepping up an elegant spiral staircase and into a burst of heavenly light. Evangeline knew the picture well. It was a reproduction of William Blake's *Jacob's Ladder,* a watercolor her father had taken her to see in the British Museum as a girl. Her mother had loved William Blake — she had collected books of Blake's poetry and prints, and her father had bought a print of *Jacob's Ladder* for Angela as a gift. They had brought it with them to America after Angela's death. It was one of the only images that had adorned their plain apartment in Brooklyn.

Evangeline opened the top left card and removed the piece of paper from inside. She opened the second card and did the same. Holding the pieces of paper side by side, she saw that her grandmother's message worked in the same fashion as the images. The message must have been written at one time, cut into squares and sealed into envelopes that Gabriella had sent in yearly intervals. If Evangeline placed the creamy pages side by side, the jumble of words came together to form comprehensible sentences. Her grandmother had found a way to keep her message safe.

Evangeline arranged the papers in the proper order, placing one sheet next to another, until a whole expanse of Gabriella's elegant writing lay before her. Reading over it, she saw that she had been correct. The fragments fit together perfectly. Evangeline could almost hear Gabriella's calm authoritative voice as she scanned the lines.

By the time you read this, you will be a woman of twenty-five and — if everything has worked according to the wishes of your father and me — you will be living a safe and contemplative existence under the supervision of our Sisters of Perpetual Adoration at St. Rose Convent. It is 1988 as I write this. You are just twelve years old. Surely you will wonder at how it came to pass that you are receiving this letter now, so long after it was composed. Perhaps I will have perished before you read it. Perhaps your father will be gone as well. One cannot glean the workings of the future. It is the past and the present that must occupy us. To this I ask you to turn your attention.

You may also wonder why I have been so absent from your life in recent years. Perhaps you are angry that I have not contacted you during your time at St. Rose. The time we spent together in New York, in those most important years before you went to the convent, has sustained me through much turmoil. As has the time we spent together in Paris, when you were but a baby. It is possible that you remember me from that time, although I doubt it very much. I used to take you through the Jardin du Luxembourg with your mother. These were happy afternoons, ones that I cherish to this day. You were such a little girl when your mother was murdered. It is a crime that you were robbed of her so young. I often wonder if you know how brilliantly alive she was, how much she loved you. I am certain your father, who adored Angela, has told you much about her.

He must also have told you that he insisted upon leaving Paris immediately after the incident, believing that you would be safer in America. And so you left, never to return. I do not fault him for taking you far away — he had every right to protect you, especially after what happened to your mother.

It may be difficult to understand, but no matter how I wish to see you, it is not possible for me to contact you directly. My presence would bring danger to you, to your father, and, if you have been obedient to your father's wishes, to the good sisters at St. Rose Convent. After what happened to your mother, I am not at liberty to take such risks. I can only hope that by twenty-five you will be old enough to understand the care that you must take, the responsibility of knowing the truth of your heritage and your destiny, which, in our family, are two branches of a single tree.

It is not in my power to guess how much you know about your parents' work. If I know your father, he has not told you a thing about angelology and has attempted to shelter you from even the rudiments of our discipline. Luca is a good man, and his motives are sound, but I would have raised you quite differently. You may be utterly unaware that your family has been taking part in one of the great secret battles of heaven and earth, and yet the brightest children see and hear everything. I suspect that you are one of these very children. Perhaps you uncovered your father's secret by your own devices? Perhaps you even knew that your place at St. Rose was arranged before your First Communion, when Sister Perpetua — in accordance with the requirements of angelological institutions — agreed to shelter you? Perhaps you know that you, daughter of angelologists, granddaughter of angelologists, are our hope for the future. If you are ignorant of these matters, my letter may bring you quite a shock. Please read my words through to the end, dear Evangeline, no matter the distress they cause.

Your mother began her work in angelology as a chemist. She was a brilliant mathematician and an even more brilliant scientist. Indeed, hers was the best kind of mind, one capable of holding both literal and fantastic ideas at once. In her first book, she imagined the extinction of the Nephilim as a Darwinian inevitability, the logical conclusion of their interbreeding with humanity, the angelic qualities diluted to ineffectual recessive traits. Although I did not fully understand her approach — my interests and background resided in the social-mythological arena — I did understand the notion of material entropy and the ancient truth that the spirit will always exhaust the flesh. Angela's second book about the hybridization of Nephilim with humans — applying the genetic research founded by Watson and Crick — dazzled our council. Angela rose quickly in the society. She was awarded a full professorship by age twenty-five, an unheard-of honor in our institution, and equipped with the latest technological support, the best laboratory, and unlimited research funding.

With fame came danger. Angela soon became a target. There were numerous threats upon her life. Security levels around her laboratory were high — I made sure of this myself. And yet it was in her lab that they abducted her.

It is my guess that your father has not told you the details of her abduction. It is painful to relate, and I myself have never been able to speak of it to anyone. They did not kill your mother immediately. She was taken from her laboratory and held for some weeks by Nephilistic agents in a compound in Switzerland. It is their usual method — kidnapping important angelological figures for the purpose of making a strategic trade. Our policy has always been to refuse to negotiate, but when Angela was taken, I became frantic. Policy or no policy, I would have traded the world for her safe return.

For once your father agreed with me. Many of her research notebooks were in his possession, and we decided to offer these in trade for Angela's life. Although I did not understand the details of her work in genetics, I understood this much: The Nephilim were getting sick, their numbers were diminishing, and they wanted a cure. I communicated to Angela's kidnappers that the notebooks contained secret information that would save their race. To my delight, they agreed to make the trade.

Perhaps I was naïve to believe they

would keep their end of the agreement. When I came to Switzerland and gave them Angela's notebooks, I was given a wooden casket containing my daughter's body. She had been dead for many days. Her skin had been badly bruised, her hair matted with blood. I kissed her cold forehead and knew that I had lost all that mattered most to me. I fear that her last days were spent in torment. The specter of her final hours is never far from my mind.

Forgive me for being the bearer of this horrible story. I am tempted to remain silent, keeping the ghastly details from you. But you are a woman now, and with age we must face the reality of things. We must fathom even the darkest realms of human existence. We must grapple with the strength of evil, its persistence in the world, its undying power over humanity, and our willingness to support it. It is little comfort, I'm sure, to know that you are not alone in your despair. For me Angela's death is the darkest of all dark regions. My nightmares echo with her voice and with the voice of her killer.

Your father could not live in Europe after what happened. His flight to America came swift and final — he cut off contact with all of his relations and friends, including me, so that he might raise you in solitude and peace. He gave you a normal childhood, a luxury not many of us in angelological families have experienced. But there was another reason for his escape.

The Nephilim were not satisfied with the invaluable information I had relinquished so foolishly. Soon after, they ransacked my apartment in Paris, taking objects of great value to me and to our cause, including one of your mother's logs. You see, of the collection of notebooks I surrendered in Switzerland, there was one that I left behind, believing it safe among my belongings. It was a curious collection of theoretical work your mother had been compiling for her third book. It was in its early stages and therefore incomplete, but upon first examining the notebook I had understood how brilliant, and how dangerous, and how precious it was. In fact, I believe that it was due to these theories that the Nephilim took Angela.

Once this information had fallen into the hands of the Nephilim, I knew that all my attempts at keeping its contents secret had failed. I was mortified by the loss of the notebook, but I had one consolation: I had copied it word for word into a leather journal that should be very familiar to you — it is the same notebook that was given to me by my mentor, Dr. Seraphina Valko, and the very same notebook that I gave to you after your mother's death. Once this notebook belonged to my teacher. Now it is in your care.

The notebook contained Angela's theory about the physical effects of music upon molecular structures. She had begun with simple experiments using lower life forms — plants, insects, earthworms — and had worked up to larger organisms, including, if her experiment log can be relied upon, a lock of hair from a Nephilistic child. She had been testing the effects of some celestial instruments — we had a number of them in our possession and Angela had full access — using Nephilistic genetic samples such as shredded wing feathers and vials of blood. Angela discovered that the music of some of these alleged celestial instruments actually had the power to alter the genetic structure of Nephilim tissue. Moreover, certain harmonic successions had the power to diminish Nephilistic power, while others appeared to have the power to increase it.

Angela had discussed the theory at length with your father. He understood her work better than anyone, and although the details are very complicated and I am ignorant of her precise scientific methods, your father helped me to understand that Angela had proof of the most incredible effect of musical vibrations upon cellular structures. Certain combinations of chords and progressions elicited profound physical results in matter. Piano music resulted in pigmentation mutation in orchids — the études of Chopin leaving a dapple of pink upon white petals, Beethoven muddying yellow petals brown. Violin music brought an increase in the number of segments in an earthworm. The incessant dinging of the triangle caused a number of houseflies to be born without wings. And so on.

You might imagine my fascination when, some time ago, many years after Angela's death, I discovered that a Japanese scientist named Masaru Emoto had created a similar experiment, using water as the medium upon which musical vibrations were tested. Using advanced photographic technology, Dr. Emoto was able to capture the drastic change in the molecular structure of water after it was subjected to certain musical vibrations. He asserted that certain strains of music created new molecular formations in the water. In essence these experiments agreed with your mother's experiments, corroborating that musical vibration works at the most basic level of organic material to change structural composition.

This seemingly frivolous experimentation becomes particularly interesting when looked at in the light of Angela's work on angelic biology. Your father was unnaturally reticent about Angela's experiments, refusing to tell me more than I saw in the notebook. But from that small exposure, I could see that your mother had been testing the effects of some celestial instruments in our possession on Nephilistic genetic samples, primarily feathers taken from the creatures' wings. She discovered that some of these alleged celestial instruments had the power to alter the very genetic building blocks of Nephilistic tissue. Moreover, certain harmonic successions played by these instruments had the power not only to alter cell structure but to corrupt the integrity of the Nephilim genome. I am certain Angela gave her life for this discovery. The invasion of my quarters convinced your father you were not safe in Paris. It was clear that the Nephilim knew too much.

But the story that occasions this letter revolves around a hypothesis buried deep within Angela's many proven theories. It is a hypothesis regarding the lyre of Orpheus, which she knew had been hidden in the United States by Abigail Rockefeller in 1943. Angela had proposed a theory connecting her scientific discoveries about the celestial instruments to the lyre of Orpheus, which was believed to be more powerful than all the other instruments combined. Whereas before the Nephilim had acquired the notebooks they had only vague notions of the lyre's importance, they learned from Angela's work that it was the primary instrument, the one that could return the Nephilim to a state of angelic purity unseen upon earth since the time of the Watchers. Angela may well have found the very solution to Nephilistic diminishment in the music of the Watchers' lyre, known in modern times as the lyre of Orpheus.

Be forewarned, dear Evangeline: Understanding the significance of Orpheus's lyre has proved to be a trial. Legend surrounds Orpheus so heavily that we cannot discern the precise outline of his mortal life. We do not know the year of his birth, his true lineage, or the real measure of his talents with the lyre. He was reputed to have been born of the muse Calliope and the river god Oeagrus, but this, of course, is mythology, and it is our work to separate the mythological from the historical, disentangle legend from fact, magic from truth. Nor is the real measure of his talents with the lyre known. Did he give humanity poetry? Did he discover the lyre on his legendary journey to the underworld? Was he as influential in his own lifetime as history claims? By the sixth century B.C., he was known through the Greek world as the master of songs and music, but how he came upon the instrument of the angels has been widely debated among historians. Your mother's work only gave confirmation to long-held theories of the lyre's importance. Her hypothesis, so essential to our progress against the Nephilim, led to her death. This you now know. What you may not know is that her work is not finished. I have spent my life striving to complete it. And you, Evangeline, will one day continue where I have left off.

Your father may or may not have told you of Angela's advances and contributions to our cause. It is beyond my power to know. He closed himself to me many years ago, and I cannot hope that he will welcome me into his confidence again. You, however, are different. If you demand to know the details of your mother's work, he will tell you everything. It is your place to continue the tradition of your family. It is your heritage and your destiny. Luca will guide you where I cannot, I'm certain of it. You must only ask him directly. And, my dear, you must persevere. With my heartfelt blessing, I urge you on. But you must be well aware of your role in the future of our sacred discipline and the grave dangers that await you. There are many who would see our work eliminated and who will kill indiscriminately to reach that end. Your mother died at the hands of the Grigori family, whose efforts have kept the battle between Nephilim and angelologists alive. I daresay you must be warned of the dangers you face and beware of those who wish you harm.

Evangeline nearly cried out with frustration at the missive's abrupt ending. The amputated letter left no further explanation of what she must do. She searched through the cards and reread her grandmother's words once again, desperate to discover something she had overlooked.

The account of her mother's murder caused Evangeline such pain that she had to force herself to continue reading Gabriella's words. The details were gruesome, and there seemed something cruel, almost heartless, in Gabriella's retelling of the horror of Angela's death. Evangeline tried to imagine her mother's body, bruised and broken, her beautiful face marred. Wiping her eyes with the back of her hand, Evangeline understood at last why her father had taken her so far away from the country of her birth.

Upon the third reading of the cards, Evangeline stopped to examine a line relating to her mother's killers. *There are many who would see our work eliminated and who will kill indiscriminately to reach that end. Your mother died at the hands of the Grigori family, whose efforts have kept the battle between Nephilim and angelologists alive.* She had heard the name, but she could not say where until she remembered that Verlaine was working for a man called Percival Grigori. At once she understood that Verlaine — whose intentions were obviously pure — was working for her greatest enemy.

The horror of this realization left Evangeline at a loss. How could she assist Verlaine when he didn't even realize the danger he was in? Indeed, he might report his findings to Percival Grigori. What she had believed to be the best plan — to send Verlaine back to New York and to carry on at St. Rose as if nothing significant had happened — had put them both in grave danger.

She began to pack the cards when, skimming the lines, she noticed one that struck her as odd: *By the time you read this, you will be a woman of twenty-five.* Evangeline recalled that Celestine had been asked to give her the cards when she turned twenty-five years old. Therefore the missive must have been conceived and written out entirely more than ten years before, when Evangeline was twelve, as each letter had been sent in an orderly progression each year. Evangeline was twenty-three years old. That meant that there must be two more cards, and two more pieces of the puzzle her grandmother had fashioned, waiting to be found.

Taking the envelopes once again, Evangeline put them in chronological order and checked the cancellation dates inked across the stamps. The last card had been postmarked before the previous Christmas, on December 21, 1998. In fact, all of the cards had a similar cancellation date — they had been mailed just days before Christmas. If the card for the present year had been posted in the same fashion, it could have already arrived, perhaps in the previous afternoon's mailbag. Evangeline wrapped the cards together, put them in the pocket of her skirt, and hurried from her cell.

Columbia University, Morningside Heights,
New York City

It had been a long and chilly walk from the
125th Street–Harlem station to his office, but
Verlaine had buttoned his coat and was determined to face the freezing winds. Once he
arrived on the Columbia University campus,
he found everything utterly quiet, more still
and dark than he'd seen it before. The holiday
had sent everyone — even the most dedicated
students — home until after the New Year. In
the distance, cars drove along Broadway, their
lights opening over the buildings. Riverside
Church, its imposing tower stretching above
even the highest of the campus buildings, sat
in the distance, its stained-glass windows illuminated from within.

The cut on Verlaine's hand had somehow re-
opened on the walk, and a fine trickle of blood
blossomed through the silk of his fleur-de-lis
tie. After some searching he found his office
keys and let himself into Schermerhorn Hall,
the location of the art history and archaeology
department, an imposing brick building in

proximity to St. Paul's Chapel that had once housed the natural sciences departments. Indeed, Verlaine had heard that it had been the site of early work on the Manhattan Project, a bit of trivia he found fascinating. Although he knew he was alone, he felt too ill at ease to take the elevator and risk being trapped inside. Instead, Verlaine ran up the stairs to the graduate-student offices.

Once in his office, he locked the door behind him and removed the folder containing Innocenta's letters from his desk, taking care not to let his bloodied hand come into contact with the desiccated, fragile paper. Sitting in his chair, he flicked on his desk lamp, and in the pale ring of light he examined the letters. He had read them numerous times before, noting every possible distinguishing innuendo and every potentially allusive turn of phrase, and yet even now, after hours of rereading them in the spooky solitude of his locked office, he felt that the letters seemed strangely, even bizarrely banal. Though the events of the past day prodded him to read the slightest detail with a new eye, he could find very little that pointed to a hidden agenda between these two women. Indeed, beneath the puddle of light from his desk lamp, Innocenta's letters appeared to be not much more than sedate tea-table discursions on the quotidian rituals of the convent and on Mrs. Rockefeller's unerring good taste.

Verlaine stood, began packing his papers into a messenger bag he kept in the corner of his office, and was about to call it a night when he stopped short. There was something uncanny about the letters. He could detect no obvious pattern — in fact, they were almost purposely jumbled. But there was an unaccountable recurrence of some very odd compliments Innocenta paid Mrs. Rockefeller. At the end of several missives, Innocenta praised the other woman's good taste. In the past, Verlaine had skimmed these passages, believing them to be a trite way to bring the letters to a close. Taking the letters from his bag, he reread them again, this time noting each of the many passages of artistic praise.

The compliments revolved around the choice of Mrs. Rockefeller's taste in a picture or design. In one letter Innocenta had written, *"Please know that the perfection of your artistic vision, and the execution of your fancy, is well noted and accepted."* At the close of the second letter, Verlaine read, *"Our most admired friend, one cannot fail to marvel at your delicate renderings or receive them with humble thanks and grateful understanding."* And yet another read, *"As always, your hand never fails to express what the eye most wishes to behold."*

Verlaine puzzled over these references for a moment. What was all this talk about artistic renderings? Had there been pictures or a design included in Abigail Rockefeller's letters to Innocenta? Evangeline hadn't mentioned finding anything accompanying the letter in the archives, but Innocenta's replies seemed to suggest that there was in fact something of that nature attached to her patron's half of the correspondence. If Abigail Rockefeller had included her own original drawings and he discovered these drawings, his professional life would skyrocket. Verlaine's excitement was so great he could hardly think.

To fully understand Innocenta's references, he would need to find the original letters. Evangeline had one in her possession. Surely the others must be somewhere at St. Rose Convent, most likely archived in their vault in the library. Verlaine wondered if it was possible that Evangeline had discovered Abigail Rockefeller's letter and had overlooked an enclosure, or perhaps had even discovered an envelope with the letter. While Evangeline had promised to look for the other missives, she had no reason to search for anything more. If only he had his car, he would drive back to the convent and assist her in the search. Verlaine fumbled through his desk, looking for the telephone number of St. Rose Convent. If Evangeline couldn't find the letters in the convent, it was more than likely that they would never be found. It would be a terrible loss for the history of art, not to mention Verlaine's career. He suddenly felt ashamed that he had been so afraid, and of his reluctance to return to his apartment. He needed to pull himself together immediately and get back upstate to St. Rose by whatever means possible.

Fourth floor, St. Rose Convent, Milton,
New York

Before the previous day, Evangeline had believed what she'd been told about her past.
She trusted the accounts she'd heard from
her father and the sequence of events the sisters had told her. But Gabriella's letter had
shattered her faith in the story line of her life.
Now she distrusted everything.

Gathering her strength, she stepped into
the immaculate, empty hallway, the envelopes tucked under her arm. She felt weak
and dizzy after reading her grandmother's
letters, as if she had just escaped from the
confines of a horrible dream. How had it been
that she'd never fully understood the importance of her mother's work and, even more
astonishing, her mother's death? What more
had her grandmother meant to tell her? How
could she possibly wait for the next two letters to understand it all? Fighting the urge to
run, Evangeline walked down the stone steps,
making her way to the one place she knew she
might find the answer.

The Mission and Recruitment offices were in the southwestern corner of the convent in a modernized series of suites with pale pink carpeting, multiple-line telephones, solid oak desks, and metal filing cabinets containing all of the sisters' personal files: birth certificates, medical records, educational degrees, legal documents, and — for those who had departed this earth — certificates of death. The Recruitment Center — combined with the Mistress of Novices' Office due to the decline in membership — occupied the left arm of the suite, while the Mission Office occupied the right. Together they formed two open arms embracing the outside world to the bureaucratic heart of St. Rose Convent.

In recent years traffic to the Mission Office had risen, while recruitment had fallen into a deep decline. Once upon a time, the young had flocked to St. Rose for the equity and education and independence convent life offered to young women loath to enter into marriage. In modern times, St. Rose Convent became more stringent, demanding that women make the choice to profess vows on their own, without family coercion, and only after much soul-searching.

Thus, while recruitment flagged, the Mission Office became the busiest department at St. Rose. On the wall of the office hung a large laminated map of the world with red flags affixed to affiliate countries: Brazil, Zimbabwe,

China, India, Mexico, Guatemala. There were photographs of sisters in ponchos and saris holding babies, administering medicine, and singing in choirs with the native populations. In the past decade, they had developed an international community-exchange program with foreign churches, bringing sisters from all over the world to St. Rose to participate in perpetual adoration, study English, and pursue personal spiritual growth. The program was a great success. Over the years they had hosted sisters from twelve countries. These sisters' photographs hung above the map: twelve smiling women with twelve identical black veils framing their faces.

Arriving at such an early hour, Evangeline had expected to find the Mission Office empty. Instead there was Sister Ludovica, the oldest member of their community, installed in her wheelchair as the early edition of a National Public Radio broadcast played from a plastic radio on her lap. She was frail and pink-skinned, her white hair springing about the bandeau edges of her veil. Ludovica glanced at Evangeline, her dark eyes glistening in a way that confirmed the growing speculation among the sisters that Ludovica was losing her mind, slipping further and further from reality with each passing year. The previous summer a Milton police officer had discovered Ludovica pushing her wheelchair along Highway 9W at midnight.

Lately her attentions had turned to botany. Her conversations with the plants were harmless but signaled further disintegration. As she wheeled through the convent with a red watering can dangling from the side of her chair, one could hear Ludovica's stentorian voice quoting *Paradise Lost* as she watered and trimmed: "'Nine times the Space that measures Day and Night / To mortal men, he with his horrid crew / Lay vanquisht, rowling in the fiery Gulfe / Confounded though immortal!'"

It was plain to Evangeline that the Mission Office's spider plants had taken to Ludovica's affection: They had grown to enormous proportions, sending shoots dripping over the filing cabinets. The plant had become so profound in its fecundity that the sisters had started snipping the baby plants and placing them in water until they sprung roots. Once transplanted, the new spider plants grew equally enormous and were stationed throughout the convent, filling each of the four floors with tangles of green spawn.

"Good morning, Sister," Evangeline said, hoping that Ludovica would recognize her.

"Oh, my!" Ludovica replied, startled. "You surprised me!"

"I'm sorry to disturb you, but I was unable to pick up the mail yesterday afternoon. Is the mailbag in the Mission Office?"

"Mailbag?" Ludovica asked, furrowing her

brow. "I believe that all mail goes to Sister Evangeline."

"Yes, Ludovica," Evangeline said. "I'm Evangeline. But I wasn't able to pick up our mail yesterday. It would have been delivered here. Have you seen it?"

"Most certainly!" Ludovica said, wheeling the chair to the closet behind her desk, where the mailbag hung from a hook. It was, as always, filled to the top. "Please deliver it directly to Sister Evangeline!"

Evangeline carried the bag to the far end of the Mission Office, to a darkened cove where she might find more privacy. Spilling the contents over the desk, she saw that it was filled with its usual mixture of personal requests, advertisements, catalogs, and invoices. Evangeline had sorted through such muddles of post so often and knew the sizes of each variety of letters so well that it took her only seconds to locate the card from Gabriella. It was a perfectly square green envelope addressed to Celestine Clochette. The return address was the same as the others, a New York City location that Evangeline did not recognize.

Pulling it from the pile, Evangeline put the card with the others in her pocket. Then she walked to the metal filing cabinet. One of Ludovica's spider plants had all but buried the tower in leaves, and so Evangeline found herself brushing aside green shoots to open the drawer containing her records.

Although she knew that her personal file existed, Evangeline had never thought to look at it before. The only time she'd needed vital records or proof of her identity had been to get a driver's license and to enroll at Bard College, and even then she'd used identification drawn up by the diocese. It struck her again as she flipped through the files that she had lived her entire life accepting the stories of others — her father, the sisters at St. Rose, and now her grandmother — without bothering to verify them.

To her consternation, the file was nearly an inch thick, much bulkier than she would have thought. Inside, she had expected to find her French birth certificate, her American naturalization papers, and a diploma — she was not old enough to have accumulated more records than this — but upon opening the folder she found a large pack of papers banded together. Sliding the rubber band from the pages, she began to read. There were sheets of what appeared to her uneducated eye to be lab results, perhaps blood tests. There were pages of handwritten analysis, maybe notes from a visit to the doctor's office, although Evangeline had always been healthy and could not recall ever having been to a doctor. In fact, her father had always resisted bringing her to the doctor's office, taking great care that she would not get sick or hurt. To her dismay, there were opalescent black plastic sheets that upon closer inspection Evangeline saw to be X-ray films. At the top of each film she read her name: Evangeline Angelina Cacciatore.

It wasn't forbidden for the sisters to look at their personal files, and yet Evangeline felt as if she were breaking a strict code of etiquette. Momentarily restraining her curiosity about the medical documents in her file, she turned to the papers relating to her novitiate, a series of run-of-the-mill admission forms that her father had completed upon bringing her to St. Rose. The sight of her father's handwriting sent a wave of pain through her. It had been years since she'd seen him. She traced a finger over his handwriting, remembering the sound of his laughter, the smell of his office, his habit of reading himself to sleep each night. How odd, she thought, pulling the forms from the folder, that the marks he'd left behind had the power to bring him back to life, if only for a moment.

Reading the forms, she found a series of facts about her life. There was the address where they had lived in Brooklyn, their old telephone number, her place of birth, and her mother's maiden name. Then, toward the bottom, written in as Evangeline's designated emergency contact, she found what she was searching for: Gabriella Lévi-Franche Valko's New York City address and telephone number. The address matched the return address on the Christmas cards.

Before Evangeline had a chance to think over the repercussions of her actions, she lifted the phone and dialed Gabriella's number, her anticipation clouding all other feelings. If anyone would know what to do, it would be her grandmother. The line rang once, twice, and then Evangeline heard it, the brusque and commanding voice of her grandmother. *"'Allo?"*

Verlaine's apartment, Greenwich Village,
New York City

The twenty-four hours since he'd left his apartment felt to Verlaine like a lifetime ago. Only yesterday he'd collected his dossier, put on his favorite socks, and run down the five flights of stairs, his wing tips slipping on the wet rubber treads. Only yesterday he'd been preoccupied with avoiding Christmas parties and putting together his New Year's plans. He couldn't understand how the information he'd collected could have led to the sorry state he found himself in now.

He'd packed the original copies of Innocenta's letters and the bulk of his notebooks into a bag, locked his office, and headed downtown. The morning sunlight had ascended over the city, the soft diffusion of yellow and orange breaking the stark winter sky in an elegant sweep. He walked for blocks and blocks through the cold. Somewhere in the mid-Eighties, he gave up and took the subway the rest of the way. By the time he unlocked the front door of his building, he had almost convinced himself that the previous night's events were an illusion. Perhaps, he told himself, he had imagined it all.

Verlaine unlocked the door to his apartment, knocked it closed with the heel of his shoe, and dropped his messenger bag on the couch. He took off his ruined wing tips, pulled away his wet socks, and walked barefoot into his humble abode. He half expected to find the place in ruins, but everything appeared to be exactly as he'd left it the day before. A web of shadows fell over the exposed-brick walls, the 1950s Formica-topped table stacked with books, the turquoise leather benches, the kidney-shaped resin coffee table — all of his Mid-century Modern pieces, shabby and mismatched, were waiting for him.

Verlaine's art books filled an entire wall. There were oversize coffee-table Phaidon Press editions, squat paperbacks of art criticism, and glossy folios containing prints of his favorite modernists — Kandinsky, Sonia Delaunay, Picasso, Braque. He owned more books than actually fit into such a small apartment, and yet he refused to sell them. He'd come to the conclusion years ago that a studio apartment was not ideal for someone with a hoarding instinct.

Standing at his fifth-floor window, he removed the silk Hermès tie he'd been using as a bandage, slowly working the fabric away from the scabbing flesh. His tie was ruined. Folding it, he placed it on the sill. Outside, a slice of morning sky hovered in the distance, lifting above rows of buildings as if propped on stilts. The snow hung upon tree branches, slouched down the slopes of drainage pipes, and tapered into daggers of ice. Water towers on rooftops dotted the tableau. Although he didn't own an inch of property, he felt that this view belonged to him. Looking intently at his corner of the city could absorb his entire attention. This morning, however, he simply wanted to clear his head and think about what he would do next.

Coffee, he realized, would be a good start. Walking to the galley kitchen, he turned on his espresso machine, packed fine-ground beans into the portafilter, and — after steaming some milk — made himself a cappuccino in an antique Fiestaware mug, one of the few he hadn't broken. As Verlaine took a sip of coffee, the flash of his answering machine caught his eye — there were messages. He pressed a button and listened. People had been calling all night and hanging up. Verlaine counted ten instances of someone simply listening on the line, as if waiting for him to answer. Finally a message played in which the caller spoke. It was Evangeline's voice. He recognized it in an instant.

"If you took the midnight train, you should have been back by now. I cannot help but wonder where you are and whether you are safe. Call me as soon as you can."

Verlaine went to the closet, where he dug out an old leather duffel bag. He unzipped it and threw in a clean pair of Hugo Boss jeans, a pair of Calvin Klein boxers, a Brown University sweatshirt — his alma mater — and two pairs of socks. He dug a pair of Converse All-Stars from the bottom of the closet, put on a pair of clean socks, and put them on. There was no time for him to think about what else he might need. He would rent a car and drive back to Milton immediately, taking the same route he'd followed yesterday afternoon, driving over the Tappan Zee Bridge and navigating the small roads along the river. If he hurried, he could be there before lunch.

Suddenly the telephone rang, a noise so sharp and startling that he lost his grip on the coffee cup. It fell against the window ledge with a solid crack, a splatter of coffee and milk spilling over the floor. Eager to speak with Evangeline, he left the cup where it landed and grabbed the phone.

"Evangeline?" he said.

"Mr. Verlaine." The voice was soft, feminine, and it addressed Verlaine with an unusual intimacy. The woman's accent — Italian or French, he couldn't tell exactly which — combined with a slight hoarseness, gave him the impression that she was middle-aged, perhaps older, although this was pure speculation.

"Yes, speaking," he replied, disappointed. He glanced at the broken cup, aware that he had diminished his collection yet again. "What can I do for you?"

"Many things, I hope," the woman said.

For a fraction of a second, Verlaine thought the caller might be a telemarketer. But his number was unlisted, and he didn't usually get unwanted calls. Besides, it was clear that this voice was not the kind to be selling magazine subscriptions.

"That's a rather tall order," Verlaine said, taking the caller's strange phone manner in stride. "Why don't you start by telling me who you are?"

"May I ask you a question first?" the woman said.

"You might as well." Verlaine was beginning to get irritated with the calm, insistent, almost hypnotic sound of the woman's voice, a voice quite different from Evangeline's.

"Do you believe in angels?"

"Excuse me?"

"Do you believe that angels exist among us?"

"Listen, if this is some kind of evangelical group," Verlaine said, bending before the window and stacking the fragments of his cup one on top of the other. The white, granular powder from the unglazed center of the cup crumbled over his fingers. "You've got the wrong guy. I'm an over-educated, left-of-left, soy-latte-drinking, borderline-metrosexual liberal agnostic. I believe in angels as much as I believe in the Easter Bunny."

"That is extraordinary," the woman said. "I was under the impression that these fictitious creatures were a threat to your life."

Verlaine stopped stacking the shards of the cup. "Who is this?" he asked finally.

"My name is Gabriella Lévi-Franche Valko," the woman said. "I have worked for a very long time to find the letters in your possession."

Growing more confused, he asked, "How do you know my number?"

"There are many things I know. For example, I know that the creatures you escaped last night are outside your apartment." Gabriella paused, as if to let this sink in, then said, "If you don't believe me, Mr. Verlaine, look out your window."

Verlaine bent before the windowpane, a strand of curly black hair falling in his eyes. Everything looked just as it had minutes before.

"I don't know what you're talking about," he said.

"Look left," Gabriella said. "You will see a familiar black SUV."

Verlaine followed the woman's instructions. Indeed, at the left, on the corner of Hudson Street, the black Mercedes SUV idled on the street. A tall, dark-clothed man — the same one he'd seen breaking into his car the day before and, if he hadn't been hallucinating, seen outside his train window — stepped out of the SUV and paced under the streetlight.

"Now, if you look to the right," Gabriella said, "you will see a white van. I am inside. I've been waiting for you since early this morning. At my granddaughter's request, I have come to help you."

"And who is your granddaughter?"

"Evangeline, of course," Gabriella said. "Who else?"

Verlaine craned his neck and spotted a white van tucked into a narrow service alley across the street. The alley was far away, and he could hardly see a thing. As if the caller understood his confusion, a window descended and a petite, leather-gloved hand emerged and gave a peremptory wave.

"What exactly is going on?" Verlaine said, abashed. He walked to the door, turned the bolt, and secured the chain. "Do you mind telling me why you're watching my apartment?"

"My granddaughter believed you were in

danger. She was right. Now I want you to gather Innocenta's letters and come down immediately," Gabriella said calmly. "But I advise you to avoid exiting the building through the front door."

"There's no other way out," Verlaine said, uneasy.

"A fire escape, perhaps?"

"The fire escape is visible from the front entrance. They'll see me as soon as I start down it," Verlaine said, eyeing the metal skeleton that darkened the corner of the window and worked its way over the front of the building. "Could you please tell me why —"

"My dear," Gabriella said, interrupting Verlaine, her voice warm, almost maternal. "You will simply have to use your imagination. I advise you to get yourself out of there. Immediately. They will be coming for you at any moment. Actually, they don't give a damn about you. They will want the letters," she said quietly. "As you perhaps know, they will not extract them gently."

As if taking their cue from Gabriella, the second man — as tall and pale-skinned as the first — stepped out of the black SUV, joining the other. Together they crossed the street, walking toward Verlaine's building.

"You're right. They're coming," Verlaine said. He turned from the window and grabbed the duffel bag, stuffing his wallet, keys, and laptop under the clothes. He took the folder of Innocenta's original letters from his messenger bag, placed them inside a book of Rothko prints, slid them gently into his duffel bag, and pulled the zipper shut with swift finality. Finally, he said, "What should I do?"

"Wait a moment. I can see them very clearly," Gabriella said. "Just follow my instructions, and everything will be fine."

"Maybe I should call the police?"

"Do nothing yet. They are still standing at the entrance. They will see you if you leave now," Gabriella said, her voice eerily calm, a strange counterpoint to the rush of blood screeching in Verlaine's ears. "Listen to me, Mr. Verlaine. It is extremely important that you do not move until I tell you."

Verlaine unlocked the window and heaved it open. A gust of freezing air swept his face. Leaning out the window, he could see the men below. They spoke in low voices and then, inserting something into the lock, pushed the door open, and entered the building with astonishing ease. The heavy door slammed hard behind them.

"Do you have the letters?" Gabriella asked.

"Yes," Verlaine said.

"Then go. Now. Down the fire escape. I will be waiting."

Verlaine hung up the phone, threw the

duffel bag over his shoulder, and crawled out the window into the icy wind. The metal froze against the warm skin of his palm as he grasped the rusty ladder. With all his effort, he pulled: The ladder clattered to the sidewalk. Pain shot through his hand as the skin stretched, reopening the wound from the barbed-wire fence. Verlaine ignored the pain and climbed down the rungs, his sneakers sliding on the ice-glazed metal. He was nearly to the sidewalk when he heard an explosive crack of wood above. The men had broken down the door of his apartment.

Verlaine dropped to the sidewalk, making sure to protect the duffel bag in the crook of his arm. As he stepped onto the street, the white van pulled to the curb. The door slid open, and an elfin woman with bright red lipstick and a severe black pageboy haircut beckoned for Verlaine to jump into the backseat. "Get in," Gabriella said, making room. "Hurry."

Verlaine climbed into the van beside Gabriella as the driver threw the vehicle into gear, rounded the corner, and sped uptown.

"What in the hell is going on?" Verlaine asked, looking over his shoulder, half expecting to find the SUV behind.

Gabriella put her thin, leather-sheathed hand over his cold, trembling one. "I've come to help you."

"Help me with what?"

"My dear, you have no idea of the trouble you've brought upon all of us."

The Grigori penthouse, Upper East Side, New York City

Percival demanded that the curtains be drawn, so as to protect his eyes from the light. He had walked home at sunrise, and the pale morning sky had been enough to cause his head to ache. When the room was sufficiently dark, he discarded his clothes, throwing the tuxedo jacket, the fouled white shirt, and his trousers on the floor, and stretched out upon a leather couch. Without a word the Anakim unbuckled his harness, a laborious procedure that he endured with patience. Then she poured oil onto his legs and massaged him from ankle to thigh, working her fingers into the muscles until they burned. The creature was very pretty and very silent, a combination that suited Anakim, especially the females, whom he found remarkably stupid. Percival stared at her as she moved her short, fat fingers up and down his legs. The burning headache matched the heat in his legs. Deliriously tired, he closed his eyes and tried to sleep.

The exact origin of his disorder was still

unknown to even the most experienced of his family's doctors. Percival had hired the very best medical team, flying them to New York from Switzerland, Germany, Sweden, and Japan, and all they could tell him was what everyone already knew: A virulent viral infection had traveled through a generation of European Nephilim, attacking the nervous and pulmonary systems. They recommended treatments and therapies to promote healing in his wings and to loosen his muscles, so that he might breathe and walk with more ease. Daily massages were one of the more pleasant elements of the treatments. Percival called the Anakim to his room to massage his legs numerous times each day, and along with his deliveries of scotch and sedatives, he had come to depend upon her hourly presence.

Under normal circumstances he would not have allowed a wretched servant woman into his private chambers at all — he had not done so in the many hundreds of years before his illness — but the pain had become unbearable in the last year, the muscles so cramped that his legs had begun to twist into an unnatural position. The Anakim stretched each leg until the tendons loosened and massaged the muscles, pausing when he flinched. He watched her hands press into his pale skin. She soothed him, and for this he was grateful. His mother had abandoned him, treating him like an invalid, and Otterley was out doing the work Percival should be doing. There was no one left but an Anakim to help him.

As he relaxed, he drifted into a light sleep. For a brief, buoyant moment, he recalled the pleasure of his late-night stroll. When the woman was dead, he had closed her eyes and stared at her, running his fingers against her cheek. In death her skin had taken on an alabaster hue. To his delight, he saw Gabriella Lévi-Franche clearly — her black hair and her powdery skin. For a moment he had possessed her once again.

As he drifted into the delicate space between waking and sleeping, Gabriella appeared to him like a luminous messenger. In his fantasy she told him to come back to her, that all was forgiven, that they would continue where they had ended. She told him that she loved him, words that no one — human or Nephilim — had said before. It was an inordinately painful dream, and Percival must have spoken in his sleep — he startled awake and found the Anakim servant staring intently at him, her large yellow eyes glimmering with tears, as if she had come to understand something about him. She softened her touch and said a few words of comfort. She pitied him, he realized, and the presumption of such intimacy angered Percival — he ordered the beast to leave at once. She nodded submissively, put the cap on the bottle of oil, collected his soiled clothing, and left in an instant, shutting him in a cocoon of darkness and despair. He lay awake, feeling the sting of the maid's touch on his skin.

Soon the Anakim returned, delivering a glass of scotch on a lacquered tray. "Your sister is here, sir," she said. "I will tell her that you are sleeping if you wish."

"No need to lie for him. I can see that he is awake," Otterley said, brushing past the Anakim and sitting at Percival's side. With a flip of her wrist, she dismissed the servant. Taking the massage oil, Otterley uncapped it and poured some in the palm of her hand. "Turn over," she said.

Percival obeyed his sister's orders, turning on his stomach. As Otterley massaged his back, he wondered what would become of her — and of their family — after the disease had taken him. Percival had been their great hope, his majestic, masculine golden wings promising that one day he would ascend to a position of power, superseding even his father's avaricious ancestors and his mother's noble blood. Now he was a wingless, feeble disappointment to his family. He had envisioned himself to be a great patriarch, the father of an expansive number of Nephilistic children. His sons would grow to be endowed with the colorful wings of Sneja's family, gorgeous plumage that would bring honor to the Grigoris. His daughters would have the qualities of the angels — they would be psychic and brilliant and trained in the celestial arts. Now, in his decline, he had nothing. He understood how foolish it had been to waste hundreds of years in the pursuit of pleasure.

That Otterley was equally disappointing made his failure even harder to face. Otterley had neglected to bring the Grigori family an heir, just as Percival had failed to grow into the angelic being his mother had so longed for him to be.

"Tell me you've come with good news," Percival said, flinching as Otterley rubbed the delicate raw flesh near the wing nubs. "Tell me that you've recovered the map and killed Verlaine and there is nothing more to worry about."

"My dear brother," Otterley said, leaning close as she massaged his shoulders. "You have really made a mess of things. First, you hired an angelologist."

"I did no such thing. He is nothing other than a simple art historian," Percival said.

"Next, you let him take the map."

"Architectural drawings," Percival corrected.

"Then you creep out in the middle of the night and put yourself in this terrible state." Otterley stroked the rotted stubs of his wings, a sensation Percival found delicious even as he wished to push his sister's hand away.

"I don't know what you're talking about."

"Mother knows you left, and she has asked

me to watch you very closely. What would happen if you were to collapse on the street? How would we explain your condition to the doctors at Lenox Hill?"

"Tell Sneja there is no need to worry," Percival said.

"But we do have reason to worry," Otterley said, wiping her hands on a towel. "Verlaine is still alive."

"I thought you sent the Gibborim to his apartment?"

"I did," Otterley said. "But things have taken a rather unexpected turn. Whereas yesterday we were simply worried that Verlaine would make off with information, now we know he is much more dangerous."

Percival sat up and faced his sister. "How could he possibly be dangerous? Our Anakim poses more of a threat than a man like Verlaine."

"He is working with Gabriella Lévi-Franche Valko," Otterley said, pronouncing each word with zeal. "Clearly he is one of them. Everything we've done to protect ourselves from the angelologists has been for nothing. Get up," she said, throwing the harness at Percival. "Get dressed. You are coming with me."

Adoration Chapel, Maria Angelorum Church,
Milton, New York

Evangeline dipped a finger into the fount of holy water, blessing herself before she ran down the wide central aisle of Maria Angelorum. By the time she entered the quiet, contemplative space of the Adoration Chapel, her breathing had grown heavy. She had never missed adoration before — it was an unthinkable transgression, one she could not have imagined committing. She could hardly believe the person she was becoming. Only yesterday she had lied to Sister Philomena. Now she had missed her assigned hour of adoration. Sister Philomena must have been astonished by her absence. She slid into a pew near Sisters Mercedes and Magdalena, daily prayer partners from seven to eight each morning, hoping her presence would not disturb them. Even as she closed her eyes in prayer, Evangeline's face burned with shame.

She should have been able to pray, but instead she opened her eyes and glanced about the chapel, looking at the monstrance, the altar, the beads of the rosary in Sister Magdalena's fingers. Yet the moment she began, the presence of the heavenly spheres windows struck her as if they were new additions to the chapel — the size, the intricacy, the sumptuously vibrant colors of the angels crowding together in the glass. If she examined them closely, she could see that the windows were illuminated by tiny halogen lights positioned around them, trained upon the glass as if in worship. Evangeline strained to make out the population of the angels. Harps, flutes, trumpets — their instruments scattered like golden coins through the blue and red panes. The seal that Verlaine had shown her on the architectural drawings had been placed at this very spot. She thought of Gabriella's cards and the beautiful renderings of angels on each cover. How had it happened that Evangeline had looked upon these windows so often and had never really seen their significance?

Below one of the windows, etched into the stone, a passage read:

If there is an angel as mediator for him,
One out of a thousand,
To remind a man what is right for him,
Then let him be gracious to him, and
  say,

"Deliver him from going down to the pit,
I have found a ransom."

— Job 33:23–24

Evangeline had read the passage every day
of her many years at St. Rose Convent, and
each day the words had seemed an unsolvable
puzzle. The sentence had slithered through
her thoughts, slick and ungraspable, moving
through her mind without catching. Now
the words "mediator" and "pit" and "ransom" began to fit into place. Sister Celestine
had been right: Once she began looking, she
would find angelology living and breathing
everywhere.

It dismayed her that the sisters had kept so
much from her. Recalling Gabriella's voice
on the telephone, Evangeline wondered if
perhaps she should pack her things and go to
New York. Perhaps her grandmother could
help her understand everything more clearly.
The hold the convent had had on her only the
day before had diminished by all that she'd
learned.

A hand on her shoulder disturbed her from
her thoughts. Sister Philomena motioned for
Evangeline to follow her. Obeying, Evangeline left the Adoration Chapel, feeling a mixture of embarrassment and anger. The sisters
had not trusted her with the truth. How could
Evangeline possibly trust them?

"Come, Sister," Philomena said once they

were in the hallway. Whatever anger Philomena must have felt at Evangeline's truancy had disappeared. Now her manner was inexplicably gentle and resigned. And yet something about Sister Philomena's demeanor seemed disingenuous. Evangeline didn't entirely believe her to be genuine, although she couldn't pinpoint why. Together they headed through the central hallway of the convent, past the photographs of distinguished mothers and sisters and the painting of St. Rose of Viterbo, stopping before a familiar set of wooden doors. It was only natural that Philomena would lead her to the library, where they could speak with some measure of privacy. Philomena unlocked the doors, and Evangeline stepped into the shadowy room.

"Sit, child, sit," Philomena said. Evangeline arranged herself on the green velvet sofa, across from the fireplace. The room was cold, the result of the perennially ill-fitting flue. Sister Philomena went to a table near her office and plugged in the electric kettle. When the water boiled, she poured it into a porcelain pot. Setting two cups on a tray, she waddled back to the sofa, placing the tray on a low table. Taking the wooden chair opposite Evangeline, she opened a metal cookie box and offered Evangeline an assortment of FSPA Christmas Cookies — butter cookies that had been baked, frosted, packaged, and sold by the sisters for their annual Christmas fund-raiser.

The fragrance of the tea — black with a hint of dried apricot — made Evangeline's stomach turn. "I'm not feeling very well," she said by way of apology.

"You were missed at dinner last night and, of course, at adoration this morning," Philomena said, choosing a Christmas-tree cookie with green frosting. She lifted the pot and poured some tea into the cups. "But I am not much surprised. This has been a great ordeal with Celestine, hasn't it?" Philomena's posture became very erect, her hand holding the teacup rigid over her saucer, and Evangeline knew that Philomena was about to cut to the heart of the matter.

"Yes," Evangeline replied, expecting the impatient and stern Philomena to return any moment.

Philomena clucked her tongue and said, "I knew that it was inevitable you would learn the truth of your origins someday. I was not sure how, mind you, but I had a vivid sense that the past would be impossible to bury completely, even in such a closed community as ours. In my humble opinion," Philomena continued, finishing off her cookie and taking another, "it has been quite a burden for Celestine to remain silent. It has been a burden for all of us to remain so passive in the face of the threat that surrounds us."

"You knew of Celestine's involvement in

this . . ." Evangeline fumbled, trying to formulate the correct words to describe angelology. She had the unwelcome thought that perhaps she was the only Franciscan Sister of Adoration who had been kept ignorant. "This . . . discipline?"

"Oh, my, yes," Philomena said. "All of the older sisters know. The sisters of my generation were steeped in angelic study — Genesis 28:12–17, Ezekiel 1:1–14, Luke 1:26–38. Bless me, it was angels morning, noon, and night!"

Philomena adjusted her weight on her chair, making the wood groan, and continued, "One day I was deep into the core curriculum prescribed by European angelologists — our longtime mentors — and the next our convent was nearly destroyed. All of our scholarship, all of our efforts toward ridding the world of the pestilence of the Nephilim, seemed to be to have been for naught. Suddenly we were simple nuns whose lives were devoted to prayer and prayer alone. Believe me, I have fought hard to bring us back to the fight, to declare ourselves combatants. Those in our number who believe that it's too dangerous are fools and cowards."

"Dangerous?" Evangeline said.

"The fire of '44 was not an accident," Philomena said, narrowing her eyes. "It was a direct attack. It could be said that we were careless, that we underestimated the bloodthirsty nature of the Nephilim here in America. They were aware of many — if not all — of the enclaves of angelologists in Europe. We made the mistake of thinking that America was still as safe as it had once been. I'm sorry to say that Sister Celestine's presence exposed St. Rose Convent to great danger. After Celestine came, so did the attacks. Not just on our convent, mind you. There were nearly one hundred attacks on American convents that year — a concerted effort by the Nephilim to discover which of us had what they wanted."

"But why?"

"Because of Celestine, of course," Philomena said. "She was well known by the enemy. When she arrived, I myself saw how sickly, how battered, how scarred she was. Clearly she had gone through a harrowing escape. And, perhaps most significant, she carried a parcel for Mother Innocenta, something meant to be secured here, with us. Celestine had something that they wanted. They knew she had taken refuge in the United States, only they did not know where."

"And Mother Innocenta knew everything of this?" Evangeline asked.

"Of course," Philomena said, raising her eyebrows in wonder, whether at Mother Innocenta or the question, Evangeline was not sure. "Mother Innocenta was the premier scholar of her era in America. She had been trained by Mother Antonia, who was the student of Mother Clara, our most beloved abbess, who had, in turn, been instructed by Mother Francesca herself, who — to the benefit of our great nation — came to Milton, New York, directly from the European Angelological Society to build the American branch. St. Rose Convent was the beating heart of the American Angelological Project, a grand undertaking, far more ambitious than whatever Celestine Clochette had been doing in Europe before she tagged along on the Second Expedition." Philomena, who had been speaking very rapidly, paused to take a deep breath. "Indeed," she said, slowly, "Mother Innocenta would never, *never* have given up the fight so easily had she not been murdered at the hands of the Nephilim."

Evangeline said, "I thought she died in the fire."

"That is what we told the outer world, but it is not the truth." Philomena's skin flushed red and then blanched to a very pale color, as if the act of discussing the fire brought her skin in contact with a phantom heat.

"I happened to be in the balcony of Maria Angelorum when the fire broke out. I was cleaning the pipes of the Casavant organ, a terribly difficult chore. With fourteen hundred and twenty-two pipes, twenty stops, and thirty ranks, it was hard enough to dust the organ, but Mother Innocenta had assigned me the twice-yearly task of polishing the brass!

Imagine it! I believe that Mother Innocenta was punishing me for something, although it completely slips my mind what I could have done to displease her."

Evangeline knew full well that Philomena could work herself into a state of inconsolable grievance about the events of the fire. Instead of interrupting her, as she wished, she folded her hands in her lap and endeavored to listen as penance for missing adoration that morning. "I am certain you did nothing to displease anyone," Evangeline said.

"I heard an unusual commotion," Philomena continued, as she would have with or without Evangeline's encouragement, "and went to the great rose window at the back of the choir loft. If you have cleaned the organ, or participated in our choir, you will know that the rose window looks over the central courtyard. That morning the courtyard was filled with hundreds of sisters. Soon enough I noticed the smoke and flames that had consumed the fourth floor, although, sequestered as I was in the church balcony, with a clear view of the upper regions, I had no idea of what was happening on the other floors of the convent. I later learned, however, that the damage was extensive. We lost everything."

"How awful," Evangeline said, repressing the urge to ask how this could be construed as a Nephilistic attack.

"Terrible indeed," Philomena said. "But

I have not told you everything. I have been silenced by Mother Perpetua on the subject, but I will remain silent no longer. Sister Innocenta, I tell you, was murdered. *Murdered.*"

"What do you mean?" Evangeline asked, trying to understand the seriousness of Philomena's accusation. Only hours before, she had learned that her mother had been murdered at the hands of these creatures, and now Innocenta. Suddenly, St. Rose felt like the most dangerous place her father could have placed her.

"From the choir loft, I heard a wooden door slam closed. In a matter of seconds, Mother Innocenta appeared below. I watched her hurry through the central aisle of the church, a group of sisters — two novices and two fully professed — following close behind her. They seemed to be on their way to the Adoration Chapel, perhaps to pray. That was Innocenta's way: Prayer was not simply a devotion or a ritual but a solution to all that is imperfect in the world. She believed so strongly in the power of prayer that I quite expect she believed she could stop the fire with it."

Philomena sighed, took her glasses and rubbed them with a crisp white handkerchief. Sliding her clean glasses onto her nose, she looked at Evangeline sharply, as if gauging her suitability for the tale, and continued.

"Suddenly two enormous figures stepped from the side aisles. They were extraordinarily l and bony, with white hands and faces that ɪmed lit by fire. Their hair and skin appeared, even from a distance, to glow with a soft white radiance. They had large blue eyes, high cheekbones, and full pink lips. Their hair fell in curls around their faces. Yet their shoulders were broad, and they wore trousers and rain jackets — the attire of gentlemen — as if they were no different from a banker or a lawyer. While these secular clothes dispelled the thought that they might be Holy Cross brothers, who at that time wore full brown robes and tonsured heads, I could not make out who or what the creatures were.

"I now know that these creatures are called Gibborim, the warrior class of Nephilim. They are brutal, bloodthirsty, unfeeling beings whose ancestry — on the angelic side, that is — goes back to the great warrior Michael. It is too noble a lineage for such horrid creatures and explains their strange beauty. Looking back, with full knowledge of what they were, I understand that their beauty was a terrible manifestation of evil, a cold and diabolic allure that could lead one all the more easily to harm. They were physically perfect, but it was a perfection severed from God — an empty, soulless beauty. I imagine that Eve found a similar beauty in the serpent. Their presence in the church caused the most unnatural state to fall over me. I must confess: I was caught completely off guard by them."

Once again Philomena took her crisp white cotton handkerchief from her pocket, unfolded it in her hands, and pressed it to her forehead, wiping the sweat away.

"From the choir loft, I could see everything very clearly. The creatures stepped from the shadows into the brilliant light of the nave. The stained-glass windows were sparkling with sunlight, as they usually are at midday, and patches of color scattered across the marble floor, creating a diaphanous glow on their pale skin as they walked. Mother Innocenta took a sharp breath upon seeing them. She reached for the shoulder of a pew to support her weight and asked them what they wanted. Something in the tone of her voice convinced me that she recognized them. Perhaps she had even expected them."

"She could not have possibly expected them," Evangeline said, baffled by Philomena's description of this horrible catastrophe as if it were a providential event. "She would have warned the others."

"I cannot know," Philomena said, wiping her forehead once again and crumpling the soiled cotton square in her hand. "Before I knew what happened, the creatures attacked my dear sisters. The evil beings turned their eyes upon them, and it seemed to me that a spell had been cast. The five women gaped at the creatures as if hypnotized. One creature placed his hands upon Mother Innocenta, and it was as though an electric charge entered her body. She convulsed and that very instant fell to the floor, the very spirit sucked from her. The beast found pleasure in the act of killing, as any monster might. The kill appeared to make it stronger, more vibrant, while Mother Innocenta's body was utterly unrecognizable."

"But how is that possible?" Evangeline asked, wondering if her mother had met the same wretched fate.

"I do not know. I covered my eyes in terror," Philomena replied. "When at last I peered over the balustrade again, I saw them upon the floor of the church, all five sisters, dead. In the time it took me to run from the loft to the church, a matter of fifteen seconds or so, the creatures had fled, leaving the bodies of our sisters utterly defiled. They had been desiccated to the bone, as if drained not only of vital fluids but of their very essence. Their bodies were shriveled, their hair burned, their skin pruned. This, my child, was a Nephilistic attack on St. Rose Convent. And we responded by renouncing our work against them. I have never comprehended this. Mother Innocenta, may God rest her soul, would never let the murder of our people go unavenged."

"Why, then, did we stop?" Evangeline asked.

"We wanted them to believe we were merely an abbey of nuns," Philomena said. "If they thought we were weak and posed no threat to their power, they would cease their search for the object that they believed we possessed."

"But we do not possess it. Abigail Rockefeller never disclosed its location before her death."

"Do you truly believe this, my dear Evangeline? After all that has been kept from you? After all that has been kept from *me*? Celestine Clochette swayed Mother Perpetua to the pacifist stance. It is not in Celestine's interest for the lyre of Orpheus to be unearthed. But I would wager my very life, my very soul, that she possesses information of its whereabouts. If you will help me find it, together we can rid the world of these monstrous beasts once and for all."

Light from the sun streamed through the windows of the library, bathing Evangeline's legs and pooling at the fireplace. Evangeline closed her eyes, contemplating this story in view of all she had taken in over the past day. "I have just learned that these monstrous beasts murdered my mother," Evangeline whispered. She pulled Gabriella's letters from her frock, but Philomena snatched them from her before she could give them over.

Philomena tore through the cards, reading them hungrily. Finally, upon coming to the last card, she declared, "This letter is incomplete. Where is the rest?"

Evangeline pulled out the final Christmas

card she had collected from the morning mailbag. She turned it over and began to read her grandmother's words aloud:

"'I have told you much about the terrors of the past and something of the dangers that you face in the present, but there has been little in my communication about your future role in our work. I cannot say when this information will be of use to you — it may be that you will live your days in peaceful, quiet contemplation, faithfully carrying out your work at St. Rose. But it may be that you will be needed for a larger purpose. There is a reason your father chose St. Rose Convent as your home and a reason you have been trained in the angelological tradition that has nurtured our work for more than a millennium.'

"'Mother Francesca, the founding abbess of the convent in which you have lived and grown these past thirteen years, built St. Rose Convent through the sheer force of faith and hard work, designing every chamber and stairwell to suit the needs of our angelologists in America. The Adoration Chapel was a feat of Francesca's imagination, a sparkling tribute to the angels we study. Each piece of gold was inlaid to honor, each panel of glass hung in praise. What you may not know is that at the center of this chapel there is a small but priceless object of great spiritual and historical value.'"

"That is all," Evangeline said, folding the

letter and slipping it into the envelope. "The fragment ends there."

"I knew it! The lyre is here with us. Come, child, we must share this wondrous news with Sister Perpetua."

"But the lyre was hidden by Abigail Rockefeller in 1944," Evangeline said, confused at Philomena's train of thought. "This letter tells us nothing."

"Nobody knows for certain what Abigail Rockefeller did with the lyre," Philomena said, standing and heading toward the door. "Quickly, we must speak with Mother Perpetua at once. Something lies at the heart of the Adoration Chapel. Something of use to us."

"Wait," Evangeline said, her voice cracking from the strain of what she must say. "There is something else I must tell you, Sister."

"Tell me, child," Philomena said, halting at the doorway.

"Despite your warning I allowed someone to enter our library yesterday afternoon. The man who inquired about Mother Innocenta came to the convent yesterday. Instead of turning him away, as you instructed, I allowed him to read the letter I discovered from Abigail Rockefeller."

"A letter from Abigail Rockefeller? I have been searching for fifty years for such a letter. Do you have it with you?"

Evangeline presented it to Sister Philomena,

who snatched it from her fingers, reading it rapidly. As she read, her disappointment became clear. Returning the letter to Evangeline's, she said, "There is not one piece of useful information in this letter."

"The man who came to the archives did not seem to think so," Evangeline said, wondering if her interest in Verlaine could be detected by Philomena.

"And how did this gentleman react?" Philomena inquired.

"With great interest and agitation," Evangeline said. "He believes that the letter points to a larger mystery, one his employer has charged him to uncover."

Philomena's eyes widened. "Did you determine the motivation for his interest?"

"I believe that his motives are innocent, but — and this is what I must tell you — I have just learned that his employer is one of those who mean us harm." Evangeline bit her lip, unsure if she could say his name. "Verlaine is working for Percival Grigori."

Philomena stood up, knocking her teacup onto the floor. "My word!" she said, terrified. "Why haven't you warned us?"

"Please forgive me," Evangeline said. "I didn't know."

"Do you realize the danger we are in?" Philomena said. "We must alert Mother Perpetua immediately. It is apparent to me now that we have made a terrible mistake. The enemy has grown stronger. It is one thing to wish for peace; it is quite another to pretend the war itself does not exist."

With this, Philomena folded the letters and cards in her hands and scuttled out of the library, leaving Evangeline alone with the empty tin of cookies. Clearly Philomena had a morbid and unhealthy obsession with avenging the events of 1944. Indeed, her reaction had been fanatical, as if she had been waiting many years for such information. Evangeline realized that she should never have shown Philomena her grandmother's confidential letter or discussed such dangerous information with a woman she had always felt to be a bit unstable. In despair, Evangeline tried to understand what she would do next. Suddenly she recalled Celestine's command about the letters: *When you have read them, come to me again.* Evangeline stood and hurried from the library to Celestine's cell.

Times Square, New York City

The driver rolled through rush-hour traffic, stopping at the corner of Forty-second and Broadway. Traffic had all but halted at the NYPD headquarters, where police were making preparations for the Millennial New Year's Eve ball drop. Through the crowds of office workers on their way to work, Verlaine could see the police welding manhole covers closed and setting up checkpoints. If the Christmas season filled the city with tourists, Verlaine realized, New Year's Eve would be a veritable nightmare, especially this one.

Gabriella ordered Verlaine out of the van. Stepping into the masses of people clustered on the streets, they fell into a chaos of movement, blinking billboards, and relentless foot traffic. Verlaine hoisted the duffel bag over his shoulder, afraid that he might somehow lose its precious contents. After what had happened at his apartment, he couldn't shake the feeling that they were being watched, that every person nearby was suspect, that Percival

Grigori's men were waiting for them at every turn. He looked over his shoulder and saw an endless sea of people.

Gabriella walked quickly ahead, weaving through the crowd at a pace Verlaine struggled to match. As people surged around them, he noted that Gabriella cut quite a figure. She was a tiny woman, barely five feet tall, extraordinarily thin, with sharp features. She wore a fitted black overcoat that appeared to be Edwardian in cut — a tight, tailored, and stylish silk jacket fastened with a line of tiny obsidian buttons. The jacket was so tight that it appeared to have been designed to be worn over a corset. In contrast to her dark clothing, Gabriella's face was powdery white, with fine wrinkles — the skin of an old woman. Although she must have been in her seventies, there was something unnaturally youthful about her. She carried herself with the poise of a much younger woman. Her sculpted, glossy black hair was perfectly coiffed, her spine erect, her gait even. She walked fast, as if challenging Verlaine to keep up.

"You must be wondering why I've brought you here, into all of this madness," Gabriella said, gesturing to the crowd. Her voice resonated with the same calm equanimity she'd had on the telephone, a tone he found both eerie and deeply comforting. "Times Square at Christmas is not the most peaceful place for a stroll."

"I usually avoid this place," Verlaine said, looking around at the neon-infused storefront windows and incessantly flashing news ticker, a zipper of electricity dripping information faster than he could read it. "I haven't been around here in nearly a year."

"In the midst of danger, it is best to take cover in the crowd," Gabriella observed. "One does not want to call attention, and one can never be too careful."

After a few blocks, Gabriella slowed her pace, leading Verlaine past Bryant Park, where the space swarmed with Christmas decorations. With the fresh-fallen snow and the brightness of the morning light, the scene struck Verlaine as the image of a perfect New York Christmas, the very kind of Norman Rockwell scene that irritated him. As they approached the massive structure of the New York Public Library, Gabriella paused once again, looked over her shoulder, and crossed the street. "Come," she whispered, walking to a black town car parked illegally before one of the stone lion statues at the library's entrance. The New York license plate read ANGEL27. Upon seeing them approach, a driver turned on the engine. "This is our ride," Gabriella said.

They turned right on Thirty-ninth and drove up Sixth Avenue. As they paused at a stoplight, Verlaine looked over his shoulder, wondering if he would find the black SUV behind them. They weren't being followed. In fact, it unnerved him to realize that he felt almost at ease with Gabriella. He had known her all of forty-five minutes. She sat next to him, peering out the window as if being chased through Manhattan at nine o'clock in the morning were a perfectly normal part of her life.

At Columbus Circle the driver pulled over, and Gabriella and Verlaine stepped into the freezing gusts of wind blowing through Central Park. She walked swiftly ahead, searching traffic and looking beyond the rotary, nearly losing her impenetrable calm. "Where are they?" she muttered, turning along the edge of the park, walking past a magazine kiosk stacked high with daily papers, and into the shadows of Central Park West. She kept pace for a number of blocks, turned onto a side street, and paused, looking about her. "They are late," she said under her breath. Just then an antique Porsche rounded a corner, stopping with a sharp squeal of tires, its eggshell white paint shining in the morning light. The license plate, to Verlaine's amusement, read ANGEL1.

A young woman bounded out of the driver's seat of the Porsche. "My apologies, Dr. Gabriella," she said, placing a set of keys in Gabriella's hand before walking quickly away.

"Get in," Gabriella said, dropping into the driver's seat.

Verlaine followed orders, squeezing into the tiny car and slamming the door. The dash was glossy burled maple, the steering wheel leather. He arranged himself in the cramped passenger seat and shifted the duffel bag so he could reach the seat belt, but found that there wasn't one to fasten. "Nice car," he said.

Gabriella gave him a cutting look and started the engine. "It is the 356, the first Porsche made. Mrs. Rockefeller bought a number of them for the society. It's amazing — all these years later we're still surviving off her crumbs."

"Pretty luxurious crumbs," Verlaine said, running his hand over the caramel-brown leather seat. "I wouldn't have suspected Abigail to like sports cars."

"There are many things about her one wouldn't have suspected," Gabriella said, and pulled into traffic, spun around in a U-turn, then headed north alongside Central Park.

Gabriella parked on a quiet, tree-lined street in the mid-Eighties. Sandwiched between two similar buildings, the brownstone to which she led him appeared to have been squeezed vertical by sheer force. Gabriella unlocked the front door and waved Verlaine through the entrance, her movements so sure that he hadn't a moment to get his bearings before Gabriella slammed the door and turned the lock. It took him a moment to register that they'd made it out of the cold.

Gabriella leaned against the door, closed her eyes, and sighed deeply. In the granular darkness of the foyer, he could see her exhaustion. Her hands shook as she brushed a strand of hair from her eyes and placed a hand upon her heart. "Really," she said softly, "I am getting too old for this."

"Forgive me for asking," Verlaine said, his curiosity getting the better of him, "but how old would that be?"

"Old enough to raise suspicion," she said.

"Suspicion?"

"About my humanity," Gabriella said, narrowing her eyes — startling sea-green eyes lined heavily in gray shadow. "Some people in the organization believe that I am one of 'them.' Really, I should retire. I've dealt with such suspicions all my life."

Verlaine looked her up and down, from black boots to red lips. He wanted to ask her to explain herself, to explain what had happened the previous evening, to tell him why she'd been sent to his apartment to watch him.

"Come, we haven't time for my complaints," Gabriella said, turning on her heel and walking up a set of narrow wooden steps. "We'll go upstairs."

Verlaine followed as Gabriella climbed a creaky stairway. At the top of the steps, she opened a door and led Verlaine into a darkened room. As his eyes adjusted, he saw a long, narrow room filled with overstuffed armchairs, floor-to-ceiling bookshelves, Tiffany lamps perched upon end tables like precarious, brightly plumed birds. A series of oil paintings in heavy gilded frames — it was too dark to make out their subjects — hung upon one wall. An unevenly canted roof peaked at the center of the room, its plaster stained yellow with water damage.

Gabriella gestured for Verlaine to sit as she drew back the curtains of a series of tall narrow windows, filling the room with light. He walked to a set of straight-backed Neo-Gothic chairs near the window, set the duffel bag lightly at his side, and sank into the rock-hard seat. The chair's legs creaked under his weight.

"Let me be clear, Mr. Verlaine," Gabriella said, taking a seat in the matching chair at his side. "You are lucky to be alive."

"Who were they?" Verlaine said. "What did they want?"

"Equally fortuitous," Gabriella continued, nonplussed by Verlaine's questions and growing agitation, "is the fact that you eluded them completely unharmed." Glancing at his raw wound, the scab of which had begun to congeal, she said, "Or nearly unharmed. You are lucky. You have escaped with something that they want."

"You must have been there for hours. How else would you have known they were watching me? How did you know they would break in?"

"I am no psychic," Gabriella said. "Wait long enough and soon the devils come."

"Evangeline called you?" Verlaine asked, but Gabriella said nothing. Clearly she was not about to divulge any of her secrets to the likes of him. "I suppose you know what they were planning to do once they found me," Verlaine said.

"They would have taken the letters, of course," Gabriella answered calmly. "Once they had them in their possession, they would have killed you."

Verlaine turned this over in his mind for a moment. He couldn't understand how the letters could possibly be so important. Finally, Verlaine said, "Do you have a theory as to why they would do this?"

"I have a theory about everything, Mr. Verlaine." Gabriella smiled for the first time in their brief acquaintance. "First, they believe, as I do, that the letters in your possession contain valuable information. Second, they want the information very badly."

"Enough to kill for it?"

"Certainly," Gabriella replied. "They have killed many times for information of much less importance."

"I don't understand," Verlaine said, pulling the duffel bag onto his lap — a protective movement that, he could see from the flicker in her gaze, did not escape Gabriella's notice. "They have not read Innocenta's letters."

This information gave Gabriella pause. "Are you certain?"

"I didn't give them to Grigori," Verlaine said. "I wasn't sure what they were when I found them, and I wanted to be certain of their authenticity before alerting him. In my line of work, it is essential to verify everything beforehand."

Gabriella opened the drawer of a small escritoire, took a cigarette from a case, fitted it into a lacquered holder, and lit it with a small gold lighter. The scent of spiced tobacco filled the room. When she held the case to Verlaine, offering him a cigarette, he accepted. He considered asking for a strong drink to accompany it.

"Truthfully," he said at last, "I don't have a clue how I got involved in this. I don't know why those men, or whatever they are, were at my place. I admit I've picked up some odd information about Grigori while working for him, but everyone knows that man is an eccentric. Frankly, I'm beginning to wonder if I might simply be going insane. Can you tell me why I'm here?"

Gabriella assessed him, as if contemplating the appropriate response. At last she said, "I have brought you here, Mr. Verlaine, because we need you."

" 'We'?" Verlaine replied.

"We ask that you help us recover something very precious."

"The discovery made in the Rhodope Mountains?"

Gabriella's face turned pale at Verlaine's words. He felt a brief flicker of triumph — for once he had surprised her.

"You know about the journey to the Rhodopes?" she said, recovering her composure.

"It is mentioned in a letter from Abigail Rockefeller that Evangeline showed me yesterday. I gathered that they were discussing the recovery of some sort of antiquity, perhaps Greek pottery or Thracian art. Although now I see that the discovery was more valuable than a few clay jars."

"Quite a bit more valuable," Gabriella said, finishing the cigarette and putting it out in an ashtray. "But its worth is assessed differently than you might think. It isn't a value that can be quantified with money, although over the past two thousand years there has been much, much gold spent trying to obtain it. Let me put it this way: It has an ancient value."

"It is a historical artifact?" Verlaine asked.

"You might say so," Gabriella said, crossing her arms against her chest. "It is very old, but this is no museum piece. It is as relevant today as it was in the past. It could affect the lives of millions of people, and, even more important, it could change the course of the future."

"Sounds like a riddle," Verlaine said, extinguishing the cigarette.

"I'm not going to play games with you. We

haven't the time. The situation is much more complicated than you realize. What happened to you this morning began many ages ago. I don't know how you became enmeshed in this affair, but the letters in your possession place you firmly at the center."

"I don't understand."

"You will have to trust me," Gabriella said. "I'll tell you everything, but it must be a trade. For this knowledge you will give up your freedom. After tonight either you will become one of us or you will go into hiding. In any case you will spend the rest of your life looking over your shoulder. Once you know the history of our mission and how Mrs. Rockefeller became involved — which is only a very minor component to a large and complex tale — you will be part of a terrible drama, one that there is no way of exiting completely. It may sound extreme, but once you know the truth, your life will change irrevocably. There is no going back."

Verlaine looked at his hands, contemplating what Gabriella had said. Although it felt as if he had been asked to step over the edge of a cliff — commanded to jump over, in fact — he could not stop himself from continuing onward willingly. At last he said, "You believe that the letters reveal what they discovered during the expedition."

"Not what was discovered but what was hidden," Gabriella said. "They went to the

Rhodope Mountains to bring back a lyre. A kithara, to be exact. Once, briefly, we had it in our possession. Now it has been hidden again. Our enemies — an extremely wealthy and influential group — want to find it as badly as we do."

"That's who was at my place?"

"The men at your apartment were hired by this group, yes."

"Is Percival Grigori part of this group?"

"Yes," Gabriella said. "He is very much a part of it."

"So in working for him," Verlaine said, "I have been working against you."

"As I told you before, you really mean nothing to them. It is detrimental and extremely risky for him to be in public, and so he has always hired disposables — that is his word, not mine — to do his research for him. He uses them to dig up information and then kills them. It is an extremely efficient security measure." Gabriella lit another cigarette, the smoke forming a haze in the air.

"Did Abigail Rockefeller work for them?"

"No," Gabriella said. "Quite the opposite. Mrs. Rockefeller was working with Mother Innocenta to find an appropriate hiding place for a case containing the lyre. For reasons we don't understand, Abigail Rockefeller ceased all communication with us after the war. It caused quite a lot of trauma in our network. We had no idea where she put the contents of the case. Some believe it was hidden in New York City. Others believe she sent it back to Europe. We have been trying desperately to locate where she hid it, if she hid it at all."

"I've read Innocenta's letters," Verlaine said, doubtful. "I don't think they will tell you what you're hoping to find. It makes more sense to go to Grigori."

Gabriella took a deep, weary breath. "There is something I would like to show you," she said. "It may help you understand the kind of creatures we are dealing with."

Standing, she slid out of her jacket. Then she began to remove her black silk shirt, her veined hands working over the buttons until each one had been unfastened. "This," she said quietly, pulling first her left arm, then her right free of the black sleeves, "is what happens when you are caught by the other side."

Verlaine watched Gabriella turn under the light of a nearby window. Her torso was covered with thick, ribboning scars that crossed her back, her chest, her stomach, and her shoulders. It was as though she had been carved with an exceedingly sharp butcher's knife. From the width of the damaged tissue and the haphazard ridges of the scars, Verlaine guessed that the wounds had not been properly sutured. In the weak light, the skin was pink and raw. The pattern suggested that Gabriella had been whipped or, worse, sliced with a razor blade.

"My God," Verlaine said, overwhelmed by the mangled flesh, the horrible yet strangely delicate oyster-shell pink of the scars. "How did it happen?"

"Once I believed I could outsmart them," Gabriella said. "I believed that I was wiser, stronger, more adept than they were. I was the best angelologist in all of Paris during the war. Despite my age I rose through the hierarchy faster than anyone. This was a fact. Believe me — I am and always have been very, very good at my work."

"This happened in the war?" Verlaine asked, trying to make sense of such brutality.

"In my youth I worked as a double agent. I became the lover of the heir of the most powerful enemy family. My work was monitored, and I was quite successful in the beginning, but ultimately I was found out. If anyone could have pulled off such an infiltration, I could have. Take a long look at what happened to me, Mr. Verlaine, and imagine what they will do to you. Your naïve American belief that good always overcomes evil would not save you. I guarantee: You will be doomed."

Verlaine could not bear to look at Gabriella, yet he could not turn away. His gaze traced the scars' sinuous pink path from her clavicle to her hip, the pallor of her skin registering through his body. He felt that he might be sick. "How can you hope to defeat them?"

"That," Gabriella said, sliding back into her

571

blouse and fastening the buttons, "is something I will explain after you have given me the letters."

Verlaine set the laptop computer on the surface of Gabriella's desk and turned it on. The hard drive clicked, and the monitor flickered to life. Soon all his files — including the research documents and scanned letters — appeared as icons on the glowing surface of the screen, bright-colored electronic balloons floating in an electronic blue sky. Verlaine clicked the Rockefeller/Innocenta folder and stepped away from the computer, giving Gabriella ample room to read. At the dust-streaked window, he observed the quiet, cold park. He knew that beyond there were frozen ponds, an empty skating rink, snow-covered sidewalks, the winterized carousel. A phalanx of taxis sped north on Central Park West, carrying people uptown. The city carried on in its usual manic fashion.

Verlaine glanced over his shoulder at Gabriella. She read the letters breathlessly, utterly absorbed in the computer screen, as if the incandescent words might disappear at any moment. The monitor cast a green-white pallor over her skin, accentuating the wrinkles about her mouth and eyes and turning her black hair a shade closer to purple. She removed a sheet of paper from the desk drawer and jotted notes on it, scribbling as she read, not once glancing up at Verlaine or down at the stream of sentences emerging from her pen. Gabriella's attention was so intently focused on the screen — the looping, pinched curves of Mother Innocenta's handwriting, the creases of the paper reproduced to an exact digital likeness — that it was not until Verlaine stood at her side, looking over her shoulder at the computer, that she noticed him.

"There is a chair in the corner," she said without taking her eyes from the screen. "You will find it more comfortable than bending over my shoulder."

Verlaine carried an antique piano bench from the corner, placed it lightly next to Gabriella, and sat.

She lifted a hand, as if expecting it to be kissed, and said, "A cigarette, *s'il vous plaît.*"

Verlaine removed one from the porcelain box, fitted it into the lacquer holder, and placed it between Gabriella's fingers. Still without looking up, she brought the cigarette to her lips. *"Merci,"* she said, inhaling as Verlaine ignited the lighter.

Finally he opened his duffel bag, took a folder from inside, and, venturing to disturb her from her reading, said, "I should have given these to you before."

Gabriella turned from the computer and took the letters from Verlaine. Sifting through them, she said, "The originals?"

"One hundred percent original stolen material from the Rockefeller Family Archive," Verlaine said.

"Thank you," Gabriella said, opening the folder and paging through the letters. "Of course, I wondered what happened to them, and I suspected that they might be with you. Tell me — what other copies of these letters are there?"

"That's it," Verlaine said. "Those are the originals in your hands." He gestured to the scans open on the computer screen. "And the scans."

"Very good," Gabriella said quietly.

Verlaine suspected that she wished to say more. Instead she stood, removed a canister of coffee grounds from a drawer, and brewed a pot of coffee on a hot plate. When the coffee bubbled into the pot, Gabriella carried it to the computer and, without a hint of warning, poured the contents of the pot over the laptop, the scalding liquid soaking the keyboard. The screen went white and then black. A horrid clicking noise wrenched through the computer. Then it fell quiet.

Verlaine hovered over the coffee-saturated keyboard, trying not to lose his temper — and failing. "What have you done?"

"We cannot allow more copies than absolutely necessary," Gabriella said, calmly wiping her hands free of coffee grounds.

"Yes, but you've destroyed my computer."

Verlaine pressed the "start" button, hoping that it would somehow come to life again.

"Technological gadgetry is easily replaced," Gabriella said, not a hint of apology in her voice. Walking to the window, she leaned against the glass, her arms crossed over her chest, her expression serene. "We cannot allow anyone to read these letters. They are too important."

Sorting through them, she placed the letters alongside one another on a low table until it was filled with yellowed sheets. There were five letters, each composed of numerous pages. Verlaine came to Gabriella's side. The pages were written in florid cursive. Lifting a soft, wrinkled sheet, he attempted to read the script — elegant, looping, exceptionally illegible penmanship that washed across the unlined paper in faded blue waves. It was nearly impossible to decipher in the dim light.

"You can read it?" Gabriella asked, leaning over the table and rotating a page, as if approaching it from a new angle might clarify the tangle of letters. "I find it difficult to make out her writing at all."

"It takes a bit of getting used to," Verlaine said. "But yes, I can manage it."

"Then you can help me," Gabriella said. "We need to determine if this correspondence is going to be of any real assistance."

"I'll give it a try," Verlaine said. "But first

I would like you to tell me what I'm looking for."

"Particular locations mentioned in the correspondence," Gabriella said. "Locations where Abigail Rockefeller had full access. Perhaps an institution where she had the authority to come and go as she wished. Seemingly innocuous references to addresses, streets, hotels. Secure locations, of course, but not too secure."

"That could be half of New York," Verlaine said. "If I'm going to find anything at all in these letters, I need to know exactly what you're seeking."

Gabriella stared out the window. Finally she said, "Long ago a band of rogue angels called the Watchers were condemned to be held in a cave in the remotest regions of Europe. Entrusted to deliver the prisoners, the archangels bound the Watchers and thrust them into a deep cavern. As the Watchers fell, the archangels heard their cries of anguish. It was an agony so great that in a moment of pity the Archangel Gabriel threw the wretched creatures a golden lyre — a lyre of angelic perfection, a lyre whose music was so miraculous that the prisoners would spend hundreds of years in contentment, pacified by its melodies. Gabriel's mistake had grave repercussions. The lyre proved to be a solace and strength to the Watchers. They not only entertained themselves in the depths of the earth, they became stronger and more ambitious in their desires. They learned that the lyre's music gave them extraordinary power."

"What kind of power?" Verlaine inquired.

"The power to play at being God," Gabriella said. She lit another cigarette and resumed. "It is a phenomenon taught exclusively in our ethereal musicology seminars to the advanced students at angelological academies. As the universe was created by the vibration of God's voice — by the music of His Word — so the universe can be altered, enhanced, or entirely undone by the music of His messengers, the angels. The lyre — and other celestial instruments fashioned by the angels, many of which we have had in our possession throughout the centuries — has the power to effect such changes, or so we speculate. The degree of power these instruments contains varies. Our ethereal musicologists believe that at the correct frequency any number of cosmic changes could occur. Perhaps the sky will be red, the sea purple, and the grass orange. Perhaps the sun will chill the air rather than heat it. Perhaps devils will populate the continents. It is believed that one of the powers of the lyre is to restore the sick to health."

Verlaine stared at her, flabbergasted at what this otherwise rational woman had just said.

"It makes little sense to you now," she said, taking the original letters and giving them to Verlaine. "But read the letters to me. I would like to hear them. It will help me think."

Verlaine scanned the sheets, found the beginning date of the correspondence — June 5, 1943 — and began to read. Although Mother Innocenta's style posed a challenge — every sentence was grandiose in tone, each thought pounded into writing as if with an iron hammer — he soon fell into the cadences of her prose.

The first contained little more than a polite exchange of formalities and was composed with a tentative, halting tone, as if Innocenta were feeling her way toward Mrs. Rockefeller through a darkened hallway. Nonetheless, the odd reference to Mrs. Rockefeller's artistry was contained even in this letter — *"Please know that the perfection of your artistic vision, and the execution of your fancy, is well noted and accepted"* — a reference that brought all of Verlaine's ambition back the instant he read it. The second letter was a longer and slightly more intimate missive in which Innocenta explained her gratitude to Mrs. Rockefeller for the important role she held in the future of their mission, and — Verlaine noted with particular triumph — discussed the drawing that Mrs. Rockefeller must have included in the letter: *"Our most admired friend, one cannot fail to marvel at your delicate renderings or receive them with humble thanks and grateful understanding."* The tone of the letter hinted that an arrangement had developed between the two women, although there was nothing concrete to be found, and certainly nothing to suggest that a plan had been arrived at. The fourth letter contained another of the references to something artistic: *"As always, your hand never fails to express what the eye most wishes to behold."*

Verlaine began to explain his theory of Mrs. Rockefeller's artwork, but Gabriella urged him to read on, clearly annoyed that he would stop. "Read the final letter," she said. "The one dated December fifteenth, 1943."

Verlaine sifted through the pages until he found the letter.

December 15, 1943

Dearest Mrs. Rockefeller,

Your latest letter arrived at an opportune moment, as we have been laboring at our annual Christmas celebrations and are now fully prepared to commemorate our Lord's birth. The sisters' annual fundraiser has been a greater success than expected, and I daresay that we will continue to draw many donations. Your assistance is also a source of great joy to us. We give thanks to the Lord for your generosity and remember you in our hourly prayers. Your name will long remain upon the lips of the sisters at St. Rose.

The charity benefit described in your letter of November has been met with great approval by all at St. Rose Convent, and I hope it will make quite a difference to our efforts to bring in new membership. After the travails and hardships of our recent battles, the great privations and declines of the past years, we nonetheless see a greater brightness emerging.

While a discerning eye is like the music of the angels — precise and measured and mysterious beyond reason — its power rests in the cast of light. Dearest benefactress, we know you chose your renderings wisely. We eagerly await further illumination and ask that you write in due haste, so that news of your work will lift our spirits.

Your fellow seeker,
Innocenta Maria Magdalena Fiori,
ASA

As he read the fifth letter, a particular phrase caught Gabriella's attention. She asked Verlaine to stop and repeat it. He backtracked and read, " '. . . a discerning eye is like the music of the angels — precise and measured and mysterious beyond reason — its power rests in the cast of light.' "

He placed the stack of yellowed papers upon his lap. "Did you hear anything of interest?" he asked, anxious to test his theory about the passages.

Gabriella appeared lost in thought, gazing past him, staring out the window, her chin resting on her hand. "It is half there," she said at last.

"Half?" Verlaine said. "Half of what?"

"Half of our mystery," Gabriella said. "Mother Innocenta's letters confirm something I have long suspected — namely, that the women were working together. I will need to read the other half of this correspondence to be certain," she went on. "But I believe that Innocenta and Mrs. Rockefeller were choosing locations. Even months before Celestine brought the instrument from Paris — even months before it was retrieved from the Rhodopes — they were planning the best way to keep it safe. It is a blessing that Innocenta and Abigail Rockefeller had the intelligence and foresight to find a secure location. Now we need only to understand their methods. We need to find the location of the lyre."

Verlaine raised an eyebrow. "Is that possible?"

"I will not be certain until I read Abigail Rockefeller's letters to Innocenta. Clearly Innocenta was a brilliant angelologist, much smarter than she's given credit for. All along she was urging Abigail Rockefeller to secure the future of angelology. The instruments were placed into Mrs. Rockefeller's care only after great forethought." Gabriella walked the length of the room, as if movement ordered her thoughts. Then she stopped short. "It must be here in New York City."

"You are certain?" Verlaine asked.

"There is no way to know for sure, but I believe it is here. Abigail Rockefeller would have wanted to keep an eye on it."

"You must see something in the letters that I can't," Verlaine said. "To me they're just a collection of friendly exchanges between two old women. The only potentially interesting element about the letters is referred to time and time again but isn't actually there."

"What do you mean?" Gabriella asked.

"Did you notice how Innocenta returns over and over to the discussion of visual images? It seems that there were drawings or sketches or other artwork Abigail Rockefeller included in her letters," Verlaine said. "These visual images must be in the other half of the correspondence. Or they have been lost."

"You are quite right," Gabriella said. "There is a pattern of some kind in the letters, and I am certain that this will be confirmed once we read the other half of the correspondence. Surely the ideas proposed by Innocenta were refined. Perhaps new suggestions were sent. Only when we can lay out the correspondence side by side will we have the whole picture."

She took the letters from Verlaine and paged through them once more, reading them over as if to memorize the lines. Then she tucked them into her pocket. "We must be extremely careful," she said. "It is paramount that we keep these letters — and the secrets they point to — away from the Nephilim. You are certain that Percival has not seen them?"

"You and Evangeline are the only people who have read them, but I did show him something else that I wish he'd never seen." Verlaine said, removing the architectural drawings from his bag.

Gabriella took the drawings and examined them with care, her expression turning grave. "This is very unfortunate," she said at last. "These give everything away. When he looked at these papers, did he understand their significance?"

"He didn't seem to think they were important."

"Ah, good," Gabriella said, smiling slightly. "Percival was wrong. We must go at once, before he begins to understand what you have found."

"And exactly what is it that I've found?" Verlaine asked, feeling that he might at last learn the significance of the drawings and the golden seal at their center.

Gabriella placed the drawings on the table and pressed them flat with her hands. "These are a set of instructions," she said. "The seal at the center marks a location. If you notice, it is at the center of the Adoration Chapel."

"But why?" Verlaine asked, studying the

seal for the hundredth time and wondering at its meaning.

Gabriella slipped into her black silk jacket and headed to the door. "Come with me to St. Rose Convent, and I will explain everything."

Fifth Avenue, Upper East Side, New York City

Percival waited in the lobby of his apartment building, his sunglasses shielding his eyes from the unbearably bright morning. His mind was wholly absorbed in the situation at hand, one that had suddenly become even more mystifying with Gabriella Lévi-Franche Valko's involvement. Her presence at Verlaine's apartment was enough to signal that they had in fact hit upon something significant. They would need to move immediately, before they lost track of Verlaine.

A black Mercedes SUV stopped before the building. Percival recognized the Gibborim that Otterley had dispatched to kill Verlaine early that morning. They sat hunched in the front seat, crude, unquestioning, without the intelligence or curiosity to wonder at Percival and Otterley's superiority. He recoiled at the thought of riding in the same vehicle with such beings — surely Otterley didn't expect that he would agree to such an arrangement. In his workings with lower life-forms, there were certain lines he would not cross.

Otterley didn't have such qualms. She emerged from the backseat composed as ever, her long blond hair tied into a smooth knot, her fur-trimmed ski jacket zipped to her chin, and her cheeks stained pink from the cold. To Percival's great relief, she said a few words to the Gibborim and the SUV sped away. Only then did Percival step outside to greet his sister for the second time that morning, happily in a less compromised position than before.

"We will need to take my car," Otterley said. "Gabriella Lévi-Franche Valko saw that vehicle outside Verlaine's apartment."

The very articulation of Gabriella's name withered his resolve. "Did you see her?"

"She has probably given every angelologist in New York the plate numbers," Otterley said. "We'd better use the Jag. I don't want to take chances."

"And what about the beasts?"

Otterley smiled — she, too, disliked working with Gibborim but would never deign to show it. "I've sent them ahead. They have a specific area to cover. If they find Gabriella, they have been instructed to seize her."

"I very much doubt they will have the skill to catch her," Percival said.

Otterley tossed her car keys to the doorman, who walked off to retrieve the car from a garage around the corner. Standing at the curb, with Fifth Avenue stretching beyond, Percival struggled to breathe. The more desperate he became for air, the more painful it was to inhale, and so he was relieved when the white Jaguar idled before them, exhaust rising from the tail. Otterley slid into the driver's seat and waited as Percival, whose body ached with the slightest irregular movement, eased delicately into the leather passenger seat, wheezing and gasping for breath. His frayed, rotting wings pressed against his back as the harness shifted. He suppressed an urge to cry out in pain as Otterley put the car in gear and sped into traffic.

While she steered toward the West Side Highway, Percival turned the heat on high, hoping that the warm air would allow him to breathe with more ease. At a traffic light, his sister turned to examine him, her eyes narrowed. She did not speak, but it was clear that she didn't know what to do with the weak, struggling being who had once been the future of the Grigori family.

Percival removed a handgun from the glove compartment, made sure it was loaded, and tucked it into the inside pocket of his overcoat. The gun was heavy and cold. Running his fingers over it, he wondered what it would feel like to point it at Gabriella's head, to press it upon the soft spot at her temple, to frighten her. No matter what had happened in the past, no matter how many times he had dreamed of Gabriella, he was not going to allow her to interfere. This time he would kill her himself.

Tappan Zee Bridge, I-87 North, New York

With its antiquated engine and low chassis, the Porsche proved to be a bumpy, loud ride. Yet despite the noise, Verlaine found the journey to be deeply calming. He looked at Gabriella sitting in the driver's seat, her arm resting against the door. She had the air of someone planning a bank heist — her manner was concentrated, serious, and careful. He had come to think of her as an extraordinarily private person, a woman who said nothing more than she needed to. Although Verlaine had pressed her for information, it took some time before she would open her thoughts to him.

At his insistence they had spent the drive in a discussion about her work — its history and purpose, how Abigail Rockefeller had become involved, and how Gabriella had spent her life entrenched in angelology, until Verlaine understood the depth of the danger he'd fallen into. Their familiarity with each other grew as the minutes passed, and by the time they drove over the bridge, an uncommon understanding had developed between them.

From their vantage above the wide expanse of the Hudson, Verlaine could see ice chunks clinging to the snowy riverbanks. Looking down upon the landscape, he felt as if the earth had split open in a great geomorphic gash. The sun burnished the Hudson so that it scintillated with heat and color, fluid and brilliant as a sheet of fire.

The lanes of the highway were empty compared to the clogged streets of Manhattan. Once across the bridge, Gabriella drove faster and faster over the open road. The Porsche sounded as tired as he felt: Its motor rattled as if it might explode. Verlaine's stomach ached with hunger; his eyes burned from exhaustion. Glancing into the rearview mirror, he saw, to his surprise, that he looked as if he'd been in a brawl. His eyes were bloodshot and his hair tangled. Gabriella had helped him to dress the wound properly, winding gauze around his hand so that it resembled a boxing glove. It seemed appropriate: In the past twenty-four hours he had become a battered, beaten, and bruised man.

And yet in the presence of such immense beauty — the river, the azure sky, the eggshell glint of the Porsche — Verlaine reveled in the sudden expansion of his perception. He could see how confined his life had become in the past years. He'd spent whole days moving along a tiny track between his apartment, his office, and a few cafés and restaurants. Rarely if ever did he step outside this pattern. He could not remember the last time he had really noted his surroundings or truly looked at the people around him. He had been lost in a maze. That he would never return to that life again was both terrifying and exhilarating.

Gabriella turned off the highway and drove onto a small country road. She stretched, arching her back like a cat. "We need to get gas," she said, scanning the road for a place to stop. Rounding a bend, Verlaine spotted a twenty-four-hour gas station. Gabriella pulled off the road and parked alongside a pump. She didn't object when he offered to fill the car, telling him to be sure to use premium.

As Verlaine had paid for the gas, he stood gazing over the neat rows of merchandise inside the station — the bottles of soda, the packaged food, the orderly array of magazines — remarking how simple life could be. Only yesterday he would not have thought much of the creature comforts of a gas-station convenience store. He would have been too annoyed by the long line and neon lights to actually look around. Now he felt a perverse admiration for anything that offered such safe familiarity. He added a pack of cigarettes to the tally and returned to the car.

Outside, Gabriella waited in the driver's seat. Verlaine took the passenger side and gave Gabriella the pack of cigarettes. She accepted them with a terse smile, but he could see that the gesture pleased her. Then, without waiting another moment, she threw the car into gear and drove onto the small country highway.

Verlaine unwrapped the pack of cigarettes, extracted one, and lit it for Gabriella. She rolled the window down a crack, the cigarette smoke dispersing in a stream of fresh air. "You don't seem to be afraid, but I know that what I told you must have some effect upon you."

"I'm still working on getting my mind around it all," Verlaine replied, thinking, even as he spoke, that this was a huge understatement. In truth, he was baffled by what he'd learned. He couldn't understand how she managed to stay so calm. Finally, he said, "How do you do it?"

"Do what?" she asked, keeping her eye on the road.

"Live like this," he replied. "As if nothing abnormal is happening. As if you've accepted it."

Keeping her eyes on the road, Gabriella said, "I became part of this battle so long ago that I am hardened to it. It is impossible for me to remember what it is like to live without knowing. Discovering their existence is like being told the earth is round — it goes against everything one senses to be true. Yet it is reality. I cannot imagine what it is like to live without them haunting my thoughts, to wake in the morning and believe that we live in a just, free, equal world. I suppose I have adjusted my vision of the world to suit this reality. I see everything in white and black, good and evil. We are good, they are evil. If we are to live, they must die. There are those of us who believe in appeasement — that we can work out a way to live side by side — but many also believe we cannot rest until they have been exterminated."

"I would think," Verlaine said, surprised by the adamancy of Gabriella's voice, "it would be more complicated than that."

"Of course, it is more complicated. There are reasons for my strong feelings. While I have been an angelologist all of my adult life, I have not always hated the Nephilim as I do today," Gabriella said, her voice quiet, almost vulnerable. "I will tell you a story, one that very few have heard before. Perhaps it will help you to understand my extremism. Perhaps you will see why it is so important to me that every last one of them is killed."

Gabriella tossed the cigarettc out the window, lit another, her eyes trained upon the winding highway.

"In the second year of my schooling at the Angelological Society in Paris, I met the love of my life. This is not something I would have admitted at the time, nor would I have made this claim in middle age. But I am an old woman now — older than I look, as a matter of fact — and I can say with great certainty that I will never love again as I did in the summer of 1939. I was fifteen then, too young to fall in love, perhaps. Or maybe it is only then, with the dew of childhood still in my eyes, that I was capable of such love. I will never know, of course."

Gabriella paused, as if weighing her words, and continued.

"I was a peculiar girl, to put it mildly. I was obsessed with my studies in the way that some become obsessed with riches or love or fame. I came from a family of wealthy angelologists — many of my relatives had trained in the academy. I was also inordinately competitive. Socializing with my peers was out of the question, and I thought nothing of working night and day in order to succeed. I wanted to be at the top of my class in every respect, and routinely I *was* at the top. By the second term of my first year, it was clear that there were only two students to have distinguished themselves — myself and a young woman named Celestine, a brilliant girl who later became a dear friend."

Verlaine nearly choked. "Celestine?" he said. "Celestine Clochette who came to St. Rose Convent in 1943?"

"It was 1944," Gabriella corrected. "But that is another story. This story begins one afternoon in April 1939, a chill, rainy afternoon, as

April afternoons tend to be in Paris. The cobblestones veritably flooded over each spring with rain, filling the sewers and the gardens and the Seine. I remember the afternoon exactly. It was one o'clock, April seventh, a Friday. I had finished my morning classes and, as usual, ventured out to find something for lunch. What was *un*usual about this day was that I had forgotten my umbrella. As I was fastidious to a fault, it was a rare spring day when I found myself unprotected in a downpour. Yet this was the case. Upon walking out of the Athenaeum, I realized that I would be soaked to the bone, and the papers and books I carried under my arm would certainly have been ruined. And so I stood under the great portico of our school's main entrance, watching the water fall.

"From out of the swirling deluge of rain, a man emerged with an enormous violet-colored umbrella, an unusual choice for a gentleman, I thought. I watched him saunter across the courtyard of the school, elegant, erect, and exceedingly good-looking. Perhaps it was the longing I felt for the hollow, dry sanctuary of the umbrella, but I stared at the stranger, hoping that he would come to me, as if I had the power to cast a spell upon him.

"Those were very different times. If it was unseemly for a woman to stare at a handsome gentleman, it was equally unseemly for him to ignore her. Only the most ill-mannered rake

595

would leave a lady in the rain. He paused halfway through the courtyard, discovered that I was staring at him, turned sharply upon the heel of his leather boot, and came to my aid.

"He tipped his hat so that his great blue eyes met mine. He said, 'May I take you safely through this torrent?' His voice was filled with a buoyant, seductive, almost cruel confidence. This one look, this single phrase, was all that it took to win me.

"'You may take me wherever you wish,' I replied. Instantly aware of my indiscretion, I added, 'Anything to get out of this terrible rain.'

"He asked me my name, and when I told him, I saw at once that the name pleased him. 'Named after an angel?'

"'The messenger of good news,' I answered.

"He met my eyes and smiled, pleased with my quick response. His eyes were the coolest, most pellucid blue I had ever seen. The smile was a sweet, delicious smile, as if he knew the power he had over me. A few years later, when it was revealed that my uncle, Victor Lévi-Franche, had disgraced our family by working as a spy for this man, I wondered if his delight at my name was tied to my uncle's position and not, as he suggested, its angelic provenance.

"He offered his hand and said, 'Come, my messenger of good news, let us go.' I gave him my hand. In that moment, with the first touch of his skin, the life I had been leading fell away and a new one began.

"He later introduced himself as Percival Grigori III." Gabriella glanced at Verlaine, to catch his reaction.

"Not the same —" Verlaine said in disbelief.

"Yes," Gabriella said. "One and the same. At the time I had no notion of who he was or what his family name meant. If only I had been older and had been exposed to more at the academy, I would have turned from him and run away. In my ignorance I was charmed.

"Under the great violet umbrella, we walked. He took my arm and led me through the narrow, flooding streets to a motorcar, a shiny Mercedes 500K Roadster, an amazing silver car that shone even in the rain. I don't know if you admire automobiles, but this was a gorgeous machine, with all the luxuries available at the time — electric wipers and locks, opulent coachwork. My family owned a car — which was quite a luxury in itself — but I had never seen anything like Percival's Mercedes. They were exceedingly rare. As a matter of fact, a prewar 500K was auctioned off a few years ago in London. I went to the event so that I could see the car again. It sold for seven hundred thousand pounds sterling.

"Percival opened the door with a grand gesture, as if placing me into a royal carriage. I sank into the soft seat, my wet skin sticking to the leather, and took a deep breath: The car smelled of cologne mixed with the slightest hint of cigarette smoke. A tortoiseshell dashboard gleamed with buttons and knobs, each one waiting to be pressed and turned, while a pair of leather driving gloves lay folded upon the dash, waiting for his hands to fill them. It was the most beautiful car I had seen in my life. Nestling deep into the seat, I was consumed by happiness.

"I remember quite vividly the feeling I had as he drove the Mercedes along the boulevard Saint-Michel and across the Île de la Cité, the rain falling with increased violence, as if it had been waiting for us to take shelter before releasing itself upon the spring flowers and green, receptive earth. The feeling, I believe, was fear, although at the time I told myself it was love. The danger Percival posed was not known to me. For all I could tell, he was just a young man who drove recklessly. I believe now that I feared him instinctively. Still, he had captured my heart without effort. I watched him, glancing at his lovely pale skin and his long, delicate fingers upon the gearshift. I couldn't speak. Over the bridge he sped, and then onto the rue de Rivoli, the wipers swishing across the windshield, cutting a porthole through the water.

"'Naturally I am taking you to lunch,' he

said, glancing at me as he slowed before a grand hotel off the place de la Concorde. 'I see that you're hungry.'

" 'And how can you see such a thing as hunger?' I replied, challenging him, although he was correct: I had not eaten breakfast and was ravenous.

" 'I have a special talent,' he said, taking the car out of gear, pulling the brake shaft, and peeling his leather driving gloves from his hands one by one. 'I know exactly what you desire before you know yourself.'

" 'Then tell me,' I demanded, hoping that he would find me bold and sophisticated, the very things I knew I was not. 'What do I want most of all?'

"He studied me for a moment. I saw, as I had in the first seconds of our meeting, the fleeting, sensual cruelty behind his blue eyes. 'A beautiful death,' he said, so quietly I was not sure that I'd heard him correctly. With that he opened the door and slid out of the car.

"Before I had time to question this bizarre statement, he opened the passenger door, helped me from my seat, and we were walking arm in arm into the restaurant. Pausing at a gilded mirror, he shed his hat and coat, glancing about as if the fleet of waiters rushing to assist him were too slow for his taste. I watched the glass as his reflection moved, examining his profile, the beautifully cut suit of light gray gabardine that in the harsh clarity of the mirror appeared almost blue, an off rhyme of his eyes. His skin was deathly pale, nearly transparent, and yet this quality had the strange effect of making him more attractive, as if he were a precious object that had been kept from the sun."

As he listened to Gabriella's tale, Verlaine tried to reconcile her description with the Percival Grigori he had seen yesterday afternoon, but he could not. Clearly Gabriella did not speak of the sickly, decrepit man Verlaine knew, but rather of the man Percival Grigori had once been. Instead of questioning her, as he wished, Verlaine sat back and listened.

"Within seconds a waiter had taken our coats and was leading us into the dining room, a converted ballroom that opened upon a courtyard garden. All the while I could feel him glancing at me with intense interest, as if searching for my reaction.

"There was no question of menus or of ordering our dishes. Wineglasses were filled and plates arrived, as if everything had been arranged ahead of time. Of course Percival achieved his desired effect. My astonishment at it all was immense, although I tried to disguise it. While I had been sent to fine schools and had been raised in the bourgeois fashion of the city, I was quite aware that this man was beyond anything I had experienced. Looking over my clothes, I realized to my horror that

I was wearing my school attire, a detail I had overlooked in the excitement of the drive. In addition to my drab clothing, my shoes were scuffed and I had forgotten my favorite perfume at my apartment.

" 'You're blushing,' he said. 'Why?'

"I merely looked down at my pleated wool skirt and crisp white blouse, and he understood my dilemma.

" 'You are the loveliest creature here,' he said, without a hint of irony. 'You look like an angel.'

" 'I look exactly like what I am,' I said, pride overruling all other emotions. 'A schoolgirl dining with a wealthy older man.'

" 'I am not so much older than you,' he said playfully.

" 'How much is not so much?' I demanded. Although he appeared to be in his early twenties — an age that was not, as he rightly said, much older than mine — his manners and the confidence with which he carried himself seemed to belong to a man of great experience.

" 'I am more interested in you,' he said, brushing away the question. 'Tell me, do you enjoy your studies? I believe you must. I own apartments near your school, and I have seen you before. You always have the appearance of someone who has been in the library too long.'

"While it should have sent a warning that

he had been aware of my existence before that day, it instead sent a ripple of pleasure through me. 'You noticed me?' I said, too eager for his attention.

"'Of course,' he said, sipping his wine. 'I could not make it through the courtyard without wishing to see you. It has become rather annoying lately, especially when you are not there. Surely you are aware of your beauty.'

"I paused to eat a sliver of roasted duck, afraid to speak. Finally I said, 'You are right — I enjoy my studies immensely.'

"'If they are entertaining,' he said, 'you must tell me everything about them.'

"And so the afternoon continued, the hours filled with course after course of delicious food, glasses of wine, and ceaseless conversation. Over the years I have had few confidants — you are perhaps the third — with whom I have spoken openly about myself. I am not the kind of woman who enjoys idle chatter. Yet not a moment of silence intruded between Percival and me. It was as though both of us had been hoarding stories to tell each other. As we talked and ate, I felt myself being drawn closer and closer to him, the brilliance of his conversation holding me in a trance. Eventually I fell in love with his body with equal abandon, but it was his intelligence that I adored first.

"Over the weeks I was drawn closer and closer to him, so close that I could not endure even one day passing without seeing him. Despite the passion I felt for my studies and the dedication I pledged to the profession of angelology, there was nothing at all I could do to keep myself from him. We met in the apartments he owned near the Angelological Society, where we lingered through the hot summer afternoons of 1939. My classes became secondary to our leisurely hours in his bedroom, the windows open to the stifling summer air. I began to resent my roommate for asking questions; I began to hate teachers for keeping me from him.

"After our first meeting, I began to suspect that there was something unusual about Percival, but I ignored my instincts, choosing to see him against my better judgment. Again, after our first night together, I knew that I had fallen into a kind of trap, although I could not articulate the nature of the danger I felt, nor did I know the damage it would cause me. It was only some weeks later that I fully understood he was Nephilistic. He had, until then, kept his wings retracted — a deception that I should have seen through but did not. One afternoon as we made love he simply opened them, encompassing me in an embrace of golden brilliance. I should have left then, but it was too late — I was completely, irrevocably under his spell. It was thus, they say, between the disobedient angels and the women of ancient time — theirs was a great passion that turned heaven and earth upside down. But I was just a girl. I would have traded my soul for his love.

"And in many ways, I did just that. As our affair grew more intense, I began to help him acquire secrets from the Angelological Society. In return he gave me the tools to advance quickly, to gain prestige and power. He asked for small bits of information at first — the location of our offices in Paris and the dates of society meetings. I gave them willingly. When his demands grew, I accommodated them. By the time I understood how dangerous he was and that I must escape his influence, it was too late: He threatened to tell my teachers of our relationship. I was terrified of being found out. It would have meant a life of exile from the only community I had ever known.

"My affair was not easy to keep secret, however. When it became clear that I would be discovered, I confessed everything to my teacher, Dr. Raphael Valko, who decided that I was in a position to be useful to angelology. I became a spy. While Percival believed that I was working with him, I was actually doing my best to undermine his family. The affair continued, growing more and more treacherous as the war continued. Despite my misery, I did my part. I fed the Nephilim misinformation about angelological missions; I brought the secrets I learned about the closed world of Nephilistic power to Dr. Raphael, who in turn educated our scholars; and I organized what was meant to be the biggest victory of our lives, a plan to give the Nephilim a replica of the lyre while we kept the authentic lyre in our care.

"The plan was simple. Dr. Seraphina and Dr. Raphael Valko knew that the Nephilim were aware of our expedition to the gorge and that they would fight us until they had the lyre in their possession. The Valkos suggested that we orchestrate a plan that would throw the Nephilim off our trail. They arranged the manufacture of a lyre with all the properties of those of ancient Thrace — the curved arms, the heavy base, the crossbars. The instrument was created by our most brilliant musicologist, Dr. Josephat Michael, who labored over each detail, finding silk strings woven with the hair of a white horse's tail. After we had unearthed the true lyre, we saw that it was much more sophisticated than the false version — its body was made of a metallic material that is closest to platinum, an element that has never been classified and cannot be considered an earthly element. Dr. Michael named the substance Valkine, after the Valkos, who had done so much to discover the lyre. The strings were made of glossy golden strands twisted into a tight cord, which Dr. Michael concluded had been made from strands of the Archangel Gabriel's hair.

"Despite the obvious differences, the Valkos

believed we had no choice but to act. We put the false lyre in a structured leather case identical to the case of the true lyre. I gave Percival a tip that our caravan would be driving through Paris at midnight, and he arranged the ambush. If all had gone according to plan, Percival would have captured Dr. Seraphina Valko and demanded that the angelological council give the lyre in exchange for her life. We would have traded the false lyre, Dr. Seraphina would have gone free, and the Nephilim would have believed that they had won the ultimate prize. But something went terribly wrong.

"Dr. Raphael and I had agreed to vote for making the trade. We assumed that the council members would follow Dr. Raphael's lead and vote to trade the lyre for Dr. Seraphina. But for reasons we could not understand, the council members voted against making the trade, throwing our plan into chaos. There was a tie, which we asked one of the expedition members — Celestine Clochette — to break. She had no way of knowing about our plans and so she voted according to protocol, which fit with her careful, meticulous character. In the end we did not make the trade. I tried to remedy the mistake by taking the false lyre to Percival myself, telling him that I had stolen the lyre for him. But it was too late. Percival had killed Dr. Seraphina Valko.

"I have lived with regret over what happened to Seraphina. But my sorrows were not to end on that terrible night. You see, despite everything, I loved Percival Grigori, or at least was terribly addicted to how I felt in his presence. It seems amazing to me now, but even after he had ordered my capture and had allowed me to be brutally tortured, I could not give him up. I went to him one last time in 1944, as the Americans were liberating France. I knew that he would flee before he could be captured and I needed to see him again, to say good-bye. We spent the night together, and some months later I learned, to my horror, that I had become pregnant with his child. In my desperation to hide my condition, I turned to the only person who knew the extent of my involvement with Percival. My former teacher, Dr. Raphael Valko, understood how much I had suffered from my involvement with the Grigori family and that my child must be kept away from them at all costs. Raphael married me, letting the world believe that he was the father of my child. Our marriage caused a scandal among angelologists loyal to Seraphina's memory, but it allowed me to keep my secret safe. My daughter, Angela, was born in 1945. Many years later Angela had a daughter, Evangeline."

Hearing Evangeline's name startled Verlaine. "Percival Grigori is her grandfather?" he said, unable to mask his incredulity.

"Yes," Gabriella said. "It was Percival Grigori's granddaughter who, just this morning, saved your life."

Rose Room, St. Rose Convent, Milton, New York

Evangeline maneuvered Celestine's wheelchair into the Rose Room and parked it at the edge of a long wooden conference table. Nine stooped and wrinkled Elder Sisters, tufts of white hair curling from under their veils and backs crooked from age, were seated around the table. Mother Perpetua sat among them, a severe, portly woman wearing the same modern attire as Evangeline. The Elder Sisters watched Evangeline and Celestine with great interest, a sure sign that Sister Philomena had alerted them all to the events of the past days. Indeed, as Evangeline took her place at the table, Philomena before them, speaking with great passion about that very subject. Evangeline's apprehension only grew when she saw that Philomena had spread Gabriella's letter on the table in front of the sisters.

"The information before me," Philomena said, raising her arms as if inviting the sisters to join her in observing the letter, "will bring about the victory we have long been hoping for. If the lyre is hidden among us, we must find it quickly. Then we will have all that we need to move forward."

"Pray, tell me, Sister Philomena," Mother Perpetua said, examining Philomena doubtfully, "move forward in what direction?"

Philomena said, "I do not believe that Abigail Rockefeller died without leaving concrete information about the lyre's whereabouts. It is time to know the truth. In fact, we must know everything. What have you been hiding from us, Celestine?"

Evangeline looked at Celestine. She was concerned for her health. Celestine had declined dramatically in the past twenty-four hours. Her face was waxen, her hands knit together at the fingers, and she hunched so deeply in her chair that there appeared a danger she might fall out of it. Evangeline had hesitated to bring Celestine to the meeting at all, but once she'd learned the truth of everything that had happened — of Verlaine's visit and Gabriella's letters — Celestine had insisted.

Celestine's voice was feeble as she said, "My knowledge of the lyre is as incomplete as your own, Philomena. These many years I have, like you, puzzled over its location. Although unlike you I have learned to temper my desire for revenge."

Philomena said, "There is more to my desire to find the lyre than simple revenge. Come. Now is the moment. The Nephilim will recover it if we don't."

"They have not found it yet," Mother Perpetua said. "I believe we can trust that they will be lost for some time longer."

"Come, now. You are fifty years old, Perpetua, too young to understand why I object to doing nothing," Philomena said. "You have not seen the destruction the creatures bring. You have not watched your beloved home burn. You have not lost sisters. You have not feared every day that they might return."

Celestine and Perpetua eyed each other with a mixture of worry and weariness, as if they had heard Philomena discoursing upon the subject before. Mother Perpetua said, "We understand that what you saw in the attack of 1944 fuels your desire to fight. Indeed, you saw the worst casualties of the Nephilim's merciless destruction. It is difficult to countenance inaction in the face of such horror. But long ago we voted to maintain peace. Pacifism. Neutrality. Secrecy. These are the tenets of our existence at St. Rose."

Celestine said, "As long as the whereabouts of the lyre are unknown, the Nephilim will find nothing."

"But we will," Philomena said. "We are so very close to finding it."

Sister Celestine lifted a hand and turned to the sisters gathered around the table, her voice so quiet that Sister Boniface, sitting across the room, adjusted her hearing aid.

Celestine clutched at the knobs of the wheel-chair's armrests, her knuckles white with the effort, as if holding herself against a steep fall. "It is true: A time of conflict is upon us. But I cannot agree with Philomena. I hold our position of peaceful resistance sacred. We should not fear this turn of events. It is the way of the universe for the Nephilim to rise and to fall. It is our duty to resist, and we must be ready to face it. But, most important, we must not become as base and treacherous as our enemies. We must preserve our heritage of civilized and dignified pacifism. Sisters, let us not forget the ideals of our founders. If we stay true to our traditions, in time we will win."

"Time is something we do not have!" Philomena said fiercely, her fervor distorting her features. "Soon they will be upon us, just as they were so many years ago. Do you not recall the destruction we endured? The foul, murderous bloodlust of the creatures? Do you not remember the horrid fate of Mother Innocenta? We will be destroyed if we do not act."

"Our mission is too precious for rash actions," Celestine said. Her face had flushed as she spoke, and for a fleeting moment Evangeline could imagine the intense young woman who had arrived at St. Rose Convent years before. The physical effort of Celestine's speech overwhelmed her. Lifting a trembling hand to her mouth, she began to cough. She appeared to consider her physical frailty with dispassionate attention, as if noting how the mind burned as brightly as ever even as the body made its way to dust.

"Your health has altered your ability to think clearly," Philomena said, the drapery of her black veil brushing her shoulders. "You are in no state to make such crucial decisions."

Mother Perpetua said, "Innocenta felt very much the same way. Many of us remember her dedication to peaceful resistance."

"And look where her peaceful resistance got her," Philomena said. "They killed her mercilessly." Turning to Celestine, she said, "You do not have the right to keep the location of the lyre secret, Celestine. I know that the means of finding it are here."

"You do not know the first thing about the lyre or the dangers that accompany it," Celestine said, her voice so frail that Evangeline could hardly hear her words. Celestine turned to Evangeline, placed her hand upon her arm, and whispered, "Come, there is no use arguing any longer. I have something to show you."

Evangeline pushed Celestine's wheelchair from the Rose Room, through the hallway, and to a rickety elevator at the far end of the convent. Squeezing the chair inside, Evangeline positioned the wheels. The doors slid shut with a soft metallic kiss. As she reached for the button marking the fourth floor, Celestine stopped her. She lifted her quivering hand and pushed an unmarked button. Jerkily, the elevator began to descend. It stopped at the basement, and the doors retracted with a screech.

Evangeline gripped the handles of Celestine's wheelchair and pushed her into an expanse of darkness. Celestine flicked a switch, and a series of dim lights illuminated the space. When Evangeline's eyes adjusted, she saw that they were in the convent's cellar. She could hear the rumbling of industrial dishwashers above and the draining water sluicing through the pipes and knew that they must be directly below the cafeteria. At Celestine's direction, Evangeline steered the wheelchair through the cellar, navigating them to the farthest edge of the basement. There Sister Celestine looked over her shoulder, to be sure that they were alone, and pointed to a plain wooden door. It was nondescript, so unremarkable that Evangeline would have guessed it to be a broom closet.

Celestine took a key from her pocket and gave it to Evangeline, who jiggled it in the lock. Only after several attempts did it finally turn.

Evangeline pulled a cord dangling before the doorway, and a lightbulb illuminated a narrow brickwork passageway angling at a sharp descending slope. Pulling back on Celestine's wheelchair to keep it from barreling downward, Evangeline measured her steps. The light grew fainter and fainter until at last the passageway opened to a musty room. Evangeline pulled a second cord, which she would have missed entirely had it not brushed against her cheek, soft as the filament of a spiderweb. Light emanated from an old-fashioned bulb, sizzling as if it might pop at any moment. Mold grew over the walls, and a number of discarded pews littered the floor. Along the wall rested cracked pieces of stained glass and a few milky slabs of marble of the same color and variety as the church altar — remnants of the original construction of Maria Angelorum. In the very center of the room sat a rusted boiler, cobwebs and dust and many years of desuetude settling upon it, heavy as an old skin. The room, Evangeline decided, had not been cleaned in many decades, if ever.

Beyond the boiler she spied another door as plain as the first. She pushed Celestine's wheelchair directly to it, took her own keys from her pocket, and tried the master. Miraculously, the door opened. Once inside, she made out the contours of a large, furniture-filled room. With the flick of a wall switch near the door, her intuition was confirmed. Long and narrow, the chamber was nearly the size of the church nave, with a low ceiling supported by rows of dark wooden girders.

Oriental carpets of various colors — crimson and emerald and royal blue — covered the floor, while tapestries of angels hung upon the walls, numerous golden-threaded weavings that Evangeline took to be quite old, perhaps medieval. A great table sat at the center of the room, its surface laden with manuscripts.

"A hidden library," Evangeline whispered before she could stop herself.

"Yes," Celestine said. "It is an angelological reading room. In the nineteenth century, visiting scholars and dignitaries took shelter with us and spent much time here. Innocenta used it for general meetings. It has been abandoned for many years. It is also," she added, "the most secure spot at St. Rose Convent."

"Does anyone even know of its existence?"

Celestine said, "Not many. When the fire of 1944 began to spread, most of the sisters ran to the courtyard. Mother Innocenta, however, went to the church to lure the Nephilim from the convent. Before this she had instructed me to come here and deposit her papers in our safe. I did not know the convent well, and Innocenta did not have the leisure to give me detailed instructions — but eventually I found this room. I secured what she had given me inside and hurried to the courtyard. To my great sorrow, everything was in flames when I returned. The Nephilim had come and gone. Innocenta was dead."

Celestine touched Evangeline's hand.

"Come," she said. "I have something else for you."

She indicated a magnificent tapestry of the Annunciation in which Gabriel, his wings tucked behind him and his head bowed, gave the Virgin the news of the coming of Christ. "The messenger of good news indeed," Celestine said. "Of course, the holiness of the news depends upon the recipient. You, my dear, are worthy. Go, roll back the cloth from the wall."

Evangeline followed Celestine's instructions, lifting the tapestry to reveal a square copper safe sunk flush with the concrete.

"Three-three-three-nine," Celestine said, pointing to a combination dial. "The perfect numbers of the celestial spheres followed by the total species of angels in the Heavenly Choir."

Evangeline squinted at the numbers of a combination dial and — as Celestine told her the combination — twisted the dial right, then left, then right, listening for the soft sweep of metal disks. Finally the safe clicked and, with a swift tug of the handle, popped open. There was a leather case in the belly of the safe. Fingers trembling, Evangeline carried it to the table and wheeled Celestine to it.

"I brought this case with me to America from Paris," Celestine said, sighing as if all her efforts had led to this singular moment. "It has been here, safe and sound, since 1944."

Evangeline ran her hands over the cool, polished leather. The brass clasps were shiny as new pennies.

Sister Celestine closed her eyes and clutched at the armrests of her wheelchair.

Evangeline remembered the extent of Celestine's illness. The journey to the depths of the convent must have taxed her enormously. "You are exhausted," Evangeline said. "I am terribly thoughtless to have allowed you to bring me here. I think it is time for you to return to your room."

"Hush, child," Celestine said, lifting a hand to stop her from protesting further. "There is one more item I must give you."

Celestine slid her hand into the pocket of her habit, removed a piece of paper, and placed it in Evangeline's palm. She said, "Memorize this address. It is where your grandmother, as head of the Angelological Society, resides. She will welcome you and continue where I have left off."

"This is the address I saw in my file in the Mission Office this morning," Evangeline said. "The same address as that on Gabriella's letters."

"The very one," Celestine said. "It is your time. Soon you will understand your purpose, but for now you must remove this case from our domain. Percival Grigori is not the only one who covets Abigail Rockefeller's letters."

"Mrs. Rockefeller's letters?" Evangeline

whispered. "This case doesn't contain the lyre?"

"The letters will lead you to the lyre," Celestine said. "Our dear Philomena has been searching for them for more than half a century. They are no longer safe here. You must take them away at once."

"If I leave, will I be allowed to return?"

"If you do, you will compromise the safety of the others. Angelology is forever. Once you begin, you cannot leave it. And you, Evangeline, have already begun."

"But you left angelology behind," Evangeline said.

"And look at the trouble that ensued," Celestine said, fingering the rosary around her neck. "One might say my withdrawal into the sanctuary of St. Rose is in part responsible for the danger your young visitor is in now."

Celestine paused, as if to let her words sink in.

"Don't be frightened," she said, gripping Evangeline's hand. "Everything has its proper time. You are giving up this life, but you are gaining another. You will be part of a long and honorable tradition: Christine de Pizan, Clare of Assisi, Sir Isaac Newton, even St. Thomas Aquinas did not shy from our work. Angelology is a noble calling, perhaps the highest calling. It is not an easy thing to be chosen. One must be courageous."

In the course of their exchange, something

about Celestine had changed — her illness seemed in retreat, and her pale hazel eyes burned with pride. When she spoke, her voice was strong and confident.

"Gabriella will be very proud of you," Celestine said. "But I will be even more so. From the minute you arrived, I knew you would make an exceptional angelologist. When your grandmother and I were students in Paris, we could pick out exactly which of our peers would succeed and which would not. It is like a sixth sense, the ability to discover new talent."

"I hope, then, that I won't disappoint you, Sister."

"It is unsettling how much you remind me of her. Your eyes, your mouth, the way you carry yourself as you walk. It is odd. You could be her twin. I pray that angelology will suit you as it has Gabriella."

Evangeline wanted desperately to ask what had happened between Celestine and Gabriella, but before she could articulate her thoughts, Celestine spoke instead, her voice cracking with emotion. "Tell me one last thing. Who is your grandfather? Are you the grandchild of Dr. Raphael Valko?"

"I don't know," Evangeline said. "My father refused to speak about the subject."

A dark expression clouded Celestine's features, but just as quickly it dispersed, replaced by anxious concern. "It is time for you to go," she said. "It will take some skill to get out of here." Evangeline tried to resume her position behind the wheelchair, but, to her surprise, Celestine drew her close and hugged her.

Whispering into her ear, she said, "Tell your grandmother I forgive her. Tell her I understand that there were no easy choices then. We did what we needed to do to survive. Tell her that it wasn't her fault, what happened to Dr. Seraphina, and please tell her that everything is forgiven."

Evangeline returned Celestine's embrace, feeling how thin and frail the old woman was under her capacious habit.

Gripping the case, feeling its weight, Evangeline slipped the leather strap over her shoulder and pushed Celestine back through the long passageways toward the elevator. Once they reached the fourth floor, her movements would need to be swift and discreet. Already she could feel St. Rose edging away from her, retreating into an unreachable place. Never again would she wake at four forty-five in the morning and rush through the shadowy corridors to prayer. Evangeline could not imagine loving another place as much as she loved the convent, and yet suddenly it seemed inevitable that she leave it.

St. Rose Convent, Milton, New York

Otterley backed the Jaguar into a cove outside the convent grounds, hiding the car deep in the foliage of evergreens. She cut the engine and stepped out into the snow, leaving the keys in the ignition. They had agreed that it would be best for Percival — who could not be of much use in any physical ordeal — to stay at a distance. Without a word to him, Otterley closed the car door and walked quickly along the icy path to the convent.

Percival knew enough about Gabriella to understand that capturing her would take a coordinated effort. At his insistence Otterley had put in a call to the Gibborim to check on their progress and had learned that they were prowling a few miles south, on the country roads north of the Tappan Zee Bridge. He doubted that they would make much headway with Gabriella, and he was prepared to step in himself if the Gibborim failed. It was imperative to stop Gabriella before she made it to the convent.

Percival stretched his legs, cramped from the narrow space of the car, and peered through the dust-flecked windshield. The convent loomed ahead, a great brick-and-stone edifice barely visible through the forest. If their timing was right, the Gibborim that Sneja had sent — she had promised at least one hundred — should be stationed in the area already, awaiting Otterley's signal to attack. Taking his phone from his pocket, Percival dialed his mother, but the line rang and rang. He'd tried to call her every hour all morning without luck. He'd left messages with the Anakim, when she bothered to answer, but she had clearly forgotten to relay them to Sneja.

Percival opened the car door and stepped into the freezing morning air, frustrated with the impotence of his position. He should have organized the entire operation himself. It should be him leading the Gibborim into the convent. Instead his younger sister was in charge and he was left to try to get through to their aloof mother, who was at that moment likely to be soaking in her Jacuzzi without a thought in her head of his condition.

He walked to the edge of the highway, looking for signs of Gabriella, before dialing his mother's line again. To his surprise, someone picked up on the first ring.

"Yes," said a hoarse, domineering voice that he recognized at once.

"We're here, Mother," Percival said. He

could hear music and voices in the background and knew at once that she was in the middle of one of her parties.

"And the Gibborim?" Sneja asked. "They are ready?"

"Otterley has gone to prepare them."

"Alone?" Sneja said, reproach in her voice. "However will your sister manage it alone? There are nearly one hundred creatures to command."

Percival felt as if his mother had slapped him. Surely she knew that his sickness prevented him from fighting. Relinquishing control to Otterley was humiliating and required a level of restraint he'd thought Sneja would admire.

"That won't be necessary," he said, keeping his anger in check. "Otterley is more than capable. I am watching the entrance to the convent, to be sure there isn't interference."

"Well," Sneja said, "whether she is capable or not is rather beside the point."

Percival considered the tone of his mother's voice, trying to understand the message it was meant to imply. "Has she proven otherwise?"

"Darling, she doesn't have anything to prove herself *with*," Sneja said. "For all her bluster, our Otterley is in a terrible predicament."

"I really have no idea what you mean," Percival said. In the distance the faintest stream of smoke began to rise from the convent, signaling that the attack had begun. His sister seemed to be managing quite fine without him.

"When was the last time you saw your sister's wings?" Sneja asked.

"I don't know," Percival said. "It's been ages."

"I will tell you the last time you saw them," Sneja said. "It was 1848, at her coming-out ball in Paris."

Percival recalled the event clearly. Otterley's wings were new, and, like all young Nephilim, she had displayed them with great pride. They had been multicolored, like Sneja's wings, but very small. It was expected that they would grow full with time.

Sneja continued, "If you have wondered why it has been so long since Otterley has shown her wings properly, it is because they did not develop. They are tiny and useless, the wings of a child. She cannot fly, and she certainly cannot display them. Can you imagine how ridiculous Otterley would look if she were to open such appendages?"

"I had no idea," Percival said, incredulous. Despite the resentment he felt for his sister, he was deeply protective of Otterley.

"That doesn't surprise me," Sneja said. "You don't seem to notice much but your own pleasure and your own suffering. Your sister has tried to hide her predicament from all of us for more than a century. But the truth of the matter is, she is not like you or me. Your wings were glorious, once upon a time. And my wings are incomparable. Otterley is a lower breed."

"You think she is incapable of directing the Gibborim," Percival said, understanding at last why their mother had told him Otterley's secret. "You think she will lose control of the attack."

"If only you could assume your rightful role, my son," Sneja said, her voice filling with disappointment, as if she had already resigned herself to Percival's failure. "If only it were you taking up our cause. Perhaps we —"

Unable to listen to another word, Percival disconnected the call. Examining the highway, he saw the blacktop stretch away from him, twisting through the trees and disappearing around a bend. There was nothing he could do to assist Otterley. He was helpless to restore the glory of his family.

Route 9W, Milton, New York

By the time they had made it to the small highway outside Milton, Gabriella and Verlaine had smoked half the pack of cigarettes, filling the Porsche with the heavy, acrid scent of smoke. Verlaine cracked the window, allowing a stream of chilled air into the car. He wished Gabriella would continue with her story, but he didn't want to press her. She appeared frail and tired, as if the very act of recounting her past had exhausted her — dark circles appeared below her eyes, and her shoulders drooped slightly. The abundance of smoke swirling through the car stung Verlaine's eyes but appeared to have little effect upon Gabriella. She stepped on the gas, intent to reach the convent.

Verlaine looked out the window as the snowy forest flashed by. Trees expanded from the highway, row upon row of winter-barren birch, sugar maple, and oak stretching far as Verlaine could see. He watched the roadside, looking for clues that they had arrived — a wooden sign marking the entrance to the convent or the church spire rising above the trees. He had mapped the course from New York City to St. Rose at his apartment, noting the bridges and highways. If his estimate was correct, the convent would be just miles north of Milton. They should be upon it at any moment.

"Look in the mirror," Gabriella said, her voice unnaturally calm.

Verlaine followed her instructions. A black SUV followed at a distance.

"They've been there for the past few miles," Gabriella said. "It seems that they are not giving up on you."

"Are you sure it's them?" Verlaine asked, looking over his shoulder. "What will we do?"

"If I try to run," she said, "they will follow us. If I continue onward, we will arrive at St. Rose at the same moment and have to confront them there."

"And then what?"

"They will not let us go," Gabriella said. "Not this time."

Gabriella hit the brakes and jerked the wheel, turning precipitously onto a gravel road. The Porsche spun on its tires, delineated a half circle over the snowy road, tipping slightly from the momentum. For a moment the car felt free of gravity, thrown into a state of weightless free fall on the ice, nothing more than a box of metal fishtailing right and left as the tires sought traction. Gabriella slowed and held the wheel, trying to gain control. As it steadied, she hit the gas again until the car sped ever faster, climbing the incline of a long, slow-rising hill, the noise of the engine deafening. Gravel crackled on the windshield in a barrage of sharp explosions.

Verlaine looked over his shoulder. The black SUV had turned onto the road, following at a distance behind.

"Here they come," he said, and Gabriella gunned the engine, taking them higher and higher along the hill. As the road crested, the thickets of trees gave way to a white sweep of valley, beyond which a dilapidated barn stood red as a splotch of blood against the snow.

"As much as I love this car, it doesn't have the capacity for speed," Gabriella said. "It's going to be impossible to outrun them. We need to find a way to lose them. Or hide."

Verlaine scanned the valley. From the highway to the barn, there was nothing but exposed frozen fields. Beyond the barn the road twisted up another hill, snaking its way into a copse of evergreens. "Can we make it to the top?" Verlaine asked.

"It doesn't look like we have much choice."

Gabriella drove past the barn, where the road tracked a slow, steady ascent. By the time they reached the evergreens, the black SUV had gained so much ground that Verlaine could make out the features of the men in the front seat.

The one in the passenger seat leaned out the window, aimed a gun, and shot, missing them.

"I can't go faster than this," Gabriella said, growing frustrated. Keeping one hand on the wheel, she tossed a leather purse to Verlaine. "Find my gun. It's inside."

Verlaine unzipped the bag, digging through a tangle of objects until his fingers brushed cold metal. He lifted a small silver handgun from the bottom of the bag.

"Have you shot a gun before?"

"Never."

"I'll walk you through it," she said. "Switch off the safety. Now roll down your window. Hold steady. Good, now level your arm."

As Verlaine positioned the gun, the man in the SUV took aim.

"Just a moment," Gabriella said. She swerved into the opposite lane and slowed, giving Verlaine a clear shot at the windshield.

"Shoot," Gabriella said. "Now."

Verlaine aimed the gun level with the SUV and squeezed the trigger. The bigger car's windshield cracked into a web of filaments. Gabriella slammed on the brakes as the Mercedes hit a guardrail and flipped over the edge of the valley road, metal crunching as it rolled. Verlaine watched the upended vehicle, its tires spinning.

"Brilliant shot," Gabriella said, pulling to the side of the road and cutting the engine. She gave him a look of pride, clearly pleasantly surprised by his aim. "Give me the gun. I need to make sure they're dead."

"Are you sure that's wise?"

"Of course," she snapped, taking the gun and climbing out of the car and over the guardrail. "Come, you might learn something."

Verlaine followed Gabriella down the icy hillside, walking in her tracks through the snow. Looking above, he saw that a mass of dark clouds had collected. They hung abnormally low, as if they might descend upon the valley at any moment. Once the two of them reached the car, Gabriella instructed Verlaine to kick out the windshield. He bashed chunks of glass with the heel of his sneaker as she crouched down and peered inside.

"You hit the driver," she said, drawing Verlaine's gaze to the dead man.

"Beginner's luck."

"I should say so." She gestured to the second man, whose body lay twenty feet away, facedown in the snow. "Two birds with one stone. The second was thrown when the car flipped."

Verlaine could hardly believe what lay before him. The man's body had transformed into the creature he'd seen through his train window the night before. A pair of scarlet wings

631

splayed open over its back, the feathers brushing the snow. As an icy wind blew over Verlaine, it was impossible to tell if his body tingled from the cold or from the shock at what lay before him.

Meanwhile, Gabriella had managed to open the door and was searching the SUV, emerging with a gym bag, the very bag he'd left in his Renault the previous afternoon.

"That's mine," Verlaine said. "They took it when they broke into my car yesterday."

Gabriella unzipped the bag, withdrew a folder, and sorted through its contents.

"What are you looking for?"

"Something that might explain how much Percival knows," Gabriella said, examining the papers. "Has he seen these?"

Verlaine peered over her shoulder. "I didn't give these files to him, but those guys might have."

Gabriella turned away from the wreckage and made her way back up the snowy hill to the car. "We had better hurry," she said. "The good sisters of St. Rose are in more immediate danger than I had feared."

Verlaine took the driver's seat, deciding that he would drive the remaining miles to the convent. He turned the Porsche around and headed back to the highway. Everything before him lay still and calm. The rolling hills appeared sedate under blankets of snow. The barn slouched in abandonment, the cloud-heavy sky vaulted above. Aside from a few scratches and a guttering in the engine, the old Porsche carried on with admirable resilience. In fact, it appeared that nothing had changed significantly in the past ten minutes but Verlaine. The leather steering wheel grew slick under his hands, and he found that his heart beat hard in his chest. Images of the dead men appeared in his mind.

Intuiting Verlaine's thoughts, Gabriella said, "You did the right thing."

"I've never even held a gun before today."

"They were brutal killers," she said, her voice businesslike, as if the dispatching of men were something she performed on a regular basis. "In a world of good and evil, one cannot shy from making distinctions."

"It isn't a distinction I've thought much about."

"That," Gabriella said softly, "will change if you remain with us."

Verlaine slowed the car, pausing at a stop sign before turning back onto the highway. The convent was only miles ahead.

"Is Evangeline one of you?" he asked.

"Evangeline knows very little about angelology. We told her nothing about it when she was a child. She is young and obedient — traits that might have been her undoing if she weren't extremely bright. Placing her in the hands of the sisters of St. Rose Convent was

633

her father's idea — he was Catholic, quite attached to the romantic notion that young ladies are best sheltered from danger by hiding them in a cloister. He could not help it. He was Italian. Such notions ran in his blood."

"And she listened to him?"

"Excuse me?"

"Your granddaughter gave up everything worth living for simply because her father told her to?"

"There is perhaps some room for debate about what is and what is not worth living for," Gabriella said. "But you are right: Evangeline did exactly as she was instructed. Luca brought her to the United States after Evangeline's mother — my daughter, Angela — was murdered. I imagine that her upbringing was rigorously religious. I imagine he must have prepared her from an early age for her eventual induction into St. Rose Convent. How else in this day and age would a young girl of her gifts go so willingly?"

Verlaine said, "It seems rather medieval."

"But you did not know Luca," Gabriella said. "And you do not know Evangeline. Their affection for each other was something to behold. They were inseparable. I believe that Evangeline would have done anything, absolutely anything, her father told her — including giving her life to the church."

They drove along the highway in silence, the Porsche's engine rattling, the forest rising on both sides. Only an hour before, it had seemed a strangely restful journey. But every cluster of trees, every bend in the road, every narrow lane funneling into their path presented the opportunity for ambush. Verlaine pressed his foot on the gas, pushing the Porsche faster and faster. He checked the mirror every few seconds, as if the SUV might appear at any moment, the assassins rising from the dead.

St. Rose Convent, Milton, New York

Evangeline and Celestine rode the elevator to the fourth floor, the strap of the leather case already weighing upon Evangeline's shoulder. When the doors opened, the old nun stopped her. "Go, my dear," she said. "I will distract the others so that you may exit unnoticed." Evangeline kissed Celestine's cheek and left her in the elevator. The moment Evangeline walked away, Celestine pushed a button and the doors swept closed. Evangeline was alone.

Upon reaching her bedroom cell, Evangeline tore open the drawers and collected the objects of value to her — a rosary and a small amount of cash she had saved over the years — which she put in her pocket. Her heart ached as she glanced around her room. Not long before, she'd believed she would never leave it. She'd imagined that life stretched before her in an endless progression of ritual, routine, and prayer. She would wake each morning to pray, and she would go to sleep each evening in a room looking out upon the dark presence of the river. Overnight these certainties had melted, dissolving like ice in the Hudson's current.

Evangeline's thoughts were interrupted by a great cacophony of rumbling from the courtyard. She ran from her room, threw open a window, and looked over the grounds as a procession of black utility vans pulled into the horseshoe driveway curling before Maria Angelorum. The van doors slid open, and a group of strange creatures climbed out onto the convent lawn. Squinting, Evangeline tried to see them more clearly. They wore uniform black overcoats that brushed the snow as they walked, black leather gloves, and military-style combat boots. As they moved across the courtyard, coming closer to the convent, she observed that their number quickly multiplied — more and more arrived, as if they had the ability to appear from the chill air. As she examined the periphery of the convent grounds, she saw the creatures step from the darkened forest, climb the stone wall, and walk through the great iron gate at the drive. They might have been waiting, hidden, for hours. St. Rose Convent was completely surrounded by Gibborim.

Clutching the leather case close, Evangeline turned from the window in fright and ran through the hallway, knocking on doors, rousing the sisters from study and prayers.

She turned the lights to full brightness, a harsh illumination that ripped away the air of coziness of the fourth floor and exposed the tattered carpeting, the peeling paint, the dreary uniformity of their enclosed lives. If there was one thing to be learned from the previous attack, it was that the sisters must leave the convent immediately.

Evangeline's efforts brought the Elder Sisters from their rooms. They stood throughout the corridor, looking about in utter confusion, their unveiled hair in disarray. Evangeline heard Philomena calling from somewhere in the distance, preparing the sisters to fight.

"Go," Evangeline said. "Take the back stairwell to the first floor and follow Mother Perpetua's orders. Trust me. You will soon understand."

Resisting the urge to lead them down herself, Evangeline pushed through the clusters of women, and, making her way to the wooden door at the end of the hall, she opened it and ran up the winding steps. The room at the top of the turret was freezing cold and shadowy. She knelt before the brick wall and pried the stone from her hiding place. In the recess in the wall, she found the metal box containing the angelological journal, the photograph tucked safely inside. She turned to the last quarter of the notebook. Her mother's scientific notes were there, copied out in Gabriella's clean, precise script. Her mother had died for these strings of numbers. Evangeline could not lose them.

The turret windows had frozen over, creating blue-white fractals upon the glass. Evangeline attempted to clear a circle in the ice with her breath, rubbing the pane with the palm of her hand, but the glass remained foggy. In a panic to see the grounds, she removed her shoe and shattered the window with the heel, swiping the barbs of glass from the frame with quick sweeps, opening a small vantage over the courtyard.

Bitterly cold air gushed into the turret. She could see the river and the forest below, framing the courtyard on three sides. The creatures had collected at the center of the grounds, a mass of dark-cloaked figures. Even at a distance, their height foreshortened, they sent a chill through Evangeline. There were fifty, perhaps a hundred of the creatures below her window, quickly composing themselves into rows.

Suddenly, as if responding to a command, they shed their great cloaks in unison. The creatures' limbs were bare, their skin throwing halos of radiance over the snow. When they stood upright, their immense height gave them the appearance of Grecian statues stationed on a desolate mall. Great, sharp-edged red wings opened on their backs, striated feathers glistening in the dull morning sunlight. In an instant she recognized the creatures, for she was gazing on beasts similar to those angelic beings she had observed in the warehouse in New York City with her father. Only in the years since she'd last set eyes on such a creature, she had grown from a girl to a woman, a change that rendered her sensitive to a seduction she hadn't experienced before. Their bodies were exceedingly lovely, so sensuous that a shock of longing passed through her. Yet even through the haze of her desire, Evangeline found that everything about them — from the way they stood to the immense span of their wings — struck her as monstrous.

Taking a deep breath to calm her thoughts she noticed a peculiar scent. Loamy and carbon-rich, it was the distinct scent of smoke. Searching the grounds she observed a group of the creatures huddled together beside the convent, fanning flames with their wings. The flickering fire rose higher and higher. The devils were attacking.

Evangeline tucked the angelology journal into the leather case and ran down the turret steps, taking the direct passage to the Adoration Chapel. The smell of fire grew more distinct as she descended, and thick drafts of smoke swirled up through the stairwell. There was no sure way to know how far the fire had blazed and, realizing she might be trapped, she quickened her pace, the leather case clutched tight beneath her arm. The air thickened as she ran down the successive flights of stairs, confirming her belief that the fire was — at least for the moment — contained in the lower regions of the convent. Even so, it seemed impossible that the flames had risen so quickly and with such force. She recalled the creatures standing before the fire, their powerful wings beating, encouraging the flames to mount. She shuddered. The Gibborim would not stop until the entire convent lay in ashes.

St. Rose Convent, Milton, New York

Verlaine could hardly make out the words ST. ROSE fashioned into the ornate wrought-iron gate, so dense was the smoke coming from the convent. Alongside the thick limestone wall sat his bludgeoned Renault, its windows smashed. It had most likely filled with snow and ice overnight, but it remained parked where he had left it. The gate to the convent was open, and as they parked the car, Verlaine saw a line of black utility vans lined up one behind the other before the church.

"Do you see that car?" Gabriella asked, pointing to a white Jaguar hidden in foliage at the end of the convent driveway. "It belongs to Otterley Grigori."

"Related to Percival?"

"His sister," Gabriella said. "I had the great pleasure of knowing her in France." Gabriella took the gun in her hand and stepped out of the Porsche. "If she is here, we can presume that Percival is here as well and that the two of them are behind this blaze."

Verlaine looked beyond Gabriella to the convent a short distance away. Smoke obscured the upper regions of the structure and, although he saw movement on the ground, he was too far away to make out what was happening. He stepped out of the car, following Gabriella toward the convent.

"What are you doing?" she asked, eyeing him skeptically.

"I'm going with you."

"I need to know you're here waiting with the car. When I find Evangeline, we will need to leave very quickly. I'm depending upon you to make sure that will happen. Promise me you'll stay here." Without waiting for a response, Gabriella started off toward the convent, tucking the gun into a pocket of her long black jacket.

Verlaine leaned against one of the vans, watching Gabriella disappear around the side of the convent. He was tempted to follow her despite her instructions. Instead he walked through the rows of utility vans to the white Jaguar. Cupping his hands over his eyes, he peered through the window. On the beige leather seat sat a folder of his research, the photocopied picture of the Thracian coin on top. He tried to open the door and, finding it locked, looked around for something to break it with. Just then he saw Percival Grigori at the side of the road, making his way toward the car.

Quickly, Verlaine ducked behind the stone wall that surrounded the convent grounds. Moving ever closer to the convent, his sneakers crunching in the ice-crusted snow, he stopped at a gap in the structure that gave onto the main lawn. He was astonished by the scene before him. Thick, dark smoke hovered above a raging fire; sheets of flames fell over the convent. Much to his amazement, an army of creatures — identical to the ones he had killed with Gabriella — swarmed over the convent grounds, perhaps a hundred winged, reptilian monsters gathered together in attack.

He strained to see the scene more clearly. The beings were a hybrid of bird and beast, part human, part monster in equal measure. Wings were mounted upon their backs, lush and red. They were shrouded in a light so intense it covered them in a gauze of illumination. Although Gabriella had explained the Gibborim to him in great detail and he had recognized them as the same beings he had seen on the train the night before, he now realized that he had not, until this very moment, believed that so many of them existed.

Through the flames and smoke, Verlaine spied more and more clusters of Gibborim. One by one they swooped upon the convent, their great wings beating hard and furious. They lifted high and buoyant in the wind, airy as kites drifting down on the building.

They appeared impossibly light, as if their bodies were insubstantial. Their movements were so coordinated, so powerful that Verlaine understood at once they would be impossible to defeat. The creatures flew in an elaborate ballet of attack, rising from the ground in an elegant orchestration of violence, one creature weaving past the other as the flames soared upward. Verlaine watched the destruction in awe.

One creature stood at a remove from the others, at the edge of the forest. Determined to examine it, Verlaine ducked into the thick foliage beyond the stone wall, moving closer to the being until he was less than ten feet away from it, hidden in bushes. He saw the elegance of its features — aquiline nose, golden curls, the terrifying red eyes. He breathed deeply, taking in the sweet aroma of its body — Gabriella had told him that the scent was called ambrosial by those who had the fortune (or misfortune) to encounter it. He was aware at once of the dangerous allure the creature held. Verlaine had imagined them to be hideous, the misbegotten children of a grand historical error, malformed hybrids of the sacred and the profane. He had not considered that he would find them beautiful.

Suddenly the creature turned. In a sweeping motion he glanced toward the forest, as if perceiving Verlaine's presence among the evergreens. The Gibborim's quick movement revealed a flash of skin at the neck, a long, thin arm, the outline of its body. As the giant moved toward the stone wall, its red wings shivering about him, Verlaine lost all sense of why he had come, what he wanted, and what he would do next. He knew he should be afraid, but as the Gibborim stepped closer, his skin casting a glow on the ground, Verlaine felt an eerie calm come over him. The harsh, scintillating light of the fire raged, throwing a glow upon the creature, mixing with its native luminescence. Verlaine stood hypnotized. Rather than run, as he knew he should, he wanted to draw closer to the creature, to touch the stark, pale body. He stepped from the safety of the forest and stood before the Gibborim, as if to give himself over. He gazed into its glassy eyes, as if searching for an answer to a dark and violent riddle.

What Verlaine found there startled him beyond reckoning. Instead of malevolence, the creature's gaze contained a frightening animal vapidity, a vacuity that was neither vicious nor benign. It was as if the creature lacked the ability to comprehend what lay before it. Its eyes were lenses into a pure emptiness. The being did not register Verlaine's presence. Rather it looked beyond, as if he were nothing more than an element of the forest, a tree stump or a clump of leaves. Verlaine understood that he was in the presence of a creature with no soul.

In a swift movement, it opened its red wings. Rotating one wing and then the other so that the fire's harsh glare slid over them, the monster gathered its strength and leaped from the ground, light and airy as a butterfly, joining the others in the attack.

Adoration Chapel, St. Rose Convent,
Milton, New York

Evangeline found the Adoration Chapel awash in smoke. She tried to breathe but was overwhelmed by hot and poisonous air. It singed her skin and stung her eyes so that within seconds her vision had blurred with tears. Through the haze she could make out the silhouettes of the sisters, arrayed through the chapel. It appeared to Evangeline that the habits blended together, forming a single patch of inviolate black. Soft, smoky light suffused the church, falling softly over the altar. Why the sisters remained in the midst of the fire was incomprehensible to her. If they didn't get out, they would die from the smoke.

Confused, she turned to escape through Maria Angelorum Church when something caught her feet and she fell heavily upon the marble floor, banging her chin. The leather case was jarred from her grip, flying off into the haze beyond. To her horror, the face of Sister Ludovica stared up from the smoke, an expression of fear frozen upon her face.

Evangeline had tripped on the body of the old woman, whose upended wheelchair lay tipped at her side, one wheel spinning. Bending over Ludovica, Evangeline placed her hands upon the warm cheeks and whispered a prayer, a final farewell to the eldest of the Elder Sisters. Gently, she pressed the lids of Ludovica's eyes closed.

Rising to her hands and knees, she inspected the scene as best she could through the smoke. The floor of the Adoration Chapel was littered with bodies. She counted four women lying at intervals along the aisles of pews, asphyxiated. Evangeline felt a surge of despair. The Gibborim had smashed great holes in the angelic-spheres windows, bombarding the bodies with debris. Pieces of colored glass were scattered from one end of the chapel to the other, lying like pieces of hard candy on the marble floors. The pews had been broken, the delicate golden pendulum clock crushed, and the marble angels tipped. The gaping hole in the window opened the convent's lawn to view. The creatures swarmed over the snowy grounds. Smoke rose into the sky, reminding her that the fire still burned. Gales of freezing wind blew through the desolate interior, sweeping across the ruin. Worst of all, the kneelers before the host were empty. Their chain of perpetual prayer had been obliterated. The sight was so terrible that Evangeline caught her breath at the sight of it.

The air along the floor was slightly cooler, the smoke less dense, and so Evangeline fell to her stomach once again and crawled over the floor in search of the leather case. Smoke burned her eyes; her arms ached with the effort. The smoke had transformed the once-familiar chapel into a place of danger — an amorphous, hazy minefield filled with unseen traps. If the smoke pressed low upon her, she risked losing consciousness like the others. If she crawled directly to Maria Angelorum to make it outside, she might lose the precious case.

Finally Evangeline caught a glint of metal — the copper clasps of the leather case sparked in the firelight. She reached out and grasped the handle, noticing, as she pulled the case closer, that the leather had been singed. Lifting herself off the ground, she covered her nose and mouth with her sleeve, trying to block out the smoke. She recalled the questions Verlaine had asked her in the library, the intense curiosity he'd shown about the location of the seal on Mother Francesca's drawings. Her grandmother's last card had confirmed his theory: The architectural drawings had been made for the purpose of marking a hidden object, something secreted by Mother Francesca and guarded for nearly two hundred years. The precision with which the maps of the chapel had been drawn could leave little doubt. Mother Francesca had placed something in the tabernacle.

Evangeline climbed the altar steps, making her way through the smoke to the elaborately decorated tabernacle. It sat atop a marble pillar, its doors crusted with golden symbols of alpha and omega, the beginning and the end. It was the size of a small cupboard, large enough to conceal something of value. Evangeline tucked the leather case under her arm and pulled at the doors. They were locked.

Suddenly a clamoring of movement alerted her to a new presence in the chapel. She turned just as two creatures broke through one of the stained-glass windows, shattering the luminous plate of the First Angelic Sphere so that shards of gold and red and blue glass scattered over the nuns. Ducking behind the altar, she felt the hair on the back of her neck rise as she examined the Gibborim. They were even bigger than they'd seemed from the turret, tall and lanky, with huge red eyes and sweeping crimson wings that draped over their shoulders like cloaks.

One of the Gibborim tore at the kneelers, throwing them to the floor and stamping upon them, while another decapitated the marble figure of an angel, separating head from body with one vicious swipe. At the far end of the chapel, another creature clutched a golden candle holder by the base and threw it with extraordinary strength at a stained-glass window, a lovely rendition of the Archangel

Michael. The glass splintered in an instant, a symphonic crackling filling the air as if a thousand cicadas sang at once.

Behind the altar Evangeline held the leather case close to her chest. She knew she must measure each movement with care. The slightest noise would alert the creatures to her presence. She was scanning the chapel to find the best route for escape when she discovered Philomena, crouched in a corner. Philomena lifted her hand slowly, gesturing to her to remain still, to watch and wait. From her hiding place near the tabernacle, Evangeline watched Philomena creep along the floor of the altar.

Then, in a movement startling in its speed and precision, Philomena grasped the monstrance poised high above the altar. The monstrance was solid gold, the size of a candelabra, and must have been extraordinarily heavy. Nonetheless, Philomena raised it over her head and smashed it upon the marble floor. The monstrance itself took no damage at the blow. The small eye of crystal at its center, the orb encasing the host, however, shattered. Evangeline heard the distinct crack of breaking glass from her hiding place.

Philomena's actions were such a gesture of sacrilege, so awful in their violation of the sisters' prayers and their beliefs, that Evangeline stood frozen in astonishment. In the midst of the destruction and the horror of the death of their sisters, there seemed no reason for

any further vandalism. Yet Philomena continued to work at the monstrance, tearing at
the glass. Evangeline stepped away from her
hiding place, wondering what madness had
overtaken Philomena.

Philomena's actions drew the creatures' attention. They moved toward her, their vermilion wings pulsing in time with their breath.
Suddenly one of them lunged at Philomena.
Possessed with the zealotry of her beliefs and
a power that Evangeline would never have
imagined her capable of displaying, Philomena stepped free of the monstrous grasp and
in an elegant sweep took the creature by its
wings and twisted away from it. The great red
wings ripped from the creature's body. The
Gibborim fell to the floor, writhing in a growing pool of thick blue fluid that poured from
the wound as it screeched in horrid, gurgling
agony. Evangeline felt that she had descended
into a version of hell. Their most sacred chapel, the temple of their daily prayers, had been
defiled.

Philomena turned back to the monstrance,
pried away the cracked crystal encasement and
then, in a moment of triumph, held something
above her head. Evangeline tried to make out
the object in Philomena's hands — it was a
small key. Philomena had cut herself on the
glass, and ribbons of blood dripped over her
wrists and arms. While the sight of such mayhem repulsed Evangeline — she could hardly

bring herself to look at the mangled body of the dismembered creature — Philomena did not seem disturbed in the least. Yet even in her fright, Evangeline marveled at Philomena's discovery.

Philomena called to her to come closer, but there was nothing she could do: The surviving creatures suddenly fell upon Philomena, tearing at her clothing like hawks feasting on a rodent. The black fabric of her habit was swallowed up in a crush of oily red wings. But then Evangeline spied Philomena pushing free from the imbroglio. As if gathering her last bit of strength, Philomena threw the key to Evangeline. Evangeline picked it off the floor and stepped back behind the marble pillar.

When Evangeline looked again, a cold light fell over the desiccated, charred body of Sister Philomena. The murderous Gibborim had moved to the center of the chapel, their great wings drawn, as if they might take to the air at any moment.

At the doorway, a crowd of sisters gathered. Evangeline wanted to call out in warning, but before she could speak, the great uniformity of habited women parted and Sister Celestine emerged from the periphery, her wheelchair pushed by attendants. She wore no veil, and her pure white hair intensified the lines of sadness etched into her face. The attendants pushed Celestine's wheelchair to the base of the altar, her pathway swallowed in a sea of black habits and white scapulars.

The Gibborim, too, watched Celestine as her attendants brought the wheelchair to the altar. They lit candles and, using pieces of charred wood from the fire, drew symbols on the floor around Celestine — arcane sigils that Evangeline recognized from the angelological journal her grandmother had given her. She had looked upon those symbols many times but had never learned their meaning.

Suddenly Evangeline felt a hand on her arm and, turning, found herself in Gabriella's embrace. For a brief moment, the terror she felt subsided, and she was simply a young woman in the arms of her beloved grandmother. Gabriella kissed Evangeline and then quickly turned to watch Celestine, examining her actions with a knowing eye. Evangeline stared at her grandmother, her heart in her throat. Although she looked older, and seemed thinner than Evangeline remembered, Evangeline felt a safe familiarity in Gabriella's presence. She wished that she could speak to her grandmother in private. She had questions she needed to ask.

"What is happening?" Evangeline asked. She examined the creatures, which had become strangely still.

"Celestine has ordered the construction of a magical square within a holy circle. It is preparation for a summoning ceremony." The attendants brought a wreath of lilies to Celestine and placed it upon her white hair. Gabriella said, "Now they are placing a crown of flowers upon Celestine's head, which signifies the virginal purity of the summoner. I know the ritual intimately, although I have never seen it performed. Summoning an angel can bring powerful assistance, clearing away our enemies in an instant. In a situation like the one at hand — the convent besieged and the population of St. Rose outnumbered — it could be a most useful measure, perhaps the only measure to bring victory. Yet it is unbelievably dangerous, and certainly for a woman of Celestine's age. The dangers usually far outweigh the benefits, especially in the case of calling forth an angel for the purpose of battle."

Evangeline turned to her grandmother. A golden pendant, an exact replica of the one she had given to Evangeline, shone upon Gabriella's neck.

"And battle," Gabriella said, "is exactly what Celestine intends."

"But the Gibborim are suddenly so placid," Evangeline said.

"Celestine has hypnotized them," Gabriella said. "It is called a Gibborish charm. We learned it as girls. Do you see her hands?"

Evangeline strained to see Celestine in her chair. Her hands were woven together over her chest, and both pointer fingers bent toward her heart.

"It causes the Gibborim to become momentarily stunned," Gabriella said. "It will wear off in a moment, however, and then Celestine will need to work very quickly."

Celestine lifted her arms into the air in a swift movement, releasing the Gibborim from the spell. Before they could resume their attack, she began to speak. Her voice echoed through the vaulted chapel.

"Angele Dei, qui custos es mei, me tibi commissum pietate superna, illumina, custodi, rege, et guberna."

The Latin was familiar to Evangeline. She recognized it as an incantation, and to her amazement the spell began to take hold. The manifestation began as a gentle breeze, the faintest bluster of wind, and grew in a matter of seconds to a gale that rocked through the nave. In a burst of blinding light, a brilliantly illuminated figure appeared at the center of the twisting wind, hovering above Celestine. Evangeline forgot the danger posed by the summoning, the danger of the creatures surrounding them on all sides, and simply stared at the angel. It was immense, with golden wings spanning the length of the high central dome and arms held outstretched in a gesture that seemed to invite all to come closer. It glowed with intense light, its robes burning brighter than fire. Light gushed upon the nuns, falling over the floors of the church, glinting and fluid as lava. The angel's body appeared both physical and ethereal at once — it hovered above and yet Evangeline was sure that she could see through it. Perhaps strangest of all, the angel began to assume Celestine's features, re-creating the physical appearance of what she must have looked like in her youth. As the angel transformed into an exact replica of the summoner, becoming Celestine's golden-hued twin, Evangeline was able to see the girl Celestine had once been.

The angel floated in midair, glittering and serene. When it spoke, its voice rang sweet and lilting through the church, vibrating with unnatural beauty. It said, "Do you call me in goodness?"

Celestine rose from her wheelchair with astonishing ease and knelt in the middle of the circle of candles, the white robe cascading about her. "I call you as a servant of the Lord to do the Lord's work."

"In His holy name," the angel said, "I ask if your intentions are pure."

"As pure as His holy Word," Celestine said, her voice becoming stronger, more vibrant, as if the angel's presence had strengthened her.

"Fear not, for I am a messenger of the Lord," the angel said, its voice pure music. "I sing the Lord's praise."

In a cataclysm of wind, the church filled with music. A celestial chorus had begun to play.

"Guardian," Celestine said, "our sanctuary

has been desecrated by the dragon. Our structures burned, our sisters killed. As the Archangel Michael crushed the serpent's head, so I ask you to crush these foul invaders."

"Instruct me," the angel said, its wings beating, its lithe body twisting in the air. "Where do these devils hide?"

"They are here upon us, ravaging His holy sanctuary."

In an instant, so quickly that Evangeline had no time to react, the angel transformed into a sheet of fire, splitting into hundreds of tongues of flame, each flame morphing into a fully formed angel. Evangeline held Gabriella's arm, bolstering herself against the wind. Her eyes burned, but she could not so much as blink as, swords raised, the warrior angels descended upon the chapel. The nuns fled in terror, running in all directions, a panic that jarred Evangeline from the trance the summoning had cast upon her. The angels struck the Gibborim dead, their bodies collapsing upon the altar and falling from the air midflight.

Gabriella ran to Celestine, Evangeline following close behind. The old nun lay upon the marble floor, her white robes spread around her, the wreath of lilies skewed. Placing her hand upon Celestine's cheek, Evangeline found her skin hot, as if the summoning had scalded her. Examining her closely, Evangeline tried to understand how a frail, soft-spoken woman like Celestine had the power to defeat such beasts.

Somehow the candles had remained lit throughout the hurricane of the summoning, as if the angel's violent presence had not translated into the physical world. They flickered brightly, casting the false glow of life upon Celestine's skin. Evangeline arranged Celestine's robes, gently folding the white fabric. Celestine's hand, which had been hot only seconds before, had gone completely cold. In the course of a single day, Sister Celestine had become her true guardian, leading her through the confusion and putting her upon the correct path. Evangeline could not be certain, but it appeared to her that tears had formed in Gabriella's eyes. "That was a brilliant summoning, my friend," she whispered as she bent and kissed Celestine's forehead. "Simply brilliant."

Remembering Philomena, Evangeline opened her hand and gave her grandmother the key.

"Where did you get this?" Gabriella asked.

"The monstrance," Evangeline said, gesturing to the shards of crystal on the floor. "It was inside."

"So that is where they kept it," Gabriella said, turning the key in her hand. Walking to the tabernacle, she fitted the key into the lock and opened the door. A small leather pouch was inside. "There is nothing more to do here," Gabriella said. Gesturing for Evangeline to follow, she said, "Come, we must leave at once. We're not out of danger yet."

St. Rose Convent, Milton, New York

Verlaine walked across the lawn of the convent, his feet sinking into the snow. Only seconds before, the compound had nearly buckled under the weight of attack. The walls of the convent had been engulfed in flames, the courtyard filled with vile, belligerent creatures. Then, to his utter bewilderment, the battle had ceased. In an instant the fire had disappeared in the air, leaving behind only charred brick, sizzling metal, and the pungent smell of carbon. The creatures' beating wings stilled midflight. They fell to the ground as if stricken by an electrical current, leaving heaps of broken bodies upon the snow. Verlaine observed the silent courtyard, the last remnants of smoke dispersing in the afternoon sky.

Walking to one of the bodies, he crouched before it. There was something odd about the appearance of the creature — not only had the radiance disappeared, but the entire physicality had changed. In death the skin had become mottled with imperfections — freckles, moles, scars, patches of dark hair. The clarified white of the fingernails had darkened, and when Verlaine pushed the body onto its stomach, he found that the wings had disappeared entirely, leaving behind a red powder. In life the creatures were half man, half angel. In death they appeared completely human.

Verlaine was distracted from the body by voices at the far side of the church. The population of St. Rose Convent filed into the courtyard and began to drag the bodies of Gibborim to the riverbank. Verlaine searched for Gabriella among them but could find her nowhere in their number. There were dozens of nuns, all dressed in heavy overcoats and boots. The women showed great determination in the face of the unpleasant work, organizing themselves into small groups and getting down to the business at hand without hesitation. As the bodies were large and unwieldy, the effort of four sisters was required to transport one creature. They dragged the corpses slowly over the courtyard to the banks of the Hudson, forming a groove of packed snow that slicked to ice. After stacking the creatures one upon another under the bower of a birch tree, they rolled them into the river. The bodies sank below the glassy surface as if weighted with lead.

As the nuns worked, Gabriella emerged from the church with a young woman, both of their faces blackened with smoke. He recognized

Gabriella's features in the young woman —
the shape of the nose, the point of the chin,
the high cheekbones. It was Evangeline.

"Come," Gabriella said to Verlaine, clutching a brown leather case under her arm. "We
haven't time to waste."

"But the Porsche has only two seats," Verlaine said, realizing the problem even as he
articulated it.

Gabriella stopped short, as if her inability
to foresee the dilemma at hand annoyed her
more than she wished to let on.

"Is there a problem?" Evangeline asked,
and Verlaine felt himself drawn to the musical quality of her voice, the serenity of her
manner, the ghostly shade of Gabriella in her
features.

"Our car is rather small," Verlaine said,
wondering what Evangeline might be thinking.

Evangeline looked at him a moment too
long, as if verifying that he was the same man
she'd met the day before. When she smiled, he
knew that he had not been mistaken. Something between them had taken hold.

"Follow me," Evangeline said, turning on her
heel and walking swiftly away. She traversed
the courtyard quickly, with purpose, her small
black shoes breaking through the snow. Verlaine knew that he would have followed her
anywhere she cared to go.

Ducking between two of the utility vans,

Evangeline led them along an icy sidewalk
and through the side door of a brick garage.
Inside, the air was stagnant and free of the
dense smell of the fire. She lifted a set of keys
from a hook and shook them.

"Get in," she said, gesturing to the brown
four-door sedan. "I'll drive."

THE HEAVENLY CHOIR

Soon, the angel began to sing, its voice climbing and falling with the lyre. As if taking cue from this divine progression, the others joined the chorus, each voice rising to create the music of heaven, a confluence akin to the congregation described by Daniel, ten thousand times ten thousand angels.

— The Venerable Father Clematis of Thrace, *Notes on the First Angelological Expedition,* Translated by Dr. Raphael Valko

December 24, 1999, 12:41 P.M.

Percival stood in his mother's bedroom, a spare, meticulously white space at the very apex of the penthouse. A wall of glass overlooked the city, a gray mirage of buildings punctuated by the blue sky. The afternoon sun slid along a series of Gustave Doré etchings on the far wall, gifts to Sneja from Percival's father many years before. The etchings depicted legions of angels basking in sunlight, tier upon tier of winged messengers arranged in rings, images magnified by the ethereal cast of the room. Once Percival had felt kinship to the angels in the pictures. Now, in his present condition, he could hardly bring himself to look at them.

Sneja lay sprawled upon her bed, sleeping. In her slumber — her wings retracted into a smooth skin upon her back — she looked like an innocent and well-fed child. Percival placed his hand upon her shoulder, and when he said her name, she opened her eyes and fixed him in her gaze. The aura of peacefulness that had surrounded her drained away. She sat up in bed, unfurled her wings, and arrayed them about her shoulders. They were perfectly groomed, the layers of colored feathers meticulously ordered, as if she'd had them cleaned before going to sleep.

"What do you want?" Sneja said, looking Percival up and down as if to take in the full scale of his disappointing appearance. "What has happened? You look terrible."

Trying to remain calm, Percival said, "I must speak with you."

Sneja threw her feet over the edge of her bed, hoisted herself up, and walked to the window. It was early afternoon. In the waning light, her wings seemed glossed in mother-of-pearl. "I should think it obvious that I'm taking a nap."

"I wouldn't disturb you if it were not urgent," Percival said.

"Where is Otterley?" Sneja said, glancing over Percival's shoulder. "Has she returned from the recovery effort? I am anxious to hear the details. We haven't employed Gibborim in so very long." She looked at Percival, and he saw at once how worried she was. "I should have gone myself," she said, her eyes glistening. "The blaze of the fires, the rush of wings, the screams of the unsuspecting — it is like the old days."

Percival bit his lip, unsure of how to respond.

"Your father is in from London," Sneja said,

670

wrapping herself in a long silk kimono. Her wings — healthy and immaterial as Percival's had once been — slipped effortlessly through the fabric. "Come, we will catch him at his lunch."

Percival walked with his mother to the dining room, where Mr. Percival Grigori II, a middling Nephilim of some four hundred years who bore a striking resemblance to his son, sat at the table. He had taken his jacket off and allowed his wings to emerge through his oxford. As a schoolboy often in trouble, Percival had frequently found his father waiting for him in his study, his wings pointed nervously in this very same manner. Mr. Grigori was a strict, ill-tempered, cold, and ruthlessly aggressive man, whose wings echoed his temperament: They were austere and narrow appendages with dull silver feathers the color of fish scales that lacked the proper width or span. In fact, his father's wings were the exact opposite of Sneja's. Percival found it appropriate that their physical appearances should be so opposite. His parents had not lived together in nearly one hundred years.

Mr. Grigori tapped a World War II–era Meisterstück fountain pen against the table's surface, another sign of impatience and irritation that Percival recognized from his childhood. Looking at Percival, he said, "Where have you been? We have been waiting for word from you all day."

671

Sneja arranged her wings about her and sat at the table. Turning to Percival, she said, "Yes, my darling, tell us — what news from the convent?"

Percival fell into a chair at the head of the table, set his cane at his side, and took a deep, labored breath. His hands trembled. He felt both hot and cold at once. His clothes were soaked through with sweat. Each breath burned his lungs, as if the air fueled a kindling fire. He was slowly suffocating.

"Calm yourself, son," Mr. Grigori said, looking at Percival with contempt.

"He's ill," Sneja snapped, putting her fat hand on her son's arm. "Take your time, dearest. Tell us what has put you in such a state."

Percival could see his father's disappointment and his mother's growing helplessness. He did not know how he would gather the strength to speak of the disaster that had befallen them. Sneja had ignored his phone calls all morning. He had tried her many times during the lonely drive back to the city and she had simply refused to pick up. He would have much preferred to tell her the news on the phone.

At last Percival said, "The mission was unsuccessful."

Sneja paused, understanding from the tone of her son's voice that there was more bad news. "But that is impossible," she said.

"I have just come from the convent," Percival said. "I have seen it with my own eyes. We have suffered a terrible defeat."

"What of the Gibborim?" Mr. Grigori said.

"Gone," Percival said.

"Retreated?" Sneja asked.

"Killed," Percival said.

"Impossible," Mr. Grigori said. "We sent nearly one hundred of our strongest warriors."

"And each one was struck down," Percival said. "They were instantly killed. I walked through the aftermath and saw their bodies. Not one Gibborim lived."

"This is unthinkable," Mr. Grigori said. "Such a defeat has not occurred in my lifetime."

"It was an unnatural defeat," Percival said.

"Are you saying that there was a summoning?" Sneja asked, incredulous.

Percival folded his hands upon the table, relieved that he had stopped trembling. "I wouldn't have believed it possible. There are not many angelologists alive who have been initiated into the art of summoning, especially in America, where they are at a loss for mentorship. But it is the only explanation for such complete destruction."

"What does Otterley say about this?" Sneja asked, pushing away her chair and standing. "Surely she doesn't believe that they have the strength to perform a summoning. The practice is all but extinct."

"Mother," Percival said, his voice strained with emotion, "we lost everyone in the attack."

Sneja looked from Percival to her husband, as if only his reaction would make her son's words true.

Percival's voice faltered in shame and despair as he continued, "I was at a distance from the convent when the attack occurred, but I could see the terrible whirlwind of angels. They descended upon the Gibborim. Otterley was among their number."

"You saw her body?" Sneja said, walking from one end of the room to the other. Her wings had pressed closed against her body, an involuntary physical reaction. "You are certain?"

"There is no doubt," Percival said. "I watched the humans dispose of the bodies."

"And what of the treasure?" Sneja said, growing frantic. "What of your trusted employee? What of Gabriella Lévi-Franche Valko? Tell me you have gained something from our losses?"

"By the time I arrived, they were gone," Percival said. "Gabriella's Porsche was abandoned at the convent. They took what they came for and left. It is over. There is no hope."

"So let me get this straight," Mr. Grigori said. Although Percival knew that his father adored Otterley, and must be in a state of unspeakable dispair, he displayed the icy calm that had so frightened Percival in his youth. "You allowed your sister to go into attack alone. Then you let the angelologists who killed her escape, losing the opportunity to retrieve a treasure we have sought for a thousand years. And you believe that you are finished?"

Percival regarded his father with hatred and yearning. How was it that he had not lost his strength with age and that Percival, who should be at the height of his powers, had become so weakened?

"You will pursue them," Mr. Grigori said, standing to his full height, his silver wings fanning open about his shoulders. "You will find them and retrieve the instrument. And you will keep me informed as the hunt progresses. We will do whatever necessary to bring victory."

Upper West Side, New York City

Evangeline turned onto West Seventy-ninth Street, driving slowly behind a city bus. Pausing at a red light, she glanced down Broadway, squinting to see the afternoon streetscape, and felt a rush of recognition. She'd spent many weekends with her father walking these streets, stopping for breakfast at any one of the cramped diners tucked along the avenues. The chaos of people slogging through the slush, the squish of buildings, the incessant movement of traffic in every direction — New York City was deeply familiar, despite her years away.

Gabriella lived only a few blocks ahead. Although Evangeline had not been to her grandmother's apartment since her childhood, she remembered it well — the subdued façade of the brownstone, the elegant metalwork fence, the slanted view of the park. It used to be that she had recalled these images with care. Now thoughts of St. Rose filled her mind. Try as she might, she could not forget how the sisters looked at her as she left the church, as if the attack were somehow her fault and their youngest member had brought the Gibborim upon them. Evangeline kept her gaze fixed upon the pathway as she left them. It was all she could manage to get to the edge of the garage without looking back.

In the end Evangeline had betrayed her instincts and looked into the rearview mirror to see the sooty snow and the baleful sisters collected at the riverside. The convent was as dilapidated as a ruined castle, the lawn coated with ash from the fires. She, too, had changed. In a matter of minutes, she had shed her role as Sister Evangeline, Franciscan Sister of Perpetual Adoration, and had become Evangeline Angelina Cacciatore, Angelologist. As they drove from the grounds, birch trees rising at each side of the car like hundreds of marble pillars, Evangeline believed she saw the shadow of a fiery angel glinting in the distance, beckoning her onward.

On the journey to New York City, Verlaine had sat in the front seat, while Gabriella insisted upon taking the back, where she had spread out the contents of the leather case and examined them. Perhaps the silence imposed upon Evangeline at St. Rose had come to wear heavily on her — over the course of the drive, she had spoken frankly with Verlaine about her life, the convent, and even, to her surprise, her parents. She told him about her childhood in Brooklyn, how it was punctuated by walks with her father over the Brooklyn Bridge. She told him that the famous walkway that runs the length of the bridge was the one place where she had felt a carefree, undiluted happiness and for that reason, it was still her favorite place in the world. Verlaine asked more and more questions, and she was amazed by how readily and openly she answered each one, as if she'd known him all her life. It had been many years since she'd talked to someone like Verlaine — handsome, intelligent, interested in every detail. In fact, years had passed since she'd felt anything at all about a man. Her thoughts of men seemed, all at once, childish and superficial. Surely her behavior struck him as comically naïve.

After Evangeline had found a parking spot, she and Verlaine followed Gabriella to the brownstone. The street was strangely barren. Snow swept the sidewalk; parked cars were encrusted with a thin layer of ice. The windows of Gabriella's apartment, however, glowed. Evangeline detected movement beyond the glass, as if a group of friends awaited their arrival. She imagined the *Times* spread in sections on thick Oriental carpets, cups of tea balanced at the edges of end tables, fires kindled in gratings — those were the Sundays of her childhood, the afternoons she had spent in Gabriella's care. Of course, her memories were those of a child, and her thoughts were filled with nostalgia and romance. She had no idea of what awaited her now.

As Gabriella unlocked the front door, someone pushed the dead bolt aside, turned a great brass doorknob, and opened the door. A bearish, dark-haired man with a hooded sweatshirt and a two-day stubble stood before them. Evangeline had never seen the man before. Gabriella, however, appeared to know him intimately.

"Bruno," she said, embracing him warmly, an uncharacteristic gesture of intimacy. The man looked to be around fifty years old. Evangeline looked at the man more closely wondering if, despite the age difference, Gabriella could have remarried. Gabriella released Bruno. "Thank goodness you're here."

"Of course I'm here," he said, equally relieved to see her. "The council members have been waiting for you."

Turning to Evangeline and Verlaine, who stood together on the stoop, Bruno smiled and gestured for them to follow him through the entrance hallway. The smell of Gabriella's home — its books and gleaming antique furniture — was instantly welcoming, and Evangeline felt her anxiety dissipating with each step into the house. The overloaded bookcases, the wall of framed portraits of famous angelologists, the air of seriousness that fell over the rooms like mist — everything in the brownstone was exactly as Evangeline remembered.

Removing her overcoat, she caught her image in a mirror in the hallway. The person standing before her startled her. Dark circles ringed her eyes, and her skin had been streaked black by smoke. She had never seemed so drab, so plain, so out of place as she did now, in the presence of her grandmother's highly polished life. Verlaine stepped behind her and put his hand on her shoulder, a gesture that only yesterday would have filled her with terror and confusion. Now she was sorry when he took it away.

In the midst of all that had happened, she found it almost inexcusable that her thoughts were drawn to him. Verlaine stood only inches from her, and as she met his eyes in the mirror, she wanted him to be closer. She wished she understood his feelings better. She wished he would say something to assure her that he felt the same shock of pleasure when their eyes met.

Evangeline turned her attention back to her own reflection, realizing as she did how utterly laughable her dishevelment made her. Verlaine must find her ridiculous with her dour black clothing and her rubber-soled shoes. The manner of the convent had been etched into her.

"You must be wondering how you got here," she said, endeavoring to understand his thoughts. "You fell into all of this by accident."

"I admit," he said, flushing, "it's certainly been a surprising Christmas. But if Gabriella hadn't found me, and I hadn't gotten involved in all of this, I wouldn't have met you."

"Perhaps that might have been for the better."

"Your grandmother told me quite a bit about you. I know that things aren't all they seem. I know you went to St. Rose as a precautionary measure."

"I went for more than that," Evangeline said, realizing how complicated her motivation for staying at St. Rose was, and how difficult it would be to explain to him.

"Will you go back?" Verlaine asked, his expression anticipatory, as if her answer mattered a great deal to him.

Evangeline bit her lip, wishing she could tell him how difficult the question seemed to her. "No," she said at last. "Never."

Verlaine leaned close behind her, taking Evangeline by the hand. Her grandmother, the work before them, everything dissolved in his presence. Then he pulled her away from the mirror and led her into the dining room, where the others waited.

There was something cooking in the kitchen — the rich smell of meat and tomatoes filled the room. Bruno gestured to the table, set with linen napkins and Gabriella's china.

"You'll need lunch," Bruno said.

"I really don't think there's time for that," Gabriella said, looking distracted. "Where are the others?"

"Sit," Bruno ordered, gesturing to the chairs. "You have to eat something." He pulled out a chair and waited until Gabriella sat. "It will only take a minute." With that he disappeared into the kitchen.

Evangeline sat in the chair next to Verlaine. Crystal glasses glimmered in the weak light. A carafe of water sat mid-table, lemon slices floating on its surface. Evangeline poured a glass of water and gave it to Verlaine, her hand brushing his, sending a shock through her. She met his eye, and it struck her that she had met him only yesterday. How quickly her time at St. Rose receded, leaving behind the impression that her old life had been little more than a dream.

Soon Bruno returned with a great steaming pot of chili. The thought of lunch hadn't crossed Evangeline's mind all day — she'd become used to the grumbling of her stomach and the light-headedness that resulted from perpetual lack of water — but once the food was before her, she discovered that she was ravenous. Evangeline stirred the chili with a spoon, cooling the beans and tomatoes and pieces of sausage, and began to eat. The chili was spicy — the heat of it hit her at once. At St. Rose the sisters' diet consisted of vegetables

and bread and unseasoned meat. The spicie[s]
thing she'd eaten in the past years had been [a]
plum pudding made for the annual Christmas
celebration. Reflexively, she coughed, covering her mouth with a napkin, heat spreading
through her.

Verlaine jumped up and poured her a glass
of water. "Drink this," he said.

Evangeline drank the water, feeling silly.
"Thank you," she said when the spell had
passed. "I haven't had food like this in quite
a while."

"It will do you good," Gabriella said, assessing her. "It looks like you haven't eaten in
months. Actually," she added, standing and
leaving her food unfinished, "I think you had
better clean up a bit. I have some clothes that
will suit you."

Gabriella took Evangeline to a bathroom
down the hall, where she directed her to step
out of the sooty wool skirt and remove the
smoke-filled shirt. Gabriella collected the
dingy clothes and threw them in a trash bin.
She gave Evangeline soap and water and clean
towels so that she could wash. She gave her a
pair of jeans and a cashmere sweater — both
of which fit Evangeline perfectly, confirming
that she and her grandmother were exactly
the same height and weight. After Evangeline
washed, Gabriella watched her dress with obvious approval of her granddaughter's transformation into a new person entirely. Upon

eir return to the dining room, Verlaine simply stared at Evangeline with wonder, as if he were not quite sure she was the same person.

After they had finished eating, Bruno led them up the narrow wooden stairway. Evangeline's heart quickened at the thought of what lay ahead. In the past her encounters with angelologists had always occurred accidentally through chance meetings with her father or grandmother, indirect and fleeting encounters that left her only half aware that something unusual had taken place. Her glimpses into the world her mother had occupied always made her curious and afraid simultaneously. In truth, the prospect of encountering the angelological council members face-to-face filled her with dread. Surely they would question her about what had happened that morning at St. Rose. Surely Celestine's actions would be an object of deep fascination to them. Evangeline did not know how she would respond to such questioning.

Perhaps sensing her distress, Verlaine brushed his fingers against Evangeline's hand, a gesture of comfort and care that once again sent electricity through her body. She turned and met his eyes. They were dark brown, almost black, and intensely expressive. Did he see how she reacted when he looked at her? Did he sense on the staircase that she lost her ability to breathe when he touched her? She could hardly feel her body as she climbed the remaining stairs after her grandmother.

At the top of the stairs, they stepped into a room that had always been locked during Evangeline's childhood visits — she recalled the carvings upon the heavy wooden door, the huge brass knob, the keyhole she had tried to peer through. Then, looking through the keyhole, she had seen only swaths of sky. Now she understood the room to be filled with narrow windows. The glass opened the space to the ashen, purple light of impending dusk. Evangeline had never suspected that such a place had been hidden from her.

She stepped inside, amazed. The walls of the study were hung with paintings of angels, bright-hued figures in brilliant robes, wings spread over harps and flutes. There were heavily laden bookshelves, an antique escritoire, and a scattering of richly upholstered armchairs and divans. Despite the grandeur of the furnishings, the room had a shabby appearance — paint peeled upon the ceiling in curls, the edges of a massive steam radiator had rusted. Evangeline recalled the absence of funds her grandmother — and indeed all angelologists — had suffered in past years.

At the far end of the room, there was a cluster of antique chairs and a low, marble-topped table, where the angelologists waited. Evangeline recognized some of them at once — she had met them with her father many years before, although at the time she hadn't understood their positions.

Gabriella introduced Evangeline and Verlaine to the council. There was Vladimir Ivanov, a handsome, aging Russian émigré who had been with the organization since the 1930s, after fleeing persecution in the USSR; Michiko Saitou, a brilliant young woman who acted as angelological strategist and international angelological coordinator while managing their global financial affairs in Tokyo; and Bruno Bechstein, the man they'd met downstairs, a middle-aged angelological scholar who had transferred to New York from their offices in Tel Aviv.

Of the three, Vladimir was most familiar to Evangeline, though he had aged drastically since she'd met him last. His face was etched with deep lines, and he appeared more serious than Evangeline remembered. The afternoon her father had placed her in Vladimir's care, he had been exceedingly kind and she had disobeyed him. Evangeline wondered what had tempted him back to the line of work he had so adamantly disavowed.

Gabriella walked to the angelologists and placed the leather case upon the table. "Welcome, friends. When did you arrive?"

"This morning," Saitou-san said. "Although we wished to be here sooner."

"We came as soon as we learned of what happened," Bruno added.

Gabriella gestured to three empty upholstered armchairs, their elaborately carved arms scuffed and dull. "Sit. You must be exhausted."

Evangeline sank into the soft cushion of a couch, Verlaine at her side. Gabriella perched upon the edge of an armchair, the leather case in her lap. The angelologists watched her with avid attention.

"Welcome, Evangeline," Vladimir said gravely. "It has been many years, my dear." He gestured to the case. "I could not have imagined that these circumstances would bring us together."

Gabriella turned to the leather case and pressed the clasps, opening them with a snap. Inside, Evangeline saw that everything remained exactly as she had left it: the angelology journal; the sealed envelopes containing Abigail Rockefeller's correspondence; and the leather pouch they had retrieved from the tabernacle.

"This is the angelological journal of Dr. Seraphina Valko," Gabriella said, taking it from the case. "Celestine and I used to refer to this notebook as Seraphina's grimoire, a term we used only partially in jest. It is filled with works, spells, secrets, and imaginings of past angelologists."

"I thought it was lost," Saitou-san said.

"Not lost, only very well hidden," Gabriella said. "I brought it to the United States. Evangeline has had it with her at St. Rose Convent, afe and sound."

"Well done," Bruno said, taking it from Gabriella. As he weighed it in his hands, he winked at Evangeline, making her smile in return.

"Tell us," Vladimir said, glancing at the leather case, "what other discoveries have you made?"

Gabriella lifted the leather pouch from the case and slowly untied the string that bound it. A peculiar metallic object rested inside, an object unlike anything Evangeline had seen before. It was as small as a butterfly's wing and made of a thin, pounded metal that shone in Gabriella's fingers. It appeared delicate, yet when Gabriella allowed Evangeline to hold it, she felt it to be inflexible.

"It is the plectrum of the lyre," Bruno said. "How brilliant to separate it from the lyre itself."

"If you recall," Gabriella said, "the Venerable Clematis separated the plectrum from the body of the lyre on the First Angelological Expedition. It was sent to Paris, where it remained in the possession of European angelologists until the early nineteenth century, when Mother Francesca brought it to the United States for safekeeping."

"And built the Adoration Chapel around it," Verlaine said. "Which would explain her elaborate architectural drawings."

Vladimir seemed unable to take his eyes

from the object. "May I?" he asked at last, delicately lifting the plectrum from Evangeline and cupping it in his hand. "It is lovely," he said. Evangeline was moved by how gently he ran his finger over the metal, as if reading braille. "Unbelievably lovely."

"Indeed," Gabriella said. "It is fashioned from pure Valkine."

"But how was it kept at the convent all this time?" Verlaine asked.

"In the Adoration Chapel," Gabriella said. "Evangeline can be more precise than I — she was the one who discovered it."

"It was hidden in the tabernacle," Evangeline said. "The tabernacle was locked, and the key was hidden in the monstrance above. I am not exactly sure how the key came to be there, but it seems that it was very well secured."

"Brilliant," Gabriella said. "It makes perfect sense that they would keep it in the chapel."

"How so?" Bruno inquired.

"The Adoration Chapel is the site of the sisters' perpetual adoration," Gabriella said. "Do you know the ritual?"

"Two sisters pray before the host," Vladimir said, thoughtful. "To be replaced each hour by two more sisters. Is that correct?"

"Exactly so," Evangeline said.

"They are attentive during adoration?" Gabriella asked, turning to Evangeline.

"Of course," Evangeline said. "It is a time of extreme concentration."

"And where is all that concentration focused?"

"Upon the host."

"Which is where?"

Picking up on her grandmother's line of thought, Evangeline said, "Of course — the sisters direct their entire attention to the host, which was held in the monstrance upon the altar and in the tabernacle. As the plectrum was hidden inside, the sisters unwittingly watched over the instrument as they prayed. The sisters' perpetual adoration was an elaborate security system."

"Exactly," Gabriella said. "Mother Francesca discovered an ingenious method of guarding the plectrum twenty-four hours a day, seven days a week. There was really no way for it to be discovered, let alone stolen, with such careful and ever-present attendants."

"Except," Evangeline said, "during the attack of 1944. Mother Innocenta was murdered on her way to the chapel. The Gibborim killed her before she could get there."

"How remarkable," Verlaine said. "For hundreds of years, the sisters have been performing an elaborate farce."

"I don't think they believed it a farce," Evangeline said. "They were performing two duties at once: prayer and protection. None of us knew what was really inside the tabernacle. I had no idea that there was more to daily

690

adoration than prayer."

Vladimir stroked the metal with his fingertips. "The sound must be quite extraordinary," he said. "For half a century, I have tried to imagine the exact pitch the kithara would make if plucked with a plectrum."

"It would be a great mistake to experiment," Gabriella said. "You know as well as I what could happen if one were to play it."

"What could happen?" Vladimir asked, although it was clear that he knew the answer to his question before he asked it.

"The lyre was fashioned by an angel," Bruno said. "As a result it has an ethereal sound, one that is both beautiful and destructive simultaneously and has unearthly — some might say unholy — ramifications."

"Well said," Vladimir told him, smiling at Bruno.

"I am quoting your magnum opus, Dr. Ivanov," Bruno replied.

Gabriella paused to light a cigarette. "Vladimir knows very well that there is no telling what might occur. There are only theories — most of which are his own. The instrument itself has not been studied properly. We have never had it in our possession long enough to do so — but we know from Clematis's account, and from the field notes taken by Seraphina Valko and Celestine Clochette, that the lyre exerts a seductive force over all who come into contact with it. This is what makes it so dangerous:

Even those who mean well are tempted to play the lyre. And the repercussions of its music could be more devastating than anything we can imagine."

"With a pluck of a string, the world as we know it could fold away and disappear," Vladimir said.

"It could transform into hell," Bruno said, "or into paradise. Legend has it that Orpheus discovered the lyre during his journey to the underworld and played it. This music ushered in a new era in human history — learning and husbandry flourished, the arts became a mainstay of human life. It's one of the reasons Orpheus is so revered. It was an instance of the benefits of the lyre."

"That's an extraordinarily dangerous bit of romantic thinking," Gabriella said sharply. "The lyre's music is known to be destructive. Such utopian dreams as yours will lead only to annihilation."

"Come now," Vladimir said, gesturing to the object on the table. "A piece of the lyre is here, before us, waiting to be studied."

All eyes fell upon the plectrum. Evangeline wondered at its power, its allure, the temptation and desire it inspired.

"One thing I do not understand," she said, "is what the Watchers hoped to gain by playing the lyre. They were doomed creatures, banished from heaven. How could music save them?"

Vladimir said, "At the bottom of the able Clematis's account, written in h hand, was Psalm 150."

"The music of the angels," Evangeline pered, recognizing the psalm instantly. It was one of her favorites.

"Yes," Saitou-san said. "Exactly so. The music of praise."

"It is likely," Bruno said, "that the Watchers were attempting to make amends with their Creator by singing His praises. Psalm 150 gives advice to those who wish to gain heavenly favor. If their attempts were successful, the imprisoned angels would have been reinstituted into the heavenly host. Perhaps their efforts were directed toward their own salvation."

"That is one way to look at it," Saitou-san said. "It is equally possible that they were trying to destroy the universe from which they had been banned."

"An objective," Gabriella added, tamping out her cigarette, "that they obviously failed to achieve. Come, let us move along to the purpose of this meeting," she said, clearly irritated. "Over the past decade, all of the celestial instruments in our possession have been stolen from our safe holds in Europe. We've presumed they were taken by the Nephilim."

"Some believe that such a symphony would free the Watchers," Vladimir said.

"But anyone who has read the literature

rees that the Nephilim care nothing about the Watchers," Gabriella said. "Indeed, before Clematis went into the cavern, the Watchers played the lyre, hoping to lure the Nephilim to their aid. It was utterly unsuccessful. No, the Nephilim are interested in the instruments for purely selfish reasons."

"They want to heal themselves and their race," Bruno added. "They want to become strong so that they can further enslave humanity."

"And they have come too close to finding it for us not to take action," Gabriella said. "It is my belief that they've apprehended the other celestial instruments for their own protection from us. But they desire the lyre for another reason altogether. They are attempting to restore themselves to a state of perfection their kind has not seen in hundreds of years. Although we have been dismayed at Abigail Rockefeller's perpetual silence, so to speak, on the matter of its location, we have not worried that the lyre would be discovered. But obviously this has failed. The Nephilim are hunting, and we have to be ready."

"It seems Mrs. Rockefeller had our best interests in mind after all," Evangeline said.

"She was an amateur," Gabriella said, dismissive. "She took an interest in angels in the way her wealthy friends were interested in charity balls."

"It is a good thing she did," Vladimir said.

"How do you suppose we received such crucial support during the war, not the least of which was her funding for our expedition of 1943? She was a devout woman who believed that great wealth should be used to great ends." Vladimir leaned back into his chair and crossed his legs.

"Which, for good or ill, turned out to be a dead end," Bruno murmured.

"Not necessarily," Gabriella said, eyeing Bruno. She slid the plectrum into its leather pouch and removed a gray envelope from inside the leather case. On the face of the envelope was the pattern of Roman letters written into a square. If Celestine's words held true, it was the envelope containing the Rockefeller letters. Gabriella placed it on the table before the angelologists. "Celestine Clochette instructed Evangeline to bring this to us."

The angelologists' interest became tangible as they spied the symbol stamped upon the envelope. Their reactions fired Evangeline's curiosity. "What does it mean?" she asked.

"It is an angelological seal, a Sator-Rotas Square," Vladimir said. "We have placed this seal upon documents for many hundreds of years. It announces the importance of the document and verifies that it has been sent by one of us."

Gabriella folded her arms across her chest, as if cold, and said, "This afternoon I had the opportunity to read Innocenta's half of her correspondence with Abigail Rockefeller. It became clear to me that Innocenta and Abigail Rockefeller were communicating about the lyre's location obliquely, although neither Verlaine nor I was able to discern how."

Evangeline watched from the edge of the upholstered chair, her spine exceedingly straight. She experienced a strange sense of déjà vu as Vladimir took the gray envelope with determined calm from Verlaine. He closed his eyes, whispered a series of incomprehensible words — a spell or a prayer, Evangeline could not say which — and tore the envelope open.

Inside, there were time-weathered envelopes the length and width of Evangeline's outstretched hand. Adjusting his eyeglasses, Vladimir raised the letters close to get a clear view of the script. "They're addressed to Mother Innocenta," he said, placing the envelopes on the table between them.

There were six envelopes containing six missives, one more than Innocenta had written. Evangeline peered at them. On the face of each envelope were canceled stamps: one red two-cent stamp and one green one-cent stamp.

Picking up one of the missives and turning it over, Evangeline saw the Rockefeller name embossed on the back, along with a return address on West Fifty-fourth Street, less than a mile away.

"The location of the lyre is surely disclosed

in these letters," Saitou-san said.

"I don't think we can come to a conclusion without reading them," Evangeline said.

Without further hesitation Vladimir opened each of the envelopes and placed six small cards on the table. The stock was thick and creamy white, a border of gold at the edges. Identical designs had been printed on the face of each of the cards. Grecian goddesses with laurel-leaf wreaths upon their heads danced amid swarms of cherubs. Two of the angels — fat, babylike cherubs with rounded moth wings — held lyres in their hands.

"This is a classic 1920s Art Deco design," Verlaine said, picking up one of the cards and examining it. "The lettering is the same font that was used by the *New Yorker* magazine on its cover. And the symmetrical positioning of the angels is classic. The dual cherubs with their lyres are mirror images of one another, which is a quintessential Art Deco motif." Leaning over the card so that his hair fell into his eyes, Verlaine said, "And this is most definitely Abigail Rockefeller's handwriting. I've examined her journals and personal correspondence many times. There's no mistaking it."

Vladimir took the cards and read them, his blue eyes scanning the lines. Then, with the air of a man who had been patient for too many years, he placed them back on the table and stood. "They say nothing at all," he said.

"The first five cards are as evocative as laundry lists. The last card is completely blank, except for the name 'Alistair Carroll, Trustee, Museum of Modern Art.'"

"They must give some information about the lyre," Saitou-san said, picking up the cards. Vladimir gazed at Gabriella for a moment, as if weighing the possibility that he'd missed something. "Please," he said. "Read them. Tell me that I am wrong."

Gabriella read the cards one by one, passing them on to Verlaine, who read through them so quickly that Evangeline wondered how he could have taken in what they said.

Gabriella sighed. "They are exactly the same in tone and content as Innocenta's letters."

"Meaning?" asked Saitou-san.

"Meaning they discuss the weather, charity balls, dinner parties, and Abigail Rockefeller's idle artistic contributions to the sisters of St. Rose Convent's annual Christmas fundraiser," Gabriella said. "They give no direct instruction for finding the lyre."

"We've put all our hope into Abigail Rockefeller," Bruno said. "What if we've been wrong?"

"I wouldn't be so quick to dismiss Mother Innocenta's role in these exchanges," Gabriella said, glancing at Verlaine. "She was known as a woman of remarkable subtlety, and she could persuade others in the art of subtlety as well."

Verlaine sat silently examining the cards. Finally he stood, took a folder from his messenger bag, and placed four letters on the table next to the cards. The fifth letter remained at the convent, where Evangeline had left it. "These are Innocenta's letters," he said, smiling sheepishly at Evangeline, as if even now she judged him for stealing them from the Rockefeller Archive. He placed Rockefeller's cards and Innocenta's letters side by side in chronological order. In quick succession he extracted four of Rockefeller's cards and, putting them before him, studied each cover. Evangeline was perplexed by Verlaine's actions, and she only became more so when he began to smile as if something in the cards amused him. At last he said, "I think Mrs. Rockefeller was even more clever than we have given her credit for."

"I'm sorry," Saitou-san said, leaning over the cards, "but I don't understand how the letters convey a thing."

"Let me show you," Verlaine said. "Everything is here in the cards. This is the correspondence in chronological order. Because of the absence of overt directions about the lyre's location, we can assume the content of Rockefeller's half of the correspondence is null, a kind of white space upon which Innocenta's responses project meaning. As I pointed out to Gabriella this morning, there is a recurring pattern in Innocenta's letters. In four of them, she comments upon the nature of some kind of design that Abigail Rockefeller has included in her correspondence. I see now," Verlaine concluded, gesturing to Mrs. Rockefeller's cards on the table before him, "that Innocenta was commenting specifically on these four pieces of stationery."

"Read these remarks to us, Verlaine," Gabriella said.

Verlaine picked up Innocenta's letters and read aloud the sentences that praised Abigail Rockefeller's artistic taste, repeating the passages he had read to Gabriella that morning.

"At first I believed Innocenta was refering to drawings, perhaps even original artworks included in the letters, which would have been the find of a century for a scholar of modern art like myself. But realistically, the inclusion of such designs would have been highly unlike Mrs. Rockefeller. She was a collector and lover of art, not an artist in her own right."

Verlaine pulled four creamy cards from the progression of papers and distributed them to the angelologists.

"These are the four cards Innocenta admired," he said.

Evangeline examined the card Verlaine had given her. She saw it had been stamped by an inked plate that left a remarkably fine rendering of two antique lyres held in the hands of twin cherubs. The cards were pleasing to look at and very much in keeping with a woman of Abigail Rockefeller's taste, but Evangeline saw nothing that would unlock the mystery before them.

"Look closely at the twin cherubs," Verlaine said. "Notice the composition of the lyres."

The angelologists peered at the cards, exchanging them so that they could see each one in turn.

Finally, after some examination, Vladimir said, "There is an anomaly in the prints. The lyres are different on each card."

"Yes," Bruno said. "The number of strings on the left lyre varies from the number on the right."

Evangeline saw her grandmother examine her card and, as if she had begun to understand Verlaine's point, smile. "Evangeline," Gabriella said. "How many strings do you count on each of the lyres?"

Evangeline looked more closely at her card and saw that Vladimir and Bruno were correct — the strings were different on each lyre — although it struck her as an oddity in the cards rather than anything of serious consequence. "Two and eight," Evangeline said, "but what does it mean?"

Verlaine took a pencil from his pocket and, in barely legible lead, wrote numbers below the lyres. He passed the pencil around and asked the others to do the same.

"It seems to me that we are making much of a highly unrealistic rendition of a musical instrument," Vladimir said dismissively.

"The number of strings on each lyre must have been a method of coding information," Gabriella said.

Verlaine collected the cards from Evangeline, Saitou-san, Vladimir, and Bruno. "Here you have them: twenty-eight, thirty-eight, thirty, and thirty-nine. In that order. If I'm right, these numbers come together to give the location of the lyre."

Evangeline stared at Verlaine, wondering if she'd missed something. To her the numbers appeared to be utterly meaningless. "You believe that these numbers give an address?"

"Not directly," Verlaine said, "but there might be something in the sequence that points to an address."

"Or coordinates on a map," Saitou-san suggested.

"But where?" Vladimir said, his brow furrowing as he thought of the possibilities. "There are hundreds of thousands of addresses in New York City."

"This is where I'm stumped," Verlaine said. "Obviously these numbers must have been extremely important to Abigail Rockefeller, but there is no way to know how they're to be used."

"What sort of information could be conveyed in eight numbers?" Saitou-san asked, as if running the possibilities through her mind.

"Or, possibly, four two-digit numbers,"

Bruno said, clearly amused by the dubiousness of the exercise.

"And all the numbers are between twenty and forty," Vladimir offered.

"There must be more in the cards," Saitou-san said. "These numbers are too random."

"To most people," Gabriella said, "this would seem random. To Abigail Rockefeller, however, these numbers must have formed a logical order."

"Where did the Rockefellers live?" Evangeline asked Verlaine, knowing that this was his area of expertise. "Perhaps these numbers point to their address."

"They lived at a few different addresses in New York City," Verlaine said. "But their West Fifty-fourth Street residence is known best. Eventually Abigail Rockefeller donated the site to the Museum of Modern Art."

"Fifty-four is not one of our numbers," Bruno said.

"Wait a moment," Verlaine said. "I don't know why I didn't see this before. The Museum of Modern Art was one of Abigail Rockefeller's most important endeavors. It was also one of the first in a series of public museums and monuments that she and her husband funded. The Museum of Modern Art was opened in 1928."

"Twenty-eight is the first number from the cards," Gabriella said.

"Exactly," Verlaine said, his excitement

rowing. "The numbers two and eight from the lyre etching could point to this address."

"If that is the case," Evangeline said, "there would have to be three other locations that match the three other lyre renderings."

"What are the remaining numbers?" Bruno asked.

"Three and eight, three and zero, and three and nine," Saitou-san replied.

Gabriella leaned closer to Verlaine. "Is it possible," she said, "that there is a correspondence?"

Verlaine's expression was one of intense concentration. "Actually," he said at last. "The Cloisters, which was John D. Rockefeller Jr.'s great love, opened in 1938."

"And 1930?" Vladimir asked.

"Riverside Church, which, to be honest, I have never found interesting, must have been completed around 1930."

"That leaves 1939," Evangeline said, the anticipation of discovery making her so nervous she could hardly speak. "Did the Rockefellers build something in 1939?"

Verlaine was silent, his brow furrowed, as if he were sifting the multitude of addresses and dates cataloged in his memory. Suddenly, he said, "As a matter of fact, they did. Rockefeller Center, their own Art Deco magnum opus, opened in 1939."

"The numbers communicated to Innocenta must refer to these locations," Vladimir said.

"Well done, Verlaine," Saitou-san said, ruffling his mess of curls.

The atmosphere in the room had shifted drastically to a buzz of restless anticipation. For her part, Evangeline could only stare at the cards in astonishment. They'd rested in a vault beneath her and the other unsuspecting sisters for more than fifty years.

"However," Gabriella said, breaking the spell, "the lyre can be in only one of these four locations."

"Then it will be most expedient if we divide into groups and search them all," Vladimir said. "Verlaine and Gabriella will go to the Cloisters. It'll be packed with tourists, so getting anything out of there will be a delicate procedure. I believe it best accomplished by one familiar with its conventions. Saitou-san and I will go to Riverside Church. And Evangeline and Bruno will go to the Museum of Modern Art."

"And Rockefeller Center?" Verlaine asked.

Saitou-san said, "It's impossible to do anything there today. It's Christmas Eve, for God's sake. The place will be a madhouse."

"I expect that's why Abigail Rockefeller chose it," Gabriella said. "The more difficult it is to access, the better."

Gabriella took the leather case holding the plectrum and the angelological notebook in hand. She gave each group the card associated with its location. "I can only hope the cards will assist us in finding the lyre."

"And if they do?" Bruno said. "What then?"

"Ah, that is the great dilemma we face," Vladimir said, running his fingers through his silver hair. "To preserve the lyre or to destroy it."

"Destroy it?" Verlaine cried. "From all that you've said, it's obvious that the lyre is beautiful, precious beyond all reckoning."

"This instrument is not just another ancient artifact," Bruno said. "It isn't something that one might put on display at the Met. Its dangers far outweigh any historical importance it may have. There is no option but to destroy it."

"Or to hide it again," Vladimir said. "There are numerous places in which we could secure it."

"We tried this in 1943, Vladimir," Gabriella said. "It is plain that this method has failed. Preserving the lyre would imperil future generations, even in the most secure of hiding places. It must be destroyed. That much is clear. The real question is how."

"What do you mean?" Evangeline asked.

Vladimir said, "It is one of the primary qualities of all celestial instruments: They were created by heaven and can be destroyed only by heaven's creatures."

"I don't understand," Verlaine said.

"Only celestial beings, or creatures with

angelic blood, can destroy celestial matter, Bruno said.

"Including the Nephilim," Gabriella said.

"So if we wish to destroy the lyre," Saitou-san said, "we must place it in the hands of the very creatures we wish to keep it from."

"A bit of a conundrum," Bruno said.

"So why hunt it down it at all?" Verlaine asked, dismayed. "Why bring something so important out of safety only to destroy it?"

"There is no alternative," Gabriella said. "We have the rare opportunity to take possession of the lyre. We will have to find a way to dispose of it once we recover it."

"If we recover it," Bruno added.

"We are wasting time," Saitou-san said, standing. "We will have to decide what to do with the lyre once we have it in our possession. We cannot risk the Nephilim's discovery of it."

Looking at his watch, Vladimir said, "It is nearly three. We will meet at Rockefeller Center at exactly six. That gives us three hours to make contact, search the buildings, and reconvene. There can be no mistakes. Plan the quickest route possible. Speed and precision are absolutely necessary."

Leaving their chairs, they put on jackets and scarves, preparing to face the cold winter dusk. In a matter of seconds, the angelologists were ready to begin. As they walked toward the staircase, Gabriella turned to Evangeline.

In our haste we must not lose sight of the dangers of our work. I warn you — be very careful in your efforts. The Nephilim will be watching. Indeed, they have been waiting for this moment for a very long time. The instructions Abigail Rockefeller left us are the most precious papers you have ever touched. Once the Nephilim understand we've discovered them, they will attack without mercy."

"But how will they know?" Verlaine asked, coming to Evangeline's side.

Gabriella smiled a sad, significant smile. "My dear boy, they know exactly where we are. They have planted informants all over this city. At all times, in all places, they are waiting. Even now they are near, watching us. Please," she said, looking pointedly at Evangeline once more, "be careful."

Museum of Modern Art, New York City

Evangeline pressed her hand to the brick wall running alongside West Fifty-fourth Street, the icy wind searing her skin. Above, sheets of glass reflected the Sculpture Garden, simultaneously opening the intricate workings of the museum and presenting the garden's image back upon itself. The lights inside had been dimmed. Patrons and museum employees moved through the interior of the galleries, visible at the outer edge of Evangeline's vision. A darkened reflection of the garden appeared in the glass as warped, distorted, unreal.

"It looks like they're closing soon," Bruno said, shoving his hands deep into the pockets of his ski jacket and walking to the entrance. "We'd better hurry."

At the door Bruno swept through the crowds and made his way to the ticket desk, where a tall, thin man with a goatee and horn-rimmed glasses was reading a novel by Wilkie Collins. He looked up, glanced from Evangeline

Bruno, and said, "We're closing in half an hour. We're closed tomorrow for Christmas, but open again on the twenty-sixth." With that he returned to his book, as if Bruno and Evangeline were no longer there.

Bruno leaned on the counter and said, "We're looking for someone who might work here."

"We are not allowed to disclose personal information about employees," the man said, without looking up from his novel.

Bruno slid two one-hundred-dollar bills over the counter. "We don't need personal information. Just where we can find him."

Peering over his horn-rimmed glasses, the man placed his palm on the counter and slid the money into his pocket. "What's the name?"

"Alistair Carroll," Bruno said, giving him the card included in Abigail Rockefeller's sixth letter. "Ever heard of him?"

He looked over the card. "Mr. Carroll is not an employee."

"So you know him," Evangeline said, relieved and a bit amazed that the name corresponded to a real person.

"Everyone knows Mr. Carroll," the man said, walking out from behind the desk and leading them to the street. "He lives across from the museum." He pointed to an elegant prewar apartment building, slightly slouched with age. A copper mansard roof punctu-

ated with great porthole windows topp_
the building, a wash of patina streaking th_
bronze green. "But he's hanging around here
all the time. He's one of the old guard of the
museum."

Bruno and Evangeline hurried across the
street to the apartment building. Once inside
the entryway, Bruno and Evangeline found
the name CARROLL written on a brass mail-
box: apartment nine, floor five. They called
a rickety elevator, the wooden cab filled with
a floral powder essence, as if it had recently
released old ladies on their way to church.
Evangeline pressed a black knob stamped
with a white 5. The elevator door creaked
closed as the car lurched, grinding slowly upward. Bruno took Abigail Rockefeller's card
from his pocket and held it.

On the fifth floor, there were two apartments, both equally quiet. Bruno checked the
number and, finding the correct door — a
brass number 9 screwed on it — he knocked.

The door opened a crack, and an old man
peered at them, his large blue eyes glistening
with curiosity. "Yes?" the man whispered, his
voice barely audible. "Who is it?"

"Mr. Carroll?" Bruno said, personable and
polite, as if he had knocked on a hundred such
doors. "Very sorry to disturb you, but we have
been given your name and address by —"

"Abby," he said, his eyes fixed on the card in
Bruno's hand. He opened the door wide and

...ved them inside. "Please, come in. I have ...een expecting you."

A pair of Yorkshire terriers with red ribbons tied into the fur over their eyes jumped off a couch and bounded to the door as Bruno and Evangeline stepped into the apartment, barking as if to frighten away intruders.

"Oh, you silly girls," Alistair Carroll said. He swooped them up, tucking one dog under each arm, and carried them down a hallway.

The apartment was spacious, the antique furniture simple. Each object appeared both treasured and neglected, as if the décor had been painstakingly chosen with the intent that it would be ignored. Evangeline sat on the couch, its cushions still warm from the dogs. A marble fireplace held a small, intense fire that sent heat through the room. A polished Chippendale coffee table sat before her, a crystal bowl of hard candies at its center. Except for a Sunday *Times* folded discreetly on an end table, it appeared as though nothing had been touched in fifty years. A framed color lithograph sat upon the mantel of the fireplace, a portrait of a woman, stout and pink, with the features of a wary bird. Evangeline had never had reason or desire to seek out a likeness of Mrs. Abigail Rockefeller, but she knew in an instant that this was the woman herself.

Alistair Carroll returned without the dogs. He had short, precisely clipped gray hair.

He wore brown corduroy trousers, a tweed jacket, and had a comforting manner that put Evangeline at ease. "You must forgive my girls," he said, sitting in an armchair near the fire. "They are unused to company. We have very few guests these days. They were simply overjoyed to see you." He clasped his hands in his lap. "But enough of that," he said. "You haven't come here for pleasantries."

"Maybe you can tell us why we *are* here," Bruno said, joining Evangeline on the couch and placing the Rockefeller card on the table. "There was no explanation — only your name and the Museum of Modern Art."

Alistair Carroll unfolded a pair of spectacles and put them on. Picking up the envelope, he examined it closely. "Abby wrote out that card in my presence," he said. "But you have only one card. Where are the others?"

"There are six of us working together," Evangeline said. "We split into groups, to save time. My grandmother has two envelopes."

"Tell me," Alistair said, "is your grand-mother named Celestine Clochette?"

Evangeline was surprised to here Celestine's name, especially from a man who could not possibly have known her. "No," she said. "Ce-lestine Clochette is dead."

"I am very sorry to hear that," Alistair said, shaking his head in dismay. "And I am also sorry to hear that the recovery effort is being done in a piecemeal fashion. Abby made specific requirements that the recovery would be accomplished by one person, either Mother Innocenta or, if time went by, as it most certainly has, a woman named Celestine Clochette. I remember the conditions very well: I was Mrs. Rockefeller's assistant in this matter, and it was I who hand-delivered this card to St. Rose Convent."

"But I thought that Mrs. Rockefeller had taken permanent possession of the lyre," Bruno said.

"Oh, my, no," Alistair said. "Mrs. Rockefeller and Mother Innocenta had agreed upon a set time to return the objects under our care — Abby didn't expect to be responsible for these items forever. She intended to return them as soon as she felt that it was safe to do so — namely, at the end of the war. It was our understanding that Innocenta, or Celestine Clochette if need be, would care for the envelopes and, when the time came, follow their instructions in a particular order. The requirements were made to ensure both the safety of the objects and the safety of the person engaged in recovery."

Bruno and Evangeline exchanged glances. Evangeline was certain that Sister Celestine had not known anything about these instructions.

"We didn't get specific directions," Bruno said. "Only a card that led us here."

"Perhaps Innocenta didn't relate the infor-

mation before her death," Evangeline sa[...]
"I'm sure that Celestine would have ma[...]
certain that Mrs. Rockefeller's wishes wer[...]
followed, had she known."

"Ah, well," Alistair said, "I see that there is some confusion. Mrs. Rockefeller was under the impression that Celestine Clochette would be leaving the convent to return to Europe. It is my recollection that Miss Clochette was a temporary guest."

"It didn't work out that way," Evangeline said, remembering how frail and sickly Celestine had become in the last days of her life.

Alistair Carroll closed his eyes, as if pondering the correct path to take in the completion of the matter at hand. Standing abruptly, he said, "Well, there is nothing to do but continue. Please join me — I would like to show you my extraordinary view."

They followed Alistair Carroll to a wall of large porthole windows, the very ones Evangeline had noticed from the street below. At their vantage, the Museum of Modern Art spread before them. Evangeline pressed her hands upon the copper frame of the porthole window and peered down. Directly below them, contained and orderly, lay the famous Sculpture Garden, its rectangular floor plated in gray marble. A narrow pool of water shimmered at the center of the garden, creating an obsidian darkness. Through wisps of snow, slabs of gray marble wept purple.

From here I can watch the garden night and day," Alistair Carroll said quietly. "Mrs. Rockefeller bought this apartment for that very purpose — I am the guardian of the garden. I have watched many changes take place in the years since her death. The garden has been torn up and redesigned; the collection of statuary has grown." He turned to Evangeline and Bruno. "We could not have foreseen that the trustees would find it necessary to change things so drastically over the years. Philip Johnson's 1953 garden — the iconic modern garden that one thinks of when one imagines it — wiped out all traces of the original garden Abby had known. Then, for some bizarre reason, they decided to modernize Philip Johnson's garden — a travesty, a terrible error in judgment. First they ripped up the marble — a lovely Vermont marble with a unique shade of blue-gray to it — and replaced it with an inferior variety. They later discovered that the original had been far superior, but that is another matter. Then they ripped the whole thing up again, replacing the new marble with one that was similar to the original. It would have been most distressing to watch, if I had not taken matters into my own hands." Alistair Carroll crossed his arms over his chest, a look of satisfaction appearing upon his face. "The treasure, you see, was originally hidden in the garden."

"And now?" Evangeline asked, breathless.

"It is no longer there?"

"Abby secured it in the hollow undersid
of one of the statues — Aristide Maillol'.
The Mediterranean, which has a great hollow
space at its base. She believed that Celestine
Clochette would arrive within months, perhaps a year at the most. It would have been
safe for a short amount of time. But at the
time of Abby's death in 1948, Celestine had
still not come. Soon after, plans were made for
Philip Johnson to create his modern Sculpture Garden. I took it upon myself to move it
before they tore the garden apart," he said.

"That seems like a difficult procedure,"
Bruno said. "Especially under the kind of security implemented at the MoMA."

"I am a lifetime trustee of the museum, and
my access — although not as complete as Abby's — was considerable. It was not difficult
to arrange its removal. It was simply a matter
of having the statue moved for cleaning and
extracting it. It was a very good thing I had
the foresight to do so: The treasure would
have been discovered or damaged had I left
it. When Celestine Clochette did not come, I
knew that I must simply hold on and wait."

Bruno said, "There must have been safer
ways of securing something so precious."

"Abby believed the treasure would be most
safe in a populated environment. Together
the Rockefellers created magnificent public
spaces. Mrs. Rockefeller, always a practi-

woman, wanted to use them. Of course, ath such priceless pieces of art inside, the museums were also the most secure locations on the island of Manhattan. The Sculpture Garden and the Cloisters are under constant scrutiny. Riverside Church was a more sentimental choice — the Rockefeller family built the church on the site of Mr. Rockefeller's former school. And Rockefeller Center, the great symbol of Rockefeller power and influence, was a nod to the Rockefellers' social standing in the city. It represented the range of their power. I suppose Mrs. Rockefeller could have thrown all four pieces into a bank vault and left it at that, but it wasn't her style. The hiding places are symbolic: two museums, a church, and a commercial center. Two parts art, one part religion, and one part money — these are the exact proportions by which Mrs. Rockefeller wished herself to be remembered."

Bruno gave Evangeline a look of amusement at Alistair Carroll's speech, but said nothing.

Alistair Carroll left the room and returned after some moments with a long rectangular metal casket. He presented it to Evangeline and gave her a small key. "Open it."

Evangeline inserted the key into a tiny lock and turned. The metal mechanism ground against itself, rust blocking its progress, and then clicked. Opening the lid, Evangeline saw two long thin bars, slender and golden, resting in a bed of black velvet.

"What are they?" Bruno asked, his surpris
apparent.

"Why, the crossbars, of course," Alistair
said. "What did you expect?"

"We thought," Evangeline said, "that you
were keeping the lyre."

"The lyre? No, no, we did not hide the lyre
at the museum." Alistair smiled as if he were
at last allowed to tell them his secret. "At least
not all of it."

"You took the liberty of dismantling it?"
Bruno asked.

"It would have been much too risky to hide
it in one place," Alistair said, shaking his
head. "And so we disassembled it. It is now in
four pieces."

Evangeline stared at Alistair in disbelief. "It
is thousands of years old," she said at last. "It
must be extraordinarily fragile."

"It is a surprisingly sturdy instrument," he
said. "And we had the help of the best profes-
sionals money could buy. Now, if you don't
mind," he said, leading them back to the
fireplace and taking a seat in the armchair.
"There are a number of pieces of information I have been entrusted to relate to you. As
I mentioned, Mrs. Rockefeller assumed that
the pieces would be collected by one person
and that they would be retrieved in a certain
order. She planned the recovery in a very
meticulous fashion. The Museum of Modern

t was the first location — thus she included card with my name for you — followed by Riverside Church, the Cloisters, and then Prometheus."

"Prometheus?" Evangeline asked.

"The statue of Prometheus at Rockefeller Center," Alistair said, straightening in his chair so that he appeared suddenly taller, more patrician than before. "The order was arranged in this fashion so that I could give you specific instructions, as well as words of advice and caution. You will find a man at Riverside Church, one Mr. Gray, an employee of the Rockefeller family. Abby trusted him with the position, but frankly I don't understand why. One cannot say if he has remained attentive to Mrs. Rockefeller's wishes after all these years — he has come to me on a number of occasions requesting money. In my book, indigence is never a good sign. In any event, if there is time, I suggest you bypass Mr. Gray altogether." Alistair Carroll removed a piece of paper from the inside pocket of his tweed jacket and unrolled it on the coffee table. "This shows the exact location of the lyre's sound chest."

Alistair Carroll gave Evangeline the paper so that she might examine the maze at its center.

"The labyrinth on the chancel of Riverside Church is similar to the one found at Chartres Cathedral in France," Alistair explained.

"Traditionally labyrinths were used as to in contemplation. For our purposes a shallc vault was installed below the central flower c the labyrinth, a seamless compartment that can be removed and replaced without damaging the floor. Abby locked the sound chest inside. It was to be removed according to these instructions."

"As for the strings of the lyre," he continued, "that is another matter altogether. They are located in the Cloisters and must be removed with the assistance of the director, a woman who has been informed of Mrs. Rockefeller's wishes and will know the best approach in circumstances such as ours. The museum will be open for another half an hour or so. The director of that space has orders to allow full access. With a call from me, it shall be done. There is simply no other way to go about it without causing mayhem. You said that your associates are there now?"

"My grandmother," Evangeline said.

"How long ago did she go there?" Alistair asked.

"She should be there now," Bruno said, checking his watch.

Alistair's complexion drained of color. "I am deeply distressed to hear it. With the order of things so upset, who can say what dangers await her? We must try to intervene. Please, tell me your grandmother's name. I will place the call immediately."

Walking to a rotary telephone, he lifted the receiver and dialed. Within seconds he was explaining the situation to another party on the line. Alistair's familiar manner gave Evangeline the impression that he had discussed the situation with the director on previous occasions. After he hung up, he said, "I am greatly relieved — there have been no unusual occurrences at the Cloisters this afternoon. Your grandmother may be there, but she has not been anywhere near the hiding place. Thankfully, there is still time. My contact will do everything in her power to find your grandmother and assist her."

He then opened a closet door and slid into a heavy wool overcoat, adjusting a silk opera scarf about his neck. Following his lead, Evangeline and Bruno rose from the couch. "We must go now," Alistair said, leading them to the door. "The members of your group are not safe — indeed, now that the recovery of the instrument has begun, none of us are safe."

"We have planned to meet at Rockefeller Center at six," Bruno said.

"Rockefeller Center is four blocks from here," Alistair Carroll said. "I will accompany you. I believe I can be of some assistance."

*The Cloisters, Metropolitan Museum of Art,
Fort Tryon Park, New York City*

Verlaine and Gabriella stepped out of a taxi
and ran up the pathway to the museum. A
cluster of stonework buildings rose before
them, ramparts lifting over the Hudson River
beyond. Verlaine had visited the Cloisters
many times in the past, finding its perfect
likeness to a medieval monastery a source of
solace and refuge from the intensity of the
city. It was comforting to be in the presence
of history, even if there was an air of fabrica-
tion to it all. He wondered what Gabriella
would think of the museum, having had the
real deal in Paris — the ancient frescoes, the
crucifixes, the medieval statues that consti-
tuted the Cloisters' collection had been put
together in emulation of the Musée National
du Moyen Âge, a place he had only read about
in books.

It was the height of the holiday season, and
the museum would be filled with crowds of
people out for an afternoon of quiet contemplation of medieval art. If they were being fol-

wed, as Verlaine suspected they were, such a crowd might shield them. He studied the limestone façade, the imposing central turret, the thick exterior wall, wondering if the creatures were hidden inside. He had no doubt that they were there, waiting for them.

As they hurried up the stone steps, Verlaine pondered the mission at hand. They had been sent to the museum without any notion of how to go about their search. He knew that Gabriella was good at what she did, and he trusted that she would find a way to bring them through their part of the mission, but it seemed a daunting task. With all his love of intellectual scavenger hunts, the immense difficulty of what lay before them was enough to make him want to turn around, find a cab, and go home.

At the arched entrance of the museum, a petite woman with glossy red hair hurried in their direction. She wore a fluid silk blouse and a strand of pearls that caught the light as she made her way to them. It seemed to Verlaine that she'd been stationed at the door waiting for their arrival, but he knew that this was impossible.

"Dr. Gabriella Valko?" she said. Verlaine recognized the accent as similar to Gabriella's and deduced that the woman was French. "I am Sabine Clementine, associate director of restoration at the Cloisters. I have been sent to assist you in your endeavors this afternoon."

"Sent?" Gabriella said, looking the woman over warily. "Sent by whom?"

"Alistair Carroll," she whispered, gesturing for them to follow her. "Who works on behalf of the late Abigail Rockefeller. Come, please, I will explain as we walk."

True to Verlaine's predications, the entrance hall overflowed with people, cameras and guidebooks in hand. Patrons waited at a cash register in the museum's bookstore, the line curling past tables stacked high with medieval histories, art books, studies of Gothic and Romanesque architecture. Through a narrow window, Verlaine caught another glimpse of the Hudson River, flowing below, dark and constant. Despite the danger, he felt his entire being relax: Museums had always had a soothing effect on him, which may have been — if he wanted to analyze himself — one of the reasons he chose art history as his field. The curatorial feel of the building itself, with its collection of disassembled medieval monasteries — façades, frescoes, and doorways taken from dilapidated structures in Spain, France, and Italy and reconstructed into a collage of ancient ruins — contributed to his growing ease, as did the tourists snapping photos, young couples walking hand in hand, retirees studying the delicate, washed colors of a fresco. His disdain for tourists, so pronounced just a day before, had transformed to gratitude for their presence.

They walked into the museum proper, through interconnected galleries, one room opening into the next. Although they didn't have time to pause, Verlaine glanced at the artwork as they passed by, looking for something that might give a clue about what they'd come to the Cloisters to do. Perhaps a painting or piece of statuary would correspond with something in Abigail Rockefeller's cards, although he doubted it. The Rockefeller drawings were too modern, a clear example of New York City Art Deco. Nevertheless, he examined an Anglo-Saxon archway, a sculpted crucifix, a glass mosaic, a set of acanthus-carved pillars — restored and cleaned to a polish. Any one of these masterpieces could hold the instrument within it.

Sabine Clementine brought them into an airy room, a wall of windows drenching the glazed wide-plank wooden floor with thick light. A series of tapestries hung on the walls. Verlaine recognized them at once. He had studied them in his Masterpieces of the World Art History course during his first year of graduate school and had encountered reproductions of them again and again in magazines and posters, although for some reason he hadn't visited the tapestries in some time. Sabine Clementine had led them to the famous Hunt of the Unicorn tapestries.

"They're beautiful," Verlaine said, examining the rich reds and brilliant greens of the woven flora.

"And brutal," Gabriella added, gesturing to the slaughter of the unicorn in which half of the hunting party looks on, placid and indifferent, as the other half drives spears into the helpless creature's throat.

"This was the great difference between Abigail Rockefeller and her husband," Verlaine said, gesturing to the panel before them. "While Abigail Rockefeller founded the Museum of Modern Art and spent her time buying up Picassos, van Goghs, and Kandinskys, her husband collected art from the medieval period. He detested modernism and refused to support his wife's passion for it. He thought it profane. It's funny how the past is so often judged sacred while the modern world is held in suspicion."

"There is often good reason to be suspicious of modernity," Gabriella said, glancing over her shoulder at the cluster of tourists, as if to ascertain whether they'd been followed.

"But without the benefits of progress," Verlaine said, "we would still be stuck in the Dark Ages."

"Dear Verlaine," Gabriella said, taking him by the arm and stepping deeper into the gallery, "do you really believe we have left the Dark Ages behind?"

"Now," Sabine Clementine said, stepping close to them so that she could speak softly, "my predecessor instructed me to memorize a clue, though I have never fully comprehended its purpose until now. Please. Listen closely."

Gabriella turned to her, surprised, and Verlaine detected the slightest hint of condescension on Gabriella's face as she listened to Sabine speak.

" 'The allegory of the hunt tells a tale within a tale,' " Sabine whispered. " 'Follow the creature's course from freedom to captivity. Disavow the hounds, feign modesty at the maid, reject the brutality of slaughter, and seek music where the creature lives again. As a hand at the loom wove this mystery, so a hand must unravel it. *Ex angelis* — the instrument reveals itself.' "

" '*Ex angelis*'?" Verlaine said, as if this were the only phrase of the clue to perplex him.

"It's Latin," Gabriella replied. "It means 'from the angels.' Clearly she is using the phrase to describe the angelic instrument — it was wrought by the angels — but it is an odd way to do so." She paused to give Sabine Clementine a look of gratitude, acknowledging the legitimacy of her presence for the first time before continuing, "Actually, the initials *E A* were often imprinted on the seals of documents sent between angelologists in the Middle Ages, but the letters stood for *Epistula Angelorum,* or letter of angels, another thing entirely. Mrs. Rockefeller could not have possibly known that."

"Is there anything else that might explain

it?" Verlaine asked, leaning over Gabriella's shoulder as she extracted Abby Rockefeller's card from the case. She turned it over, looking at the reverse side.

"There is a drawing of some sort," Gabriella said, rotating the card in an attempt to get a better view. There was a series of lightly sketched lines arranged by length, a number written next to each one. "And that explains exactly nothing."

"So we have a map without a key," Verlaine said.

"Perhaps," Gabriella said, and asked Sabine to repeat the clue.

Sabine repeated it word for word.

"The allegory of the hunt tells a tale within a tale. Follow the creature's course from freedom to captivity. Disavow the hounds, feign modesty at the maid, reject the brutality of slaughter, and seek music where the creature lives again. As a hand at the loom wove this mystery, so a hand must unravel it. Ex angelis — *the instrument reveals itself."*

"Clearly she's telling us to follow the order of the hunt, which begins in the first tapestry," Verlaine said, stepping through clusters of people to the first panel. "Here a hunting party makes its way to the forest, where they discover a unicorn, chase it vigorously, and then kill it. The hounds — which Mrs. Rockefeller advises us to ignore — are part of the hunting party, and the maid — whom we should also bypass — must be one of the women hanging around watching. We're supposed to ignore all that and look where the creature lives again. That," Verlaine said, leading Gabriella by the arm to the last tapestry, "must be this one."

They stood before the most famous of the tapestries, a lush green meadow filled with wildflowers. The unicorn reclined at the center of a circular fence, tamed.

Gabriella said, "This is most definitely the tapestry in which we should 'seek music where the creature lives again.'"

"Although there doesn't seem to be anything at all referring to music here," Verlaine said.

"Ex angelis," Gabriella said to herself, as if turning the phrase over in her mind.

"Mrs. Rockefeller never used Latin phrases in her letters to Innocenta," Verlaine said. "It's obvious that the use of it here has been meant to draw our attention."

"Angels appear in nearly every piece of art in this place," Gabriella said, clearly frustrated. "But there isn't a single one here."

"You're right," Verlaine agreed, studying the unicorn. "These tapestries are an anomaly. Although the hunt for the unicorn can be interpreted, as Mrs. Rockefeller mentioned, as an allegory — most obviously a retelling of Christ's Crucifixion and Resurrection — it's one of the few pieces here without overt Christian figures or images. No depictions of

Christ, no images from the Old Testament, and no angels."

"Notice," Gabriella said, pointing to the corners of the tapestry, "how the letters A and E are woven everywhere throughout the scenes. They're in each tapestry and always paired. They must have been the initials of the patron who commissioned the tapestries."

"Perhaps," Verlaine said, looking more closely at the letters and noticing that they had been stitched with golden thread. "But look: The letter E is turned backward in each instance. The letters have been inverted."

"And if we flip them," Gabriella said, "we have E A."

"Ex angelis," Verlaine said.

Verlaine stepped so close to the tapestry that he could see the intricate patterns of threads composing the fabric of the scene. The material smelled loamy, centuries of exposure to dust and air an inextricable part of it. Sabine Clementine, who had been standing quietly nearby, waiting to be of assistance, came to their side. "Come," she said softly. "You are here for the tapestries. They are my specialty."

Without waiting for a response, Sabine walked to the first panel. She said, "The Hunt of the Unicorn tapestries are the great masterpieces of the medieval era, seven panels woven of wool and silk. Together the panels depict a courtly hunting party — you can see

731

for yourself the hounds, knights, maidens, and castles, framed by fountains and forests. The precise provenance of the tapestries remains something of a mystery, even after years of study, but art historians agree that the style points to Brussels around the year 1500. The first written documentation of the Unicorn Tapestries emerged in the seventeenth century, when the tapestries were cataloged as part of the estate of a noble French family. They were discovered and restored in the mid-nineteenth century. John D. Rockefeller Jr. paid over one million dollars for them in the 1920s. In my opinion it was a bargain. Many historians believe them to be the finest example of medieval art in the world."

Verlaine gazed at the tapestry, drawn to its vibrant color and the unicorn that reclined at the center of the woven panel, a milk-white beast, its great horn raised.

"Tell me, mademoiselle," Gabriella said, a hint of challenge in her voice, "have you come to help us or to give us a guided tour?"

"You will need a guide," Sabine replied pointedly. "Do you see the block of stitches between the letters?" She gestured to the *E A* initials above the unicorn.

"It looks like there was pretty intensive restoration work," Verlaine replied, as if the answer to Gabriella's question were the most obvious one in the world. "It was damaged?"

"Extensively," Sabine Clementine said. "The

tapestries were looted during the French Revolution — stolen from a château and used for decades to cover peasants' fruit trees from frost. Although the fabric has been lovingly, painstakingly restored, the damage is apparent if one looks closely."

As Gabriella examined the tapestry, her thoughts appeared to take a new turn. She said, "Mrs. Rockefeller was given the enormous challenge of hiding the instrument, and according to the clue she gave as instructions, she indeed chose to hide it here, in the Cloisters."

"It would seem that way," Verlaine said, gazing at her expectantly.

"To accomplish this she would have needed to find a location that was well guarded and yet exposed, safe yet accessible, so that the instrument could eventually be recovered." Gabriella took a deep breath and looked about the room — crowds had gathered in clusters before the tapestries. She lowered her voice to a whisper. "We can see firsthand that hiding something as unwieldy as a lyre — an instrument consisting of a large body and crossbars, which are generally of sizable proportions — in an intimate museum like the Cloisters would be almost impossible. And yet we know she has managed it."

"Are you suggesting that the lyre isn't really here?" Verlaine asked.

"No, that's not what I'm saying at all," Gabriella said. "It is exactly the opposite. I don't think Abigail Rockefeller would send us on a wild-goose chase. I have been thinking over the dilemma of there being four locations for one instrument and have come to the conclusion that Abigail Rockefeller was extremely savvy about hiding the lyre. She found the safest locations, but she also put the lyre in its more secure form. I believe that the instrument may not be in the form we expect."

"Now you've lost me," Verlaine said.

Sabine said, "As any angelologist who has spent a semester in Ethereal Musicology, the History of the Angelic Choruses, or any of the other seminars that focus upon the construction and implementation of the instruments would know, there is one essential component to the lyre: the strings. While many other heavenly instruments were fashioned from the precious celestial metal known as Valkine, the lyre's unique resonance arises from its strings. They were made of an unidentifiable substance that angelologists have long believed to be a mixture of silk and strands of the angels' own hair. Whatever the material, the sound is extraordinary because of the substance of the strings and the way they are stretched. The frame is, for all intents and purposes, interchangeable."

"You have attended the academy in Paris," Gabriella said, impressed.

"*Bien sûr,* Dr. Valko," Sabine said, smiling

slightly. "How else would I be entrusted with such a position as this? You may not recall, but I attended your Introduction to Spiritual Warfare Seminar."

"What year?" Gabriella asked, studying Sabine, attempting to recognize her.

"The first term of 1987," Sabine responded.

"My last year at the academy," Gabriella said.

"It was my favorite course."

"I am very glad to hear it," Gabriella said. "And now you can repay me by helping me solve a puzzle: 'As a hand at the loom wove this mystery, so a hand must unravel it.'" Gabriella watched Sabine as she repeated the line from Mrs. Rockefeller's letter, searching for a spark of recognition.

"I am here to assist in the unraveling," Sabine said. "And I now know what it is that I'm meant to free from the tapestry."

"Mrs. Rockefeller wove the strings into this tapestry?" Verlaine said.

"Actually," Sabine replied, "she hired a very adept professional to do the work for her. But yes, they are there, inside the Unicorn in Captivity tapestry."

Verlaine stared at the weave skeptically. "How in the hell will we get them out?"

Nonplussed, Sabine said, "If I am informed correctly, the procedure was skillfully performed and will leave no damage vhatsoever."

"It is odd that Abby Rockefeller would choose such a delicate piece of art as a shield," Gabriella noted.

Sabine said, "You must remember that once upon a time these tapestries were the private property of the Rockefellers. They hung in Abigail Rockefeller's living room from 1922, when her husband bought them, until the late 1930s, when they were brought here. Mrs. Rockefeller had a very intimate knowledge of the tapestries, including their weak spots." Sabine pointed at a heavily repaired patch on the weave. "See how it is irregular? One snip of the repair thread and it will open in a seam."

A museum security guard stationed at the far side of the room walked casually over to them. "Are you ready for us, Ms. Clementine?" he asked.

"Yes, thank you," Sabine responded, her manner becoming crisp and professional. "But we will need to clear the gallery first. Please call in the others." Sabine turned to Gabriella and Verlaine. "I have arranged to block off the area for the duration of the procedure. We will need complete freedom to work on the tapestry, a task that would be impossible in such a crowd."

"You can do that?" Verlaine asked, looking at the congested hall.

"Of course," Sabine said. "I am the associate director of restorations. I can arrange pairs as I see fit."

"What about that?" Verlaine asked, nodding to the security camera.

"I have taken care of everything, monsieur."

Verlaine gazed at the tapestry, realizing that they had very little time to locate the strings and remove them. As he'd originally suspected, the repaired fabric above the unicorn's horn, located in the upper third of the tapestry, contained the largest defect. It was high off the floor, perhaps six feet. One would have to stand upon a chair or a stool to reach it. The angle wouldn't be ideal. There was every possibility that the seam would be too difficult to open and that it would be necessary to remove the tapestry from the wall, spread it flat on the floor, and work it open there. This, however, would be the last resort.

A number of security guards entered the gallery and began directing people from the room. Once the space had been cleared, the guards stood watch at the door.

With the gallery emptied, Sabine escorted a short, bald man past the guards and to the tapestry, where he placed a metal case on the floor and unfolded a stepladder. Without so much as a glance at Gabriella or Verlaine, he climbed the stepladder and began to examine the seam.

"The glass, Ms. Clementine," the man said.

abine opened the case, revealing a row of alpels, threads, scissors, and a great magnifying glass, the last of which collected a bright swirl of light from the room and condensed it into a single ball of fire.

Verlaine watched as the man worked, fascinated by his confidence. He had often wondered at the skills of restoration and had even been to an exhibit that demonstrated the chemical processes used to clean fabrics such as these. Holding the magnifying glass in one hand and a scalpel in the other, the man worked the tip of the blade into a row of tight, neat stitches. With the slightest pressure, the stitches split apart. He opened one stitch after another in this fashion until a hole the size of an apple appeared in the tapestry. The man continued his work with the concentration of a surgeon.

Standing on tiptoes, Verlaine peered up at the unbound fabric. He could see nothing but a fray of colored threads, fine as hair. The man requested a tool from the case, and Sabine handed him a long, thin hook, which he inserted into the hole in the fabric. Then he slipped his hand directly between the *A* and the *E*. He tugged, and a bright spark caught Verlaine's eye: Twisted about the hook, there was an opalescent cord.

Verlaine counted them as the man handed him the strings. They were capillary-thin and so smooth that they slid between Verlaine's fingers as if waxed. Five, seven, ten strings limp and sumptuous, draped over his arm. The man climbed down the ladder. "That is all," he said, a look of sobriety upon his face, as if he had just desecrated a shrine.

Sabine took the strings, rolled them into a tight coil, and zipped them into a cloth pouch. Pressing it into Verlaine's palm, she said, "Follow me, madame, monsieur," and led Gabriella and Verlaine to the entrance of the gallery.

"Do you know how to attach them?" Sabine asked.

Gabriella said, "I will manage, I'm sure."

"Yes, of course," Sabine said, and with a snap of her finger the security guards collected around them, three on each side. "Be careful," Sabine said, kissing Gabriella on each cheek in the Parisian manner. "Good luck."

As the security guards escorted Gabriella and Verlaine through the museum, pushing past the ever-present crowd, it seemed to Verlaine that the studies he had undertaken, the frustrations and fruitless searches of academic life — somehow, all of it had delivered him to this moment of triumph. Gabriella walked at his side, the woman who had brought him to understand his calling as an angelologist and his future — if he dared to hope — with Evangeline. They passed under archway after archway, the heavy Romanesque architecture ielding to the light trelliswork of the Gothic, the pouch containing the strings of the lyre held tightly in his hand.

Riverside Church, Morningside Heights, New York City

Riverside Church was an imposing Gothic Revival cathedral rising above Columbia University. Together Vladimir and Saitou-san mounted the steps to a wooden door adorned with disks of iron, Saitou-san's high-heeled boots crunching upon the salt-strewn ice, a black shawl wrapped snugly about her shoulders.

As they walked inside, the light diminished to a honeyed glow. Vladimir blinked, his eyes readjusting to the ambience of the foyer. The church was empty. Straightening his tie, Vladimir walked past an alcove with an empty reception desk, up a set of steps, and into a large antechamber. The walls were creamy stone that rose to a confluence of jointed arches, one meeting another like wind-filled sails hoisted in a crowded harbor. Beyond, through a set of wide double doors, Vladimir ascertained the deepening hollow of the church nave.

His first impulse was to search the church,

he held back, his attention drawn to two
pper plaques hung on a wall. The first com-
emorated John D. Rockefeller Jr.'s generos-
ty in the building of the church. A second
plaque was a dedication to Laura Celestia
Spelman Rockefeller.

"Laura Celestia Spelman was Abigail Rockefeller's mother-in-law," Saitou-san whispered,
reading the plaque.

Vladimir said, "I believe the Rockefellers
were devout, especially the Cleveland generation. John D. Rockefeller Jr. paid for the construction of this church."

"That would explain Mrs. Rockefeller's access," Saitou-san said. "It would be impossible
to keep anything here without inside help."

"Inside help," a whining, high-pitched voice
said, "and a lot of cash."

Vladimir turned to find that a toadlike
old man in an elegant gray suit and neatly
combed gray hair had appeared in the hallway. A monocle encircled his left eye, its
gold chain hanging over his cheek. Vladimir
stepped back instinctively.

"Forgive me for startling you," the man
said. "My name is Mr. Gray, and I could not
help but notice you here." Mr. Gray appeared
to be half blind with anxiety. His eyes bulged
wildly as he looked about the hallway, his gaze
settling at last upon Vladimir and Saitou-
san.

"I would ask who you are," Mr. Gray said,

pointing to Abigail Rockefeller's card in Vladimir's hand. "But I know already. May I?" Mr. Gray took the card from Vladimir, looked it over carefully, and said, "I have seen this before. In fact, I helped arrange for the printing of these cards when I worked as Mrs. Rockefeller's errand boy. I was merely fourteen. I once overheard her say that she liked my obsequious manner, which I tend to believe was a compliment. She had me running her errands — downtown for paper, uptown to the printers, downtown to pay the artist."

"Then perhaps you will tell us the meaning of the card?" Saitou-san said.

"She believed," Mr. Gray said, ignoring Saitou-san, "that angelologists would be coming."

"And we have arrived," Vladimir said. "Can you tell us how we're meant to proceed?"

"I will answer your questions directly," Mr. Gray said. "But we must first go to my office, where we might speak with more ease."

They descended a stone staircase off the antechamber, Mr. Gray moving downward at a rapid pace, skipping steps in his haste. At the bottom a darkened hallway opened before them. Mr. Gray threw open a door and ushered them into a narrow office piled high with papers. Stacks of unopened mail tipped from the edge of a metal desk. Curled pencil shavings were scattered across the floor. A wall calendar from the year 1978 hung next to a filing cabinet, the month of December left open.

Once they were inside the office, Mr. Gray's manner became one of indignation. "Well! You have certainly taken your own sweet time in coming," he said. "I was beginning to think there was some misunderstanding. Mrs. Rockefeller would have been furious at that — she would turn in her grave if I'd died without delivering the package in the fashion she wished. An exacting woman, Mrs. Rockefeller, but very generous — my children and my children's children will feel the benefit of the arrangement, even if I, who have been waiting half of my life for your arrival, will not! I was but a young man when she hired me to oversee the workings of the church office — fresh from England, without a position in the world. Mrs. Rockefeller gave me my place here in this office, instructing me to await your arrival, which I have done, ceaselessly. Of course, provisions were made should I have expired before your arrival — which I must say could have happened any day now, since clearly I'm not growing any younger — but let's not allow ourselves to ponder such morbid thoughts, no, sir. At this important hour, it is only the wishes of our benefactress that must concern us, and her thoughts turned upon a single solemn hope: the future." Mr. Gray blinked and adjusted his monocle. "Come, let's get down to business."

"An excellent idea," Vladimir said.

Mr. Gray went to the filing cabinet, pulled a ring of keys from his pocket, and proceeded to work through the number until he discovered the match. With a turn of the key, the cabinet drawer popped open. "Let me see," he said, straining to see the files. "Ah, yes, here! The very documents we need." He flipped through the pages, stopping at a long list of names. "This is a formality, of course, but Mrs. Rockefeller specified that only those appearing on this list — or the descendants of these persons — would be authorized to receive the package. Is your name, or the name of one of your parents or grandparents, or indeed your great-grandparents, among this number?"

Vladimir scanned the list, recognizing all the major angelologists of the twentieth century. He found his own name in the middle of the final row, next to Celestine Clochette's.

"If you don't mind, you will sign here and here. And then once more here, on this line at the bottom."

Vladimir examined the paper, a long legal document that, from a cursory view, affirmed that Mr. Gray had performed the task of delivering the object.

"You see," Mr. Gray said by way of apology, "I receive my remuneration only after the delivery has been performed, as evidenced by your signature. The legal document is quite specific, and the lawyers are unrelenting — it has been inconvenient, as you might imagine, living without recompense for my labors. All these years I have scraped by, waiting for you to arrive so that I might retire from this wretched office. And here you are," Mr. Gray said, giving Vladimir a pen. "Simply a formality, mind you."

"Before I sign," Vladimir said, pushing the document away, "I must have the object you're holding for me."

An almost imperceptible chill hardened upon Mr. Gray's features. "Of course," he said tersely. He slipped the contract under his arm and tucked the pen into the pocket of his gray suit. "Just this way," he said, his voice clipped as he led them out of the office and up the stairs.

As they returned to the upper level of the church, Vladimir hung back, shadowed in the recesses of the hall. His study of ethereal musicology had consumed his youth, driving him deeper and deeper into the closed world of angelological work. After the war he'd left the discipline. He had run a humble bakery, making confections and cakes, the simplicity of which gave him comfort. He had believed that his work was futile, that there was little humanity could do to stop the Nephilim. He returned only after Gabriella had come to him herself, pleading with him to join their efforts. She had said that they needed him.

At the time he'd been doubtful, but Gabriella could be quite persuasive, and he could see the dark changes that had begun to occur. He could not say how he knew — perhaps it was the rigorous training of his youth or perhaps simple intuition — but Vladimir understood that Mr. Gray was not to be trusted.

Mr. Gray walked haltingly up the central aisle of the nave, bringing Vladimir and Saitou-san into the cool dark church. The scent was instantly familiar to Vladimir, the mossy fragrance of incense filling the air. Despite innumerable stained-glass windows, the space remained dark, nearly impenetrable. Above, Gothic candelabras hung by thick ropes, oxidized-iron wheels of intricate fretwork topped with candles. A massive Gothic pulpit, ring after ring of sculpted figures climbing the sides, rose at the altar, while Christmas poinsettias, bright red ribbons tied about their pots, stood on pedestals throughout the church. Separated from the nave by a thick maroon cord, the apse lay in shadows before them.

Mr. Gray unclipped the velvet rope and dropped it to the floor, the buckle echoing through the nave. Worked into the marble floor was a stonework labyrinth. Mr. Gray tapped his toe upon it, nervous, creating a frantic rhythm. "Mrs. Rockefeller placed it here," Mr. Gray said, sliding his shoe over the chancel. "At the center of the labyrinth."

Vladimir walked the length of the pattern, examining the lay of the stones with care — it seemed impossible that anything could be hidden in it. It would have required breaking the stones, something he could not imagine that Mrs. Rockefeller, or anyone else involved in the care and preservation of art, would condone. "But how?" Vladimir asked. "It looks perfectly smooth."

"Ah, yes," Mr. Gray said, moving to Vladimir's side. "That is simply an illusion. Come, look closely."

Vladimir squatted to the floor and examined the marble. A thin, fine seam had been cut along the border of the central stone. "It is practically invisible," Vladimir said.

"Step away," Mr. Gray said. Positioning himself over the stone, he applied pressure to its center. The stone lifted from the floor as if on springs. With a twist of his hand, Mr. Gray removed the central stone of the labyrinth.

"Amazing," Saitou-san said, watching over his shoulder.

"There is nothing a fine stonemason and an abundance of funds cannot achieve," Mr. Gray said. "You were acquainted with the late Mrs. Rockefeller?"

"No," Vladimir said. "Not personally."

"Ah, well, a pity," Mr. Gray said. "She had a keen sense of social justice marked with the folly of a poetic nature — a combination quite rare in women of her stature. Originally she designated that when angelologists arrived to claim the object under my care, I was to lead whoever came here to the labyrinth and ask for a series of numbers. Mrs. Rockefeller assured me that whoever came would know these numbers. I have them memorized, of course."

"Numbers?" Vladimir said, baffled by this unexpected test.

"Numbers, sir." Mr. Gray gestured to the center of the labyrinth. Below the stone there was a safe, a combination lock at its center. "You will need numbers to open this. I suppose you might think of yourself as the Minotaur making your way into the stone labyrinth." He smiled, enjoying the bafflement he had caused.

Vladimir stared at the safe, its door perfectly flush with the floor beneath the labyrinth as Saitou-san bent over it. Saitou-san said, "How many numbers in each combination?"

"That, I cannot tell you," Mr. Gray said.

Saitou-san turned each of the dials in succession. "Abigail Rockefeller's cards were made specifically for Innocenta to decode," she said, speaking slowly, as if searching her thoughts. "Innocenta's responses affirmed that she had counted the lyre strings on the cards and had — I assume — written down the numbers."

"The sequence," Vladimir said, "was twenty-eight, thirty, thirty-eight, and thirty-nine."

Saitou-san turned each of the four dials to correspond with the numbers and pulled at the safe. It didn't open.

"This is the only sequence of numbers we have," Saitou-san said. "They must work in some combination."

"Four numbers and four dials," Vladimir said. "That makes twenty-four different possible combinations. There is no way we can try all of them. There isn't time."

"Unless," Saitou-san said, "there was a designated order to the numbers. Do you remember the chronology in which they were given? Verlaine told us the sequence in which numbers appeared on the cards."

Vladimir thought for a moment. "Twenty-eight, thirty-eight, thirty, and finally thirty-nine."

Saitou-san moved each dial, aligning the numbers carefully. Wrapping her finger around a metal lever, she pulled the handle of the safe. It lifted without resistance, exhaling a soft gush of air. Reaching into the cavity, she withdrew a heavy bundle of green velvet and unwrapped it. The sound chest of the lyre threw waves of golden illumination over the stone labyrinth.

"It is lovely," Saitou-san said, turning it to examine it from all angles. The base was round. Two identical arms bowed out and then curled, like the horns of a bull. The golden surfaces were smooth and polished to a gleam. "But there are no strings."

"Nor is there a yoke," Vladimir said. He knelt by Saitou-san's side and looked at the instrument cradled in her hands. "It is just one piece of the lyre. A most important piece, but alone it is useless. This must be why we were sent to four locations. The pieces have been scattered."

"We need to tell the others," Saitou-san said, carefully returning the lyre's body to the velvet bag. "They need to know what they are looking for."

Vladimir turned and faced Mr. Gray, who stood trembling between them. "You didn't know the combination. You've been waiting for us to come and give it to you. If you had known, you would have taken it yourself."

"There is no need to worry about what I know or do not know," Mr. Gray said, his face growing red from perspiration. "The treasure belongs to neither of us."

"What do you mean?" Saitou-san asked, incredulous.

"His meaning," said a voice at the far end of the apse, a familiar voice that sent chills of terror through Vladimir, "is that the game has been over for many years. It is a game that the angelologists have lost."

In his fright Mr. Gray's monocle fell from his eye, and without a moment of hesitation, he scurried from the apse and into a side aisle of the nave, the fabric of his gray suit appearing and disappearing as he traversed puddles of light and shadow. Watching Mr. Gray flee, Vladimir made out bands of Gibborish creatures along the aisles of the church, their white hair and red wings visible in the dull light. The creatures turned to watch as Mr. Gray passed, avid as sunflowers to the movement of the sun. Before he could escape, however, a Gibborim seized Mr. Gray. As Vladimir watched, all doubt cleared about the nature of the meeting: The angelologists had fallen into a trap. Percival Grigori had been waiting for them.

The last time Vladimir had met Grigori was many decades before, when Vladimir was a young protégé of Raphael Valko. He had seen firsthand the atrocities the Grigori family had perpetrated during the war. He had also witnessed the great pain they'd inflicted upon angelologists — Seraphina Valko had lost her life because of Percival Grigori's machinations, and Gabriella had come close to dying as well. Back then Percival Grigori had cut a startling, fearsome figure. Now he was a sickly mutant.

Grigori gestured and the Gibborim brought Mr. Gray forward.

Without warning, Grigori cracked the ivory head of his cane from the shaft, twisting the steel blade of a dagger from its mooring. For a second the knife glinted in the weak light. Then, in one swift movement, Grigori stepped forward and plunged the dagger into Mr. Gray's body. Gray's expression changed from surprise to disbelief and then to wilting, disconsolate anguish. As Percival Grigori withdrew the knife, Mr. Gray collapsed to the floor, whimpering softly, blood collecting about him. In a matter of moments, his eyes held the watery gaze of death. As swiftly as he'd unsheathed the knife, Percival wiped it clean on a white square of silk and inserted it back into the shaft of the cane.

Vladimir saw that Saitou-san had edged away from him with the sound chest in hand, slinking silently toward the rear of the church. By the time Percival noticed, she was within reach of the door. Percival lifted his hand and ordered the Gibborim after her. Half of the creatures turned upon her, while the remaining Gibborim stepped forward, the hems of their robes brushing against the floor as they surrounded the apse. With a second gesture, Percival instructed these creatures to take hold of Vladimir.

Clutched tightly in their grasp, Vladimir inhaled the scent of the creatures' skin; he felt the chill of their bodies behind him. A cool gust of air swept the nape of his neck as the creatures beat their wings, steadily, rhythmically.

"She will take the lyre to Gabriella!" Vladimir cried, struggling against the hold of the creatures.

Percival looked upon Vladimir with contempt. "I was hoping to see my dear Gabriella. I know that she is behind this little recovery mission. She has become quite elusive over the years."

Vladimir closed his eyes. He recalled that Gabriella's infiltration into the Grigori family had been a sensation in the angelological community, the largest, most influential undercover job of the 1940s. Indeed, her work had paved the way for modern surveillance of the Nephilistic families and brought them useful information. But it had created a dangerous legacy for all of them. After so many years, Percival Grigori still wanted revenge.

Leaning heavily upon his cane, Grigori hobbled to Vladimir. "Tell me," he said. "Where is she?"

Percival leaned close to Vladimir, so that he could see the purple pouches under Percival's eyes, thick as bruises on his white skin. His teeth were perfectly even, so white they seemed plated in pearl. And yet Percival was aging — a net of fine lines had developed about his mouth. He must have reached at least three hundred years.

"I remember you," Percival said, narrowing his eyes as if comparing the man before him with one in his memory. "You were in my presence in Paris. I recall your face, although time has changed you almost beyond recognition. You helped Gabriella to deceive me."

"And you," Vladimir said, recovering his

equilibrium, "betrayed everything you believed in — your family, your ancestors. Even now you haven't forgotten her. Tell me: How badly do you miss Gabriella Lévi-Franche?"

"Where is she?" Percival said, staring into Vladimir's eyes.

"That I will never tell you," Vladimir said, his voice catching as he spoke. He knew that with those words he had chosen to die.

Percival released the ivory-headed cane from his grip. It fell to the floor, sending a sharp echo through the church. He placed his long, cold fingers upon Vladimir's chest, as if to feel his heartbeat. An electrical vibration surged through Vladimir, shattering his ability to think. In the last minutes of his life, his lungs burning for air, Vladimir was drawn into the horrifying translucency of his killer's eyes. They were pale and ringed with red, intense as a chemical fire stabilized in a frozen atmosphere.

As Vladimir's consciousness dissolved, he remembered the delicious sensation of the lyre's body, heavy and cool in his hands, and how he had longed to hear its ethereal melody.

Rockefeller Center Ice Skating Rink, Fifth Avenue, New York City

Evangeline glanced at the rink, following the skaters' slow, circular progress. Colored lights fell upon the glossy surface of the ice, skittering under blades and disappearing in the shadows. In the distance a tremendous Christmas tree rose against a solid gray building, its red and silver lights glinting like a million fireflies captured in a glass cone. Rows of majestic herald angels, their wings delicate and white as lily petals, stood below the tree like a legion of sentries, their wire bodies illuminated, their elongated brass trumpets raised in choral praise to the heavens. The shops along the concourse — bookstores and clothing stores, stationery shops and chocolatiers — had begun to close, sending customers into the night with gifts and shopping bags tucked under their arms.

Pulling her overcoat close, Evangeline wrapped herself in a cocoon of warmth. She cradled the cold metal casket — the crossbars of the lyre tucked safely inside — in her hands.

756

At her side, Bruno Bechstein and Alistair Carroll scanned the masses beyond the rink. Hundreds and hundreds of people filled the plaza. "White Christmas" played through a tiny overhead speaker, its melody punctuated by laughter from the skating rink. Fifteen minutes remained until the designated meeting time, and the others were nowhere to be found. The air was crisp, smelling of snow. Evangeline inhaled, and a fit of coughing overtook her. Her lungs were so tight she could hardly breathe. What had begun as simple discomfort in her chest had grown in the past hours to a full-blown hack. Each breath she took felt labored, giving her only the slightest bit of air.

Alistair Carroll removed his scarf and placed it gently around Evangeline's collar. "You are freezing, my dear," he said. "Protect yourself from this wind."

"I've hardly noticed it," Evangeline said, drawing the thick, soft wool about her neck. "I'm too worried to feel anything. The others should be here by now."

"It was at this time of year that we came to Rockefeller Center with the fourth piece of the lyre," Alistair said. "Christmas 1944. I drove Abby here in the middle of the night and helped her through a terrible storm. Luckily, she had the foresight to call the security personnel herself, informing them that we would be coming. Their assistance proved most useful."

"So you are aware of what is hidden here?" Bruno said. "You've seen it?"

"Oh, yes," Alistair said. "I packed the tuning pegs of the lyre into the protective case myself. It was quite an ordeal, finding a case that would allow us to hide the pegs here, but Abby was certain that this was the best place. I carried the case in my own hands and assisted Mrs. Rockefeller in locking it away. The pegs are tiny, and so the case is merely the weight of a pocketwatch without its fob. It is so very compact that one cannot conceive that it could hold something so essential to the instrument. But it is a fact: The lyre will not produce a note without the pegs."

Evangeline tried to imagine the small knobs, envisioning how they fit onto the crossbar. "Do you know how to reassemble it?" Evangeline asked.

"Like all things, there is an order one must follow," Alistair said. "Once the crossbar is fitted into the arms of the lyre's base, the strings must be wound about the tuning pegs, each at a certain tension. The difficulty, I believe, is in the tuning of the lyre, a skill that requires a trained ear."

Directing their attention to the angels collected before the Christmas tree, he added, "I assure you that the lyre looks nothing at all like the stereotypical instruments held by the herald angels. The wire angels at the base of the Christmas tree were introduced to Rockefeller Center in 1954, one year after Philip Johnson completed the Abby Aldrich Rockefeller Sculpture Garden and ten years after the treasure's interment here. Although these lovely creatures' appearance here was purely coincidental — Mrs. Rockefeller had passed away by then, and nobody, save myself, knew about what had been hidden here — I find the symbolism rather exquisite. It is fitting, this collection of heralds, wouldn't you say? One feels it the moment one enters the plaza at Christmastime: Here is the treasure of the angels, waiting to be uncovered."

"The case was not placed near the Christmas tree?" Evangeline asked.

"Not at all," Alistair replied, gesturing to the statue at the far end of the skating rink, where the statue of Prometheus rose above the rink, its smooth gilded-bronze surface wrapped in light. "The case is part of the Prometheus statue. There it lies, in its gilded prison."

Evangeline studied the sculpture of Prometheus. It was a soaring figure that appeared to be caught in midair. The fire stolen from the hearth of the gods blazed in his tapering fingers, and a bronze ring of the zodiac encircled his feet. Evangeline knew the myth of Prometheus well. After stealing fire from the gods, Prometheus was punished by Zeus, who bound him to a rock and sent an eagle to peck at his body for eternity. Prometheus's punishment was equated with his crime: The gift of fire marked the beginning of human innovation and technology, harkening the gods' growing irrelevance.

"I have never seen the statue up close," Evangeline said. In the light of the skating rink, the skin of the sculpture appeared molten. Prometheus and the fire he'd stolen were one incendiary entity.

"It is no masterpiece," Alistair said. "Nevertheless, it suits Rockefeller Center perfectly. Paul Manship was a friend of the Rockefeller family's — they knew his work well and commissioned him to create the sculpture. There is more than a passing reference to my former employers in the myth of Prometheus — their ingenuity and ruthlessness, their trickery, their dominance. Manship knew that these references would not be lost on John D. Rockefeller Jr., who had used all his influence to build Rockefeller Center during the Great Depression."

"Nor are they lost on us," Gabriella said, surprising Evangeline as she appeared among them, Verlaine at her side. "Prometheus holds fire in his hands, but thanks to Mrs. Rockefeller he holds something even more important as well."

"Gabriella," Evangeline said. Relief overcame her as she hugged her grandmother. Only then, feeling Gabriella's frail embrace, did she realize how worried she'd been.

"You have the other pieces of the lyre?" Gabriella said, impatient. "Show them to me."

Evangeline opened the casket holding the crossbar, showing her grandmother the contents. Gabriella unfastened the leather case, where she had kept the cloth pouch containing the lyre's strings, the plectrum, and the angelological notebook, then set the casket inside. Only after collecting the pieces of the instruments in the case and making sure that it was securely closed did Gabriella notice Alistair Carroll standing at the periphery of the group. She examined him warily until Evangeline introduced him, explaining his relationship with Mrs. Rockefeller and the assistance he had offered them.

"Do you know how to remove the pegs from the statue?" Gabriella inquired, her manner one of intense purpose, as if a lifetime of expertise had been distilled into this one moment. "You know where they have been hidden?"

"The precise location, madam," Alistair said. "It has been etched upon my mind for half a century."

"Where are Vladimir and Saitou-san?" Bruno asked, suddenly realizing that they were missing two angelologists.

Verlaine checked his watch. He stood so close to Evangeline that she could read the time. It was 6:13.

"They should be here by now," Evangeline said.

Bruno looked at the Prometheus statue

761

glinting at the far end of the skating rink. "We can't wait much longer."

"We can't wait another second," Gabriella said. "It is too dangerous to expose ourselves in this fashion."

"Were you followed?" Alistair asked, clearly alarmed by Gabriella's anxious manner.

"Gabriella believes we were," Verlaine said, "although we were fortunate enough to complete our work at the Cloisters without trouble."

"This was part of their plan," Gabriella said, scanning the crowd as if she might find the enemy lurking in the mass of shoppers. "We left the Cloisters unmolested because they chose to let us do so. We can't wait another moment. Vladimir and Saitou-san will be here soon enough."

"In that case let us proceed immediately," Alistair said, displaying a calm Evangeline found admirable, reminding her of the stalwart sisters of St. Rose Convent she'd left behind.

Alistair led them along the edge of the plaza and down a concrete stairway to the rink. Walking alongside the plastic wall bordering the ice, they made their way toward the statue. The GE Building soared before them, its great façade broken by a row of flags — American, British, French, Portuguese, German, Dutch, Spanish, Japanese, Italian, Chinese, Greek, Brazilian, Korean — the unrelenting wind lifting them into the air in whorls of color. Perhaps the years of isolation at St. Rose had made Evangeline sensitive to crowds — she found herself examining the people gathering around the rink. There were teenagers in tight jeans and ski jackets; there were parents with little children; there were young lovers and middle-aged couples, all skating around and around one another. The crowd made her see how far away from the world she had lived.

Suddenly she spotted a dark-cloaked figure not five feet from her. Tall, pale-skinned, with great red eyes, the creature stared intently at her, a menacing expression on its face. Evangeline turned in all directions, panic coursing through her. Gibborim had mixed within the crowd, each tall, dark figure standing in silent attention.

Evangeline grasped Verlaine's hand and drew him closer. "Look," she whispered. "They're here."

"You have to leave," he said, meeting her eye. "Now, before we're trapped."

"I think it's too late for that," Evangeline said, glancing around them, her terror growing. The number of Gibborim had multiplied. "They are everywhere."

"Come with me," he said, pulling her away from the cluster of angelologists. "We can leave together."

"Not now," Evangeline said, leaning close

so that only he could hear her. "We have to help Gabriella."

"But what if we fail?" Verlaine said. "What if something happens to you?"

She smiled slightly and said, "You know, you are the only person in the world who knows my favorite place. Someday I'd like to go there with you."

Evangeline heard her name and they both turned. Gabriella was beckoning to them.

As they joined the angelologists, Alistair was examining the crowd. His expression solidified into one of horror. Evangeline followed his gaze to the end of the skating rink, where a cluster of the stark white creatures, their wings carefully hidden under long black cloaks, had gathered at the statue of Prometheus. In the middle of it all stood a tall, elegant man leaning heavily upon a cane.

"Who is that?" Evangeline asked, pointing to the man.

"That," Gabriella said, "is Percival Grigori."

Evangeline recognized his name at once. This was Verlaine's client, Percival Grigori of the infamous Grigori family. This was also the man who had killed her mother. She watched him from a distance, transfixed by the terrible spectacle. She'd never met him before, but Percival Grigori had destroyed her family.

Gabriella said, "Your mother looked very like him. Her height, her coloring, and her

big blue eyes. I was always worried that sh
was too much like him." Her voice was so
quiet that Evangeline could hardly hear her.
"It terrified me how Nephilistic my Angela
appeared. My biggest fear was that she would
grow to be like him."

Before Evangeline could respond to this
cryptic message — and the horrifying impli-
cations it foretold — Grigori raised a hand
and the creatures embedded in the crowd
stepped forward. They were more numerous
than Evangeline had initially thought — row
upon row of black-cloaked figures, pale and
skeletal, appeared from nowhere, as if they
had materialized out of the cold, dry evening
air. Evangeline watched, awestruck, as they
pushed toward her. Soon the periphery of the
ice darkened with a nimbus of creatures. A
collective consternation appeared to immobi-
lize the skaters as the Gibborim encroached.
They left off from their hypnotic circling and
looked askance at the growing population
looming around them, pausing to examine
the strange figures with curiosity rather than
fear. Children pointed to them in wonder,
while adults, perhaps inured by the everyday
spectacles of the city, endeavored to ignore
the strange events entirely. Then, in one swift
motion, the Gibborim swarmed the railings of
the plaza. The collective trance of immobility
shattered in an instant. Masses of frightened
people were suddenly surrounded on all sides.

he angelologists were caught at the center of an elaborate net.

Evangeline heard someone call her grandmother's name and turned to find Saitou-san making her way through the throng. Evangeline knew instantly that something terrible must have happened at Riverside Church. Saitou-san had been injured. Cuts covered her face, and her jacket was ripped. Worst of all, she was alone.

"Where is Vladimir?" Gabriella asked, looking over Saitou-san with concern.

"He isn't here yet?" Saitou-san asked, out of breath. "We were separated at Riverside Church. Gibborim were there, with Grigori. I don't know how they would know to come here, unless Vladimir told them."

"You left him?" Gabriella asked.

"I ran. I had no choice." Saitou-san pulled out a velvet bundle that had been hidden inside her coat and cradled an object against her body as if it were a baby. "It was the only way to get out with this."

"The base of the lyre," Gabriella said, taking it from Saitou-san. "You found it."

"Yes," Saitou-san said. "Did you recover the other pieces?"

"All but the tuning pegs," Evangeline said. "Which are there, in the middle of the Gibborim."

Saitou-san and Gabriella gazed at the skating rink, which had become filled with

Gibborim.

Calling Bruno to them, Gabriella spoke to him in a low, commanding voice. Try as she might, Evangeline could not make out her grandmother's words, only the urgency with which they were uttered. Finally Gabriella took Evangeline by the arm. "Go with Bruno," she said, placing the leather case containing the pieces of the instrument in Evangeline's hands. "Do exactly as he tells you. You must take these as far from here as you can. If all goes well, I will be with you soon."

The contours of the skating rink wavered at the edges of Evangeline's vision as her eyes filled with tears — somehow, despite her grandmother's assurance to the contrary, she felt that she would not see Gabriella again. Perhaps Gabriella understood her thoughts. She opened her arms and took Evangeline into them, hugging her tightly. Kissing her lightly upon the cheek, Gabriella whispered, "Angelology is not simply an occupation. It is a calling. Your work is just beginning, my dear Evangeline. Already you are everything I hoped you would be."

Without another word, Gabriella followed Alistair through the crowd. Making their way alongside the ice rink, they disappeared into the chaotic crush of movement and noise.

Bruno took Verlaine and Evangeline by the arms and guided them up the concrete steps to the main plaza, Saitou-san following close behind. They did not stop until they were standing among the rows of flags behind the statue of Prometheus. From above, Evangeline saw the danger Gabriella and Alistair were in: The skating rink had become a solid swarm of creatures, a horrifying congregation that stopped Evangeline cold.

"What are they doing?" Verlaine asked.

"They are walking into the center of the Gibborim," Saitou-san said.

"We have to help them," Evangeline said.

"Gabriella was clear about what we should do," Bruno said, although the worry in his voice and the deep furrows lining his brow belied his words. It was obvious that Gabriella's actions terrified him as well. "She must know what she's doing."

"Perhaps she does," Verlaine said. "But how in the hell is she going to get out of there?"

Below, the Nephilim parted, making a path for Gabriella and Alistair to walk unimpeded to Grigori, who stood near the statue of Prometheus. Gabriella appeared smaller, more fragile in the shadow of the creatures, and the reality of their situation hit Evangeline with full force: The same passion and dedication that drove the Venerable Father Clematis to descend into the depths of the gorge and face the unknown and the drive to knowledge that had sealed her own mother's murder — these were the forces that brought Gabriella to fight Percival Grigori.

In a distant part of her consciousness, Evangeline understood the choreography of h[er] grandmother's plan — she saw Gabriella arguing with Grigori, diverting his attention as Alistair ran to the statue of Prometheus — yet she was shocked by the directness of Alistair's execution. Stepping gingerly into the pool of water, he waded to the statue's base, mist soaking his clothes and hair as he climbed to the golden ring encircling Prometheus's body. Ice must have made the edge slippery: instead of climbing farther, he reached along the interior of the ring and grasped at something behind it. From her vantage directly above the statue, Evangeline could not be certain of the mechanics of the procedure. And yet it appeared that Alistair was unfastening something from behind the ring. As he lifted it free, she saw that he had detached a small bronze box.

"Evangeline!" Alistair called, his voice almost drowned out by the fountain, so that she hardly hear him. "Catch!"

Alistair threw the box. It flew over the Prometheus statue, over the transparent plastic barrier between the skating rink and the concourse, and fell at Evangeline's feet. She scooped it from the sidewalk and held it in her hand. The box was oblong and as heavy as a golden egg.

Clutching the case to her chest, Evangeline assessed the plaza once more. On one side, the ice rink was blocked by people removing tes with studied nonchalance. The Gibborim had begun to slowly encircle Alistair n the ice. He appeared frail and vulnerable compared to the Gibborim, and when the creatures descended upon him, Evangeline touched the soft woolen scarf he had given her, wishing she could do something to help him escape. But it was impossible to get close to him. Within minutes, the creatures would finish their gruesome business with Alistair Carroll and turn upon the angelologists.

Aware of the dire turn in their predicament, Bruno looked about the concourse for an escape route. At last he appeared to arrive at a conclusion. "Come," he said, gesturing to Verlaine and Evangeline to follow him along the plaza.

Grigori barked something to them and, drawing a gun from his pocket, put it to Gabriella's head.

"Come, Evangeline," Bruno said, his voice filled with urgency. "Now."

But Evangeline could not follow him. Looking from Bruno to her grandmother, held captive at the center of the ice, she understood that she had to act quickly. She knew that Gabriella would want her to follow Bruno — there was no doubt that the case containing the lyre was more important than the life of any one of them — and yet she could not simply turn and leave her grandmother to die.

She squeezed Verlaine's hand and, pulling

herself away, ran to her grandmother. Dow
the steps and onto the ice she ran, knowing
even as she went that she was putting their
lives — and much more — in danger. Even
so, she could not just leave Gabriella. She had
lost everyone. Gabriella was all she had left.

On the ice, Gibborim held Gabriella at
Grigori's side, one gruesome creature to each
of her arms. Gibborim closed in behind Evangeline as she made her way across the skating rink, sealing her path. She could not go
back.

"Come," Grigori said, gesturing to Evangeline with his cane. Eyeing the bronze box
Alistair had thrown her, he said, "Bring it
here. Give it to me."

Evangeline walked closer until she stood
before Grigori. Looking him over, she took in
his appearance, shocked at his condition. He
was nothing at all as she had imagined him
to be. He was hunched, frail, and gaunt. He
extended his withered hand, and Evangeline
placed the bronze box from the Prometheus
statue in his palm. Grigori held it up to the
light and examined it, as if unsure what such a
tiny box could contain. Smiling, he dropped it
into his pocket and, with a sweep of his hand,
snatched the leather case from Evangeline.

Verlaine knew that the creatures' wings were tucked under their black cloaks, and he understood the destruction they were capable of inflicting if they were to deploy them. Yet to the ordinary person the creatures appeared to be little more than a band of oddly dressed men performing some bizarre ritual on the ice. They followed Grigori's orders, assembling around him at the center of the rink, creating an impenetrable wall between Grigori and the angelologists. The orchestrations of the Gibborim would have absorbed Verlaine's entire attention if it were not for the fact that Evangeline stood surrounded by this dark horde of creatures.

"Stay here," Bruno said, gesturing for Verlaine to remain where he stood, above the Prometheus statue. "Saitou-san, take the stairs. I'm going to go to the other side of the rink and see if I can divert Grigori."

"It's impossible," Saitou-san said. "Look at how many of them there are."

Bruno paused, staring out over the rin. "We can't leave them out there," he said his anguish apparent. "We have to try some thing."

Bruno and Saitou-san ran off, leaving Verlaine to watch helplessly from his perch. He could hardly keep himself from jumping over the barrier onto the ice. He felt sick at the sight of Evangeline in danger, and yet he could do nothing at all to rescue her. He had known her only one day and yet the thought of losing whatever future awaited him with her terrified him. He called her name, and through the chaos of creatures she looked up at him. Even as Grigori pushed her ahead, steering her and Gabriella from the ice, she had heard Verlaine calling to her.

For a second, Verlaine felt as if he were outside himself, watching his misery from a distance. The irony of his position wasn't lost on him: He had become the destitute tragicomic leading man watching the woman he loved be swept away by a dastardly villain. It was amazing how love had the power to make him feel that he was both a Hollywood cliché and an utter original at once. He loved Evangeline, this he knew for certain. He would do anything for her.

At the opposite end of the rink, Bruno was watching the creatures. It was plain that he would be vastly outnumbered if he went into the mêlée of Gibborim. Even if the three of

em went in at once, it would be impossible
 reach Gabriella and Evangeline. From her
position at the stairs, Saitou-san awaited a signal to go in. But Bruno, like Verlaine, could
see the hopelessness of their position. There
was nothing they could do but watch.

A rumbling noise consumed the din of city
sounds. At first Verlaine was unable to discern
the source of the noise — it began as a soft
stirring in the distance and grew in a matter
of seconds to the distinct growl of an engine.
Scanning the plaza, he saw that a black utility
van, identical to the vans he'd found parked
outside of St. Rose Convent, was driving over
the concourse to the skating rink, cutting a
path through the crowd.

As the van approached, Grigori waved the
gun at Gabriella and Evangeline, pushing
them up the steps. Verlaine strained to see
Evangeline, but Gibborim stood on each side
of her, blocking his view. As the entourage
passed Saitou-san, he could detect a moment
of indecision in her manner. For an instant it
appeared as if she might push past the Gibborim and tackle Grigori herself. Realizing
that she was far too weak she did nothing.

Grigori forced Evangeline and Gabriella into
the van, pushing them inside with the gun and
swinging the door closed in one quick motion.
As the van drove away, Verlaine called out to
Evangeline, desperately, his helplessness filling him with anger. He ran after the van, past

Christmas lights, past the herald angels wi their golden trumpets raised to the black nigh sky, past the immense evergreen tree adorned with colored lights. The van turned into traffic and disappeared. Evangeline was gone.

The Gibborim dispersed, climbing the stairs and disappearing into the crowds of confused people, sliding away as if nothing had happened at all. When the ice was clear, Verlaine ran down the stairs and walked onto the rink where Evangeline had been. He slipped forward and back on the soles of his sneakers, balancing himself as he went. The spotlights trained over the ice left a swirling polish upon its surface, gold and blue and orange, like an opal. Something at the center of the rink caught his eye. He squatted on his haunches. Running his finger over the cold surface, he lifted a glimmering golden chain. A lyre pendant had been pressed into the ice.

East Forty-eighth Street and Park Avenue, New York City

Percival Grigori ordered the driver to turn onto Park Avenue and head north to his apartment, where Sneja and his father would be waiting for him. The wide avenue was clogged with traffic; they moved forward in incremental lurches. The black branches of winter trees had been strung with thousands of colored lights that rose and fell along the median, reminding him that human sects were still celebrating their holiday gatherings. Holding the case, its aged, scuffed leather rough under his fingers, Percival knew that for once Sneja would be pleased. He could almost imagine the pleasure she would show when he placed the lyre and Gabriella Lévi-Franche Valko at her feet. With Otterley gone, he was Sneja's last hope. Surely this would redeem him.

Gabriella sat across from him, glaring with pure contempt. It had been more than fifty years since their last meeting, and yet his feelings for her were as strong — and as conflicted — as they'd been the day he'd ordered her capture. Gabriella hated him now, [much] much was clear, but he had always admi[red] the strength of her feelings: Whether it [is] passion or hatred or fear, she felt each emotio[n] with the entirety of her being. He'd believed that her power over him had ended, and yet he could feel himself grow weak in her presence. She had lost her youth and beauty, but she was still dangerously magnetic. Although he had the power to take her life in an instant, she appeared utterly unafraid. This would change once they reached his mother. Sneja had never been intimidated by Gabriella.

As the van slowed and stopped at a traffic light, Percival studied the young woman at Gabriella's side. It seemed absurd, but her resemblance to the Gabriella he'd known fifty years before — her creamy white skin, the shape of her green eyes — was uncanny. It was as if the Gabriella of his fantasies had materialized before him. The young woman also wore a golden lyre pendant about her neck, the identical pendant Gabriella had worn in Paris, a necklace he knew she would never part with.

Suddenly, before Percival had the chance to react, Gabriella flung open the door of the van, grabbed the case from Percival's lap, and leaped out into the street, the young woman following close behind.

Percival screamed for the driver to follow them. Cutting through the red light, the turned right onto Fifty-first, driving the ong way on a one-way street — but even as e van was upon them, the women evaded ., running across Lexington Avenue and disappearing into a staircase down to the subway. Percival grabbed his cane and jumped through the door Gabriella had left open, pushing himself forward with all his strength. He ran as best he could through the crowds, his body aching with each halting step.

He had never been inside a subway station in New York City, and the MetroCard machines and the maps and the turnstiles were strange and unreadable. He was at a loss for how it all worked. Many years ago he'd been to the subway in Paris. The opening of the Métro at the turn of the last century had drawn him underground out of curiosity, and he'd taken the trains more than once when it was the fashion, but the appeal had worn off quickly. In New York such transport was out of the question. The thought of standing next to so many human beings, all of them crushed together, made him nauseous.

At the turnstiles he paused to catch his breath, and then he pushed at the metal bar. It was locked in place. He pushed a second time, and once again the bar caught. Smashing his cane on the turnstile, he cursed in frustration, noticing as he did how people in the crowd paused to examine him, as if he were insane. Once he would simply have scaled the metal

barriers with ease. Fifty years ago it wou
have been only a matter of seconds befo
he would have caught Gabriella — who als
could not move as quickly as she once had —
and her associate. But now he was left helpless. There was nothing to do but get around
these ludicrous metal barriers.

A young man in a tracksuit entered the
station and pulled a plastic card from his
pocket. Percival waited, letting him come to
the turnstile, and then, just as he was about
to swipe his card, Percival slid the knobbed
handle of his cane from the shaft and, pressing the tip into the man's back, jabbed with all
his might. The man's body lurched forward,
slamming into the turnstile and falling back
at Percival's feet. As the man moaned in pain,
Percival snatched the card from the injured
man's fingers, swiped it, and pushed through
the gates of the subway. In the distance he
heard the thundering of a train approaching
the platform.

As the train came into the station, a whoosh
of hot air brushed against Evangeline's skin.
She took a deep breath, taking in the smell of
stale air and hot metal. The doors slid open,
and a stream of passengers stepped onto the
platform. She and Gabriella had run less than
a block to the station, but the effort had rendered her grandmother breathless. As Evangeline assisted her into a glossy plastic seat,
she saw how weakened Gabriella had become.
Her grandmother leaned back against the
seat, trying to recover her equilibrium, and
Evangeline wondered how long they would be
able to continue if Percival Grigori had followed them.

The car was empty except for a drunk man
stretched across a row of seats at the far end,
and within a few sniffs Evangeline understood why there were no other passengers
in their proximity. The man had vomited all
over himself and the seats, leaving a pungent
stench. She almost gagged from the odor, but

there was no way she could risk stepping o
onto the platform. Instead she tried to figur
out which train they were on and, finding a
map, she deduced their position: They were on
the 4-5-6 green line. Tracing the line south,
she saw that it ended at the Brooklyn Bridge–
City Hall station. She knew the streets near
the bridge intimately. If they could only get
there, she would have no trouble finding them
a place to hide. They must leave at once. And
yet the doors, which Evangeline expected to
close immediately, stood open.

A loud, jarring voice came onto the inter-
com system, speaking in a rapid string of
words, each one running into the next. The
announcement, Evangeline surmised, must
have something to do with a delay at the station, although she couldn't be sure. The doors
sat open, leaving them exposed. Panic surged
through her at the thought of being trapped,
but her grandmother's sudden agitation over-
shadowed her thoughts.

"What's wrong?" Evangeline asked.

"It's gone," Gabriella said, grasping at her
throat, clearly startled. "My amulet has fallen
off."

Evangeline instinctively touched her own
throat, feeling the cold metal of her golden
lyre pendant. At once she began to unfasten
the clasp, to give the necklace to her grandmother, but Gabriella stopped her. "You will
need your pendant now more than ever."

Pendant or no pendant, it was too dangerous to remain standing there, waiting. Evangeline looked out at the platform, measuring the distance to the exit. She was about to take her grandmother by the arm and escort her off the train when, through a graffiti-etched window, the shape of their pursuer appeared. He limped from the stairwell and onto the platform, searching the train. Evangeline ducked below the window, pulling Gabriella with her, hoping he hadn't seen them. To her relief, a bell sounded and the doors began to close. The car pulled away from the station, its wheels grinding on metal as they gained speed.

But when Evangeline looked up, her heart sank. A bloodied cane filled her vision. Percival Grigori leered down at her, his face twisted in rage and exhaustion. His breathing was so labored that Evangeline calculated they would be able to outrun him once they made it to the next station. She doubted he'd be able to follow them up even the smallest flight of stairs. But as Percival removed the gun from his pocket and gestured for Evangeline and Gabriella to stand, she knew that he'd caught them. Grasping a metal bar for support, Evangeline held her grandmother close.

"Here we are again," Percival said, his voice little more than a whisper as he leaned over and took the leather case from Gabriella. "But perhaps this time we are dealing with th thing."

As the train made its way through the da ness of the tunnels, swaying with the cur of the underground passage, Percival placec the case on the plastic seat and opened it. The train stopped at a station and the doors opened, but as passengers stepped inside, they took one smell of the drunk man and changed cars. Percival didn't appear to notice. He unwrapped the lyre's body from the green velvet cloth, removed the plectrum from its leather satchel, withdrew the crossbar from its casket, and unwound the lyre's strings. From his pocket he took the small bronze case Alistair Carroll had recovered from Rockefeller Center, worked it open, and examined the Valkine tuning pegs. The pieces of the lyre lay before them, rocking with the movement of the train, waiting to be fitted together.

Percival lifted the journal from the bottom of the case, its leather cover and golden angel clasp moving in and out of the flickering light. He turned the pages, flipping past the familiar sections of historical information, magic squares, and sigils and pausing at the point where Angela's mathematical formulas began.

"What are these numbers?" he asked, examining the notebook with careful scrutiny.

"Look closely," Gabriella said. "You know exactly what they are."

he read over the pages, his expression ...ged from consternation to delight. "They ... the formulas you withheld," Percival said ... last.

"What you mean to say," Gabriella said, "is they are the formulas you killed our daughter for."

Evangeline caught her breath, finally understanding the cryptic words Gabriella had uttered at the skating rink. Percival Grigori was her grandfather. The realization filled her with horror. Grigori appeared equally stunned. He tried to speak, but a fit of coughing overtook him. He struggled for air until at last he said, "I don't believe you."

"Angela never knew her paternity. I spared her the pain of learning the truth. Evangeline, however, has not been spared. She has witnessed firsthand the villainy of her grandfather."

Percival looked from Gabriella to Evangeline, his haggard features hardening as he fully understood Gabriella's meaning.

"I am certain," she continued, "that Sneja would be quite pleased to know that you have given her an heir."

"A human heir is worthless," Percival snapped. "Sneja cares only for angelic blood."

The car rushed into a station, the platform's white lights flooding the interior, and jerked to a halt at Union Square. The doors opened, and a party of people trickled inside, merry

from holiday celebrations. They didn'
pear to notice Percival or the stench in th
and took seats nearby, talking and laugh.
loudly. Alarmed, Gabriella moved to shie.
the case from view. "You must not expose th
instrument in this fashion," Gabriella said. "It
is too dangerous."

Percival gestured to Evangeline with the gun.
She picked up the pieces one by one, pausing
to examine them before replacing them in
the case. As her fingers brushed against the
metal base of the lyre, a strange sensation
fell upon her. At first she ignored the feeling,
thinking that it was simply the fear and panic
Percival Grigori inspired in her. Then she
heard something unearthly — a sweet, perfect
music filled her mind, notes rising and falling,
each one sending a shiver through her. The
sound was so blissful, so exhilarating, that she
strained to hear it more clearly. She glanced
at her grandmother, who had begun to argue
with Grigori. Through the music Evangeline
could not hear what Gabriella said. It was as
if a thick glass dome had descended around
her, separating her from the rest of the world.
Nothing at all mattered but the instrument
before her. And although the dizzying effect
had mesmerized her alone, she knew that the
music was not a figment of her imagination.
The lyre was calling to her.

Without warning, Percival slammed the
top of the case shut and yanked it away from

geline, breaking the spell the instrument cast upon her. A violent surge of despair k hold of her as she lost her grasp upon e case, and before she understood her ac- ions, she fell upon Percival, wrenching the case from him. To her surprise, she had been able to take the instrument with ease. A new strength moved through her, a vitality she had not known only moments before. Her vision was sharper, more precise. She held the case close, ready to protect it.

The train car stopped at another station, and the group of people sauntered off, aloof to the spectacle. A chime rang, and the doors slid shut. They were alone again with the mal- odorous drunk at the far end of the car.

Evangeline turned away from Gabriella and Percival and opened the case. The pieces were there, waiting to be assembled. Quickly, she fastened the crossbar to the lyre's base, screwed the tuning pegs into the crossbar, and attached the strings, winding them slowly about the pegs until they were taut. While Evangeline had expected the procedure to be complicated, she was able to fit each new piece to the previous one with ease. As she tightened the strings, she felt vibrations under her fingers.

She ran her hand over the lyre. The metal was cold and smooth. She slid a finger over the firm silk of a string and adjusted the tun- ing peg, listening to the note change register.

She withdrew the plectrum, its surface g ——
ing under the harsh lights of the subway ——
and drew it over the strings. In an instant t——
texture of the world changed. The noise ——
the subway, the menace of Percival Grigori,
the uncontrollable beating of her heart — everything stilled and a lilting, sweet vibration
filled her senses once again, many times more
powerful than before. She felt both awake and
asleep at once. The crisp, vivid sensations of
reality were everywhere around her — the
rocking of the train, the ivory handle of Percival's cane — and yet she felt as if she'd fallen
into a dream. The sound was so pure, so powerful that it disarmed her entirely.

"Stop," Gabriella said. Although her grandmother stood only inches away, her voice
sounded to Evangeline as if it had come from
a distant room. "Evangeline, you don't know
what you're doing."

She looked at her grandmother as if through
a prism. Gabriella stood close by her side, and
yet Evangeline could hardly see her.

Gabriella said, "Nothing is known about
the correct method of playing the lyre. The
horrors you could bring upon the world are
unimaginable. I beg you, stop."

Percival stared at Evangeline with a look
of gratitude and pleasure. The sound of the
lyre had begun to work its magic upon him.
Stepping forward, his fingers trembling with
lust, he touched it. Suddenly his expression

...ged. He fixed her with a look of horror
... awe, equal parts terror and admiration.
Gabriella's eyes became filled with fear. "My
...ear Evangeline, what has happened?"

Evangeline could not understand what Gabriella meant. She looked at herself and saw no change. Then, turning, she saw her reflection in the wide, dark glass of the window and caught her breath. Curling about her shoulders, glittering in a nimbus of golden light, hung a pair of luminous, airy wings so mesmerizing in their beauty that she could do nothing but stare at herself. With the slightest pressure of her muscles, the wings unfurled to their full expanse. They were so light, so weightless, that she wondered for a moment if they might be an illusion of the light. She angled her shoulders so that she might look upon them directly. The feathers were diaphanous purple veined with silver. She breathed deeply, and the wings shifted. Soon they beat time with her breathing.

"Who am I?" Evangeline said, the reality of her metamorphosis suddenly dawning upon her. "What have I become?"

Percival Grigori edged close to Evangeline. Whether from the workings of the lyre's music or his new interest in her, he had changed from a withered, bent figure to an imposing creature whose height dwarfed Gabriella. His skin appeared to Evangeline to be lit by an internal fire, his blue eyes glittered, his back

788

straightened. Throwing his cane to the
of the subway car, he said, "Your wings
the likeness of your great-great-grandmotl
Grigori's wings. I have only heard my fathe
speak of them, but they signify the very purest
of our kind. You have become one of us. You
are a Grigori."

He placed his hand upon Evangeline's arm.
His fingers were icy, sending shivers through
her, but the sensation filled her with pleasure
and strength. It was as though she'd been living in a constrictive shell all her life, one that
had, in an instant, fallen away. All at once she
felt strong and alive.

"Come with me," Percival said, his voice
silken. "Come to meet Sneja. Come home
to your family. We will give you all that you
need, everything that you have longed for,
anything you might wish to have. You will
never want again. You will live long after the
world of here and now has disappeared. I will
show you how. I will teach you all that I know.
Only we can give you your future."

As she looked into Percival's eyes, Evangeline understood all that he could bring her.
His family and his powers could belong to
her. She could have everything she had lost
— a home, a family. Gabriella could give her
none of these things.

Turning to her grandmother, she was startled to see how Gabriella had changed. She
appeared suddenly to be little more than a

and insignificant woman, a frail human ~ng with tears in her eyes. Evangeline said, ~ou knew I was like this."

Gabriella said, "Your father and I had you examined as a little girl, and we saw that your lungs were formed like those of a Nephilistic child, but from our studies — and the work Angela had conducted on Nephilistic decline — we knew that a large percentage of Nephilim do not grow wings at all. Genetics are not enough. There have to be many other factors present."

Gabriella touched Evangeline's wings as if taken in by their shimmering beauty. Evangeline pulled away, repulsed.

"You meant to trick me," Evangeline said. "You believed I would destroy the lyre. You knew what I would become."

"I had always feared that it would be Angela — her resemblance to Percival was so strong. But I believed that even if the worst happened and she became like him physically, she would transcend him in spirit."

"But my mother wasn't like me," Evangeline said. "She was human."

Perhaps sensing the conflict raging in Evangeline's thoughts, Gabriella said, "Yes, your mother was human in every way. She was gentle, compassionate. She loved your father with a human heart. Perhaps it was a mother's delusion, but I believed that Angela could defy her origins. Her work led us to believe that the

creatures were dying out. We hoped for a n
race of Nephilim to rise, one in which huma
traits would overcome. I believed that if he
biological structure was Nephilistic, it would
be her fate to be the first of this new breed.
But it was not Angela's destiny. It is yours."

As the train rattled to a stop, and the doors
slid back, Gabriella drew her granddaughter
close. Evangeline could hardly make out Gabriella's words. "Run, Evangeline," she whispered urgently. "Take the lyre and destroy it.
Do not fall prey to the temptations you feel.
It is up to you to do what is right. Run, my
darling, and do not look back."

Evangeline rested a moment in Gabriella's
arms, the warmth and security of her grandmother's body reminding her of the safety she
had once felt in the presence of her mother.
Gabriella squeezed her once more and, with a
small push, released her.

Brooklyn Bridge–City Hall station, New York City

Percival took Gabriella by the arms and pulled her from the train. She was light in his grasp, her wrists thin and breakable as twigs. She had never been a match for him, but in Paris she'd been strong enough to put up some resistance. Now she was so feeble, so unresisting that he could harm her without effort. He almost wished she were stronger. He wanted to watch her struggle as he killed her.

The terror in her eyes as he dragged her along the platform would have to suffice. When he clutched her collar, the tiny buttons of her black jacket broke free, scattering across the concrete of the platform like so many beetles fleeing the light. Her exposed skin was pale and wrinkled, except where a thick pink scar curved along the upper edge of her breastbone. Once he had reached a darkened stairwell at the far end of the platform, he threw her down the steps and bounded after her until his shadow cut across her. She tried to roll away, but he held her to the cold concrete floor, pinning her with his knee. would not let her go.

He placed his hands over her heart. It bea quick and strong against his palms, the pulse as rapid as a small animal's. "Gabriella, my cherub," he said, but she would not look at him or speak to him in return. Yet as he slid his hands across her tiny rib cage, he could feel her fear: His palms became wet with the sweat that coated her skin. He closed his eyes. He'd been starving for her for many decades. To his delight, she turned under him, twisting and writhing, but there was no point in the struggle. Her life belonged to him.

When he gazed upon Gabriella again, she was dead. Her great green eyes were fixed open, as clear and beautiful as the day he'd met her. He could not explain it, but a moment of tenderness fell over him. He touched her cheek, her black hair, her small hands encased in tight leather gloves. The kill had been glorious, and yet his heart ached.

A sound drew Percival's attention to the platform. Evangeline stood watching at the top of the stairs, her spectacular wings extended from her body. He had never seen anything like them — they rose from her back in perfect symmetry, pulsing in rhythm with her breath. Even at the height of his youth, his wings had not been so regal. Still, he, too, was growing stronger. Exposure to the lyre's music had given him renewed strength. When possessed the lyre for himself, he would be ore powerful than he'd ever been before.

Percival approached Evangeline. His muscles did not cramp; the bite of the harness no longer slowed him. The lyre was cradled in Evangeline's hands, its metal gleaming. Fighting an urge to snatch the instrument from her, Percival measured his movements. He must remain calm. He mustn't frighten her away.

"You have waited for me," he said, smiling down at Evangeline. Despite the power her wings gave her, there was something childlike in her manner. She was hesitant as she met his gaze.

"I couldn't leave," she said. "I had to see for myself what it means —"

"What it means to be one of us?" Percival said. "Ah, there is much to learn. There is much I will teach you."

Drawing himself up to his full height, Percival placed his hand on Evangeline's back, sliding his fingers on the delicate skin at the base of her wings. As he pressed the point where the appendages met her spine, she felt suddenly vulnerable, as if he had hit upon a hidden weakness.

Percival said, "Retract them. Someone may see you. You must only open them in private."

With Percival's instruction Evangeline retracted the wings, their airy substance collapsing as they slipped from view.

"Good," he said, leading her along the p... form. "Very good. You will understand ever... thing soon enough."

Together Percival and Evangeline made their way up the stairs and through the mezzanine of the station. Leaving the neon behind, they walked outside and into the cold, clear night. The Brooklyn Bridge lifted before them, its massive towers illuminated by floodlights. Percival searched for a taxi, but the streets were deserted. They would need to find a way back to the apartment. Sneja was surely waiting. No longer able to contain himself, Percival eased the lyre from Evangeline's grasp. He held it close to his chest, basking in his conquest. His granddaughter had brought him the lyre. Soon, his strength would return. He only wished Otterley were there to witness the glory of the Grigori. Then, his triumph would have been complete.

Brooklyn Bridge–City Hall station,
New York City

Without the lyre, Evangeline's senses returned and she began to understand the spell the lyre had cast upon her. She had been captive to it, held in a mesmerism that she only fully comprehended once the lyre had been taken from her. Horrified, she recalled how she had simply stood by as Percival killed Gabriella. Her grandmother had struggled under his grasp, and Evangeline — who was near enough to hear the exhalation of Gabriella's last breath — had merely observed her suffering, feeling nothing at all but a removed, almost clinical interest in the kill. She'd noted how Percival had placed his hands upon Gabriella's chest, how Gabriella had struggled, and then, as if the life had been sucked from her, how Gabriella had become perfectly still. Watching Percival, Evangeline understood the pleasure he'd taken from the kill. To her horror, she longed to experience the sensation for herself.

Tears came to her eyes. Had Gabriella died as Angela had? Had her own mother struggled

and suffered at Percival's hands? In disg[...]
Evangeline touched her shoulders and the f[...]
of her back. The wings were gone. Althoug[...]
she remembered clearly that Percival had
taught her to retract them and that she had
felt them settle under her clothing, resting
lightly against her skin as she'd tucked them
away, she was not quite certain that they had
existed at all. Perhaps it had been a terrible
nightmare. And yet the lyre in Percival's possession proved that everything had happened
just as she remembered.

"Come, assist me," Percival ordered. Un-
buttoning his overcoat and then the silk shirt
beneath, he revealed the front of an intricate
black leather harness. "Unbuckle it. I must
see for myself."

The buckles were small and difficult to unfasten, but soon she had worked them open.
Evangeline felt that she might be sick as her
fingers brushed her grandfather's cold, white
flesh. Percival stripped away his shirt and let
the harness fall to the floor. His ribs were
lined with burns and bruises from the leather.
She stood so close to Percival that she could
smell his body. His proximity repelled her.

"Behold," Percival said, his manner trium-
phant. He turned, and Evangeline saw small
nubs of new pink flesh scaled with golden
feathers. "They are returning, exactly as I
knew they would. Everything has changed
now that you have joined us."

vangeline watched him, taking in his words, eighing the choice before her. It would be asy to follow Grigori, to join his family and become one of them. Perhaps, he had been right when he said that she was a Grigori. Yet, her grandmother's words echoed through her mind: *"Do not fall prey to the temptations you feel. It is up to you to do what is right."* Evangeline looked beyond Grigori. The Brooklyn Bridge rose against the night sky. It made her think of Verlaine, how she had trusted him.

"You are wrong," she said, her anger uncontainable. "I have not joined you. I will never join you or your murderous family."

Evangeline lunged forward and, recalling the intense feeling of insecurity she'd felt when Percival had touched her at the base of her wings, grasped the soft flesh on his back, took hold of the wing nubs he'd taken such pride in showing her, and thrust him to the floor. She was surprised at her strength — Percival hit the concrete hard. As he writhed in agony at her feet, she used her advantage to hoist him to his stomach, exposing the nubs. She had broken one of the wings. The torn flesh oozed a thick blue fluid. The flesh hung agape, and a great wound opened where the wing had been, allowing her to witness the gruesome collapse of his lungs.

As Grigori died, his body transformed. The eerie whiteness of his skin dimmed, his golden hair dissolved, his eyes turned into

black vacancies, and the tiny wings crum...
to a fine metallic dust. Evangeline bent...
pressed her finger to the dust and, hold...
it aloft, so that she could see the glitteri...
grains sparkle against her skin, she blew ...
into the cold wind.

The lyre lay tucked under Percival's arm.
Evangeline eased it away from his body, relieved to have it in her possession even as the
hypnotic power it might cast terrified her.
Overcome with disgust at the sight of the
corpse, she ran from Percival's body, as if it
might contaminate her. In the distance the
intersecting cables of the bridge wove across
her line of vision. Floodlights illuminated the
granite towers that rose into the frigid night
sky. If only she could cross the bridge and
find her father waiting for her to come home.

Climbing the concrete ramp, she emerged
on a wooden platform that brought her to
the pedestrian walkway at the center of the
bridge. Holding the lyre close, she ran. The
wind hit her full force, thrusting her back,
yet she struggled forward, keeping her vision
trained on the lights of Brooklyn. The walkway was deserted, while a stream of cars sped
by on either side of her, their headlights flickering between the slats of the guardrail.

As she reached the first tower, Evangeline
paused. Snow had begun to fall. Thick, wet
flakes drifted through the mesh of cables,
alighting upon the lyre in her hand, upon the

way, upon the dark river below. The city ched around her, its lights glimmering on obsidian surface of the East River as if it ere a single dome of life in an endless void. canning the length of the bridge, she felt her heart break. No one was waiting for her. Her father was dead. Her mother, Gabriella, the sisters she'd grown to love — they were all gone. Evangeline was utterly alone.

With a flex of her muscles, she unfurled the wings on her back, opening them to their full span. It surprised her how easily she could control them; it was as though she'd had them her whole life. She stepped up onto the railing of the walkway, girding herself against the wind. Concentrating on the stars glinting in the distance, she steadied herself. A gale threw her off kilter, but with an elegant twist of her wings, she kept her balance. Stretching her wings, Evangeline pushed away from the solid world. The wind lifted her into the air, past the thick steel cables, and up toward the abyss of sky.

Evangeline guided herself to the top of the tower. The pavement far below had been blanketed in a layer of pure white snow. She felt strangely immune to the freezing air, as if she'd gone numb. Indeed, she no longer felt much of anything at all. Gazing at the river, Evangeline drew herself inward, and in a moment of determination she knew what she must do.

She brought the lyre between her h.
Pressing her palms around the cold edge
the base, she felt the metal soften and gi
warm. As she added pressure, the lyre gre
less resistant in her hands, as if the Valkin.
had reacted chemically with her skin and had
begun a slow dissolution. Soon the lyre began
to glow with a molten heat against her flesh. In
Evangeline's grasp it had transformed into a
ball of fire brighter than any of the lights glowing in the sky above. For a fleeting moment,
she was tempted to keep the lyre intact. Then,
remembering Gabriella's words, she thrust the
fire forth. It fell like a shooting star to the river.
Its light dissolved into the inky darkness.

Gabriella Lévi-Franche Valko's brownstone, Upper West Side, Manhattan

Although Verlaine wanted to be of assistance to the angelologists, it was clear that he hadn't the training or the experience necessary to be of much help and so he stood at a remove, observing the frantic efforts to locate Gabriella and Evangeline. The details of the abduction replayed in his mind — the Gibborim swarming the rink, Gabriella and Alistair descending to the ice, Grigori's escape. But as he withdrew into himself, his thoughts grew strangely still. Recent events had left him numb. Perhaps he was in shock. He couldn't reconcile the world he had lived in the day before with the one he had now entered. Sinking onto a couch, he stared through the window at the darkness beyond. Only hours before Evangeline had sat at his side on that very couch, so close he could feel her every movement. The strength of his feelings for her baffled him. Was it possible that he had met her only yesterday? Now, after so little time, she filled his thoughts. He was desperate to find her. To locate Evange-

line, however, the angelologists would
to pin down the Nephilim. It seemed as
possible as grasping a shadow. The creatu.
had virtually disappeared at the skating rir.
dispersing into the crowd the instant Grigor
had left. This, Verlaine understood, was their
greatest strength: They appeared from nowhere and evaporated into the night, invisible
and deadly and untouchable.

After Grigori had left Rockefeller Center,
Verlaine joined Bruno and Saitou-san on the
main concourse and the three of them fled.
Bruno flagged a taxi and soon they were
speeding uptown to Gabriella's brownstone,
where they were met by a van of field agents.
Bruno took over, opening the rooms at the
top of the house to the angelologists. Verlaine
watched his gaze stray intermittently to the
windows, as if he expected Gabriella to return
any moment.

Soon after midnight they learned of Vladimir's death. Verlaine heard the news — delivered by an angelologist dispatched from
Riverside Church — with an eerie feeling of
equilibrium, as if he'd lost the ability to be
shocked by the Nephilim's violence. The dual
murders of Vladimir and Mr. Gray had been
discovered not long after Saitou-san had escaped with the sound chest. The bizarre state
of Vladimir's body, left charred beyond recognition, not unlike Alistair Carroll's, in what
Verlaine was beginning to see as the Neph-

signature, would surely be reported
ywhere the next morning. With one an-
ologist dead and two missing, it was clear
at their mission had ended in disaster.

Bruno's determination only increased after
learning of Vladimir's death. He began barking orders at the others while Saitou-san
stationed herself at the gilded escritoire and
made phone calls, requesting assistance and
information from their agents on the street.
Bruno hung a map at the center of the
room, divided the city into quadrants, and
dispatched agents throughout the city, taking every possible approach to finding a clue
about Grigori's whereabouts. Even Verlaine
knew that there were hundreds if not thousands of Nephilim in Manhattan. Grigori
could be hiding anywhere. Although his Fifth
Avenue apartment was already under surveillance, Bruno sent additional agents across the
park. When it became clear that he wasn't
there, Bruno went back to the maps and more
fruitless searching.

Bruno and Saitou-san each voiced theories,
one more unlikely than the next. Though
they didn't let up for a moment, Verlaine
sensed that they were getting nowhere. All
at once, the angelologists' efforts to locate
Grigori seemed pointless. He knew that the
stakes were high and the consequences of not
finding the lyre incalculable. The angelologists cared about the lyre; Evangeline hardly

registered in their efforts. Only now, on this couch they had shared the pr... afternoon, was he struck by the truth o. matter. If he wanted to find Evangeline al. he would have to do something himself.

Without a word to the others, Verlaine slipped into his overcoat, took the stairs two at a time, and ducked out the front door. He inhaled the freezing night air and checked his watch: It was after two o'clock on Christmas morning. The street was empty; the entire city was asleep. Gloveless, Verlaine shoved his hands in his pockets and began trekking south along Central Park West, too lost in thought to notice the biting cold. Somewhere in this bleak, labyrinthine city, Evangeline waited.

By the time he'd made his way downtown and had begun moving toward the East River, Verlaine had grown increasingly angry. He walked faster, passing blocks of darkened storefronts, turning possible plans over in his mind. Try as he might, he could not reconcile himself to the reality that Evangeline was lost to him. He cycled through every strategy to find them he could imagine but — like Bruno and Saitou-san — he came up with nothing at all. Of course, it was insane to think he might succeed where they had not. In this haze of frustration, the scars woven over Gabriella's skin rose in his mind and he shuddered in the miserable cold. He could not allow himself to entertain the possibility angeline was in pain.

...e distance, he saw the Brooklyn Bridge ...inated from below by floodlights. He ...alled Evangeline's nostalgic attachment ...the bridge. In his mind's eye, he saw her ...profile as she drove them from the convent toward the city and shared the memory of childhood walks with her father. The purity of her feelings, and the sadness in her voice, had made his heart ache. He had seen the bridge hundreds of times before, of course, but suddenly it had an undeniable personal resonance.

Verlaine checked his watch. It was now nearly five in the morning and the faintest hint of light colored the sky beyond the bridge. The city seemed eerie and still. Headlights from the occasional taxi flickered over the bridge's ramparts, breaking the gauzy darkness. Runnels of warm steam coiled in the brittle air. The bridge rose stark and powerful against the buildings beyond. For a moment he simply looked at it, this steel and concrete and granite edifice.

As if he'd reached an unintended but final destination, Verlaine was about to turn away and head back to the brownstone when a movement high above caught his eye. He looked up. Perched on the west tower, its wings extended, stood one of the creatures. Raised in the half-light of dawn, he could just make out the tapering elegance of the wings. The creature was standing upon the edge of a tower as if examining the city. As he strained to examine its otherworldy magnificence more closely, he detected something unusual in its appearance. Whereas the other creatures had been enormous — much taller and stronger than human beings — this one was tiny. Indeed, the creature seemed almost fragile under its great wings. He watched in awe as it extended them, as if in preparation for flight. As it stepped to the edge of the tower, he caught his breath. The monstrous angel was his Evangeline.

Verlaine's first impulse was to call out to her, but he could not find his voice. He was overwhelmed by horror and a poisonous sense of betrayal. Evangeline had deceived him and worse, she had lied to all of them. Repulsed, he turned and ran, blood thrumming in his ears, his heart pounding with the effort. The freezing air filled his lungs, singeing them as he breathed. He could not tell if the pain in his chest was from the chill or from losing Evangeline.

Whatever his feelings, he knew he must warn the angelologists. Gabriella had told him once — was it only the previous morning? — that if he became one of them, he could never go back. He understood now that she had been right.

West tower, Brooklyn Bridge, between Manhattan and Brooklyn, New York City

Evangeline woke before the sun rose, her head nestled upon the soft cushion of her wings. The disorientation of sleep clouded her thoughts, and she half expected to see the familiar objects of her room at St. Rose — her starched white sheets, the small wooden dresser, and, from the corner of her window, the Hudson River flowing by beyond the glass. But as she stood and gazed over the darkened city, her wings unfolding around her like a great purple cloak, the reality of everything that had happened hit her. She understood what she was and that she could never go back. All that she had been, and all that she had thought she would become, had disappeared forever.

Looking below, to be sure that there was no one to witness her descent, Evangeline climbed up on the granite edge of the tower. The wind lifted her wings, whistling through them, filling them with buoyancy. At such tremendous height, all the world at her feet, a moment of trepidation took hold of her. Flight

was new to her, and the fall appeared e
But as she took a deep breath and stepp
the tower, her heart rising to her throat a
depths before her, she knew that her wi
could not fail her. In a sweep of weightles
ness, she rose into the currents of icy air.

ABOUT THE AUTHOR

Danielle Trussoni is the author of the critically-acclaimed memoir *Falling Through the Earth*. Her first novel, *Angelology,* is being published in over thirty countries. Film rights were purchased by Sony Pictures.

The employees of Thorndike Press hope you have enjoyed this Large Print book. All our Thorndike, Wheeler, and Kennebec Large Print titles are designed for easy reading, and all our books are made to last. Other Thorndike Press Large Print books are available at your library, through selected bookstores, or directly from us.

For information about titles, please call:
(800) 223-1244

or visit our Web site at:
http://gale.cengage.com/thorndike

To share your comments, please write:

Publisher
Thorndike Press
295 Kennedy Memorial Drive
Waterville, ME 04901